**Acclaim for
JULIE B...**

'A sweeping tale of family secrets, betrayal, jealousy, ambition and forbidden romance . . . Fans of *The Thorn Birds* and *Downton Abbey* will love the epic scope of this novel'
Ali Mercer

'I thoroughly enjoyed this immersive story which spans both generations and continents. The evocative details and impeccable research make for a delightful reading experience and I can pay it no greater compliment other than to say, *I wish I'd written it*'
Kathryn Hughes

'This is an epic dual-time novel which draws the reader in right from the start and keeps you in thrall until the very last page. The writing is superb, the descriptions detailed, lush and evocative'
Christina Courtenay

'A gripping story full of family secrets: the price of love and loss within two generations . . . convincing and poignant'
Leah Fleming

'Rich in evocative detail – the complex mystery kept me guessing right up to the last page'
Muna Shehadi

Julie Brooks was born in Brisbane, Australia, but has lived most of her life in Melbourne. She taught English and Drama in secondary schools before working as an editor of children's magazines. She has been a full-time author since 1999 and is the author of several young adult novels as well as children's fiction and non-fiction. *The Heirloom*, *The Keepsake* and *The Secrets of Bridgewater Bay* are her first novels writing as Julie Brooks.

To find out more, visit **juliebrooksauthor.com** and follow her on Instagram **@juliebrooks_books**.

By Julie Brooks

The Secrets of Bridgewater Bay
The Keepsake
The Heirloom

THE HEIRLOOM

Julie Brooks

H
REVIEW

Copyright © Carol Jones 2025

The right of Julie Brooks to be identified as the Author of
the Work has been asserted by her in accordance with the
Copyright, Designs and Patents Act 1988.

First published in 2025 by Headline Review
An imprint of Headline Publishing Group Limited

This paperback edition published in 2025

1

Apart from any use permitted under UK copyright law, this publication may
only be reproduced, stored, or transmitted, in any form, or by any means, with
prior permission in writing of the publishers or, in the case of reprographic
production, in accordance with the terms of licences issued
by the Copyright Licensing Agency.

All characters in this publication are fictitious and any resemblance
to real persons, living or dead, is purely coincidental.

Cataloguing in Publication Data is available from the British Library

Paperback ISBN 978 1 0354 1482 6

Typeset in Minion by CC Book Production

Printed and bound in Great Britain by Clays Ltd, Elcograf S.p.A.

Headline's policy is to use papers that are natural, renewable and recyclable products
and made from wood grown in well-managed forests and other controlled sources.
The logging and manufacturing processes are expected to conform to
the environmental regulations of the country of origin.

Headline Publishing Group Limited
An Hachette UK Company
Carmelite House
50 Victoria Embankment
London EC4Y 0DZ

The authorized representative in the EEA is Hachette Ireland,
8 Castlecourt Centre, Castleknock Road, Castleknock,
Dublin 15, D15 XTP3, Ireland (email: info@hbgi.ie)

www.headline.co.uk
www.hachette.co.uk

For my mother, Lorna Jones,
from whom I inherited my love of reading

1

Brisbane, Australia

2024

The parcel sat unopened on Mia's kitchen table for a second day running. Each time she entered the kitchen her eyes were drawn towards the table despite all intentions to ignore the parcel. Something about it bothered her. She couldn't put a name to the feeling, only that since the courier had delivered it two days earlier her hands had felt twitchy, her neck itchy, and the dermatitis was flaring on her chest again. The white plastic package rested innocently enough alongside a fruit bowl of ageing lemons and a single overripe banana, but she found the red Royal Mail logo unsettling. That and the way the address label spelled out her name in capital letters, as if admonishing her. So much so that last night she had lain awake puzzling over how she had offended the unknown sender. She had always been prone to these rambling midnight debates of the self-flagellating variety.

'Stop being so ridiculous,' she told herself, as she fixed a bowl of muesli with a splash of oat milk and a sprinkle of almonds. 'It's just a parcel.'

In the middle of these deliberations, her phone erupted into peals of laughter and a message from her friend Kate flashed across the top of the screen. Last month, in a moment of whimsy, she had downloaded a kookaburra ringtone from some dubious app, and now it was haunting her.

Open it!

Yesterday, when she mentioned the arrival of the parcel, her friend had asked why she hadn't opened it already. A perfectly reasonable question since, unlike Mia, Kate wasn't riddled with uncertainties. She never had a 'bad' feeling about anything and always operated on the principal of deserved gratification.

A second message followed.

You know you want to

Maybe she should ignore both her friend and the parcel's unknown sender and consign the package to her cache of out-of-sight, out-of-mind objects at the back of the wardrobe where she put everything she wanted to relegate to the past. It could languish there with the birthday card from her seventeen-year-old high school sweetheart and the acceptance letter for the fine arts degree that mocked her from inside its yellowing envelope. Things she didn't want to think about but couldn't quite face throwing out.

Except those things were the past. This parcel wasn't anything – yet. It was just a parcel.

The kookaburra laughed again and she glanced at her phone, expecting further instructions from Kate. Except this time, it was her mother checking in on her.

Hi darling.

For some reason, her mother's messages had the uncanny habit of arriving at the exact moment Mia was poised on the cusp of a decision. She knew this apparent prescience was illusory, for it showed little discrimination between major life decisions and inconsequential choices. A message could just as easily arrive when she was choosing what shoes to wear for a night out, or finally deciding to give her latest lover the toss after refusing to recognise his serial infidelities for months.

Clearly her mother messaged her too often.

Don't do anything hasty today. Xoxo

She put the phone face down in disgust. Her mother was prone to cryptic messages. When questioned as to their meaning she usually explained them away by saying she was only passing on the daily horoscope and laughed them off with an airy wave. (Celia had long ago perfected the art of the airy wave and the shoulder shrug as if to say you could believe as you liked but that wouldn't change the facts.) Except, Mia did not believe in astrology. She believed that the future was governed by the intersection of past events with the random nature of the world. Nine times out of ten she could safely predict that today she would cycle to the café, make three hundred cups of coffee and then cycle home again at four thirty. Because that's what she did most days. Of course, there was always the chance that she might come down with chickenpox, be hit by a falling crane, or the creek might flood and the bridge would prove impassable. In her experience no horoscope ever predicted events like these. And Celia knew that as well as she did. Her mother was just being her usual overprotective, overly imaginative self.

She stowed the phone in her backpack where she couldn't hear it, where she could safely ignore both her mother and her friend. Then she grabbed the overripe banana for later, knocking over His Majesty's package in the process. The sender's name and address reproached her with its neat businesslike font.

Ellis and Associates
High Street
Lewes
BN7 1XG
UNITED KINGDOM

'You're such a baby. It won't bite.' She could almost hear Kate's voice teasing in her head.

She supposed she would have to open it sooner or later, so why not now? After all, it might be important. She picked up the package between thumb and forefinger, dangling it as if it were contaminated. Then she settled on one of the cane chairs she had inherited from a former housemate who had decamped to Perth in the name of love, and proceeded to tear open the plastic seal.

She was just about to open the thick yellow envelope inside when she heard the sound of rapping on the back door. Her flat was situated at the rear of a 1920s weatherboard house that had been divided into two sometime in the 1970s, judging by its olive-green kitchen cupboards and geometric brown and white floor tiles. It might be expected that by the age of thirty she would have graduated to something newish – or at least renovated – but so far, her lifestyle had not lent itself to permanence.

The colour scheme wasn't her favourite but the rent was cheap, the ceilings high, and she loved the cedar-lined walls of the old Queenslander. It even came with a box room she had turned into a studio, ignoring the way tendrils of bougainvillea kept finding their way in through the weatherboards. From the back veranda she could look out over a tangle of lush sub-tropical greenery to the houses climbing an adjacent hillside in one direction, with brown glimpses of river in another. Her friends all agreed that it was perfect for house parties, of which it had seen quite a few.

She set aside the envelope and ambled to the back door in her Uggs and saggy-bottomed trackpants, secure in the notion that it wouldn't be *him* of Friday night's woeful encounter. For *he* hadn't been heard from since he demolished the last two slices of bread in her pantry before exiting in a flurry of 'I'll DM you' early on Saturday morning. The feminine silhouette on the other side of the ribbed glass panel proved her correct. In fact, a halo of dark brown hair and a certain restless impatience told her that Kate had decided to take parcel matters into her own hands.

'Hi, lovely, I thought you might turn up,' she said, smiling as she opened the door.

'The suspense was driving me crazy, even if you're a pillar of indifference. I mean, if it isn't something you ordered, what could it be?'

Kate pushed past her down the pale lemon hall Mia had spent two weekends painting when she moved in last summer. Even paupers couldn't live with brown walls.

'I don't know.' She didn't mention the anonymous British stranger she may or may not have offended, or His Majesty's debt collector chasing down some long-forgotten parking fine from her now distant working holiday. These were the imaginings of an insecure person, obsessive thoughts her friend tended to dismiss with a wrinkle of her perfectly snub tanned nose or a flourish of her expertly manicured hand.

'Anyway. I googled it.'

'What did you google?'

'The name and address. I could read it on the photo you posted.'

Of course, she could read it! – If she enlarged it enough.

'I don't know why you're so fascinated by a package,' Mia said.

'The fact that you won't open it is what fascinates me. It reminds me of the times you decide not to go on a picnic for no discernible reason, and then it pours with rain and the sky electrifies. Or when you change your jeans for a slip dress at the last minute, and an old boyfriend turns up unexpectedly at the same party. That's what fascinates me,' Kate said, turning to stare at her friend over the top of her rose-coloured sunglasses before heading towards the kitchen.

Mia followed. 'I don't know what you're talking about,' she insisted.

'Yes, you do. Anyway, it turns out that Ellis and Associates are probate genealogists,' her friend said cheerily as she perched on a chair, her hand inching towards the yellow envelope peeking out from the white plastic.

Mia frowned. 'What's a probate genealogist? I mean, I know what a genealogist is but—'

'Did you never watch that reality show *Heir Hunters* when you lived in London?'

'No. I remember being tormented by several episodes of *Love Island* but . . . no.'

'Well, probate genealogists trace missing heirs,' Kate announced with a flourish of the yellow envelope. 'So, if one is writing to you, it probably means that you, my dear Miss Curtis, are somebody's heir.'

Mia was silent for a few moments, digesting this piece of information.

'I don't know anyone who would leave me money,' she said after a while. 'And I can't think of anyone related to me.'

One or two of the friends she'd made in London had stayed with her for a few days when they passed through Brisbane on their way to somewhere else. And she still kept in touch with a few others on social media, but the tyranny of distance couldn't make up for boozy lunches, snug road trips and group hugs. The truth was, they had grown apart.

'Maybe . . . but apparently, they know you. You must have a distant relative or something,' Kate said, her voice rising excitedly, her fingers drumming on the table, itching to open the envelope.

'Not that I know of.'

'I mean your mum did come from there.'

'So she says.'

'You could be heir to a fortune. Or a title . . . just don't forget your friends when you move into your grand estate.'

Mia tried to focus on her friend's words but she was somehow stuck on the idea of having British relatives. Her mother had been born in Sussex and moved to Australia straight after uni. But her mother's parents had died long before Mia was born, and Celia had no siblings. While Mia's father came from a long line of Aussie battlers – descended, according to family legend, from British convicts and Prussian peasants. So, who could possibly be hunting *her*?

'I can see you drifting about in a ruined Highland castle with your plaid shawl and your heaving bosoms.'

'What?'

'Aha, I knew you were listening!'

'Honestly, Kate, you're such a fantasist. Don't go all *Outlander* on me over some stupid parcel. And my bosoms aren't large enough to heave.'

No, not a castle. She closed her eyes, trying to picture the ruined grandeur of her friend's imagination, but all she could conjure was a cobbled street lined with quaint Tudor buildings and a charming old pebbled cottage, like something out of a movie set. Probably one of the many picturesque villages she remembered from her time in the UK.

Kate clicked her tongue, shaking her head in reproof. 'You're so frustrating. Just open it,' she said in a slow hiss. 'Maybe some elderly cousin twice removed has left you a few pounds in his will. You're not exactly rolling in money, hon.'

She was right, of course. Mia put up a hand to the long unkempt locks that had last seen a hairdresser – well, she couldn't remember when. Plus, she hadn't bought any new clothes for at least a month, and she really should pay some of those outstanding fines now that she had sold her car. She had been saving her money for ... well, she wasn't quite sure why, but it had seemed like a good idea. You never knew when you might need it. Maybe she would actually go back and finish her degree one day. Or buy a house. Or something.

Kate was right. She was acting like a child haunted by unfounded fears. It was only a package, after all. 'You do it,' she said, relenting.

Her friend didn't need telling twice. She snatched up the envelope and inserted one perfect pearl nail beneath the flap. Then, with a brief sideways glance, she tore it open, withdrew a wad of documents and placed them squarely on the table in front of Mia with a questioning look.

Mia shook her head. 'You read it, please.'

'Okay, here goes . . .'

Dear Ms Curtis, she read aloud, pausing every few sentences to check on Mia, whose tanned and freckled features grew more puzzled with each revelation, her deep blue eyes narrowing, her fingers raking unconsciously through the dark tangle of strands framing her heart-shaped face, her small neat lips pressed tightly together.

We have been retained by Thayer and Daughter, Solicitors, executors for the decedent, Ms Henrietta Foord Sutton, to locate missing beneficiaries to her estate in the county of East Sussex, England. After a thorough search of our extensive databases, records of births, deaths and marriages, digital archives, and by pursuing local enquiries, we believe that you may be a beneficiary.

Ellis and Associates has been in the business of probate genealogy and asset recovery for more than a decade. Unlike some probate researchers, who work on a speculative basis, in most cases solicitors or estate executors will retain our firm to trace missing heirs and trust beneficiaries for a negotiated fee. We will not and do not ask you for payment.

Our work includes proving the relationship to the decedent of any beneficiaries located by us. The Treasury Solicitor requires evidence of kinship. To that end, we may ask you

for copies of such documents as birth certificates, parental marriage certificates et cetera, should you wish to proceed.
I'd be pleased if you would contact me by email, telephone or letter in order to expedite this matter.
Kind regards,
Reid Ellis

'Who is Henrietta Foord Sutton?' Kate asked, when she reached the end of the letter.

While her friend was reading, Mia's thoughts had been in disarray, so much so that she didn't reply at first. The shiny white parcel had landed on her doorstep with a metaphorical thud, an unwanted intrusion into the quiet world she had built around herself these last few years, one where routine was a bulwark against any unwelcome thoughts from the past.

'It's probably a scam,' she said after a while, taking a deep breath. She had known it wasn't 'just' a parcel, after all.

'They're not asking you for money, or to sign anything . . .'

And yet the deceased's name sent fingers of alarm creeping up Mia's spine. She didn't know who the dead woman was, she had never heard her mentioned, or seen her name written anywhere. But she knew the family name, and she had an undeniable feeling that she should know who she was. That *someone* should have told her and, for whatever reason, they hadn't.

'. . . and they enclose a letter from the solicitors. So maybe it is legit,' Kate added, shuffling through the pages enclosed with the letter. 'Maybe you really are an heiress.'

Maybe she was . . . but heiress to what exactly? Money? Property? A family heirloom? Or something less tangible, such as – a bunch of lies? And more to the point, did she want to find out? Yet despite her reluctance, she couldn't resist glancing down at the ream of papers Kate was now poring over in fascination. As well as the two letters there was a glossy brochure and a chart.

'What's this?' she asked, drawing the single sheet of paper with its little orange boxes and grey arrows closer, even as her eyes zeroed in on the lone blue box labelled with the ominous heading 'Deceased'.

And directly below that heading a single name. A solitary direct descendant.

'Table of Consanguinity.' Mia read the title of the chart aloud.

'It looks like a kind of sideways family tree,' Kate said. 'And there *you* are, right below your mum, who's right below . . . oh, I see . . .' her voice trailed off.

'Mmm, there's my mum sitting right below the deceased. Funny about that.'

And there were other names and relationships stretching out to the right of the deceased. Parents, grandparents, great-grandparents, brothers, sisters, uncles, aunts, nephews, nieces, first cousins . . . first cousins once removed, second cousins, third cousins . . . so many boxes. Some already occupied by names, others waiting to be filled. All those relations. And yet there she was, right below her mother, who was right below *her* mother who was, apparently, the 'Deceased' – Henrietta Foord Sutton. Suddenly, she could barely breathe.

And right on time, her phone chortled with laughter once more and her mother's name lit the top of the screen again.

'You've got to get rid of that ringtone,' Kate said, jumping in surprise.

'I don't know. It's kind of apt, don't you think? Since it seems *someone* has been laughing at me my entire life.' How could she?

Well, it appeared that for whatever reason, her mother had lied. And if she had lied about her own mother's existence, what else had she lied about? *Who* else had she lied about? Who else had she wiped from her lineage – their lineage?

'Sutton was my mother's maiden name and Foord is her middle name too,' Mia said, frowning. 'An old family name . . . she always said. Handed down to the eldest daughter through the generations.'

Except that the custom had petered out by the time it came to Mia. Her mother had decided to erase custom and heritage. The question was why? What possible harm could a granny cause? What possible harm could your ancestors bring? Those pesky Suttons and Foords. Who knew what other denizens of Sussex might lurk on the heir hunter's Table of Consanguinity?

Her mother had denied Mia that kinship.

The thought was like a punch in the eye – her dark blue eyes that came from neither her father nor her mother. The real question was, whose legacy were those eyes? And what else had she inherited?

She looked down at the Table of Consanguinity sent by the probate genealogist. The coloured boxes dropped off the page with the deceased's great-great-grandparents, but Mia could still see them in her mind's eye, stretching out into eternity. All those boxes filled with people who each shared a sliver of her DNA. People her mother had assured her were of no importance, since she had no living relatives. People whose lives had begat hers.

Yes, someone definitely had a lot of explaining to do.

2

Sussex, England
1821

Philadelphia was hunting a spool of ribbon to trim the dame's second-best bonnet when she entered the workshop that morning, little expecting her life was about to become a public spectacle. For rather than ribbon, she found her husband draped over a spindle-back chair. His shears lay splayed on the floor while his nephew stood forlornly beside him. Her first thought was that Jasper would be furious with the apprentice who had been so careless with his shears. Then she noted that his neckcloth was awry, his chin flecked with spittle and his complexion pale as a perch's belly, and she realised more was amiss than the discarded shears. It was the fixed and staring eyes that told her he was dead.

'He is gone,' Isaac said, when he saw her hesitating at the foot of the stairs. She must have been standing there for some time, frozen by the sight of her husband in such a state. Her nephew's words broke the trance. 'And I did not save him,' he cried, his shoulders slumped.

His cry was reminiscent of a fox kit calling for its mother, and she felt its tug in her breast. Poor lad, he was eighteen and already a man in body, yet for all his broad shoulders and square chin, a child still in many ways. He looked to her for comfort as he would have looked to his mother, yet she did not know if she had such comfort in her with her husband lying dead in his workshop.

'What should we do?' he asked, his eyes begging her to take charge even as he straightened his shoulders and lifted his chin.

The question jolted her out of her trance. She was seeking ribbon, a length of yellow silk jacquard from France. She had not expected to find her husband dead on a chair when she rose that morning. She had not expected to be made a widow before she broke her fast. Already, her legs were trembling beneath the printed India cotton of her gown. Her heart was racing beneath her corset. But Isaac looked to her for reassurance and she must find it, despite her shaking legs. He was only a boy, no matter how harsh his father's discipline or how stern his uncle's tutelage, and she a woman grown. She must put aside her fears, for there was no one else to help them.

'Hush, now,' she said after a moment, coming to his side.

She made to lay a hand upon his shoulder, then thought better of it, bending instead to retrieve the shears and place them upon the low platform that served as the tailor's work table. She sighed as she glanced through the casement window to the street. It promised to be a long day, for already sunshine poured through the open drapes, saturating the workroom with soft light. And if the day began with death, how might it end and who might it touch?

'You have opened the drapes already.' The damask drapes, which shielded the shop window at night, had been raised. Left open, any passer-by could see that Death had come to the Boadle household.

'I didn't think. I always open them, readying the shop for the day.'

'It doesn't matter,' she said, the tears only a blink away. 'They will know soon enough.'

She risked a glance at her husband's face, swallowing the

bitterness that rose to her throat and quelling the impulse to cry out. She must be strong. Jasper always expected her to be strong.

'We must think on what to do.'

She must think, and clearly, for the household's sake: the two apprentices and Jenny, the maidservant, who depended upon the tailor's workshop for their livelihoods. And then there was Marjory. How would she explain her father's death to his daughter? She was such a loving child, and Philadelphia had always tried to protect her from life's harshest realities, from things she did not need to know. The child was Jasper's own sweet dove. She must safeguard her daughter's inheritance too, for there were those who would take advantage of a widow whose husband owned a thriving tailor's workshop. Especially if that man had a book of debts totalling 27 pounds 2 shillings and 6 pence at last tally, debts that might be overlooked if turmoil were to consume them. A man whose wife – nay, widow now – many in the village misliked, though her family had lived in the parish for generations.

She shook herself, shrugging off the old bitterness. There was no place for that here. Nor fear. Nor, indeed, grief. So many things must be considered, and so little time. Some might think it cold, but she must act swiftly to protect her little family.

'We must think upon what your uncle would have us do,' she said to her nephew, for Jasper had always known best. Except her husband's pale eyes, which had been quick to flash in both anger and delight, now stared back at her, flat and lifeless. His complexion, which tended to ruddiness, appeared deprived of all blood. And apart from a yellowish crust at one corner, his fine lips cast a blue tinge.

'What would you have me do?' she whispered to the dead man.

Of course, he could not answer. He would never speak again.

She forced herself to look away and gather her thoughts, noting that apart from the shears all else was in its place. Spools of thread and ribbon lay neatly wound. Bolts of cloth were shelved.

Cushions bristled with needles arranged according to their size. The tailor's mahogany candlestand rested on one corner of the work table, kept within easy reach as he sat cross-legged at his work. Nothing was out of place. All was in order except her husband. And, possibly, her family's future.

Perhaps she was dreaming still. She had always been prone to vivid dreams. Yes, that must be it. But it did not feel like a dream. It was all too real, even the smell of vomit that lingered in the air. She glanced at Isaac, considering him with a sigh of affection. He had grown so tall this last year, his shoulders broadening so as to burst the seams of his jacket twice. His boyish cheeks had sprouted whiskers that glinted red in the morning light. He promised to be quite handsome in a year or two and already seemed to know it. As did her maid, Jenny, from the way she trailed after him with her eyes. Silly child.

When she returned her attention to her husband, she discovered he was still dead. She was not dreaming.

'Did you find him like this?' she asked his nephew.

'When I came down from the attic at dawn, he was gasping and clawing at his neck. The others were yet sleeping.' He made to reach for her then, the poor motherless boy, his head lowered as if he might find comfort at her breast.

'You did not think to raise the alarm?' she asked, stepping back half a pace.

She wasn't his mother; although she had cared for him since the day his father apprenticed him to his uncle, some five years earlier. Cared for him, tended his hurts, even taught him what she could of her garden and its secrets when he showed an interest. No one else cared for the herbs she cultivated and the flowers she nurtured. Only her mother, Susanna, who had perished of the dropsy two years past. Susanna, who was sorely missed. She would have known how to be going on with this predicament. Susanna always knew. Philadelphia swallowed another sob.

'I did not know what to do. I loosened his neckcloth. I fetched a cup of water. I . . .' He nodded to a stoneware cup sitting on the corner of the work table. 'He vomited copious amounts. All down his shirt. I tried to wipe it up and then . . . and then I watched over him . . .' he paused to inhale deeply, 'in case he should come to himself and have need of me. I did not want to wake you. You do not like to be woken.'

'I would have made an exception in this case,' she said, gently.

Isaac's eyes glazed over as he continued. 'Before I knew it, he was clutching at his heart and then . . .' He could not complete the sentence, so great was his distress.

'And then he-he was g-gone?' She stumbled over the question.

'Yes . . . it was too late. He . . . he was gone.'

A clattering of pots from the kitchen at the rear of the house told her that Jenny was awake and setting porridge to cook and bread to bake. Soon the entire village would be out and about. Soon every householder within a mile would know that her husband was dead and begin asking why a strong and vital man like Jasper Boadle had died, so suddenly, so swiftly. In a chair, of all places. They would be looking for someone to blame, and who would come to mind first? If she was not careful, there would be a hue and cry, calling for the coroner, and there were plenty in the village who were fond of a good inquest. Why, the blacksmith had been paid as a juror three times last year, and yet all three of the deceased were proven to have died of natural causes.

'You were greatly shaken,' she said to her nephew, the hint of a question in her voice.

'Yes. I *was* greatly shaken.' He nodded, the tremor in his right hand proving the truth of her words.

'Poor boy, you were not thinking clearly.' This time there was more certainty in her voice. How else could they explain his slowness to act? There must be no room for uncertainty, no taint for the gossips and slanderers to seize upon.

The Heirloom

'No, I could not think straight,' he said, taking up her theme. 'Not with my uncle writhing on his chair as if he was being strangled from the inside out. He . . .'

She put up a hand, shooing ineffectually at the air. 'Have a care for the feelings of his poor wi . . . widow.' She faltered over the untried word. She was a woman without a husband now. A woman without protection.

'I am sorry, Aunt, I did not think.' He stared down at his uncle's stiffening body then back at her. There was longing in that look, longing that must be put to rest before another saw it. They might mistake it for something it was not.

'We should attend to your uncle.'

She returned her gaze to her husband. Jasper had always been a fine figure of a man, full of manly vigour and so elegant in his dress. Now he lay crumpled in a chair and not yet forty years of age. Now he had dropped dead before breakfast, when she had expected to have him by her side for decades. She was ill prepared for such an occurrence, for how does one prepare for the death of one's partner? She felt all awry with the shock of it. Now her bed would be cold . . . and her hearth too, if she was not careful.

'I think we must summon aid,' she said to her nephew, who had covered his eyes with his hand.

It was too late now to help Jasper, but she sensed that she would need allies in the days to come. She closed her eyes momentarily, trying to think. They would need witnesses, friends at their backs when the whispers began, as they surely would. As they always did. But who in the village could be trusted with such a business? And what was the proper course of action when a man had died all of a sudden, with no inkling of ill health. Her mother would have known how to deal with it, but she was gone. The folk of this village had not fully trusted Susanna Foord, anyway – lest they were in direst need.

'Perhaps we should fetch the constable,' she mused aloud. 'But your uncle complained of a treacherous stomach last night, did he not?' It was true Jasper had complained of stomach ache last night. 'So, the surgeon might suit better . . .'

Then again, the surgeon would prove superfluous to a dead man.

'I could fetch my father. He will know what to do in a case such as this,' Isaac said, peering at her from downcast eyes.

She stood a moment considering the boy's suggestion. Jasper's brother, Enoch, was a respected carrier with two carts and six horses. He was well known in the village, having married a farmer's daughter whose family had lived in the parish as long as Philadelphia's. And he had arrived there a good ten years before his brother, Jasper, established his tailoring business. The carrier's word would be heeded, and he above all others should have their interests at heart. Yet *should* and *would* were not always one, and Enoch had not welcomed her into the Boadle family. Even after ten years of marriage, he rarely showed her any sign of affection, though she saw him every other day. Sometimes she suspected he misliked her still.

'Mr Earle might be prevailed upon to assist us,' she said, surprised to find she spoke the words aloud.

'But why would a man like Thomas Earle wish to involve himself with our troubles, Aunt?'

Why indeed? She had been milliner and confidante to his wife for years, except poor Marianne Earle was gone now too. Why should Thomas Earle remember his wife's milliner with anything more than a passing nod simply because he had smiled at her on occasion? Because he had spoken to her kindly once or twice? He was one of the greatest landowners in the parish and far above a mere milliner or tailor in his standing.

No, she wasn't thinking straight. Enoch's voice was loud enough to be heard the length of the parish. And, despite his misgivings about the suitability of her marriage, and his wish that his brother had married elsewhere, he would do right by his brother's widow and child, surely? For the past could not now be undone. It was too late for any other plans he may have harboured.

'What shall you tell him?' she asked, glancing up at her nephew. Though she could not blame him, he seemed all topsy-turvy with events, and might say anything if questioned harshly. The constable, for one, could be excessively righteous if he took against you.

'I shall tell the truth. That my uncle felt sickly last night but believed he would be well by morning. That the squire was expecting him to fit his new riding breeches this morning.'

Jasper would never have delegated the squire to one of his apprentices, that was sure. And he was usually of a robust constitution, not one to make a fuss of a little stomach ache. Why, he had once hobbled three miles with a sprained ankle to attend upon the squire. Even so, there were those who would find fault no matter what course she took. Those who had always looked askance at the Foord women.

'I should have fixed him a posset last night,' she decided, dabbing at a fleck of vomit on his collar with her apron, but the vomit had dried already and would not budge, no matter how hard she rubbed.

Isaac stared down at his uncle. 'I do not think one of your possets would have helped him.'

Perhaps not, and yet she could not ignore her disquiet at this small neglect. Jasper had not been himself last night. He had returned home late after a prolonged meeting with a certain local smuggler – negotiating the purchase of French silk, so he had said. Smuggling was an integral part of the local economy and could not be avoided altogether, although she could not say her husband's recent dealings sat comfortably with her. Still, she should have at least offered a posset for his poor stomach. Then again, Jasper had never been one to trust in her possets. Indeed, he often questioned the hours she spent in the garden tending even the most common of herbs.

Well, she must not dwell on it, there would be regret enough in the coming days. Guilt, grief and regret . . . the customary widow's garb. Besides, despite this small neglect, she had always striven to be a good wife, even in the face of her husband's sometimes less than warm affection. She had done her best. From the moment the tailor had presented her with a golden thimble as a token of his affection, a token that had once belonged to his mother, she had striven to be the woman he desired. The woman he respected. A woman he would honour.

'Shall I fetch my father then?'

She still was not sure that Enoch would do right by her. There was much to consider, bygones that yet lingered like rotting memories. She sighed, leaning over her husband to stroke his cheek with a forefinger and finding it cold. She had loved and admired this man from the moment she set eyes upon him, ten years before. A mutual attraction. Fate, some would have called it. The Lacy sisters could bleat all they wished that she had stolen him.

'Perhaps,' she said to her nephew. 'But first we shall make him more comfortable.' Her husband had been such a fastidious person in life, he deserved no less in death. 'He would not like to be seen in such a state,' she added, looking up to discover that her nephew had already disappeared.

3

Sussex, England
1811

The mud was so deep that Philadelphia held her petticoats high as she passed by Farmer Sutton's wagon, on the morning she met the man who would later become her husband. The wagon was rickety with hay, the path clodgy with the morning's rain, and she did not wish to arrive at the inn splattered in mud. Her ankles were trim and her feet nimble in new wool stockings and she avoided the churned mud on the high street by skipping sideways. She had donned a new petticoat of pale green linen – stitched by rushlight after her mother was abed – worn with her second-best short gown in dark blue, and a newly washed apron. A handkerchief of printed yellow cotton was tucked into the low neckline of her gown and her cap was spotless. In any case, Mistress Tupper, the innkeeper, was bound to have words for her tardiness. Best not give her cause for more.

The King's Head fronted directly on to the high street, built of flint rubble like her mother's cottage, although far larger and boasting three floors altogether. Her employer was fond of telling anyone who would listen that old King Hal, the eighth of that name, had once stepped in for a cup of ale after a hunting trip to Ashdown Forest. She was as proud of the visit as she was of the chatelaine she wore chained at her waist, tinkling with keys, a silver case of sewing needles, a tiny embroidered purse and a nib pen (although Philadelphia knew for a fact that she signed her name with an X).

Spotting her mistress's plump figure in a window of the half-timbered upper storey, Philadelphia avoided the front entry and headed for the arched gateway to the walled yard with its well and stables, small orchard and kitchen garden beyond. The King's Head wasn't situated on one of the great roads, nor was theirs a popular seaside village, so there was no need for a coach house, an ostlers' room or a forge, yet it was on a well-travelled local route. She thanked the Lord they did not have so many customers that they must keep their own hogs, for she knew who would be put to caring for the creatures.

Her pattens clattered across the cobblestones and she stopped to hang them by the rear door alongside Joan's, the other serving maid, before entering the kitchen. The smell of roasting meat greeted her, a half lamb turning upon a spit powered by Laddie, the poor turnspit dog, who trotted a dozen miles a day upon his wheel but never managed to escape Mistress Tupper's kitchen. She reached up to stroke his long, dangling ears, wishing she could set him free, then set about finding him some tasty morsel. She was feeding him a sliver of cheese, small enough that the mistress would not notice it missing from the great wheel of cheddar, when she heard her name echoing through the inn and quickly wiped a wet hand upon her apron.

'Philadelphia Foord! I will box your ears, you slatternly maid!' The landlady growled as she trundled into the kitchen from the hall. 'Never here when you are needed . . .'

'Beg pardon, Mistress Tupper,' she said, bobbing a curtsey, 'but my mother was late to home last night and—'

'I am not interested in your excuses, miss, you are lucky I do not send you packing . . .' She paused to inspect Philadelphia from head to toe, frowning at the almost imperceptible mark upon her apron. 'Well, at least you are almost clean. I declare young Joan must have rolled in mud when she emptied the chamber pots this morning.'

''Tis a clean apron, mistress.'

'Well, do not stand there. The master has a guest in the parlour. You are to prepare a pot of coffee and take it in to them with a plate of my gingerbread. Use the Davenport rather than the plain stoneware. But no more than a dessertspoon of coffee, mind.'

It must be a fine guest, indeed, if the mistress were serving coffee rather than ale, for despite the busy smuggling trade on the nearby coast, coffee remained a luxury. Philadelphia set to work boiling two heaped spoons of coffee in a pot of water, then added a shaving of isinglass for clarity. She let the pot stand by the fireside while she assembled a plate of her mistress's famous gingerbread, laden with treacle and spices, and set a jug of cream (the master preferred more cream than coffee), a bowl of Lisbon sugar and two cups on a tray. Once the coffee had stood for several minutes she placed it on the tray with the gingerbread, tweaked the kerchief at her neck so that it covered all but the barest glimpse of skin, and headed for the parlour on the further side of the common room.

Even at this early hour several customers slumped before tankards of her master's home-brewed ale, while a couple of travellers broke their fasts upon fresh baked rolls, ham, cheese and dishes of tea. She hurried past them, careful not to spill a drop of the precious coffee, veering around the stout oak pillars, black with age, which propped up the massive roof beams, before stepping through a low doorway to the parlour where the more affluent travellers took their refreshment. This morning there were no well-to-do merchants or gentry staying at the inn. Only the master and a single guest occupied the room, both with their backs turned to her.

Mr Tupper was garbed in his best coat, a tight-fitting cut-away in brown-and-yellow striped linen with an enormous collar, so high it covered him to his cheeks. He wore it with a blue-and-yellow plaid waistcoat peeking out below, and dark brown breeches. When she entered, his arms were extended as if about to take flight so that his coat threatened to burst at the seams, while the tails parted across his large backside. Clearly, he had expanded somewhat since the coat was made. In contrast, the other gentleman was a picture of elegance in his coat of dark blue wool, and cream pantaloons tucked into high black boots.

'Good morning, Mr Tupper,' she said. 'The mistress bade me bring coffee.'

'You can put it there, girl,' he said, indicating a spot on the trestle table. 'Mr Boadle is making me a new suit. What d'ye think, Philadelphia? Shall I be the next Beau Brummell?'

She caught her breath at the realisation that the elegant young man in the blue morning coat must be none other than the new tailor who had set up shop in the village – the man it was rumoured the brick maker's daughter, Lettice Lacy, had set her cap at. The same man who was now turning to face her, a long strip of paper cut with tiny notches draped in his hand.

'I am sure, sir,' she managed at last. Mr Brummell and his circle's doings had reached even here, on the Downs.

'He has me measure now, don't you, Boadle?' The innkeeper slapped his knee in high good humour at his pun.

'I believe I will soon, Mr Tupper, if you will hold still for one last measure. We do not wish to make the waist too tight, do we?'

The tailor helped the other man out of his coat, with only the slightest fuss when it came to squeezing free of the shoulders. When Tupper stood in his shirtsleeves, Boadle held one end of his paper strip just above the man's belly button and reached it around his waist to his spine, before cutting a final notch with a small pair of scissors and standing back with a satisfied smile.

'Now we have your measure, sir,' the tailor said.

'What do you say, girl? You always have an eye for a frock,' Tupper said, with a wink. 'Shall we choose the green-and-brown plaid for me coat or the fine red wool?' He gestured towards a thick book lying upon the trestle.

'I would not know, sir,' she said with a shrug, for all books were enigmas to one who cannot read.

'It would be my pleasure to show you, Miss . . .?' the tailor said, with a questioning look.

'Foord. Philadelphia Foord, sir,' she replied, glancing up at him through lowered lashes. 'Of Puckridge Cottage.'

Had he heard tell of her mother's shame? Of her inherited shame? Anybody in the village would have been happy to inform him that her name was written in the bastard registry. Yet he did not blink at her introduction, merely nodded.

This was the first time she had seen the man for herself, close to, and she found it difficult not to stare. He was taller than her master by a head although half his width. His hair was brown with a reddish tint, curling about his ears and forehead with only a lick of pomade to keep it in place, so different to Tupper's moth-eaten old wig. His eyes were pale grey with a hint of blue, and she could not help noticing his fine legs in their fitted pantaloons. The man looked altogether too splendid for their village. Little wonder that Lettice Lacy was so taken with him.

Still, she hesitated when he beckoned her closer to where the book lay in wait upon the table beside him. She was not the only girl in the village who could not read, but that did not make her less self-conscious. The Lacy sisters had a tutor come to teach them their letters but there was no charity school in their village for the likes of Philadelphia.

Squaring her shoulders and lifting her chin, she took a step closer, with quaking arms. Man, or book, either might prove a threat to her peace of mind, but the heavy tray was the greater risk. Her employer would have her hide if she dropped it.

'Here is my book of cloth samples, Miss Foord,' said the tailor, opening the book to a place marked with a length of green ribbon. 'See, here is the plaid your master prefers.' He touched a small square of bright green and brown check, his hand pale and well-shaped, except for calluses on his thumb and several fingers. It was strangely incongruous, set against his fine apparel and clean-shaven chin.

'And here,' he added, turning a page, 'is the preferred red wool.' He glanced up, catching her staring at his hands. 'Tailor's hands, from holding scissors and the like, a hazard of our trade.'

She felt heat flush her cheeks and tried to look away but he caught her eye quicker than an otter snares a trout, and she could not wriggle free. He kept her there for a moment, his grey eyes holding hers of deep blue, before she gave two quick shakes of the head and broke free.

'What think you, Philadelphia?' asked Tupper.

'Both are very fine, sir.'

'Perhaps you have another preference?' the tailor asked, turning over the pages, inviting her inspection.

The cloths were all beautiful in their own way. She knew without even touching them that they would be soft and closely woven. More beautiful than anything she was ever likely to wear.

'Do not be afraid to feel their texture,' the tailor said, as if reading her thoughts.

Balancing the heavy tray, she tentatively reached out a hand to touch a sample that caught her eye as he flipped through the pages. It was of a blue so dark that it almost matched her eyes, and woven in a worsted so fine that it shone with a subtle lustre.

'I think . . . I think this dark blue wool would look very distinguished, sir,' she ventured after a while.

'Miss Foord has excellent taste. This cloth is the finest French shalloon, a lightweight twill suitable for every season. It would indeed set your figure to advantage. And these darker hues are all the fashion in London.'

'You do not think it too . . . dull . . . for a man of my stature?' Tupper asked, unconvinced.

'Not at all. You will be the envy of all your clientele. A coat cut from this cloth would put Mr Brummell to shame.'

'Well, the girl does have good taste. Even my dear wife has commented upon her caps and aprons. "Too fine for a serving maid," she told me just the other day. "That girl has designs above her station," she said.'

"'Tis only white embroidery that I fashion by my own hand,' Philadelphia protested, thinking herself in trouble again.

'Yet it has the delicacy of lace with those exquisite van Dyck points,' Jasper Boadle said, inspecting the cap – and the face beneath it – with such a pleased smile that she returned her attention to the tray and its contents lest her expression reveal more than she wished. 'The right costume can turn a washerwoman into a lady,' he added.

'Hah! Do you aim so high then, Philadelphia?' asked Mr Tupper.

'Or an innkeeper into an earl,' the tailor said, with a wink for his patron. 'I could not have chosen better myself.'

'Then we must have it!' her master said, with a clap of his hands so loud that she almost spilled the coffee.

'Yes. We certainly must,' said the tailor, but his gaze was all for Philadelphia. The cloth of finest quality was forgotten in the depths of her midnight-blue eyes.

She lowered her lashes to escape his gaze but could not rid herself of the thought of him, a thought that stayed with her all through that day and the next as she scrubbed floors and served ale to the Tuppers' customers. She kept seeing an image of the handsome tailor standing by her side, his arm looped about her waist, holding her as if she were too precious to release.

Was this the foresight her mother always warned her to treat with care – or mere wishful thinking? She supposed she would have to let matters take their course. One way or another, the future would reveal itself.

4

Brisbane, Australia
2024

It was almost dark by the time Mia wheeled her bike up the path to her parents' house. She'd had plenty of time to fume and stew while she brewed cup after cup of latte and macchiato at work. And after the long ride to their house from the café, she was literally steaming in the humid January dusk. She leaned her bike against the iron railing, looped and locked the cable, then took the steps to the front veranda two at a time. Her father had finally finished repainting the weatherboards of their 1970s ranch-style house, and the scent of Dulux Weathershield filled the air. Not bothering to knock – for what could they possibly be doing that warranted privacy? – she turned her key in the lock and headed straight for the kitchen at the rear of the house.

'*Ow!* That hurts!'

Sunday was roast night at the Curtis household and her father was cutting up pumpkin. Badly, it seemed.

'I told you not to slice towards you, it's suicidal,' her mother could be heard trilling from the living room.

'Hi, Dad,' she said, plucking a tissue from the box on the kitchen bench, before removing his thumb from his mouth and wrapping it in the tissue. 'Hold tight while I fetch you a Band-Aid.'

'Thanks, darling, I don't think it's very deep.' Her father grimaced and clung to his thumb obediently.

'Oh, hello, Mia,' her mother said as she entered the kitchen, cradling an empty wine glass. As usual, she wore her old gardening shorts with an unfashionable T-shirt from the 'Class of 19' with the names of her former Year 12 English students printed on the back. 'I didn't hear the door.'

'I thought you'd know I was coming,' Mia said, reaching into the cupboard above the sink where a jumble of medical stuff lived. 'You usually do.'

'Well, I did think you *might* call by on your way home from work. We haven't seen you for a couple of weeks. I did a nut roast.'

Mia couldn't see her mother's face as she dabbed her father's thumb with disinfectant, but she could feel her gaze zinging the back of her scalp as if burrowing into her thoughts. What did she know?

'Thanks, love,' her father said when she'd finished applying the Band-Aid. He picked up his Tooheys and saluted her, adding, 'I hope you'll stay for dinner despite the bloodied pumpkin.'

'I'm sure it'll be fine after a wash. And so will you,' she said, frowning at her mother, who was topping up her glass from a bottle of Pinot Grigio on the counter. Her mother's freckles were blooming through sunburned skin, and her chin-length brown bob hosted several scraps of leaf litter.

'Don't look so disapproving, it's only my second. As you can see, your father isn't too badly wounded and he's quite capable of putting on a sticking plaster by himself. Besides, I've been slashing at that overgrown bougainvillea on the shed all afternoon and developed quite a thirst.'

'It's not the wine I disapprove of, Mum.'

'Well, something's niggling you, I can see that,' Celia said, concentrating on her glass. 'I could swear I saw puffs of steam coming from your ears a minute ago.'

'I just remembered I left the ... um ... the ... um ... thingamabob turned on in the office,' Mike said, his eyes shifting from one woman to the other. 'I'd better go turn it off.'

'You do that, darling, we can't risk leaving the thingamabob on, can we?' Celia took a sip of wine, waving to her husband with a resigned expression.

'Go ahead, Dad. Mum and I will survive without you for a bit.'

'I might do a bit more on the Curtis family tree while I'm in there. I've hit a bit of a road block in the mid 1800s.' He considered both women over the top of his black-rimmed glasses, raised his sandy eyebrows questioningly, and when neither tried to stop him, gave wife and daughter a friendly wave and headed for the study.

'Your father does hate confrontation,' Celia said with a resigned lift of her eyebrows, when he was gone. 'Remember that year he went camping with your uncle for a week when you were sitting your Year Twelve exams and I was feuding with my principal? And he always did hate camping.'

Mia sighed. In many ways, her mother was Mia's rock. Unfortunately, rocks can be crushing if you don't take suitable precautions. 'And who could blame him for hating confrontation?' she said, with an exaggerated shrug.

'So, are you going to tell me what the problem is?'

Mia rested her hands on her hips, considering how to broach the subject of her mother's betrayal. She had always assumed they possessed an unspoken mother-daughter pact of at least moderate honesty. If they couldn't bring themselves to tell the truth, then they wouldn't say anything at all. Celia didn't need to know the details of Mia's worst mistakes, and she didn't need to know all her mother's youthful indiscretions. Or did she? Now she was discovering she had been fooled all these years. It wasn't only that Celia had confided almost nothing about her family in Mia's three decades, it was that she always claimed her parents were no longer living. Now it turned out that, until recently, Henrietta at least had been very much alive.

She decided to get straight to the point. 'Who is Henrietta Foord Sutton?'

If it were possible to pale beneath her sunburn, Celia's face would have turned white. As it was, she drew a surprised breath, her fingers clenching the wine glass so tightly the knuckles paled.

'Name ring a bell, Mum?' Mia prodded. 'The Sutton bit sounds familiar to me. And, oh yeah, Foord is an old family name, isn't it?' Except there had been no mention of a Henrietta. Why had Mia never asked? Or had her mother waved away her enquiries with a practised hand? Her memory was strangely fuzzy on the subject. Who didn't know their grandmother's name, dead or not?

'Has she written to you?' Celia asked, an expression of alarm in her pale blue eyes.

'Not exactly. More to the point, has she written to *you*?'

For a few moments Celia appeared dazed, shaking her head slowly and staring into space. 'She doesn't know where I am,' she said after a while. 'At least, I hoped she didn't. Given what you've just said, I'm not so sure.'

'You still haven't answered my question. Who *is* Henrietta Foord Sutton?' Mia glared, defying her mother to evade the truth, for Celia was an expert at evading truths she neither liked nor approved of, almost as adept as Mia, who was practised at ignoring things she did not want to remember.

'Henrietta is my mother. But I suspect you know that already.' Her voice was steady but the tension was noticeable in the muscles of her arms.

Unlike Mia, her mother was wiry rather than curvy. In fact, she had often wondered where her curves came from, given both her parents and her paternal grandparents verged on skinny. Of course, she had never met or even seen a photograph of her maternal grandparents, had she?

'*Was* your mother. Henrietta *was* your mother. Parents dead. No siblings. No family at all. Remember?'

Celia frowned and reached for a second wine glass that rested on the counter beside the open bottle, as if awaiting Mia's arrival. She poured a generous splash and handed it to her daughter. 'You might need this.'

'Better top up your own then, too,' Mia suggested. 'So . . . are you going to tell me how I suddenly come to have a grandmother?'

As she uttered the words, she remembered that Celia probably did not know her mother was dead and she flinched at her own callousness in not breaking the news immediately. Before she launched into any accusations. Imagine if someone held back on telling her that Celia was dead? No, she couldn't imagine it. It was too awful. She wasn't usually so insensitive. In fact, her last boyfriend, the serial philanderer, always complained that she was too sensitive. (Not that she believed him – well, not truly.) It was just that . . . Henrietta wasn't real to her yet, she supposed. She couldn't just conjure a real-life grandmother out of nowhere and then tell that grandmother's daughter she was dead. Apparently, to all intents and purposes, Henrietta had been dead to Celia for thirty years.

How did you tell someone their mother was dead?

'I think we need to take this outside,' Celia said, picking up the bottle and heading towards the back veranda.

Words quivered on the tip of Mia's tongue. She should tell her mother the news now, but she didn't know how she would react after all these years. Celia might have renounced her past, but Henrietta was still her mother, and not even being on another continent could change that. She deserved to know. Unfortunately, it appeared that Mia was the only one able to tell her.

Maybe the news could wait a few minutes, to give them both time to acknowledge Henrietta's existence first.

5

As Celia led the way outside, she took a deep breath of perfumed air, inhaling the scent of eucalypt and tea tree. Her garden and the bush beyond always had a calming effect on her, and she was in desperate need of that calm now. The rear of their house was situated on a ridge looking out over remnant bushland towards the Brisbane River, the river that coiled like a giant brown snake through Queensland's capital. When she and Mike first moved to the suburb, twenty years before, the reserve had been a neglected jungle of overgrown lantana and potato vine. A small army of committed volunteers, themselves included, had transformed it into a tract of dry rainforest, a haven for more than a hundred species of bird, and a favourite haunt of their adventurous daughter as she grew older and more difficult to keep at home.

She took a seat in one of the rattan armchairs while Mia took another opposite her. Then she waited silently for her daughter to explain in more detail what was bothering her. Usually, silent waiting did the trick with her students. But when nothing was forthcoming from her daughter, she bit the bullet and opened negotiations. Getting started was the tensest part of any conversation with Mia. It seemed like she was always on tenterhooks around her daughter lately.

'I did message you not to do anything hasty today,' she began, realising as soon as the words left her mouth that they were probably a mistake.

'Really? This is how you explain why for thirty years I didn't know I had a grandmother alive and well and living in Sussex?'

'Well, as far as we know she's alive and well. I haven't seen her for almost forty years.'

Henrietta could be dead but Celia didn't let herself think about that. After all, it would be forty years next February since she left England. She had called a halt years ago to her secretive, almost compulsive annual enquiries directed to the one friend she had sworn to secrecy about her whereabouts. They had gone so quickly, those forty years, flown through her hands, even when she tried to hold fast and savour them. Although not at first. At first, the place in her heart where her mother had once lived festered like an open wound. She had wanted it to heal yet she had wanted to punish herself with the pain too.

'Mum!'

She snapped back to the present. She must have closed her eyes for a second.

'You can't go to sleep on me now. We're arguing.'

Celia sighed. 'Do we have to?'

'You've kept my grandmother secret from me my whole life. Of course we have to argue. You *lied* to me.'

Celia placed her glass on the table and leaned forward with clasped hands resting on her knees. 'I only did what I thought best for your welfare . . .' she began, 'yours and mine. I have to be honest. I truly believed your grandmother would be a danger to you if she was allowed into our lives. Just as she had been a danger to me.'

'That's funny,' Mia said sarcastically. 'Here I've been imagining an elderly lady with short white hair and a web of wrinkles. Or maybe long blond hair and that shiny look that comes from too much Botox. But I never considered for a moment a dangerous monster. Tell me, how can a grandmother be a "danger"? Especially if she's safely on the other side of the world?'

'She had her ways.'

'Mum, you've kept my grandmother from me all my life. You have to give me more than "she had her ways".'

Celia took a deep breath, then exhaled slowly. 'I don't know how to explain. I don't know what to say.'

'Maybe start with the truth.'

The truth was the problem, though. Painful, complicated, subjective. Best kept locked away. She took another deep breath, glancing up at the blue gums shadowing the twilit sky for inspiration. 'All right. You know I grew up in a small village in the south of England.'

'In East Sussex. I know. I went there once. White cliffs, cute medieval pubs, the scenic rolling Downs, picturesque commuter villages, et cetera. I never heard any mention from you of an evil mother, though.'

'You grew up in Brisbane. You can't know what it's like to grow up in a village where everyone knows everyone else. Where everyone knows that your mother is quite simply – for want of a better word – mad.'

She took a gulp of wine and leaned back in her chair, staring out at the darkening sky. Her jaw tensed as her eyes drifted unseeing over the bushland below, as if some part of her was still back in Sussex, a small child wrapped in her mother's arms. No matter how mad. No matter how dangerous.

'How was she "mad"?' Mia invoked fingers of inverted commas around the word.

'Some people would say she was delusional. Others might

simply call her deluded. It wasn't only her beliefs, though; it was the people she mixed with. All of which would have been okay, except she kept forcing them and their ideas on to me.'

It was fifty years ago, but she could still vividly remember being ten years old, wrapped in blankets and bundled yawning into the car for one of her mother's midnight excursions. She couldn't forget waking to the sound of chanting voices in the middle of the night. Or her childhood peopled with strange 'aunties' and 'uncles' who drifted about the cottage, consulting with her mother.

'What do you mean? Was your mother in a cult or something?'
Celia shrugged. 'You could say that. It felt like one.'
'What kind of cult?'
From the tone of her voice, she couldn't tell whether her daughter's question was sympathetic or merely curious.
'I don't really know now. It was all so long ago.'
'Did she . . .' Mia hesitated, her expression horrified. 'Did she abuse you?'

'No. No, not physically. And she loved me in her way.' Celia took another gulp of wine, as if she could wash away the taste of the past. 'How about I tell you another time, hmm? That's enough about Henrietta for one day. Let's just say that, although I loved her, I believed the only way I could escape her world was by leaving. So, I came to Australia, fell in love with your father, and never went back.'

Even so, she had been filled with the bitterness of denial for so long it had become a constant taste in the back of her throat. Denial . . . and guilt. She had left England but the regret had not left her. Not in forty years.

'I don't understand. How could you shrug off your own mother like that? Even if she was in a cult?'

Celia shook her head, her reticence becoming defiance despite her intention to remain calm as she dredged up the past. 'You don't know what it was like. You don't know how crazy she made me with her obsessions . . . I didn't want that for you . . . I *don't* want that for you.' She had wanted her daughter to be free of that inheritance.

'I'm sorry, Mum, but you won't need to worry about any of it any more.' It was her daughter's turn to search the sky, searching for the right words, and Celia wondered what on earth she might be about to tell her. Or did she?

'I'm sorry to tell you that Henrietta is dead. She died two months ago.'

Celia greeted her daughter's revelation with silence. Why hadn't she known? She should have known. She had felt uneasy lately, but she had thought that uneasiness related to Mia. She hadn't considered it might be her mother she sensed. Her mother's passing.

'It must be a shock. I'm really sorry.'

The world speaks of love taking your breath away, and in that moment, Celia felt a flood of grief like nothing before. It took away her breath, her hearing, her voice. It made her heart beat faster, her limbs quiver, the blood rush to her head. She needed time to come back to herself. To return to the world where her mother no longer existed.

'Mum?'

She knew that Mia was waiting for her to speak but she still couldn't locate her voice. And the only sounds she could bear in this moment were the singing of cicadas in the Moreton Bay fig at the bottom of the garden and the muffled groan of a distant car engine. Henrietta was dead. Before her granddaughter had the opportunity to meet her. Before her daughter had a chance to say goodbye. Before she had a chance to tell her mother . . . what? There weren't enough words to fill forty years.

'I thought you might have known somehow.' Mia leaned forward, as if about to take her mother's hand, but an invisible shield enveloped Celia's body, repelling any comfort.

'How did you find out?' she said at last. Her voice was flat, but this wouldn't fool her daughter.

Celia had always kept her secrets close and her losses closer, for being open made you vulnerable to all kinds of . . . influences. Only her husband truly knew the intricacies of her heart but her daughter was perceptive enough to hazard a pretty good guess. She would know that whatever Celia and Henrietta's history, news of her mother's death would be a dagger to both her composure and her heart.

'An heir hunter contacted me,' Mia said, her voice equally monotone. 'Apparently, Grandmother has remembered me in her will.'

Despite her pretence of calm, Celia felt her face drop. The jaw she usually kept tight, with a half-smile or a displeased grimace, sagged as her mother's bequest found its true objective.

'I'm sorry, Mum. I don't know why she didn't name you in her will.'

'Oh, I think I do.'

It seemed that her mother's legacy was about to skip a generation, if Henrietta had her way. She only hoped that she could somehow control it before it did any further harm.

'You must be doubly sad that she didn't at least remember you in her will.'

'Don't worry, I'm not sad because she disinherited me. I did that to myself a long time ago. In many respects, my mother has been dead to me for forty years. No, I'm sad because I waited too long to try and make my peace with her.' She had always thought there was more time. That eventually she would go back. When her mother was so old that she . . . she could do no more harm. Harm Celia had spent forty years avoiding. Harm to her daughter and possibly all the daughters who would follow.

'You were really young when you left.'

'Yes, young and not strong enough to simply say no, which is

The Heirloom

what I should have done.' Before the rift grew so wide that she just didn't know how to cross it. How to go back. The past was so far away now. And yet, so dogged in its pursuit.

'Maybe her legacy to me is her way of trying to reconnect with you,' Mia said.

Celia caught her daughter's midnight-blue eyes, so like Henrietta's. 'Well, I hope you won't be sorry, darling. I hope neither of us will be. Henrietta's legacy may prove more dangerous than you think.'

'I'm a big girl, Mum. A lot older than you were when you left England.'

'I know.'

And yet, Henrietta always told her that you couldn't escape your ancestry, no matter how vehemently you denied it. You carried pieces of it in your very cells. And sometimes you kept more tangible reminders long after you vowed that they meant nothing. A photograph tucked into an old book. A tiny golden token wrapped in a silk scarf. A teacup blooming with flowers.

'Still . . .'

'Still, what?'

'Nothing. Only, be careful.'

6

The cicadas had gone quiet by the time Mia slipped through the gate in her parents' back fence and set out along the trail down to the river, but she could hear the chatter and screech of flying foxes roosting nearby. The trail wasn't official, merely a narrow path made by the passage of feet over decades. Her father kept the most intrusive of undergrowth discreetly at bay with his snippers, otherwise it was left to all manner of creatures: human, mammal, bird and reptile. More than once she had surprised a carpet python in all its metres of mottled beauty, and once an eastern brown snake slithering from the bushes had surprised them both.

The moon emitted enough light for her to scramble down the slope to the river, brushing against the low-hanging branches of casuarinas and acacias, with the lofty spires of blue gums scattered against the night sky. Although she was deep in suburban Brisbane, she may well have been hiking in some faraway bushland. The river lapped against its banks, swollen and brown, an immutable presence, its soft gush broken by the '*boo-book*' call of an owl or the scolding of a Noisy Miner. She had always been drawn to the river, growing up alongside it, even now living close enough to glimpse its wide brown waters above the treetops of her inner-city neighbourhood. Despite what had happened that day by another river, she kept returning to the water. Or perhaps because of it; picking at old scabs, keeping them fresh. More than a decade had passed since that other river – thirteen years, in fact – yet she still thought about it every single day. She was still adrift, still struggling to find direction. Still silently blaming herself. But we all end up blaming ourselves for something, she supposed.

'You've got to get your life together, Mia.' Her voice sounded small in the vast night, even to her own ears.

Most of her friends were settled with partners, in fulfilling careers, while she was only beginning to work out who she was and what she wanted. She had been mired in the past for more than a decade, wading through a thicket of mangroves to reach the present, when all her friends had swum the years like champions. Last week, she might have said that she *was* finally finding her feet, finding a semblance of equilibrium after years of being unsettled – of abandoned studies, abandoned art projects, dead-end jobs, dead-end love affairs, aimless travel – then the parcel arrived and knocked her off balance.

Now, it turned out she didn't know anything about herself at all. She didn't know who her mother really was and, apparently, her grandmother had been in a cult. What was she supposed to do with that titbit of information? And what might she find out next – that she was descended from aliens? It seemed just as probable as her mother growing up in a cult.

But the river was still here, same as ever. Constant, yet always changing.

She emerged on to the path that meandered alongside the water, stretching one way to the bush reserve, the other way through parkland, and beyond that to a manicured river walk. Hugging her arms across her body, she set out at a brisk pace towards the more open ground. Maybe she could walk off some of this uneasiness before she cycled home.

Ten minutes later, she found herself at the boat ramp park, a lone fisherman her only company, his hunched shape visible at the far end of the pontoon, lit by the moon and a single street lamp. She took a seat on one of the picnic tables looking out over the pontoon to the river, vaguely watching the fisherman as he cast his line, but really she was still simmering with anger at her mother and her secrets. Anger and sadness. For both of them, she supposed. Dipping her hand in the pocket of her jeans, she pulled out the by now much-folded letter from the heir hunter in England. She spread the paper on the table and switched on her phone torch; her eyes were drawn inexorably to the words *the decedent, Ms Henrietta Foord Sutton*. Decedent. Deceased. Dead. Gone before Mia had a chance to meet her, or even know of her existence.

According to her mother, this grandmother she had never met was mad. Was she really mad, or merely eccentric? And did her mother really grow up in a cult, or were these friends just so odd that it felt like that to a child? Something about her mother's description of Henrietta's madness reverberated through Mia's head, setting her thoughts ricocheting into the past, memories flashing before her like a waking dream. Memories of her ten-year-old self sitting bolt upright in the middle of the night, inconsolable with tears for some unfathomable reason, only to discover next morning that her grandfather had passed in the night. Memories of informing her Year 9 teacher that she didn't need a note for the excursion the next day because they wouldn't be going, then having the excursion cancelled at the last minute because hailstones the size of golf balls had made a hike out of the question. Memories of arguing with her friends about getting into a car as the sound of heavy rain pounded on the roof. No, she wouldn't think about any of that. It was all just coincidence or hindsight. She wasn't mad. And maybe . . . maybe her grandmother had not been mad either.

Out on the pontoon the fisherman was standing now, his rod bowing with the struggles of some poor creature. She watched as he fought to reel in his prey, silently hoping that it might escape.

'I thought I might find you here,' Celia said, walking towards her from the car park and sliding on to the bench opposite. Clearly, their fight was still too raw for her to sidle in beside her daughter. 'I saw your bike was still at home.'

'I was watching the fisherman,' Mia said.

Celia shuffled sideways out of her line of sight. 'You disappeared while we were washing up.'

'Sorry. I was tired after standing all day.'

'That's all right. I was just worried. I know you were upset.'

'I suppose that's one way of putting it. How did you know where to find me?'

'You've always liked this park.' Catching the moonlight, her mother's short, light brown hair was a nimbus of light around her face but her eyes were in deep shadow.

They sat in silence for a time. Mia didn't look at her mother, instead keeping her eyes fixed on the fisherman who was leaning way back and hauling on his line in an effort to land the fish. She didn't know what else to say, how to comfort her mother for the loss of someone she hadn't known existed until today.

'My mother wasn't evil, darling, I know that. But she was deluded. She was intractable. She was . . . she was fanatical. And she was determined that I should be like her. I was twenty-one. She wouldn't let me go and I couldn't stand up to her. I could only . . . leave.'

Her mother's voice faltered on the last few words so that Mia saw she was choking back tears. Despite her confusion, the mixture of anger and sorrow she felt, she found herself saying, 'I'm sorry your mother's gone. And I'm sorry you had to find out the way you did.'

'And I'm sorry I kept my family a secret from you,' Celia said.

'But I'm not sorry that I kept you away from Henrietta. She could charm the stinger from a wasp if she wanted to. A sensitive girl like you wouldn't have stood a chance.'

'You didn't have even an inkling about her?' Mia asked, remembering her reluctance to open the parcel. That feeling of foreboding, as if whatever it contained was somehow a threat.

'What do you mean?'

'That she'd died.'

'I could say that she was dead to me a long time ago. But that wouldn't be true. She was always there, haunting me. Don't think I didn't feel bad about abandoning her,' her mother said.

But she didn't answer Mia's question. Not really.

'I thought you might like this,' Celia added, still sniffing back tears. She placed one hand on the table and Mia realised that all the while she had been holding something.

'What is it?' she asked automatically but even in the darkness she could see that the object was a photograph.

'It was taken not long before I left. Mum came up to London, insisting on a girls' day out. We wandered through Portobello Road market and then we just had to make a detour to Brompton Cemetery so that she could look at the gardens. I think she was hoping to run into some dead people. Henrietta always liked a good cemetery.'

Mia snatched up the photograph in case it was whisked away. She switched on her phone torch again and aimed the beam at the small rectangle. Even before she noticed the enormous, elaborate tomb that the woman posed beside, her face, her hair, her very posture struck Mia.

'She looks like me!'

'Yes . . . she looks just like you,' her mother said slowly, emphasising each word. 'Or you look like her.'

Long black hair, a little wild, as if it refused to be tied down. Dark eyes, the colour impossible to determine in this light.

Strong brows framing the eyes like dark archways. Long limbs, with womanly hips and thighs. A certain defiance in her lifted chin.

Mia tore her eyes away from the photograph to consider her mother. Her grandmother didn't look much like Celia – who had always been skinny and athletic, with her light blue eyes and light brown hair, now threaded with grey beneath its artful restoration.

'I suppose I must take after my father, whoever he was,' Celia said, with a shrug. 'Now do you understand?'

Mia was still reeling from the remarkable resemblance. How could she look so much like someone she had never met? It was uncanny.

'Understand what?'

'It doesn't matter any more,' Celia said with a sniff, fumbling in her pocket and pulling out a scrap of yellow fabric.

'Don't tell me you've started using a handkerchief. Next, you'll be ironing the tea towels.'

'I have something else for you.'

'Another peace offering?'

'Maybe . . . an heirloom, I suppose you'd call it. Now that you know about your grandmother, I can give it to you.'

For an instant, Mia felt a tremor through her body, like the flutter of a thousand tiny wings against her skin.

'It's very old. Eighteenth century, I think. Your grandmother gave it to me on my twenty-first birthday. It's been handed down from mother to daughter for more than two hundred years. I would have given it to you sooner, but that would have meant explaining . . .'

Not that she had actually explained much. Only hinted. Mia wondered what her mother would have done if she had never found out about her grandmother. Bequeathed the gift in her will?

Celia set the yellow fabric on the picnic table and unwrapped its contents, her shadow casting the small object into darkness.

Even so, Mia could see that it was vaguely spherical and possibly made of metal. Not a ring, or a brooch. Perhaps a locket?

She reached out for it. But before she could grasp it, Celia caught her hand in hers. 'It's only an object,' she warned, squeezing her daughter's hand.

Mia wondered what she meant but she didn't ask. And then her hand was released and she took the small object in her fingers and held it up to the haze of light from the moon and the nearby street lamp. She saw that it was a thimble, golden and shiny and glowing in the night, pricked all over with indentations and embellished with a single flower. Peering closer, she saw that old-fashioned writing was engraved around its rim.

'What does the engraving say?' she asked.

'Thine heart be mine.' Her mother had the words by heart.

'That's a bit Hallmark-y for a piece of sewing kit, isn't it?'

'Well, thimbles could be more than dressmaking tools once upon a time. If a man gave his sweetheart a thimble it meant that he was serious, not just playing around. By keeping it, she indicated that she was serious too.'

'A love token.'

Even with her face in shadow she could sense her mother smile.

'Yes, exactly. A love token.'

'I wonder which of our ancestors—' She broke off as a shout rent the night.

Both women turned towards the sound. A hundred metres away, out on the pontoon, the fisherman had landed his prey. Or was trying to. The prey, longer than the fisherman's leg, flopped about uncooperatively as it fought to escape.

'It looks like a bull shark,' her mother said, for even kilometres from the river's mouth, the water was teeming with them.

The fisherman attempted to grasp the shark by its tail but it slipped free, sliding back into the water and dragging out the line as it swam for its life, pulling the fisherman with it, so that

The Heirloom

it was difficult to tell who was the hunter and who was the prey. And as they watched the man run the length of the pontoon, trying to reel his catch back in, she discovered that she had been clutching the thimble so hard that the rim dug into her flesh. She opened her hand where the thimble rested, warm and glowing in the moonlight, a red crescent marking the mound of her palm.

'Come on,' her mother said, resting a hand on her shoulder. 'Let's put your bike in the back of the car and I'll give you a lift home to yours. You must be exhausted after everything that's happened.'

She was exhausted, yes, but her blood also fizzed with energy. As if for the first time in years, anything might happen. Good or bad, she couldn't be sure.

7

Sussex, England
1821

The tailor's hands hung limp at his sides. Philadelphia could discern their pallor even by candlelight, for after Isaac left, she had drawn the drapes to keep out prying eyes. She was tempted to pick up a hand and squeeze it. Or prick it with a needle to test if he were truly dead. Despite the evidence of her eyes, she could not quite believe it. Yet the coldness of his flesh suggested it must be true. So, she kept a vigil while her nephew fetched his father, her hand too shaky to hold a needle or braid straw for a bonnet.

The boy had been gone a half-hour at least, a half-hour in which she sat motionless upon a stool except to shoo away Martin, the other apprentice, or instruct Jenny to put the kitchen in order before her brother-in-law arrived, for Jasper always insisted upon a tidy house. But mostly she just sat.

'Good God, woman, I cannot tell if your husband be living or dead in this gloom,' a gruff voice called as the door facing the street swung open with a groan.

The voice was not that of her husband's brother, Enoch, for he was a regular visitor to her home and she knew his voice better than she might sometimes wish. She turned to find the bulky figure of Mr Puttick, the village ironmonger and parish constable, filling her doorway. He must have dressed in a hurry, for even in this light she saw that his wig was crooked – having not adopted the fashion for undressed hair as yet – and his cuffs unbuttoned. Luckily, her husband had repaired his tailcoat the week before, so at least he did not look a complete scarecrow.

Behind him loomed the tall figure of her brother-in-law, silhouetted by the sun edging through the doorway. She could not see his expression but when he spoke, his voice held its usual chilly timbre. She had been wedded to his brother these ten years and still he had not warmed to her. Now here he was, arriving at her home with the constable in tow before she had a chance to say a word to him in private. What did he mean by it? She wished now that she had sent Isaac to call on Thomas Earle, despite her misgivings as to its rightness. She felt sure that he would have come himself before resorting to the constable and the law. Before events were stitched up so tight, they could not be undone.

'Good day to you, Philadelphia,' Enoch said, with barely a nod of greeting, as the two men entered the workshop.

They consumed the small shop with their presence, so that she must take a step back to make room. Her nephew did not meet her eyes as he followed a few paces behind them.

'Let some light in, boy,' ordered the ironmonger, gesturing to the drapes that were kept open during daylight hours to display the caps, gloves, stockings and ribbons, of which they kept some few items in stock. Jasper did not care to sell used clothing. He was too fine a tailor for that.

'And good day to you, Mrs Boadle,' Puttick added after several moments, with a modest bow, as if he had just thought of it. His eyes were all for the prone man. Her husband. As if he could not wait to get his hands on him.

She returned their greetings by rote, rising shakily from her stool to make her curtsey, knocked asunder by the appearance of the ironmonger when she had been expecting only her brother-in-law. Perhaps, in his confusion, her nephew had not made their situation clear and his father had brought along the ironmonger with his crowbar to free them from some imagined predicament. Except with the drapes now opened, she saw that it was no crowbar Puttick carried but the yard-long truncheon of the constable's office.

'Well, what do we have here?' he asked, directing his query to her poor husband. 'I saw you at the King's Head only yesterday, taking an ale with one of the Alfriston gang before your dinner. You looked in excellent spirits.'

He shifted closer, narrowing his eyes and staring quizzically into the dead man's face so that Philadelphia half expected her husband to sit up and reply. She still did not quite believe he could be dead. Puttick was taking no chances either, for he grasped Jasper's shoulder and shook him gently. When that received no response, he put his ear close to her husband's mouth and listened.

'Just as I thought,' he said after a while. 'The poor man is dead. Although he has not been dead so very long,' he added, lifting one of Jasper's arms and then letting it drop, 'as the stiffness has not yet set in.'

'My nephew, Isaac, found him like this when he came downstairs at dawn,' she sobbed, for she could hold back her tears no longer. Not when these men were filling her home with their ... with their ... what were they doing here? She had thought to protect herself and her household, and now Enoch had summoned the constable and who knew what might come to pass.

'I was still abed and the boy was so shocked he did not know what to do. Is that not so, Isaac?' she managed through her tears.

'I . . . er . . . I—'

Isaac was interrupted by an eruption of words spurting from his father's lips in a spray of spittle, as if he had been working up to a high dudgeon. 'Who could have done this?' he spat. 'My brother was a man in the prime of his life. He bore no sign of illness. Why, I spoke with him just two days since. He has no reason to be dead.'

'A man does not need a reason to be dead, Boadle. It can happen to the best of us,' Puttick said calmly, peering intently at Jasper's hand. 'I would say your brother has been dead at least this hour past, perhaps two. See how his fingertips have begun to purple. No doubt his feet will be turning too.'

Philadelphia clutched her hands to her heart so that both men wrested their attention from the corpse and stared in her direction.

'Forgive me, Mrs Boadle. I should not speak so plain in your presence. It is not fitting. Not everyone is as accustomed to death as a constable.'

'I am sure my dear sister-in-law has encountered death before this, Puttick. Her mother, after all, attended to the ills of the village for years. And Philadelphia was her right hand before my brother married her, were you not, my dear? No doubt she has knowledge of all kinds of cures and charm stuff,' Enoch said, with a shiver he made no attempt to disguise. 'She has probably seen all manner of deaths.'

'Not so many, dear brother.' Philadelphia managed to rouse herself sufficiently to find the words. 'I have been too busy fashioning hats these last ten years to ... to ...' She felt tears imminent once again.

Oh, why was he speaking of cures and charm stuff when her husband lay dead on a chair? It was unseemly. It was callous. Did he not understand that despite her years of service to the women of the parish there were many in the village who misliked her? Some who were indebted to her husband for their waistcoats and jackets – the very clothes upon their backs – might be pleased to see her in trouble, hopeful that their debts might be mislaid. She had thought to have her brother-in-law's help and here he was casting doubts as to the manner of Jasper's death.

'I have been my husband's partner in all ways, as you know.'

But the constable was no longer listening to either of them, his attention caught by something about her husband's face. He squatted next to the body, his breeches straining, and sniffed at Jasper's chin.

'Has someone wiped his face?' he asked. 'For he smells of puke. And see here, there are signs of it upon his shirt.' He pointed to a yellowish spot on her husband's shirt.

Philadelphia leaned closer, noticing several specks of vomit marring the otherwise pristine linen shirt.

'We merely wiped Uncle's face,' Isaac said. 'He would not like to be seen with spittle on his chin.'

'My husband is . . . was a proud man, Constable Puttick.'

'And why has he a blanket covering his lower body?' he asked, pulling aside her best Witney blanket, banded in indigo blue, which she had draped over her husband's legs for modesty. Then he looked to the floor, noticed the puddle by the chair leg and nodded.

'Hmm, I see, well, 'tis best not to disturb the body in cases of this kind. I must ask you not to touch anything further until I have had a chance to complete my inspection.'

'We only sought to make my husband . . .' She paused to sniff back another tear. 'To make him more comfortable.'

'I should like to see the kitchen now,' Puttick said, ignoring her protest as he levered himself to his feet, knees buckling with the effort.

'The kitchen?' she asked.

'To begin with.'

8

Isaac followed his aunt as she ushered the constable past the stairs which led to the upper chambers, through the hall open to the gallery above, and on to the kitchen at the rear of the house. She padded softly over the chalk floor in her new nankeen half-boots – the ones whose cost his uncle had been so wroth about – clutching her apron in one hand. He wished he'd had a chance to speak with her before his father brought the constable. He knew from the look she gave him that she was upset, and he did not like being the one to cause her distress, especially not on this day of all days.

His aunt might ply her trade as a milliner, order the household and minister to certain other needs of her clients, but beneath her calm appearance she was as fragile as any woman, as afeared as any new widow. She hid her fragility well – the only time he had seen her shed a tear before this day was when her pet raven was taken by a fox – but he knew. He felt it when he stood alongside her while she kneaded dough in this very kitchen or sat to embroider a linen cap in the workroom. She was so small and delicate, the expression in her deep blue eyes so sad-like, even before the events of this morning. Beneath her crisp demeanour she was . . . all sweet loving.

Except for some strange reason, his father had never liked her.

'She brought nothing but her cunning ways to the marriage,' he once overheard his father say to his uncle. 'You could have had the brick maker's daughter if you'd bided your time.' Still, despite anything his father had said, despite any harsh words or thoughts he had directed at his aunt, Isaac thought he would help her for the sake of his dead brother, for the sake of his young niece. For Isaac's sake.

With his uncle gone, it would be up to him to protect his aunt, if she would let him. So far, he was not making a very good job of it. He had not meant for the constable to be summoned. He had thought his father would come and testify to his uncle's death from natural causes. He had tried to tell him that Uncle Jasper had complained of illness the night before. He had thought his father would be distressed at news of his brother's death. Not angry. Not blundering about the house in a rage. He had not given his son a chance to explain. Instead, an expression of fury had crossed his face and he had set off for the ironmonger's shop before Isaac could utter more than the word 'dead'.

When they entered the kitchen, Jenny was standing stiffly by the brick hearth, but he could tell from the way her eyes darted from one man to the other that she had been in the hall listening a moment before. She bobbed a curtsey to his father and another to the constable and then looked worriedly to her mistress for instruction. She was wearing one of his aunt's old frocks, a simple printed calico – although she did not look half so fine in it, and its longer waistline had fallen out of fashion since the French modes returned after the war. His aunt wore one of her newer gowns that morning, a pretty light-blue printed cotton, with a very high waist and a ruffled neck that he had helped her stitch when his uncle did not need him in the evenings. She had an eye for the cut of a frock that did not need a book of fashion plates.

The Heirloom

'There's little to see here, Mr Puttick, except porridge and yesterday's loaf,' his aunt said, gesturing towards the pot warming upon a trivet by the fire, a half-eaten loaf of bread and a pat of crock butter awaiting their breakfast upon the table.

The constable wasn't listening. He strode about the room, tipping up his aunt's green-glazed earthenware jugs to peek inside; opening the doors of the oak dresser; sniffing at the contents of a half-empty mug; even raking at the fire with the wrought-iron poker. Isaac thought for a moment that he might go so far as to taste the porridge but he merely examined it and moved on. What was he looking for?

'My sister-in-law keeps an extensive herb garden,' Isaac's father said, with a grim smile for his aunt. 'She has all manner of plants growing there. Plus, those she still tends at her mother's cottage.'

'All good housewives keep a herb garden, Brother,' Philadelphia answered. 'We must see to the ills of our household as best we can.'

'And you more than most.'

The constable looked up from a trug of herbs that Jenny must have set upon a bench by the door to the yard. He picked up one or two sprigs, sniffed at them a moment, before asking, 'What are you suggesting, Boadle?'

'I am only saying that there are all manner of plants in the garden that could have caused illness, or even death if improperly applied.'

Isaac stood in place, as if his feet were mired in thick mud. He did not like his father's meaning. He feared his intent but, as always, the cat had got his tongue where Enoch was concerned and he remained silent, though his breathing quickened and his eyes flicked from one man to the other. Communication with his uncle had not been much better, but he had relied upon his aunt to speak up for him at the tailor's house, although his uncle did not much like it. At his father's farm, there was none to plead his case since his mother died. There was only his father and his elder brother, who aped their father in all ways.

'No one has given any herbs to my husband, improper or otherwise, Constable. He complained of a stomach illness last evening but did not ask for a posset. Is that not so, Isaac?' She leaned forward and placed a hand upon his arm to stay its quivering.

He felt the warmth through his linen shirt and looked up, searching for reassurance in her eyes. But she gave all her attention to the constable; only Jenny gazed back at him from her refuge by the hearth.

'Yes, my uncle insisted on finishing a pair of buckskin breeches he had promised to the squire. He would not let Sir Toby down,' he croaked, avoiding his father's eye. Even so, he could feel his father's fury burning the back of his neck.

'And yet I did not see any breeches on the work table in the shop,' Puttick said.

'He must have put them away when he felt the sickness coming on,' Isaac suggested, before his father could comment. 'He would not want to ruin such expensive buckskin. It was imported from America.'

'Oh, but I put them away while you went for your father, Isaac,' Philadelphia said, her voice noticeably shaky. 'He had finished them, but for the lacings at the waist.' She looked to the constable as she added, 'Jasper always insisted upon a tidy workroom.'

Isaac could testify to that. He had lost count of the times his uncle had taken the rod to him because he left out a length of silk lustring or a bolt of velvet. And heaven help him if he left his uncle's favourite shears lying about.

'You are to be complimented upon your industry, Mrs Boadle,' Puttick said. 'And now, perhaps you will lead the way to the upstairs chambers.'

Philadelphia nodded and turned towards the hall once more,

the constable following. But before they gained the plank door between the two rooms, his father bent over to reach for something on the floor. Isaac could not quite make it out, for his father's legs blocked his view.

'What have we here?' Enoch asked, a jubilant note in his voice that his son recognised from the times he had been discovered in some misdeed or other.

'Oh, has Jenny not swept the floors yet this morning?' his aunt said, a slight frown puckering her brow.

'But I did, mistress, just as you asked,' Jenny said.

'See here, Puttick. It is a plant of some kind. And still quite green and fresh.'

He held out his hand, displaying a sprig of leaves shaped like broad spearheads. Isaac knew those leaves, for they were a common sight with their purple flowers, growing in the dry hilly fields above the village. His aunt grew a yellow variety in her garden too, for the beauty of their towering spikes of golden flowers like thimbles or tiny bells. Close to, his father would find the leaves were covered in fine hairs. If he cared to look.

'Perhaps you prepared a posset for my brother last night, after all, Philadelphia? To calm his angry stomach?'

The constable produced a linen handkerchief from his coat pocket and took the proffered leaves with tight lips.

'Not I,' his aunt answered. 'It is nothing but a few leaves tracked in upon someone's shoes. Why, the plant grows everywhere hereabouts. Jenny will tell you that.'

'That may be,' said Puttick. 'That may well be. But a man's death in the prime of his life is a grave matter, Mrs Boadle, not something we can take lightly. And I think we must summon the coroner.'

A rush of air escaped Isaac's lips and he realised he had been holding his breath. Jenny noticed too, for she gave him a strange sideways look. Her face was flushed from standing near the hearth and her curls stuck damply to her cheeks as she mirrored his gasp with her own intake of breath.

'Yes, we must leave him to decide what is to be done,' the constable announced, brandishing the handkerchief-wrapped sprig of foxglove leaves in one hand and his truncheon in the other. 'It is possible there has been a grave crime done here. We must leave it to the coroner and the surgeon to discover the truth, whatever it may be. And if it be deemed a crime, the assize court to decree the punishment.'

As a child, Isaac had seen an accused murderer hanged once when his father took him to Horsham on a mission to buy a new horse. He remembered the stallholders selling pies and ale to the spectators. There were jugglers and acrobats entertaining the crowd and a festive air to the proceedings. Some in the crowd cheered when the man trembled and wailed upon the gallows, but not Isaac. Nor when the man gasped out his hunger for air and his body jerked like a mad thing from the rope.

Isaac did not find it so jolly then.

He risked a glance at his aunt, hoping his father would not notice. Her face held the pale sheen of Marjory's wax doll, and she returned his stare with fear in her eyes. *He* had brought his father to her house. *He* had brought the constable. Oh, what had he done? And how, in the good Lord's name, could he fix it?

9

Brisbane, Australia

2024

By lunchtime, the rhythm of the espresso machine had lulled Mia into a dreamlike state so that she barely noticed her sore feet and back. Grind the beans, fill the basket, tamp the coffee. Pull the shot, purge the steam, swirl the milk, pour the milk . . . grind the beans, fill the basket . . . The repetitive motions were interspersed with calling out customers' names and offering a smile and a few words to her regulars. Sometimes, lulled by the soft whoosh of steaming milk, she found her mind drifting to other places and times. Some of these daydreams she recognised as memories; others arrived like flashes of elsewhere, conjured by her imagination – emerald-green Downs, swift running streams, winding cobbled lanes and ancient woodlands – disappearing too quickly for her artist's eye to properly capture them.

'Jason!' She called the owner of the soy latte's name.

She was surprised to hear her own name in response from the lips of the stranger who came to collect it. Tall, burly, dark-skinned with curly, dark brown hair, and a tattoo peeking out from beneath his T-shirt, inked on his inner biceps, he grinned as if they were old friends.

'Mia, good to see you, mate.'

'Hi... um...' She trawled her memory for those brown eyes, finding them in an image of a skinny kid with sun-streaked hair and an inability to stand still for more than a minute at a time. *'Jase!'* She started in surprise.

'Ah, so you remember now.' He leaned forward on his toes, as if he might hug her if a counter hadn't separated them.

'How could I forget?' She hid the lie behind the broadest smile she could muster. How could she not?

'What is it? Ten years?'

'More like thirteen?' Thirteen years since they finished secondary school and she had weaned herself off their tight little clique, to get lost among the hordes at the Queensland College of Art.

'What have you been up to since... ah... since school?'

'Oh, you know, a bit of study, a bit of travel, and a lot of coffee making,' she answered with a shrug, concentrating on his face, so that her mind obeyed her command not to panic. It was one of those situations where you are going about your normal day – out for a run by the river, foraging the supermarket shelves for dinner, or flipping through old magazines at the dentist – when your past barrels around a corner and collides with your present. Nice-guy Jase. Once-upon-a-time friend. Now a bogeyman from the past, through no fault of his own. Jase. The parcel. Her dead grandmother. The photograph. The golden thimble. She felt like the past, the present and the future were all whirling around her.

'What about you?' she asked, trying to keep her hand steady as she handed over the paper cup.

'Same, same, except not so much coffee. I'm working near here. Building roads and bridges.'

'So, you're in construction?'

'Yeah. An engineer. Civil.'

Of course he was an engineer. Of course he would be building bridges. He had always been interested in how things worked.

The Heirloom

He was the only one she knew at school who had a clue how to assemble an Ikea bookcase or restart a stalled car – and her friends had all driven ancient cars. Ancient cars that stalled easily.

'Hey, listen, I can see you're busy, but maybe we could catch up later, if you're free?'

She caught his eye and smiled. Briefly, she entertained the idea of making excuses, suddenly discovering an appointment, a class, or even a date. But despite her sense of rising panic, that would be a betrayal of their shared past. And he was looking so happy to see her, she couldn't do it.

'What do you think?'

Besides, he worked nearby – so presumably she would have to change jobs to escape him completely. Better to face the pesky demons his presence conjured up, head on. She would just have to close her mind to everything else that came with it, and focus on his teasing grin and laughing brown eyes.

'Sure. That'd be great. I finish at five, but I'm supposed to be meeting my friend Kate for a drink after.'

'I'll tag along, if you'll have me.'

'We're meeting at the Osbourne in the Valley, at six.'

'I'll see you there, then.' He raised his coffee in a salute before threading his way through the tables as if nothing out of the ordinary had just happened.

'Yeah. See you there.'

Except something out of the ordinary *had* just happened. And suddenly, the past was swirling around her like a maelstrom so that she scalded the milk on her next three orders before she could bring her thoughts under control. Jason. Funny, lanky Jase. Bane of Ms Jones's English class, captain of the school rugby team, all-round nice guy. One of their gang of four.

Jase and Amy. Mia and Nick.

And then there were two.

* * *

Kate waved to her from across the other side of the beer garden. Good, she had managed to snare a table amid the usual post-work rush. Not always a given. The glass roof soared high above the wide space furnished with lush greenery and warm timber, giving the bar an open vibe even when crowded. She navigated a path through the crush, snatching a stray chair on the way through.

'Is someone joining us?' Kate asked when she set the chair beside her friend and took the one opposite.

'Maybe. We'll see.'

'New friend?' Kate eyed her speculatively.

Her friend had watched a procession of love interests dance their way through her life. Mia supposed she should have learned by now that men who were quick on their feet could be just as quick out the door. And men for whom words came too easily could just as easily fall silent. Except she hadn't, had she?

'Old friend,' she said.

'Before *moi*?'

She and Kate had met serendipitously on a beach in Mykonos nine years ago and shared the cost of a hotel room to eke out their dwindling euros. They'd been best friends ever since. 'Long before *toi*,' she answered. 'Old schoolmate.'

'I thought you hadn't kept in touch with any of your school friends. Weirdly.'

'He came into the café today and wanted to catch up. I couldn't say no,' she said, checking out the crowd so she didn't have to meet her friend's eye.

'So, you're using me as a buffer zone?' Kate rolled her eyes as she shook her head in exaggerated disbelief.

'No.'

'Your nose is growing as we speak, Mia.'

'Maybe. Anyway, he's nice. You'll like him.' Everybody liked Jase. At least they had when they were at school, and she didn't see any reason why they wouldn't now. He had that kind of open face and glint of fun about him.

'But not so nice that you bothered to keep in touch with him?'

Mia shrugged. She had always avoided talking about her school days, even with Kate, other than to say there wasn't much to tell. And for the most part Kate let her be, once she realised it would take more effort than it was worth to drag the details out of her friend. Still, she remained curious, digging a little here and there when the topic arose, as if she sensed there was something important to Mia, something *verboten* waiting to be dug up.

Maybe it hadn't been such a good idea to invite Jase along tonight. It might just open the floodgates of interrogation when there were two to the party. The coward in Mia was actually contemplating standing him up when she realised it was too late, for there he was, making his way through the crowd towards them, hugging a jug of beer and three glasses.

'The bar was so busy, I took a punt. Hope you still like beer, Mia. Otherwise, I'll have to drink up.' He set the beer on the table and offered his hand to Kate. 'Hi, I'm Jase. I hope she's been talking me up.'

'She hasn't stopped talking about you since we sat down.' Kate smiled and tucked a curl behind one ear. 'But she didn't tell me how cute you were.'

'You'll get used to Kate. She always says what she thinks.'

'Don't let me stop you,' Jase said, his eyes fixed on Kate.

An hour and a second jug of beer later, Mia was feeling quite redundant. Her friends had hardly taken their eyes off each other, meaning no hard questions and no reminiscing aimed her way, which suited her fine. She could lean back in her chair, sip her beer and allow that pleasant state of just-drunk-enough to envelop her. She had even relaxed enough to enjoy her Pacific Ale when Jase tore his attention from Kate and turned to her with a sloppy grin.

'It almost feels like old times, being here with you and the lovely Kate.'

'Here's to old times,' Kate said, lifting her glass.

'You know, I often wondered what happened to you, Mia. We heard you went to art school and then . . . nothing much. You went off Facebook, and some stranger ended up with your mobile number. I ran into your mum at the supermarket one day and she said you were travelling, but apart from that . . . *nada*. I used to joke that your name really suited you. MIA. Missing in action.' He finished with a laugh.

The beer in Mia's mouth suddenly turned bitter, and she swallowed so quickly that she breathed in a mouthful.

'I wasn't missing, Jase. I was hiding,' she spluttered, coughing up at least a partial truth.

'You didn't need to hide from me, mate.'

Kate stared from one to the other. 'Am I missing something?'

The coughing had brought tears to Mia's eyes. 'I'll tell you later. It's too noisy here for confessions,' she said, slurring her words slightly.

'Anyway, how's the art?' Jase asked, trying to salvage the mood.

'I think I do my best art on a latte these days,' she said, attempting a smile in return. Except for some reason, this last week, all her hearts and ferns had been morphing into crescent moons. She'd thought it was just a lack of precision, but maybe it was something else. Who knew?

'I had a job in a gallery for a while but it didn't pan out. I've been working on a few things, though – photography, mixed media. Not sure where they're going yet.'

'I don't know about her art, but *she's* going to England,' Kate announced.

'I never said that.' Mia scowled at her friend.

'You know you want to,' Kate said, echoing her earlier text message. 'Apparently, she's an heiress,' she added for Jason's benefit.

'We don't know that.'
'A certain Mr Reid Ellis says so, and he should know.'
'An heiress? Good for you,' Jase said, giving her the thumbs up.
'Well, I've probably inherited some ratty old fur coat or a family Bible with a broken spine.'
'If you say so, but then again, you can't actually know until you answer the letter,' Kate said, stabbing the air with her finger. 'You are going to answer it, aren't you?'
'Mmm . . . maybe.'
'Well, let's make s-s-sure.' Kate fished her phone from her bag and began scrolling through it, her fingers sliding drunkenly off the screen.
'What are you doing?'
'Just . . . being . . . a . . . good . . . friend.'
Mia reached across the table for the phone but Kate was too quick for her, snatching it away even in her semi-drunken state. 'Uh-uh. Here it is. The infamous letter. Lucky, I took a pic of it.'
'*Nooo!*'
Jason looked from one to the other, with a bemused smile on his face. 'Do you always fight over your phones?'
'Only when she's threatening severe personal trauma,' Mia said. 'Gimme that!'
But it was too late. Her former friend was already dialling.
'Hello, Ellis and Associates?' she said clearly, after a few moments, belying the volume of alcohol she had drunk. 'I have a call from Ms Mia Curtis, in response to your letter dated March third. Shall I put her through?'
When Kate thrust the phone into her hands, mouthing, 'Don't be a pussy,' Mia's mouth went dry, despite the beer swilling around in her stomach (and up her nose, come to that).
Meanwhile, Jason was nodding at her, as if offering encouragement, when at the same moment her own phone buzzed and a message from her mother flashed across the top of the screen.

This is not the time for . . .

Not the time for what? Her mother's message was cut off mid-sentence, but now was not the time to open her messages and deal with it. In fact, Celia's usual horoscope warning (or whatever it turned out to be) was enough to goad her into taking the call.

'Hello . . . Mia s-s-peaking.' Suddenly, the words felt too big for her mouth.

'Good morning, Ms Curtis. Reid Ellis. I'm pleased that you got in touch.'

'My friend made me,' she blurted. 'I mean . . . my friend made the call on my behalf.'

'I'm pleased you have such a persuasive friend, then. I was beginning to think I might have the wrong address for you. Usually, prospective beneficiaries contact us more quickly.'

His voice was low, with a professionally friendly manner, and she imagined him sitting at his antique desk with his proper ergonomic chair, earbuds in, several screens on, while continuing to work on whatever genealogical mystery was currently puzzling him.

'I'm not sure that I . . . that I . . .'

'That's perfectly all right. There's no need to be sure of anything at this stage. Sometimes a prospective inheritance like this can come as a shock,' he said, sympathetically, as Kate shook her head dramatically from side to side so that her curls flicked Jason's face. Not that he seemed to mind.

'You . . . are . . . sure,' Kate mouthed.

'I never knew my grandmother,' she said, her voice crumpling to a sob. 'I never knew she existed.'

'Ah . . . I wondered about that. According to my sources, your mother hasn't returned to the village since she left as a young woman. But that isn't any bar to your inheritance.' His voice soothed at the same time as it asserted competence.

'What exactly might I have inherited?'

'The solicitors acting for your grandmother's estate will give you the details but they have permitted me to say that there are some bank deposits, although much of that might be eroded by death duties. Some furniture, personal effects . . .'

She felt for the thimble she had tucked away in her pocket that morning, risking its loss, leaving its fate to the gods.

'You mean like books, and clothes and . . .'

'Yes, that too. And then, of course, there's Puckridge Cottage.'

'A cottage.'

'Yes. Apparently, it's been in the family for generations. I've only gone back about a century in the records, so I'm not sure exactly how many generations.'

A cottage. Generations. A heritage.

'We will need some identification from you: photo ID, birth certificate, et cetera. Now that we've made contact, I shall ask your grandmother's solicitor to get in touch. You'll probably want to do your due diligence before you send us any documents,' he was saying pleasantly, while her head was whirling and her stomach threatening to object to the confusion.

'And of course, you'll want to know more detail about the extent of the inheritance before you arrive.'

'Arrive where?' she cried out, although part of her could guess. Had probably guessed some days ago. Her cry was loud enough that Kate and Jason stopped staring at each other and looked towards her.

'In Sussex,' he replied, as if speaking of somewhere just across the river from her house. 'There's a condition attached to your late grandmother's will. You must visit the cottage and accept your inheritance in person. Otherwise, the estate will be bestowed elsewhere.'

Elsewhere. As opposed to somewhere. As opposed to *somebody*. She was that somebody. A somebody her grandmother had never met. A somebody Henrietta may not even have been sure existed. The question was . . . why? Why had she left her estate to someone she had never met? And why was it so important for Mia to visit this cottage – Puckridge Cottage – that had been in her mother's family for generations?

Maybe the cottage would tell her, if she let it.

10

Sussex, England
1821

The constable had finally left her house after inspecting every leaf and blade of grass in the garden and searching each of the upstairs chambers. He devoted particular care to rifling through Philadelphia's chest that she had inherited from Susanna, and inspecting the oak bureau where she kept her writing materials and her 'finery', as Jasper called it. Her husband had taught her the rudiments of writing and numbers when they married, so she could keep an account of her millinery business. She often sat of an evening while he met with his associates at the inn, recording her accounts or writing in her book of receipts. Some of the recipes and remedies in her receipts book she gathered from her clients but most she had learned at her mother's knee. Jasper's tuition had given her the means to record them for her own daughter. Her precious Marjory.

She waited until she could no longer hear Puttick's heavy footsteps upon the stairs before she opened the drop front of the bureau, caressing the decorative brass keyhole as she did so. The bureau had been a wedding gift from her husband – the second most beautiful thing she had ever owned – and she kept it buffed to a mellow shine with a polish of beeswax from her own hives and a dollop of mineral oil. She scanned the central cupboard, the half-turned columns and the pigeonholes, but found nothing out of place. Nor were her accounts book or her husband's ledgers missing when she opened the cupboard door and peered inside. Before closing the bureau's drop front once more, she ran her hand over the nooks and crannies to satisfy herself that nothing had been disturbed. Then she breathed a sigh of relief.

'My father is still downstairs.'

She turned with a jolt at the sound of her nephew's voice. He stood at the door, his eyes fixed upon her face, one foot encroaching upon their chamber. *Her* chamber now, she remembered, glancing away from Isaac and letting her eyes rest upon the bed, with its oak-panelled headboard darkened by time, and the richly coloured counterpane. She had sewn the woollen hangings herself, and filled the bed covers with down she collected from the geese at her mother's cottage. Her only dowry.

'Now you shall sleep alone, Aunt,' he said, as if reading her mind.

'I suppose I shall.'

'Perhaps not for long. You are young yet. Why, you are but ten years my senior,' he said, staring at her, so like a puppy that she wondered he did not lick her hand.

'I have only just been widowed, Isaac.'

'Of course, I only meant . . .'

'Never mind. Let us go downstairs and thank your father for what he has done for us,' she said, making little effort to disguise the bitterness in her voice.

She swept from the room, brushing past him in the doorway. He was so tall now that his head almost touched the lintel, for like most houses in the village theirs had been built centuries earlier, half-timbered with a tiled roof, and the doorways did not accommodate a boy as tall as Isaac. Her shoulder grazed his as she passed, and she thought she felt him shiver.

The Heirloom

'Are you cold, nephew?'

'No,' he said, his eyes wandering to the smoke-blackened beams above the bed.

'Perhaps you should fetch your coat,' she said, for he was clad only in his linen shirt. He must have removed his coat for some reason when he showed the constable to the chamber he shared with Martin, the other apprentice. The shirt was partly untucked from his pantaloons, and he had left off his waistcoat too.

'I did not have time to wash this morning, and I know you do not like us to come to breakfast unwashed.'

'It is not seemly for a young man to go about without his coat, Isaac. And please ask Martin to join us in the hall. He has been languishing in his chamber long enough.'

'Yes . . . Aunt.'

When she came downstairs, Enoch was hunched over the candlestand case that usually sat within reach upon the work table. With its candleholder and compartments for holding threads and needles, it was well used when the light grew dim in the late afternoon. Her brother-in-law did not hear the soft tread of her slippers and she was almost upon him when he looked up, his hand holding an object he had removed from the small drawer inside the stand. She caught a glint of gold as his fingers closed about it.

'What is that you hold, Brother?'

'Nothing that need concern you, Sister.' He said the word 'sister' as if it held some taint.

She crossed to his side to inspect the drawer for herself, perturbed to find that amongst the pillowed needles, boxes of buttons and tailor's chalk, something was missing.

'You have my thimble,' she said, too shocked to disguise the note of alarm and not a little fear in her voice. If he took such a thing as a thimble, what might he take next?

'It was my mother's thimble,' he announced, not an ounce of kindness in him for her grief. He opened his hand and held the thimble out teasingly in front of her. The gold looked dull in the palm of his brown leather glove, and his broad back blocked the light from the window so that she could not make out the patterns pricked into the gold, nor the words engraved on its rim. She made to pluck it from his palm but he snatched the hand away before she could rescue it.

'Jasper gave it to me as a betrothal gift. I have worn it every day these past ten years.'

'It was not his to give,' he said with a snort. 'I am the elder brother. Our mother meant to give it to me, but he charmed it from her finger before she could bequeath it.'

'If that is so, why did you not take the matter up with your brother before this?' And why bring it up on the day when her husband lay dead in this very house? Carried to the cellar by the constable and two apprentices. Why now, when she was a widow alone? 'It was made for a woman's finger. And you have no need of it, in any case.'

He shrugged. 'It is a keepsake. A memento to remind me of my mother.'

'Every woman of standing in the parish has seen that thimble upon my hand,' she said, drawing back her shoulders and pretending to a height she did not own. 'Every woman in the parish knows that I wear a golden thimble upon my finger when I sew their caps or trim their bonnets. And what of my widow's bench?' By law and custom she had rights to a share of her husband's estate beyond what she had brought to the marriage.

For the first time in the conversation, he looked unsure.

'What will they say when they learn that my brother-in-law stole it from me on the day of my husband's death?'

'You mistake me, Philadelphia, I meant only to ensure its safety. I am not the dishonest one in this room.'

She took a step back from him, but not before she had secured the thimble into her possession once more.

'What are you suggesting?' She clenched the keepsake so hard that its rim dug into the flesh of her hand.

'Do you think Jasper was unaware of your doings behind his back?'

Philadelphia flinched at the venom in his voice. He had never liked her, but this was more than dislike.

'Do you think he did not know what other services you performed, along with the trimming of bonnets and making over of gowns?' He leaned over her, as if he would cow her with his size.

'An occasional remedy for gout, or syrup for a cough, is not a crime,' she said, 'it is a kindness.'

'My brother made you promise when you wed that you would give up your mother's calling. That you would renounce her superstition and cunning. And that is not the full extent of your dishonesty. Nothing remains secret for long in this village . . .'

Philadelphia could not prevent the shiver that overtook her, but she disguised it as well as she could by crossing her arms and raising her chin defiantly.

'I have nothing to reproach myself with.'

'. . . no matter how cunning the perpetrator. Certainly not adultery. You know of what I speak.'

A loud gasp caused them both to turn towards the hall, where they discovered Isaac standing by the stairs, looking bereft. They had been so intent on their argument they had not heard him return.

'Come with me, Isaac,' his father ordered. 'With your uncle gone, this is no longer a fit place for a lad to dwell.'

As if the events of the day had not been grievous enough already, her nephew took this news like a blow. She watched his shoulders sag beneath its force; his face crumple with despair. Hurrying to his side, she took his hands in hers, chafing warmth into them. If it weren't for his father's presence, she would have relented and taken the poor boy in her arms. She knew how he feared his father, how cruel was the man's discipline, with his whiplike tongue and his birch of hazel twigs – the most painful of all rods.

'Your father is sad and wants you by his side, that is all. He does not mean anything more. You are a man now, and your uncle was about to make you his journeyman. When the inquest is done, you will come back and take up his work. He would want you to continue his legacy,' she said, squeezing his hands.

'Come away, son. I will not let you be corrupted by this woman.'

'He does not mean it, Isaac,' she pleaded, but Enoch had reached the pair already and was wrenching his son's arm from her clasped hands and towing him towards the entrance, the boy trailing him like a sleepwalker.

She followed them to the door, dismayed to hear that her brother-in-law continued to pour venom into his son's ear.

'I warned my brother about her cunning ways, but he was too trusting to listen. She bewitched him into marrying her. Just as she has bewitched you into following her around like a lap dog, doing her bidding, fetching her bits of twig and leaf. I would not put it past her to be having dealings with Old Nick.'

'But Father—'

Philadelphia heard a slap as Enoch continued, 'And now it's plain to see she has set her cap at Thomas Earle. I have seen her. I have watched her. Let her look to her paramour for comfort, rather than to my son.'

When they had gone, their voices fading into the sounds of the village, their tall figures shrinking to the size of twin marionettes, she slumped down upon the low work table where the tailor and his apprentices sat cross-legged to clothe the parish. Her hand moved of habit to replace the thimble in its usual resting place. But the small wooden case with its tiny drawer was no longer safe. She would need to find another hiding place, somewhere to keep it safe for her daughter.

The Heirloom

She closed her eyes, clutching the thimble tight. Jasper's face swam before her eyes but she willed it away. Instead, she searched the blackness for some sign of Susanna.

'Where are you, Mother? I need you.' She could almost feel her mother's presence like a warm shawl about her shoulders. But she could no longer hear her. She could no longer seek her help.

Today she had lost her husband. And now his brother had stolen away the only person who might have helped her retain their business. Isaac. She was alone. This was not the course she had imagined her life taking, the day Jasper had first shown her the thimble, dangling it before her like a prize. She had known even then that *he* was the true prize.

And now he was gone.

11

Sussex, England
1811

A fence of sharpened hazelwood poles enclosed the garden at Puckridge Cottage. One of Philadelphia's ancestors had built it long ago, and subsequent generations had replaced the poles and mended the woven hurdles with twigs cut from coppiced hazel in the woods beyond the cottage. The fence, like the knowledge passed from mother to daughter, might last forever. Or at least until the woods were no more and the women gone. For now, the fence kept the goats at bay while warding away unwelcome visitors who strayed where they weren't wanted.

A path meandered past the garden gate; shrunk to a narrow bridle path so far from the village, distance being another deterrent to anyone without proper business with the Foord women. Yet despite its remoteness, the garden, fragrant with blossom and ripe with fruit, was an invitation to some, as was her mother's renown for cunning and a certain unwanted repute for magic. Philadelphia had heard that in other parts of the country, wise women were once hanged or put to the torture as witches. But here in Sussex, there had been few such cases brought to trial. Apparently, her neighbours, for all their gossip and malice, preferred their witches alive. Nevertheless, her mother Susanna remained cautious. She always insisted, when quizzed on the magical properties of her tonics, that there was no magic involved. If it helped to whisper a few words to the saints as she dished out her cures, then she did not mind indulging her clients. Belief could be a powerful tool in healing and a most propitious cure for bewitchment. But the Foords did not actually practise magic, and Philadelphia's visions were only dreams, after all. At least, that is what she told herself at those moments when the next world ventured too close. And no one but Susanna knew of her 'dreams', in any case.

She was alone in the garden when the visitor arrived. She and her mother had returned from church, a short while earlier, when Susanna was called to attend Farmer Philpott's sick cow. He had tried dosing the poor creature with a tincture of wormwood, to no avail, and now sought further advice. Meanwhile, Philadelphia watered the herbs and harvested those in danger of going to seed. Her mother had particularly asked her to cut back the knitbone and gather its leaves. Although the roots were most effective in a poultice for sprains and the like, the leaves were plentiful too, and old Goody Collins swore by them as a cure for her gout.

The first she knew of the visitor was a slow *clip-clop* of hooves coming down the lane and, before she could turn, a voice hailing her with the greeting, 'Mrs Foord, how d'ye do this fine morning?'

The voice sounded familiar but she could not quite place it, until she turned to discover a fine-looking gentleman dismounting by the gate. Not so fashionably dressed as Mr Boadle, perhaps – whose profession demanded he look smart – but well turned out, all the same. His breeches were of buckskin, buttoning just below the knee, with high-topped black riding boots, a dark olive tailcoat and snowy cravat. She could not help noticing how well his breeches fitted him, and wondered who had made them.

'Mr Earle, how d'ye do?' she answered, rising from her knees and brushing leaves from her skirts, too flustered to remember to curtsey.

Thomas Earle lived in a tall gabled manor house, and his family owned much of the land in the neighbourhood. And here was Philadelphia wearing her oldest apron with grass stains upon its skirt.

He touched the brim of his hat before looping the reins of his mount over a fence pole and turning to face her with a broad smile. 'I mistook you for your mother,' he said, and then, realising perhaps that a young woman might not take this kindly, added, 'before I saw your face, of course, Miss Foord.'

'My mother is out, sir,' she said, coming to the gate.

'Ah, 'tis a pity. I had thought to ask her advice upon a matter.'

'I can ask her to call upon you when she returns.'

He smiled again, less widely this time, yet there remained a kindly glimmer in his eyes, light brown to match his hair, and the glow of summer upon his wide-cheeked face.

'I do not wish to trouble you . . . except my wife is . . . erm . . . with child and suffering greatly. The sickness is with her all hours of the day and night. I had thought Mrs Foord may have . . .' he trailed off, perhaps not knowing exactly what he had thought or indeed sought. Few gentlemen took an interest in women's business. In fact, Philadelphia wondered that he had come to seek out her mother himself, rather than sending one of his grooms or his housekeeper on this errand.

'Some women do suffer something terrible with the puking,' she said, with a sympathetic smile.

'Her physician has prescribed a diet of fruits and vegetables and advised she drink no wine or coffee . . .' He paused to run a hand through his hair. 'He says the vomiting is a good sign.'

'Well, he might, for *he* does not have to suffer for it.' She regretted the words as soon as they were out of her mouth. Mr Earle might take offence that she spoke this way of the doctor who tended his wife, and she did not wish to bring the wrath of the medical men down upon her mother. Most took umbrage at her work, in any case.

'No, he does not. She has grown so thin and weak and keeps to her bed most of the day. I cannot think this dreadful purging can be good for her. Nor the lack of exercise. I hate to see her in such distress.' The smile had disappeared, replaced by a troubled frown, and for a moment Philadelphia envied poor Marianne Earle that she had such a doting husband.

'I am sorry, Miss Foord. I did not mean to burden you with my woes,' he said, tipping his hat and reaching for the reins looped about the fence post. 'If you would ask your mother to call, I would be grateful.'

'Wait . . . sir.' He looked like a lost boy, standing at her gate; his shoulders slumped with such an air of helplessness about him. 'Perhaps I can find something to help Mrs Earle until my mother can visit. Please, come into the garden and wait while I fetch some herbs to make a healing tea.' She indicated a rough bench beneath a cherry tree laden with ruby fruit.

While she busied herself plucking handfuls of tender spearmint leaves, she watched him from the corner of her eye. He removed his top hat and sat with it in his hands beneath the cherry tree, watching the cloud of yellow butterflies that enjoyed the garden at this time of the year, the dark-rimmed white spots on their wings like a swarm of winking eyes.

'Your cherries promise to be sweet this year,' he said, when she returned, her trug brimming with fragrant leaves.

'Would you like some, sir?' she asked, reaching up with her free hand to pluck a few stems of ripe fruit from a low-hanging branch and offering them to him.

'Thank you, I shall take them home with me. Perhaps I can tempt my wife.'

'And here is some mint and a few other herbs,' she added,

placing the cherries alongside the herbs and presenting him with the trug. 'If your cook prepares a tea with the leaves—'

She was interrupted by the squeak of the gate announcing a new arrival and turned in surprise that the cottage should receive two visitors in one morning. When she discovered the identity of the caller, she broke into a wide smile.

'Mr Boadle, good morning. I had not thought to see you again so soon.'

'I can see that I have surprised you.' The tailor glanced enquiringly at the two people standing beneath the cherry tree. 'Forgive me for arriving unannounced.'

The two men stood awkwardly for a moment before Philadelphia realised that they must not have met and were waiting for her to introduce them.

'Mr Earle, may I present Mr Boadle, who has set up his tailoring business in the village.'

'How d'ye do?' the landowner said, with a slight bow.

'Good morning, Mr Earle.' The tailor returned the compliment, with a deep bow and a flourish that set the tails of his coat dancing. 'If I may say so, several of my customers speak admiringly of you, sir.'

'Is that so, Boadle? Well, my compliments to them. And now, I must be returning home. My thanks again for your help, Miss Foord.' He accepted the trug and cherries, bowed to Philadelphia, nodded to the tailor, before striding towards the gate and his horse. Once mounted, he gave a last wave of his gloved hand before turning his horse and setting off at a trot in the direction of the village.

'What did he want?'

Philadelphia was startled by the tailor's tone. This being only their fourth meeting, she had heard nothing but sweetness in his tone thus far. He had called at the inn twice after their first introduction, and asked after her most particularly, so that she left work with a bounce in her step all that week. Still, she did not like this curtness and wondered what had caused it.

'I only meant that I am surprised to find such an eminent visitor at your cottage. A gentleman would not normally call upon a young woman alone.' His glance wavered towards the ripe cherries hanging over her head.

'He was seeking my mother.'

'On what matter?' he asked, smiling so that his eyes seemed to glisten in the dappled light under the tree.

She was not sure that she should divulge Mr Earle's business, but he smiled at her so prettily that she found herself saying, 'He looked for a physic to calm the stomach of his wife who is with child.'

'Aah, your mother is a physician, is she?'

Philadelphia frowned, not knowing how to reply. He knew that her mother was not and could not be a doctor, for what woman could?

'I only mention it because I have heard that your mother sometimes ventures into territory that she would do better to avoid, for your sake, if nothing else. What would happen if she were to be blamed for the woman's illness or even her death? Childbirth can be so unpredictable.'

'My mother seeks only to help people,' she said, taking a step back from him.

'I have also heard in the village that the very people she helps believe her potions to be magic. That she brews her charm stuff with the aid of magic words.'

'Magic? No, sir, neither my mother nor I deal in magic.' She blinked at him, feeling the hairs on her arms lift and goosebumps pepper her limbs. 'That is only the prattling chavish of superstitious folk.'

'Unfortunately, there are those unsophisticated souls hereabouts who still believe that witches fly at night, casting spells upon the unwary, consorting with the Devil. Nonsense, I know, but . . .' He spread his hands wide and leaned his head to one side with a shrug.

'It is not true. There are no witches here. That is just a tale to frighten children!' she exclaimed.

'Dear Miss Foord, please forget I mentioned it. The last thing I would wish is to distress you.'

Perhaps she had misjudged him. Perhaps he truly had her interests at heart, for he held out his right hand, clothed in the softest yellow kid, as if he wished her to take it. She looked down at her own, nails rimed with earth and palm stained by leaves, and did not know what to do. Indignation and embarrassment warred within her, for he had criticised her mother and chastised her, however gently. While she debated, he solved her dilemma by taking her hand in both his and staring into her eyes.

'Such a sweet little hand,' he murmured, 'and always so hard at work. A perfect hand for delicate work.'

'Delicate work?'

'Such as a seamstress or a milliner might do. How would you like that? To work as a milliner, for example?'

'I should think I would like that very much.' Much more than swabbing floors at the inn.

'I would see you happy, not sad.'

'I'm not sad.'

'And I thought you well disposed towards me.'

'I am,' she said. He had asked for her in particular to wait upon him at the King's Head. He had spoken to her most kindly. And Joan had told her that he had no business with Mr Tupper on those days.

'Such fair skin and dark hair.' He smiled as he inspected her from the top of her head to the bare feet peeking from beneath her petticoat. 'You would look so elegant dressed in a gown of muslin, with a cream straw bonnet to enhance those lovely eyes. I know just the thing, a white-on-white weave of the most delicate muslin. All the ladies would be green with envy.'

'They would?'

'Undoubtedly. Oh, we would make a fine pair, m'dear.' He squeezed her hand as her drew her towards him, and for one brief moment she thought he might kiss her, but he only brought his handkerchief to her cheek and wiped away a smudge. 'There, now you are perfect again,' he said, releasing her.

She breathed out with a sigh, a slight shiver running through her body. Philadelphia was young but far from ignorant in such matters. One part of her knew that she should send him away before he took more than a smudge from her cheek. Another part wished he had not let her go.

'My mother will return soon,' she said, and waited to see how he would reply.

'Then I must not tempt fate by keeping you from your work.' This time he was the one to step back from her.

'Good day then, Mr Boadle.' His name tarried on her breath like a soft breeze.

'I have something for you, if you will have it from me,' he said, regarding her expectantly.

Perhaps he had brought her a posy or a ribbon, she thought, a small token to win her favour. He wanted her favour, she could see that, although what he would do with it, she wasn't so sure. But every time he looked at her, she remembered last Midsummer's Eve and the dreams which followed it, and she could not resist finding out.

'I cannot say until I know what it is, sir.' Still, she would not make it too easy for him.

'Here then, I will show you.' He fished in his waistcoat pocket and brought out a small object hidden in his clenched fist. It could not be a posy, then. And if it were ribbon, it was of a paltry length.

'What is it?' she asked, leaning forward despite herself.

For answer he opened his gloved hand and held the object towards her. On the flat of his palm sat a trinket, catching the light filtering through the cherry-laden boughs.

A thimble. A golden thimble to fit a woman's finger.

''Twas my mother's once,' he said. 'Too small for any but my smallest finger.'

It was a tool of his trade, but more than that; it was a token of intent, if she read him right. She looked up, frowning in confusion. That he liked her, it was clear, but the thimble was precious. The thimble meant more than 'like'. The thimble was a serious gesture. She took it in her hand to inspect it more closely. She had never held an object so precious. The few metal objects in their cottage were cast of iron or worked from copper, utilitarian items to cook upon a fire or latch a door. Only her mother possessed a single object made of silver, a ring given her by her mother. Now here was another tool, all glittering and golden.

'There is writing upon the rim,' she said, frowning that she could not read it.

'It says, "Thine heart be mine."'

Is that what he wished? For her to give him her heart? When she thought about her future husband, she imagined receiving rather than giving. And yet . . . should they not be one and the same?

'There is no need to decide anything now. If you will allow, I shall call again. And then we shall see, my dear Philadelphia. Then we shall see.'

Realising that he still held his palm open, she returned the thimble to its owner, but not without a longing glance as he closed his fist around it once more and returned it to his pocket. She could see the thimble's outline pressing against the fine jacquard silk of his waistcoat.

Yes, they would see.

12

Brisbane, Australia
2024

It was sweltering in the studio. She had left everything open but the breeze was playing hard to get that afternoon. Sun lanced through the glass so that her T-shirt was already damp and her forehead filmed with sweat. The studio was the first room she had painted when she moved into the flat, trading the dirty brown paint of its timber-lined walls for white so that the room was washed with light. (Unfortunately, light and heat often went hand-in-hand in Brisbane's subtropical climate.) It was probably the neatest room in the house too, although she wasn't sure if this was a sign of serious commitment or evidence that it was underused. Possibly the latter.

Two Ikea trestle tables were arranged underneath a row of windows overlooking the back garden. She used one for cutting, pasting, drawing and painting. The other held a large computer screen connected to her laptop. Alongside one trestle table she kept a drinks trolley that held olive and pickle jars from the café, brimming with brushes, pens and pencils, the lower shelves filled with various tools and supplies. A tall bookcase occupied an end wall while a plan drawer topped with tubs of acrylic paints took the other. Apart from an easel and a stack of canvases, the long wall opposite the windows was left clear of furniture, giving her enough space to move around. Instead, she had filled the wall with old frames displaying paintings and photographs she had collected on her travels, plus Blu-tacked images of people and places which had caught her eye. She seemed to be drawn to historical images, and some from her father's family tree collection had found their way on to the wall. Scattered amongst the found images were photographs she had taken herself, images she had scanned and digitally manipulated, and the very few drawings she had done that weren't half bad.

She was sitting on an adjustable stool, supposedly sketching from a photograph, but mostly swivelling about the room on castors, procrastinating. Several balls of crumpled paper littered the floor. Ever since her mother had given her the photograph of her grandmother, she couldn't shake the image of this woman she had never met from her mind. So, in an effort to clear her head, she had decided to try sketching her grandmother's likeness. An exorcism of sorts. For once, the head and face bore some resemblance to life; the hair fell in a charcoal tangle around high cheekbones, the eyes were long and wide set, the eyebrows winged, the nose and lips in proportion. More than that, they suggested character. There was determination in the chin, a steely resolve in the eyes that seemed to say this woman wouldn't be taken in by charmers and ratbags. But no matter what Mia did, the clothes just didn't look right.

In the photograph, her grandmother had been wearing a black kaftan with red embroidery. It was loose and shapeless with wide sleeves that added to the bohemian air of her wild hair. But in Mia's sketch her grandmother was dressed in a high-waisted garment with a snug bodice, and a handkerchief tucked around her neck to cover a low-cut neckline. The sleeves were long and narrow, and the skirt beneath the bodice was draped rather than full. To add to Mia's confusion, she had drawn her grandmother wearing a mob cap with a frill. None of this was by design. Her hand seemed to have developed a mind of its own. Maybe the kaftan was the problem; the shapeless black garment just didn't lend itself to a drawing, and her inner critic was sending her a message. Or maybe . . .

She scooted back to the trestles, this time pulling up in front of her computer. She would google her grandmother. There was sure to be an image of her online. There were images of everyone online, weren't there? Even elderly Englishwomen who may or may not have belonged to a cult. Her fingers tingling in anticipation, she entered her grandmother's name, giving her full name for full effect, and her location – Sussex – and pressed enter.

The first thing she discovered was that there were more Foord families in Sussex than she had imagined, given the unusual spelling; genealogy pages, the Sussex Record Society and the Australian Cemeteries Index being the main sites that surfaced. (Clearly, at least one family of Foords had found their way to Australia in the nineteenth century, even here in Brisbane.) She decided to give Google more to go on, adding the name of the village, a date range and the search term 'village news'. She trawled the results that appeared, leaving the genealogy sites for later, while searching for something, anything, that might contain a photograph of her grandmother. She was feeling quite dejected by the third page of results, when she decided to narrow her search to images only – something she had neglected initially.

She scrolled and clicked and there, amongst a row of strangers, was Henrietta staring back at her granddaughter. She was older and more defiant than in the photograph Celia had shown her, but undoubtedly the same person. The same cloud of hair, greyer, but just as untamed. And she was still wearing a kaftan-like garment; only this time it was forest green with a band of silver embroidery at the neck and cuffs. (Mia suspected her late grandmother might have been something of a drama queen.) She clicked on the article that accompanied the photograph and began to read.

> *Always one of our most popular stalls, 'Henrietta's Tent of Good Fortune' was again bustling. Those of you familiar with the fair will know that Henrietta Foord Sutton has been a regular since the 1990s, reading palms and on occasion peering into teacups to tell our futures.*

So . . . her grandmother was a notable personage in East Sussex, judging by what Mia saw as she scanned the page archived from a blog celebrating people and events in the village. This particular article concerned a certain 2010 village fair.

> *This year was no exception, one happy villager divulging to this scribe that, 'Henrietta predicted last year that I would marry soon – and look at this,' as she held up her ring finger. It seems that our Ms Foord Sutton's fame is only eclipsed by her ancestor's notoriety. Thankfully for local residents, her talents are considerably more benevolent than her infamous ancestor.*

She read the article a second time before she could properly take it in. What did this Sussex scribe mean by 'her ancestor's notoriety'? Cryptic, to say the least, and Henrietta must have chosen her outfit to match the fortune-teller vibe. Clearly, she wasn't one to shy away from publicity, if not notoriety. Mia scrolled to the bottom of the page to see if any more would be said about Henrietta amongst the descriptions of the dog show, tug-of-war contest, pony rides and Pimm's by the lake. But there was nothing further to be discovered about her grandmother, or the 'notorious' ancestor, and nothing to suggest why a decade and a half later Mia was sketching Henrietta in an obscure historical costume rather than her customary boho look.

Well, her mother may not have enjoyed being the daughter of an eccentric but she quite liked the idea that her grandmother was doing her own thing well into her seventies.

'Good on you, Henrietta,' she muttered.

'She always did please herself.'

Mia turned to find that Celia had entered the studio on stealthy cat's feet and was standing behind her, staring over her shoulder at the computer screen.

'What are you doing here?' she asked, swivelling on her stool.

'I knocked on your screen door but you didn't answer, so I let myself in. I brought snacks.' She held up a package from Mia's favourite patisserie.

'You can't just let yourself in, Mum.'

'Darling, any old stranger can let themselves in when you leave the screen door unlatched. Your mother is the least threatening.'

Personally, Mia wondered whether this was strictly true.

'I see you've been googling Henrietta. She doesn't look much different to how I remember her,' Celia said, her voice tinged with regret.

'In all these years, haven't you been tempted to do the same?' Mia asked. Sometimes it was hard to read her mother.

'Tempted, maybe. But it always felt too … risky,' Celia answered, with a frown.

'Did you think she would use her powers to find you if she sensed you were looking? Plant cookies to track you or something?' Mia scoffed, while secretly wondering whether it might be true.

If her grandmother was a fortune-teller, did she also have a sixth sense, was that part of her mother's fear of her? Suddenly, so many things began to make 'sense' to Mia. Her strange dreams, sleeping and waking. Her sudden certainties, out of nowhere. She had a sixth sense, too. What's more, maybe her mother also had some kind of psychic sensibility – hence the uncannily prescient texts. No, she found herself shaking her head, it couldn't be true. She wouldn't let it. She had spent so long denying it.

Celia laid a hand on her daughter's shoulder and squeezed. 'No, darling. It might seem hard to you, but it took decades of self-restraint not to contact her. I couldn't afford to give in to the urge, even online. I knew she was all right, because I kept in touch with an old school friend – one who vowed on her life not to tell, by the way. Besides, I knew my mother would always be okay. She was like a cat. A black cat,' she added, ruefully, 'with at least nine lives.'

'Why didn't you mention the fortune-telling?'

'Oh,' Celia answered, making a shooing motion with her hand, 'just one of her many eccentricities.'

'And the cult?'

'Well, it wasn't really a cult so much as a c—' She broke off mid-sentence.

'A what?'

'A coven.'

Well, this wasn't what Mia had been expecting. 'As in a witches' coven? You're joking,' she snorted, even as bits and pieces of memory started joining together in her head. 'First a cult. Now a coven? Really?'

'Yep. My mother was a witch.'

'Like in Wicca?'

'Nuh-uh, as in the old-fashioned kind of witch. She always said Gerald Gardner made up all that stuff about the New Forest Coven. Although, I wouldn't say that to a Wiccan or she might put a hex on me,' her mother added, with a warning look.

'What do you mean?'

'I was joking about the hex, you know. But Henrietta always insisted that the New Forest witches were just a group of Masonic, intellectual wannabes. Whereas she and her associates had been witches for generations. The kind who passed their secrets on to their daughters. The kind they once burned for selling cures and love potions and telling fortunes. Not surprisingly, my mother wasn't well liked in *certain* quarters. Personally, I think most of it was a con,' she added, with a cynical chuckle. 'And very competitive.'

'Mum, you do realise that you're talking about this as if it's all quite normal. As if you knew these people.' She almost sounded a bit snobby about it, to tell the truth.

'Well, I did grow up with it,' Celia explained, with a huff. 'And I did meet Gerald Gardner once when I was a kid, the so-called "father of Wicca". According to my mother, the Foord women were witches long before Gardner had his "meeting" with the New Forest Coven. Anyway, maybe now you can begin to see why I left.'

'She sounds intriguing to me.'

'Of course, she does,' Celia said. 'She could be charming and eccentric, if you didn't have to live with her. That's what made her so dangerous. People didn't see how misguided it all was. How . . . how . . . frightening it could be to a child. Besides, that would have been fine,' her mother was on a roll now, 'if she hadn't forced her beliefs on to me. Except she just couldn't help herself. She had to make my life a misery.'

'How? By putting a hex on you?'

'Oh,' Celia scoffed, 'I could have handled a hex. No, this was much worse. This was Sussex in the 1970s, don't forget, not London. We were all helmet hairdos, hats and shirtdresses. Henrietta, with her weird hippy clothes and mystical ideas, terrified the parents at the school gate, so none of my friends were allowed to visit me or invite me over. She banned all technology from the house, so I couldn't even listen to the radio, and then she made me read dingy old books about wizards instead. And I do *not* mean Harry Potter.'

'Sounds like a lot of parents,' Mia muttered under her breath, which her mother chose not to hear.

'Not to mention dragging me to all kinds of strange gatherings where she explored her "powers". Then there was the constant stream of sad romantics knocking on the door to have their fortunes read or buy a love amulet.'

'So, in other words, she was odd.'

'Once, she got us *both* arrested for desecrating graves in the churchyard. Even when I went off to London, to university, she kept turning up on my doorstep with her tarot cards and her witch's brews. No, the only way I could keep her out of my life was by escaping to somewhere she couldn't find me.'

Celia stopped to draw breath. Suddenly, she looked haggard, the faint lines above her mouth and around her eyes made prominent by the afternoon sunlight. The white strands of encroaching age visible in the parting of her hair. Her mother was getting old, Mia realised. She had always thought of her as youthful, with her gardener's litheness and her teacher's curiosity. But the heir hunter's letter had brought back too many memories, clearly too many to unpack in one conversation. This was the most her mother had told her about her childhood in Mia's entire life. Now she seemed to have run out of language, while Mia had so many words bottled up inside that she didn't know where to start. Questions bobbing up against questions which suddenly needed urgent answers.

'Mum, who was our "notorious ancestor"?' she asked, after a short silence. Maybe the distant past was the safest place to begin. 'It says in this article that Henrietta's fame was "only eclipsed by her ancestor's notoriety".'

'Oh, that ancient gossip.' Celia shook her head. 'Sussex is full of stories of witches who lived down the lane, or up the hill or on the common.'

'But the article speaks of a *particular* "notorious ancestor".'

'I don't know, darling,' she said, deflated now, and bereft of words. 'You'd have to ask the person who wrote it.'

What Celia meant was she didn't want to know. Or she didn't want to talk about it any longer. 'You've been sketching,' she said instead, ever the mistress of deflection.

'Trying. That's why I was looking for another image of Henrietta. In my head, I keep seeing her dressed in really old-fashioned clothes, and those clothes keep creeping into the drawing. I mean who wears a mob cap?'

Someone from the past, obviously.

'It's probably your subconscious at work. You're always collecting pictures of something or other,' Celia said. 'You probably saw a picture of someone dressed in something similar. Or one of those Jane Austen movies.'

But Mia knew the image was more visceral than that. She felt it in her bones. Maybe she wasn't sketching Henrietta at all. Maybe she was sketching a more distant relative . . . one of her earlier ancestors.

Yes, that must be it. But exactly *who* was she sketching? Her grandmother, or the notorious ancestor?

She closed her eyes, all too conscious of her mother's hand still resting on her shoulder, and alongside it the tiny hairs on the back of her neck twitching into life. Delivering a message. Just as they had done once before, thirteen years ago. That time, the silent message had been accompanied by the sound of rushing water and an icy chill. That time, she had ignored the message, and people had died. For years, she had been telling herself that hindsight had made her imagine she'd had a vision; conjured that creepy feeling of dread out of survivor guilt after the event. She hadn't wanted to believe that people had died and she could have saved them. That she could have done something.

Denial had seemed like the only way she could move on with her life. At least after a fashion. But two years ago, when the floods came again, the memories had come with them. Those memories were so overpowering that she had decamped Brisbane to escape them, too. She had abandoned a job at the gallery that she was growing to love, and moved north for six months to work as a barista in Port Douglas. She couldn't face the rising waters; the ever-present threat of being washed away. Higher ground wasn't enough for Mia; she had to move a thousand miles away. When she returned to Brisbane, she had promised herself she would ignore her fears next time, that she really would get her life in order and grow up.

But what if her fears were real? What if her fears were really warnings? What if Jase turning up was a sign? And what if this vision of her ancestor in her anachronistic costume was sending her another warning?

She sighed. One way or another, she needed to accept the possibility that her 'feeling' might be real and have the courage to act on it – whatever it meant – or she might never get beyond the past.

'Maybe I will,' she whispered, half to herself.

Maybe, rather than a warning, she was being sent a call to action. One she couldn't afford to ignore.

'Will what?' Celia asked.

'Speak to the person who wrote it. Maybe I will go to Sussex and ask the writer of the blog what they meant. I've been invited.'

She looked up into her mother's face, expecting to find surprise, but instead she saw resignation.

'You knew? You knew Grandmother's will stipulated I had to come in person to claim it.'

'No. I didn't know, but it sounds like Henrietta. She always liked to wave her magic wand and bend people to her will. No, let's just say it was a mother's instinct.'

That evening, after Celia had departed in a flurry of warnings and advice that her daughter would inevitably ignore, Mia returned to her studio to sit staring at her half-finished sketch. The light was almost gone. Even so, it was as if the face staring back at her glowed in the last flickers of sunlight in the pink sky.

'Who are you?' she whispered. 'And what do you want?'

There was something about the woman's face that suggested determination; a certain tilt to the chin, a defiance in the eye, the wild hair that would not be contained by the pretty white cap. The contradiction between the demureness of her clothes and the wilfulness of her attitude compelled Mia's attention.

'You wouldn't take the easy road, would you?'

Mia sighed; a sound that issued from somewhere deep in her chest. What had *she* been doing with her life? Drifting from one job to another, one place to another, one love affair to another? Never really getting anywhere, still mired somewhere back in the past – despite her denials. Well, it had to stop. She had to make it stop; no fairy godmother was going to wave her magic wand and stop it for her. And the only way to do it was to make some changes. Drastic changes.

She breathed in a great gulp of Brisbane's moist subtropical air, scraping her sticky hair back from her face. So . . . she needed to get her finances and her career in order and become a grown-up. And if that meant slaying her demons, then she would need to find a way to do that, too. She just didn't know how yet. Still, she did have a few clues. Taking up one of her Copic markers, she tore a sheet from her sketch pad with a determined flourish. Then, without stopping to think it through, she scrawled:

MIA'S RULES OF ENGAGEMENT
No falling in love for at least ~~one~~ two years
No sex for at least ~~six months~~ one year

She paused, marker in the air. Ending her trail of disastrous, short-lived boyfriends was a good place to start. She wasn't sure when exactly she had lost her talent for true love, but it was probably around the time . . . around the time she left school. She still had a talent for falling in love, she just didn't have the knack for staying there. The men she chose, however, had a knack for breaking her heart. Her poor little heart had been broken so many times that it was thick with scar tissue and had nearly lost all feeling.

> *Must make art, no matter how bad*
> *Get a job and stick to it for ~~a while~~ at least a year*

Sticking to things was another area that needed vast improvement. Funny how her relationship and employment history were similarly choppy.

> *Find out for self, truth of grandmother*

She paused again, chewing the end of her marker. So far, her rules were all objective, attainable. But there was something else, a feeling that seeing Jase again had provoked in her. Truthfully, a feeling that had never quite gone away, despite all her efforts to suppress it. She put her purple marker to paper again.

> *Listen to intuition*

Yes. This time, instead of ignoring her instincts, Mia would listen to them. And her instincts were telling her to make the journey to her mother's birthplace and become acquainted with her heritage. She would learn what she could about her eccentric grandmother, and perhaps even discover for herself the story of this notorious ancestor. In the process, maybe she would find out more about who *she* was – and, more importantly, – who she wanted to become.

How could it hurt to find out?

13

Sussex, England
1821

From the window of her bedchamber, Philadelphia looked down upon the scene below with a sinking heart. The street bustled at this early hour. In the market square, farmers packed up their baskets of cabbages, peas and beetroots until next week's market. Pedlars of tin goods, brooms and fancy shawls hawked for customers amongst the women gossiping with neighbours or visiting the shops lining the high street. Men who had breakfasted early were out and about, taking coffee or ale at one of the two inns, seeing the farrier about a horse that wanted shoeing or commissioning a new pair of top boots from the shoemaker. And there, parading about the street, his truncheon at his belt, was Constable Puttick in earnest conversation with the village mercer.

Jasper had died only yesterday, but already Puttick marched the street, assiduous in his hunt for jurors. For the coroner had arrived on her doorstep with the surgeon the previous afternoon, demanding to inspect her husband's body. Philadelphia had ushered them down the narrow stone stairs that led to the vaulted cellar where Jasper lay amongst the sacks of parsnips and potatoes. She apologised to him silently for the indignity, glancing away when Surgeon Goodenough drew back the length of black crêpe she had draped over her husband's body. But not quickly enough to miss a glimpse of green-hued skin. Jasper would have scorned the way it clashed with the red and blue stripes of his silk waistcoat.

The men had taken their time considering Jasper's body before Mr Honeycett, the coroner, issued the constable with a warrant to call a jury. Puttick must present the coroner with suitable names, enough to select fourteen men of good character. Men who would be charged with deciding whether her husband had died of natural or unnatural causes. The usual choices as jurors were the farmers and tradesmen of the parish, with only the occasional professional man or gentleman. Those particular men claimed exemption for one reason or another; belonging to the gentry was usually reason enough. Jasper had served several times, his brother also, although her husband enjoyed the task far less than his brother Enoch.

Most of the men Puttick might approach had been Jasper's customers at one time or another. Some of them still owed him money, owed her money now, she recalled. And many did not approve of either Philadelphia or her mother, Susanna. Certainly not the brick maker, who Puttick just now accosted outside the shoemaker's shop across the street. She recognised the man by the cut of his yellow tailcoat, a colour Jasper had tried valiantly to dissuade him from choosing, with little success. The coat was as yet unpaid – and unlikely to be paid at all, now. Her heart sank even lower as she watched the brick maker nod agreeably and tip his hat to the constable. Edgar Lacy was a man of means, that was a fact, and his daughters had never liked Philadelphia. They frowned upon her entire profession; affecting a knowing nod, a raised eyebrow, even a snigger whenever the 'milliner' was mentioned.

Everyone in the parish knew that Lettice had always wanted Jasper for herself.

She continued to watch from her window as the constable enlisted several more men; the shoemaker himself, Farmer Sutton who was passing by, and the apothecary three doors down, who was known to dislike the Foord women on principle for encroaching upon his business. Puttick did not take his task lightly and had been known to interrupt a likely candidate at his dinner. With each meeting, her trepidation grew.

'See how you have left me,' she whispered to her dead husband, not without a hint of resentment. Alone. Without allies, except for young Isaac – and that was no certainty now that his father had dragged him home. She could not be sure what the lad might say under pressure from Enoch Boadle, whether he would be strong enough to protect her interests and honour Jasper's memory, even if he wanted to.

A soft rap, little more than a scratch at the door, drew her attention from the window.

'Mama?' came a muffled plea through the heavy oak wood.

'Marjory.' Her spirits lifted at the sound of her daughter's voice, and with it her resolve hardened. Whatever the future held, she must face the scrutiny of the inquest and overcome it for her daughter's sake. Jasper would concur with that at least.

'Jenny is scrubbing pots.' Clearly, her daughter had concluded that scrubbing pots was no pastime for a child of eight years.

'Come in, my cherub.' She opened her arms as the small face, a twin to her own, appeared around the door. 'Come sit with your mother.' She patted her lap, clad in her one good black dress. She had sewn it for Susanna's mourning, a good bombazine made up in the military style, with frogging at its bodice, long sleeves *à la mamalouk*, and three broad tucks at the hem. It would have to do for Jasper. She must guard her pennies now, for who knew how far they must stretch in the coming months?

Marjory took her at her word, flying across the floor to throw herself into her mother's arms. 'I could not find you. You were not at your workbench.'

'I'm sorry, sweeting. I have been busy with my own concerns. Has Jenny given you breakfast?'

'Porridge again,' the child said, squirming with distaste. 'Is Papa still in the cellar?'

'I'm afraid so.' Philadelphia bit her lip, trying to banish the memory of that green face. His staring eyes had seemed to glare at her in reproach, although she could not be sure if he reproached her for putting him in the cellar or for the fact of his demise. He would have found something.

'Is he coming back?'

'No. Papa will not be coming back. I told you, remember, that he has gone to be with God in Heaven. It is just you and me, and cousin Isaac now.'

'And Jenny and Martin.'

'Yes. And Jenny and Martin.' Although she could make no pledge for how long.

'You will not go to God, will you, Mama? I should not like to be left alone without you *and* Papa.' She pushed herself from Philadelphia's lap and stood with her blue eyes flashing beneath a cloud of ebony hair. 'I need you more than God does.'

'They would have to drag me to Heaven in chains,' Philadelphia replied, patting her lap again. She saw that her daughter had left a trail of tears, or snot, upon the bodice of the bombazine. 'We will miss Papa very much but we will remember him in our prayers.'

'Is he with Grandmama?'

'I should not think so.'

She hugged the child to her chest before planting a kiss on her forehead and setting her on her feet, saying, 'Now, I am about to make damson cakes and would be glad of your help.'

The murmur of voices beneath the window drew her attention and she stood to peer out over the window ledge to the street below. Only a few feet beyond the timber awning that sheltered customers to the tailor's shop, the constable was in earnest conversation with a tall man in a narrow-brimmed beaver hat – genuine beaver felt, by the look of it, from this distance – and a morning coat of tan with a dark brown collar. She could not see the man's face, for she viewed him from above, and did not recognise the coat as one Jasper had fashioned. It was certainly well cut, if a little worn, and even from this height she could see that it was of a fine worsted.

The two men seemed to have come to some arrangement, for they bowed agreeably and took their leave of one another, the constable resuming his hunt for jurors while the second man remained standing below her window. There was something familiar about the way he tapped his riding whip against his leg in a slow rhythm, his head bowed, as if deep in thought. Not a hasty man, then. A considered one. She was still watching him when he raised his head and glanced up at the window. She almost recoiled, for it would not help her reputation to be caught staring at a gentleman, except the intensity of his gaze held her captive. She could not see the colour of those eyes from her perch above the street, but she knew them to be keen and hazel-flecked, with the warm tone of their namesake wood.

She was about to withdraw from the window when she saw that he was approached by another, a man with a wiry frame and purposeful stride, hands clasped tightly behind his back, chin jutting. She could not see the new arrival's face but she knew his walk, and watched warily as he presented his greetings with a deep bow and a flourish of his hat. She would have recognised the brown hat, even if she did not recognise his gait, for it had once been owned by Jasper and had seen better days; fashioned by a Lewes hatter of some renown, and made of rabbit felt in the 'chimney' style popular ten years earlier. Jasper had worn it with a rakish tilt to the brim.

'Come, Marjory,' she said, grasping her daughter's hand a little too firmly so that the girl squeaked in surprise. 'Come, we must speak to that gentleman about your poor dear papa.'

She flew to the door, pausing at the top of the narrow staircase to pick up her daughter and carry her down, before setting her on her feet again at the bottom. Then she almost dragged Marjory through the workshop, slamming the front door behind her. Enoch had finished his business with the gentry by this time – and she could not help wondering how many of Puttick's worthies he had already accosted – so that the gentleman stood alone in the street, frowning up at her window. He must have heard the slamming door, or Marjory's protest of 'Mamaaa!' for he turned his attention to them when they were about ten feet distant.

She slowed her pace, conscious that her hair was yet untamed and covered by neither cap nor bonnet, and her own eyes were brimming with unshed tears for her husband – may he rest in peace – but mostly for herself and her daughter. It also occurred to her that she did not know what she meant to say to him, only that upon seeing Enoch casting his spell of malice, she felt compelled to say something. Thomas Earle was one of the foremost personages in the parish. But more than this, he was respected for his considered judgement and well liked for his kindness.

'Good day to you, Mrs Boadle,' he said, tipping his hat so that the morning sun caught the chestnut hints in his hair.

'Good day to you, Mr Earle,' she replied. 'We are closed today, as you can see.'

'Yes, I was most sorry to hear of your loss.' A loss he would understand only too well, she knew.

'Thank you.' She slipped an arm about Marjory's shoulders, who had sidled nearer as she spoke.

'And your daughter, too. A very sad day for you both.'

'The coroner has called for an inquest,' she said, though he

The Heirloom

knew that already. 'He believes there are questions to be answered about my dear Jasper's death.'

'So Puttick tells me.'

'I fear some in the parish may be unkind in their . . . opinions, if called to testify.'

He did not respond for several moments. Then, with a nod and the merest shadow of a smile, he said, 'That may be. However, there are those to whom you have been of great service, too. My wife, Marianne, had nothing but gratitude for you, Mrs Boadle, for your excellent hats and your other skills.'

'Mrs Earle was always most kind to me, sir, even in the depths of her illness,' she said. Then, in case he did not quite understand the ramifications of the skills she had employed for his wife, she added, 'And if you remember, sir, I did but offer herbal tea and a listening ear. Only herbal tea and a listening ear. Anyone would have done the same.'

'That is true, of course. Although, not all would have done the same.' He tilted his head almost imperceptibly, adding, 'Some folk grow tired in the face of a terrible grief. Not that I blame them.'

He had not wearied, though, despite his own sadness; he had comforted his wife in her grief over her lost babies. Two miscarriages, one stillborn that Philadelphia knew of, and a six-month-old boy dead of a fever. Too many losses for one poor woman.

She smiled, saying, 'I was very fond of Mrs Earle, if I may be so bold, sir.'

'Well, I hope that I can be of some service to you at this difficult time, Mrs Boadle,' he said, and she saw from the crinkles at the corners of his eyes that he spoke the truth.

'That is very kind of you. I admit the prospect of an inquest fills me with alarm. Not everyone looks upon me with such kindness.'

'You must trust that some jurors won't be swayed by gossip and unfounded opinion.'

'You will serve on the jury then?' He had not done so before, as far as she knew.

'I will.' He spoke the words as if he had just then made up his mind, and she breathed a sigh of relief.

With these two simple words of reassurance, he took his leave of her. She followed him with her eyes all the way down the high street until he disappeared around the corner in the direction of the stables. Her heart still thrumming, she hugged her daughter to her chest.

'At least there will be one on the jury who we might trust, Marjory.'

'Who, Mama? Who shall we trust?'

'Mr Thomas Earle. For he has said we must. And if a gentleman such as Mr Earle asks for our trust, then we must give it, must we not?'

Despite the difference in their stations, he had ever been a friend to her, she realised. In his own way. And she had done her very best to be a friend to his poor dead wife, Marianne. Tried to bring her every comfort a simple milliner could offer, until it was too late.

14

East Sussex, England
1819

The Earles' butler kept Philadelphia standing in the entry a good half-hour before he ushered her into the drawing room to wait upon Mrs Earle. Still, she stepped into the room as graciously as possible, her head held high, her arms burdened by a tumble of bandboxes brimming with samples and the leather satchel containing the tools of her trade. She found her client reclining on a daybed of green damask, her muslin dress draped about her legs like a flurry of fresh snow and her face seeming even whiter for its frame of pale curls and delicate lace cap.

'Mrs Boadle, how kind of you to come at such short notice.'

Marianne Earle beckoned Philadelphia closer, indicating an elaborate carved chair beside her, its seat upholstered in the same green fabric as the sofa. 'I had a sudden yen for a new bonnet.'

'I am always happy to oblige you, Mrs Earle. In fact, I have some new fashion plates from Paris with the most charming of bonnets to show you,' Philadelphia answered, placing her boxes upon the floor and taking a seat. She did not bring her hat blocks, or her flower irons and dies, when visiting clients, but she brought her sewing kit with its shears, pins, needles and chalk, useful if they should require a small adjustment to the hem of a gown or a repair to a torn sleeve. A milliner was often called upon to repair and refurbish garments as well as create hats. Plus, she carried samples of the latest ribbons, straws and fabrics that might suit her customers, and she always brought her golden thimble, as a talisman if nothing else. It reminded her of how far she had come since the day Jasper had first tantalised her with his intent. And how far she might fall if all were taken from her.

She smiled as she waited for the other woman to divulge the real reason for the visit. Marianne Earle wasn't the sort of woman to summon her with such urgency in need of a new hat. There was more to the request, she felt sure. Since the death of her only living child two years earlier, she had sought out Philadelphia more often, a new bonnet or cap being a convenient pretext.

'I woke this morning with the sudden notion that one of your creations might cheer me,' Marianne said, with a smile. The smile was a tentative thing, as if she hadn't used it for some time.

'I have only this week finished crafting some silk fruits that might be just the thing for that plain straw bonnet we fashioned for you last summer. We could make it over anew. What say you to a bunch of grapes and some juicy plums to decorate the brim? Or perhaps a confection of apples and pears atop the crown? We might even tie it all together with some plaid ribbon.'

'I could as well place an entire bowl of fruit upon my head, although Cook might frown upon it,' Marianne replied, with a laugh. 'See, you have cheered me already.'

Philadelphia was glad to see that her words had the desired effect. 'Then perhaps I can show you the latest fashion plates from Paris instead.' Now that the war was finally over, French fashions were all the rage again.

'But first some tea, I think,' Marianne said, as a maid appeared with a tray of silver tea things and set it on the table in front of her mistress. Marianne made to rise from the daybed before sinking back with a sigh. 'Forgive me, I cannot seem to summon the strength. Could you pour, Mrs Boadle?'

'Of course.' Philadelphia considered the other woman more closely. She hadn't called upon her for several weeks, and she had been absent from church of late. She realised now that the limbs hiding beneath the muslin gown and fine Kashmir shawl were bone thin. And her pallor may have sprung from illness rather than a fine complexion. 'I would have brought a tonic if I had known you were unwell,' she said.

Marianne shivered, her shoulder bones knifing the wool of her shawl. 'Forgive me. I should think my friends grow tired of my malaises.'

'A friend's illness, whether of spirit or body, is not something to tire of.' So, Marianne Earle, one of the most respected women in the parish named Philadelphia her friend. It was unexpected but welcome. 'Perhaps I might help, if I knew more.'

'The surgeon advises it is a woman's lot and I must bear it.'

'Perhaps that is because the surgeon is not a woman.'

Marianne glanced towards the door, listening for the sound of servants, before whispering, 'I bleed so heavily, Mrs Boadle. And with the bleeding comes such pain that I cannot leave my bed.'

'Has this been happening for very long?'

'I have always bled heavily but it has become so great that I fear I may run dry of blood. And when the bleeding wanes, I am so tired. So tired that I drag myself through the days.' She frowned; her years of suffering were apparent in the fine lines feathering her forehead. 'Is this a woman's lot?'

'Some of us suffer more than others, but not so much that we run dry,' Philadelphia answered, with a concerned smile. 'I can prepare a tonic that may help. If my mother, Susanna, were still with us, she might do more. Unfortunately, I don't have her knowledge. I would suggest you consult a physician, perhaps in London. But in the meantime, I will do my best to bring the tonic as soon as I can, and I will scour my memory for any other of my mother's remedies.' Though she would have to wait until Jasper visited one of his more far-flung clients, for he had long ago forbidden the brewing of remedies in his house.

'You are very kind.' Marianne extended a hand, the fingernails pale moons, as wan as her complexion, the weight of her hand like a baby chick in Philadelphia's with its milliner's calloused palm.

'And now for tea,' the other woman said, a smile flitting briefly across her lips.

The scalloped teapot, set upon the side table, shone like a silver shell; the cream jug and sugar bowl glowed with their gilt linings. Set beside the tea service, the cups and saucers were like a garden in full bloom: lilies, tulips, lilac and iris, bordered by a rim of gold. Philadelphia spooned tea from the caddy into the pot and filled it with hot water from a silver urn. After allowing the tea to brew for several minutes – while discussing the latest fashion plates in *Ackermann's Repository* – she poured a cup for her hostess, added the required milk and sugar, and set it in her hand. Then she poured another for herself. They chatted amiably of this and that, until Marianne took her final sip, twisted her cup thoughtfully upon its saucer several times, before returning it to the milliner's hand.

'Oh, how clumsy of me,' Philadelphia said, with a conspiratorial glance, having knocked the cup so that it fell upon its side on the saucer. She upended it, swivelled it upon the saucer once more, before setting it upright again.

'What do you see?' Marianne asked, an excited edge to her voice. She leaned forward as far as she could manage, peering into the teacup sitting in its dregs upon the tea tray. The pale blue interior of the Jasperware cup was painted with a trail of wet tea leaves.

Philadelphia considered the cup, a furrow forming between her brows. 'There is not much to see or tell. You have swallowed most of the leaves this time, I think.'

The Heirloom

'You must see something, surely. I had hoped ... I had hoped ... well, I had hopes for the future ...' Her excitement dampened, she trailed off into silence, though her eyes remained focused on Philadelphia's face.

'I see ... I see ... that you shall soon be feeling better,' Philadelphia answered after a few moments, sorry that she could not give the other woman what she wanted. Sorry that no one could.

A fleeting expression of disappointment crossed Marianne's face, before she sank back on to her sofa with a resigned smile. 'Well, perhaps your tonic will do the trick, then.'

'I certainly hope so, Mrs Earle.'

The butler had almost succeeded in shepherding her out the door (the front door, upon his mistress's explicit instruction) when it was flung open and the master of the house entered, his spaniel at his heels and a younger man at his side. Philadelphia was accustomed to seeing Thomas Earle as she pursued some errand in the high street, or on occasion when he called at the workshop to make a small purchase of socks or such. She was not accustomed to almost colliding with him, dropping her bundles and bandboxes upon the Turkey rug in the hall, and all in view of the butler and this well-turned-out gentleman. She felt her cheeks flame, which only added to the consternation brought about by her visit with his wife and her resulting feeling of helplessness.

'Mrs Boadle! I have brought you unstuck,' he said cheerfully, appearing unfazed by their near collision. 'Here, let me help you collect your packages.' He bent to pick up a box as she retrieved a bundle.

'Phillip, may I present Mrs Philadelphia Boadle, friend and milliner to Marianne,' he said as he handed up the box containing her fabric samples. 'My nephew, Mr Sparrow. Mr Sparrow is my sister's son.'

'How d'ye do, Mrs Boadle?' the young gent said, tipping the brim of his hat and offering a token bow.

'How d'ye do, Mr Sparrow?' Philadelphia curtseyed clumsily, weighed down by her packages.

The pair appeared to be returning from a walk. Earle's trousers and boots were splattered with mud and his hair was tousled beneath his country straw hat, while his nephew's nose was red from the wind.

'I shall see you inside, if you do not mind, Phillip,' Earle said, to a lifted eyebrow from the younger man, who glanced Philadelphia's way in a manner she could only describe as appraising. 'You may go, Robertson,' he added, waving away the hovering butler. 'I will see Mrs Boadle out.'

'Did my wife offer you tea?' he asked, when the pair had gone indoors.

'She did, sir.'

'And how did she seem to you?'

For a moment she was taken aback by the question and did not know how to answer. But he regarded her so intently that she blurted out the truth before she thought to temper it with kindness.

'She looked terrible, sir. She has become so thin and pale since I last saw her. And I fear . . .'

'And you fear?'

'I am sorry, it is not my place.'

'Please.'

Still, she hesitated. 'I fear for her.'

He was silent for several seconds, before saying, 'As do I. I would have appealed to your mother – may she rest in peace – but . . .'

He bent down to stroke his spaniel's ears so that she could not see his face. 'But perhaps you might have some suggestion? The surgeon has proved of little help.'

'I am only a milliner, sir.'

'And yet you have proved yourself more than that. My wife values your advice, Mrs Boadle.'

'I have offered to bring her a tonic. My mother sometimes used this remedy for a lady's particular problems.' How else could she describe a woman's bodily functions to a man, a gentleman at that? 'Luckily, it can be brewed from flowers that grow in nearby meadows.'

'What is the plant you need called? I can have my groom search for it when he is out exercising the horses, if that would help.'

Again, she hesitated, but he looked to her so intently that she answered, 'It is known as the Devil's bit, sir. The flowers are shaped like purple balls, sweet-scented to the nose.'

'And do you truly think the tea may help?'

'I do not know for certain. But we may try.'

Despite her encouraging words, Philadelphia could not banish the image of Marianne's cup with its coil of tea leaves decorating the rim. The serpent, omen of misfortune. And below that a shape resembling a tipping kettle. The black spout and handle – an augury of death. She shuddered, trying to banish the image from her mind.

'The waters at Bath might provide a cure. I have heard they may restore a woman to health,' she suggested.

A cup scattered with a graveyard of tiny crosses, portents of death and disaster.

'Or perhaps she might consult a physician in London?'

Poor Marianne, how could she hope to escape so many harbingers of death? So many portents of doom rallying against her? She who had already suffered the death of a beloved child and the loss of those others before she had the chance to meet them. Philadelphia regarded the man standing before her with a grave expression. She could not put the truth into words, but perhaps he saw it in her eyes.

'I will do everything I can,' he said, taking her gloved hand in his and shaking it. 'Everything.'

'That is all any of us can do, sir.'

15

East Sussex, England
2024

Mia didn't know where to look first; at the ancient cottage rising from the ruin of a neglected garden or the man standing just inside its fence of twigs. The cottage looked like something out of a fairy tale, with its flint walls and thatched roof, tiny white-framed windows and a doorway of handmade red bricks. The overgrown garden could have been a thicket of briars, while the tall man surveying the cottage – whip of brown hair sweeping across his forehead, broad shoulders stretching his grey hoodie, white polo, worn jeans, and *very* clean runners – could have been preparing to do battle with its hidden monsters. He certainly wasn't what she had been expecting. He was much better looking, and not nearly so old.

'Hi!' she called.

He turned to regard her with a frown. The frown threw her for a moment so that she took an involuntary step backwards. She wasn't that late, was she? Although, the walk from the hotel *had* been longer than she thought, plus she had taken her time to enjoy the sunken country lane with its overhanging trees and scent of recent rain. It wasn't every day she travelled ten thousand miles to claim an inheritance.

'You're Mia,' the unexpected man said, stepping forward to open the gate before she could reach it.

The gate had seen so many decades that the twigs forming its rails seemed to have grown into each other.

'That's me.'

He held the gate open, his eyes fixed on hers, inspecting her closely, almost as if she were some unearthly being. At first, she presumed his eyes were brown but, closer to, she discovered flecks of green reflected by the surrounding garden.

'Reid,' he said, blinking and offering his hand once he had closed the gate behind her.

She took his hand in a firm grip, disconcerted by the spark of warmth that shot up her arm as her hand rested briefly in his. This too was unexpected. He wasn't her type at all. She usually went for the arty boys and the musicians, the ones with a penchant for breaking hearts. Maybe the windswept athletic vibe had caught her off guard when she had been expecting a middle-aged man in a suit.

'Are you playing tennis later?' she asked, aiming for casually friendly but instead achieving awkward, which wouldn't have happened if he had been a fifty year old in a suit and tie, would it? She had sworn off men the moment she stepped aboard flight QF2 for London, vowing to give herself a clean slate, a chance to start anew without entanglements. Given that most of her past relationships had been uninspiring at best, and damaging at worst, it shouldn't have proved too great a sacrifice. So, her response to his handshake left her a bit unsettled.

Of course, her past choices might conceivably have been the problem rather than the men themselves – but that was a question for another day and years of future therapy. Love had not been her forte, she had to admit. Each time she began a relationship, she was sure he was the one, only to discover that he was probably the one for someone else. She had never managed to find the closeness that many of her friends found – that her parents had found – and she had begun to accept that *she* was the problem. After all, she was the common denominator. She was the one who chose the butterfly men who flitted from flower to flower. Or the loveable puppy dog men who wanted to know all her secrets and were hurt when she divulged little more than her favourite authors. She had that much self-knowledge. But why? That she didn't know. So for now, she was going to give love the flick and concentrate on the future. Or the past. The two might very well turn out to be the same thing.

Reid was glancing down at his trainers. 'I wanted to put you at ease. Some of our clients get jumpy if I turn up in a pinstripe suit.'

She wondered if he was making fun of her but decided to take his answer at face value, at least for now. Did anyone under forty own a pinstripe suit?

'Too casual?'

'Nope. I'm suitably at ease.'

'Well, let's get started, then. I thought we could take a look around while I explain the process in more detail.'

'Do you usually give your heirs a guided tour?'

'Occasionally. If I have access. In this case, since the will stipulated you had to travel so far to claim the inheritance, your grandmother's solicitor thought it might be a good idea to show you around before you meet with her.'

'Thanks, then.'

He set off up a weed-choked gravel path to a heavy oak door, inserting an old-fashioned key in the lock and jiggling it this way and that, before turning the iron door knob, lifting the door a fraction and heaving it open.

'You've been here before.'

'A few times, during our search for clues to your whereabouts.'

He said 'our'. Did that imply staff?

'Or possibly my actual existence?' she said. 'Mum might not have produced any children.'

'That too. I'm not sure if the power has been reconnected yet,' he said, flipping an old-fashioned brass light switch. 'Ah, there we go.'

The lights illuminated a low-beamed hall facing wooden stairs. The floor was paved with wide, handmade bricks and the walls were bare white plaster. Rooms led off to both sides, the brick floor spread with several tribal rugs. The room to her left was clearly the living room, furnished with a long elm sideboard beneath the near window, tall bookcases on either side of the far window, an elm occasional table, an Indian sofa with brightly patterned (if somewhat faded) cushions and two Queen Anne armchairs. In the room to her right, she spotted a long dining table surrounded by antique timber chairs, and beyond that a door to another room, where she caught a glimpse of pale green kitchen cupboards and shelves overflowing with ceramics and glass jars.

'Those beams look ancient,' she said, staring up at the ceiling of exposed boards and beams.

'The cottage is listed. I hope that doesn't put you off.'

'Not yet,' she said, smiling up at him. Standing alongside him in the narrow hall, she realised that his shoulder was actually level with her nose. 'How *did* you find me, by the way?'

'We knew your mother existed, so it became a matter of tracing her first. We traced her to university in London, but after that she seemed to disappear.'

'That's because Mum had already left for Australia by then.' Although, despite her mother's half-arsed explanations, Mia still didn't understand why she had cut off all contact with Henrietta. It just didn't make sense. Celia would have to do a lot more than cast spells for Mia to disown her.

'Exactly, and your grandmother also instructed her solicitors that she'd had no contact with her daughter after that time, apart from a letter with a UK postmark asking her not to contact the police or search for her . . .' He paused to allow her time to digest this, before continuing. 'After our UK online search proved fruitless, we presumed she'd left the country. But where to?'

'The world is a big place.'

'True. So, when our enquiries among your grandmother's friends and neighbours came to nothing, we began a search through some of the documents and memorabilia at the cottage. We found a photograph of your mother with some friends amongst a shoebox full of old photographs. Luckily, someone had pencilled names on the back and we traced one of those friends who was still living locally.'

Who was this 'we' he kept referring to? Or was it really some kind of royal 'we'. It was really starting to get on her nerves.

'When we interviewed the friend and explained our search, she divulged that your mother had sent her a postcard from Queensland back in the late eighties. But she'd sworn her to secrecy concerning her whereabouts, other than to let your grandmother know she was all right.

'After that, it was a matter of searching electoral rolls in Queensland and other resources we subscribe to . . . newspaper archives and the like. Until we located your mother,' he finished, gracing her with a smile that lit his eyes and made him seem almost boyish.

She wondered how old he was actually. Several years older than her, probably.

'And then you found me.'

'Yes. And then I found you.'

This time they both smiled at each other, seemingly misplacing their words for long seconds, until Mia broke the silence by asking, 'And what if I didn't exist?'

He blinked, as if the idea was preposterous, before saying, 'Ah well, that's a bit more complicated, since the will stipulated that the estate was not to be inherited by your mother, under any circumstances.'

'So, the government would have got it?'

'In this case . . . no. Since our family tree research showed several other living relatives. Cousins.'

Cousins. She had cousins. It was a strange idea to someone who had always been an only child.

'How about we finish the tour?' he suggested, while she silently digested this news.

'Sure. Let's do it.'

She followed him into the living room, wondering about these mythical cousins and if Celia had known about them. Maybe her mother had even met them. Grown up with them.

As he led her through the three downstairs rooms with their monster fireplaces, Aga cooker and eclectic furnishings from around the globe, she kept imagining the cottage as her mother's childhood home. Somehow, she couldn't reconcile Celia's contemporary style with the charming, rustic vibe of her grandmother's house. But maybe that was the point. Maybe her mother had wanted to excise all reminders of her earlier life. The walls throughout the house, covered with historic prints and photographs, were a case in point.

'Is this somewhere nearby?' she asked, pausing beside a print of two horsemen riding by a crumbling castle.

'That's Battle Abbey. And that one over there is Bodiam Castle.'

Other prints were less grand in scale. A medieval cottage, not unlike this one, an old inn, an ancient church, a rustic wooden bridge over a stream. Alongside the prints, Henrietta had hung black and white photographs of women in long dresses and men in hats, posed outside buildings that would have looked at home in the Middle Ages.

The Heirloom

She lingered over her grandmother's gallery until Reid broke the spell, asking, 'Upstairs?'

There turned out to be two bedrooms, a bathroom (thankfully modernised) and a study upstairs, the study containing a very old, very beautiful, possibly wormy desk. But it was when they came back downstairs and walked through the kitchen to a stone-flagged terrace outside that her heart skipped a beat. Finally, recognition. Here, here was her mother. Here in this rampant jungle of a garden with its fruit trees, herb and vegetable plots gone feral. And there, encased in a glass conservatory abutting the rear of the cottage, was Mia herself. Or would be, if the cottage truly became hers. A light-filled studio-to-be surrounded by a magical garden.

'It's gorgeous,' she said.

'Needs a lot of work.'

'I don't mind work.'

He turned from gazing at the garden to look directly at her. Standing side by side in the shelter of the shaded terrace, she could see herself reflected in the pupils of his hazel eyes. And for one tiny moment, she felt an irresistible urge to touch him, to make sure he was real. Except just as she was about to reach out, her phone pinged, breaking the spell.

It's midnight in the garden of good and evil! Just joking. It's a beautiful night here and your father and I are sitting on the terrace enjoying the air. What are you up to, darling?

'I gather, from something your grandmother's neighbour told me, that the garden was once a veritable Eden,' Reid said, when she closed her messages with a stab of her finger.

She had been distracted by her mother's text and wasn't aware they had waded into a tangled thicket. It was clear no one had tended it for some time, yet it remained beautiful, heady with the scent of summer, verdant with new growth and a ragtag of blossom. As they strolled through the garden, unruly tendrils whipped her ankles. She recognised the scents of lavender, mint and rosemary, and rearing above the smaller plants, the white pinwheels of yarrow flowers and the tall spears of yellow foxgloves with their flowers like rows of golden thimbles. Fairy thimbles. For a moment she felt disorientated: she had left behind a Brisbane winter, where the scent of wattle was just beginning to sweeten the air and the banksia candles were aflame, to arrive in this land of sweet summer herbs.

The foxglove flowers were level with her chin, her nose almost within reach of the yellow bells. She leaned over, intending to inhale their perfume, when she stepped back in surprise. Although the flowers had no discernible scent, the leaves stank of mouse droppings. Except it wasn't the smell that had caused her surprise, it was the sudden powerful sensation that she had been here before. A sensation that left her hand shaking. For some reason, the foxgloves had conjured a vision of herself in this very garden, plucking these same flowers, a cloud of black hair escaping a straw hat tied beneath her chin, a basket of woven twigs over her arm, a long white summer dress floating about her legs. But of course, she had never been here before.

Who, then, was she seeing? And was she seeing the past – or the future?

'Mia?'

With an effort, she shook off the strange vision and returned to the present.

'Sorry, what did you say?'

'What do you think?'

He was staring at her again, as if he would read her mind if he could.

'What *don't* I think?' she muttered, more to herself than him.

'Cryptic.'

'If you could see inside my head,' she said, casting him a dubious glance, 'you'd soon realise that's because I have way too many thoughts to untangle a single one.'

'Fair enough.' They stood in itchy silence for several seconds, before he added, 'I guess I'll have to be more specific, then.'

'About the cottage?'

'I was asking how you feel about moving in while you wait for probate.'

'Oh, is that allowed?'

'As executor, your grandmother's solicitor assumes you'll need somewhere to stay. Plus, the cottage really could do with a caretaker,' he said, glancing around at the neglected garden.

'Really?' she almost squealed. 'I can stay here *now*?'

'Really,' he said, with a grin that seemed to relax his whole body. 'Probate could take six to twelve months.'

'So long? Okay, then. When do I move in?' she asked, squashing the other thought that flashed through her mind – what would she live on for the six to twelve months that probate might take? She had budgeted for weeks, not months.

'We can pick up the keys from the solicitor after your meeting tomorrow, if you like.'

Maybe it was the fragrance of summer infusing the garden, maybe it was the excitement of realising that this wasn't a dream, that her grandmother's cottage might truly soon be hers, but she found herself twirling in a circle, her arms outstretched, her face lifted to the sky. Something she couldn't remember doing since she was a teenager.

'I do like.'

16

Brisbane, Australia

2024

The shrieking of lorikeets in the lemon myrtles at the bottom of the garden brought Celia back to the present. She had been far from Brisbane, drifting through the past in the low-ceilinged cottage of her childhood, all musty thatch and narrow wooden stairs that announced every step, no matter how surreptitious. Another mother might have pounced on her seventeen-year-old daughter sneaking up the stairs at two in the morning, but not Henrietta. She merely called out, reminding Celia to switch off the hall light and bring the cat in. Another daughter might even have been grateful. Except the freedom to return after midnight went hand in hand with the expectation that the daughter was made in her mother's otherworldly image. And that, Celia had vowed never to be.

She took a deep breath, releasing it in a long, slow exhale. Her garden was fizzing with the loamy scent of that afternoon's rain and the citrus-perfumed air of the lemon myrtles. She should go down and pluck a few leaves to put in the fish tagine she was planning for dinner. Like most herbs the lemon myrtle was multi-purpose: culinary and medicinal. Sometimes she would crush a handful of leaves to her nose if she felt a cold coming on, or add

The Heirloom

some to her tea for a sore throat, just as the Aboriginal people had done for thousands of years. Her garden had grown into a strange and wonderful hybrid of Australian natives intermingled with the plants of her childhood, at least those that thrived in Brisbane's subtropical climate. Herbs trailed vigorously over rocks; peas and beans climbed trellises of eucalyptus twigs; a riot of wonga-wonga vine twined around the wire fence; and winter-flowering native shrubs bloomed in a rainbow of colours.

Strangely, Henrietta would have felt right at home.

'What are you up to out here, love? You've been staring into that teacup for at least half an hour.' Mike opened the screen door and stepped out on to the back deck, bearing two glasses of white wine. 'Here, I'll swap you.'

She took the proffered glass with a sigh. 'Oh, nothing much. Just thinking.'

'And no teabag. You made a pot.'

'The tea leaves were going stale.'

'I see. I suppose this little tea ceremony has nothing to do with our daughter being so far away,' he said, clinking glasses with her. 'Cheers.'

In a fit of madness, gladness, sadness – she wasn't sure which – she had rummaged through the tumble of boxes in the spare bedroom for the teacup handed down from her great-great-however-many-times-grandmother. A teacup with a gilded curlicue of a handle, lavishly painted with an array of brilliant flowers, the cup she had always begged Henrietta to let her use. Its matching saucer was rimmed with gold and decorated with posies of similarly bright flowers. She suspected it might be quite valuable.

'I haven't seen that cup for a while,' Mike continued, picking up the cup and inspecting the tea leaves still clinging to the inside.

Henrietta had given her the cup on her thirteenth birthday, along with her first lesson in how to read the leaves. She hadn't used it in years. Hadn't felt the need to. Now, the cup and its blossoms had transported her back to the past, as much as they offered a glimpse into the future.

'I found it when I was looking for some old teaching notes.'

The lorikeets screeched again, as if remarking upon the lie.

'Uh-huh, and what's it telling you?' he asked, replacing the teacup on the table and taking a sip of wine.

'What do you mean? It's just a cup.'

Mike almost sprayed his wine into the teacup. 'Darl, we've been married for thirty-five years,' he said, an expression of incredulity animating his face. 'Do you think I don't know about your occasional forays into tasseomancy? Come on, what do the leaves say?'

She eyed him with a frown. 'Nothing. You know I don't really believe in fortune-telling.'

'And I don't believe in gambling, but I still put a bet on the ponies now and then. Come on, out with it. You'll feel better once you've told me.'

She sighed, knowing that he wouldn't let up until she relented. He could be annoyingly determined when he wanted to be, belying the blandly agreeable demeanour he wore like camouflage. Other people might be taken in by it, but not her.

'Oh, all right,' she agreed, with a shrug. 'But it's make-believe, you know that. You can't live your life by make-believe.'

He considered her, his eyebrows raised, brow furrowed, brown eyes shadowed by a hint of sadness. 'Sometimes I think you're trying to convince yourself, not me, when you deny your heritage. So, your ancestors believed they were witches? So what? Mine were convicts.'

'It's not the same. You wear yours like a badge of honour.'

'Maybe you should, too. I've heard a whisper that witches are legit again.'

'Not in any circles I move in,' she said, with a roll of her eyes. Her friends were far too sensible – and even she only resorted to those old skills when anxiety got the better of her. In a way, it was compulsion rather than choice that drew her back to the past she had rejected in search of . . . what . . . comfort? She had fought so hard not to believe in it, and yet, when under duress, something in her nature kept drawing her back.

'The world is full of wonder and very little is too strange to be contemplated,' Mike was saying, looking over the top of his glass, out to the river flowing inexorably towards the sea.

'Do you want to know what I see in the leaves, or not?'

The words were out before she could bite her tongue. What was wrong with her? She knew she was being testy, but she didn't want to think about her 'heritage', acceptable or not. She had run away from it more than forty years ago, yet sometimes she felt like she had never truly escaped. That no matter how far she fled – even to the other side of the world, cutting off all contact with her mother, and denying her daughter a grandmother – her heritage would follow her.

Because it was inside her.

Her husband was regarding her patiently. He knew her too well. He knew that she was angry with herself, not him.

'Sorry.'

'If it's not real, there's no need to worry.'

'True.' Not true. She stared into the cup but she already knew it by heart. The specks of tea dust and smaller leaves were the first thing she had noticed. They formed a wavy line around the cup. A journey then, but one that wasn't smooth and didn't appear to return home. She had been thinking about Mia as she turned the cup, anxious about her future as any mother would be, but it was she who drank the tea and she who asked the question. Were the leaves simply reflecting her own journey forty years before, or did they refer to her daughter's trip to England?

'Someone may not return from a journey,' she said, her voice flat.

'Well, clearly the leaves are talking about you then, since you have no intention of returning to England.'

'Maybe. There's also a crescent moon hanging over the wavy path, so the journey may bring good fortune.'

'Simple, you met me.'

'You're very cute when you're being cocky,' she said, flashing him a smile, 'but the path leads towards the bottom of the cup – towards the future – and my journey to Australia is ancient history.'

'Maybe you and I are going to take a trip. Second honeymoon?'

'I see a flag, which warns of an enemy.'

Mike reached for her hand across the table. 'She's going to be fine. She's a big girl. She's travelled before. And if you're worried about Henrietta's influence,' he said, squeezing her hand, 'she's gone now. Besides, you don't believe in fortune-telling, remember?'

Mike was right. She didn't believe in any of her mother's nonsense. She had forsaken the past, forsaken Henrietta. And yet she couldn't deny the tingle in her fingers, the tremor in her hand when she twisted the cup upon its saucer, as if her hand hadn't forgotten at all. She stared out over the treetops to the glimpse of river winding through Brisbane's leafy suburbs, towards its city towers and riverside parklands, its busy port and wide estuary leading to the ocean. Her daughter was somewhere across the seas. Mia had journeyed to the place from which Celia had fled. She was in search of the heritage her mother had forsaken. Now Celia was afraid for her daughter but also for herself. What if Mia didn't come back? Daughters did not always return. Even if they meant to, one day. Sometimes, the longer they waited while they grew their armour, the harder it became to go back, for in the process they had become a different person, with a different life. And then suddenly, without them realising, it was too late.

'I'm a terrible person,' she said, her throat tight with regret.

The Heirloom

'No, you're not.'

'I abandoned my mother – and for what? Because I wasn't strong enough to stand up to her.'

'You were young.'

'I haven't been young for a long time.'

Mike shook his head in silence. Even her husband believed she should have gone back to make peace with Henrietta. And now it was too late.

'Mia will come home when she's ready,' Mike offered, summoning his most reassuring smile, the one that had caught and held her attention all those years ago. 'Just let her be, love. She has her own path to forge.'

He was right. Her daughter had her own journey to make, and if it took her in the opposite direction to Celia, took her back to the heritage she had rejected, then she must accept that – even if it caused her sleepless nights. If Mia could stand up to her living mother, she should be strong enough to resist her dead grandmother.

She closed her eyes, picturing Mia's heart-shaped face with its halo of dark curls, eyes the colour of the ocean depths, lips parted in a knowing smile. A smile totally unlike any she had ever witnessed on her daughter's face. Was it her mother's face she was seeing, smiling back at her? Or some other Foord ancestor altogether?

17

Sussex, England

1821

'On the day following his death, I was called to examine the body of the deceased, Jasper Boadle, which was then lying in the cellar of his premises on the high street,' the surgeon began, addressing his remarks to the fourteen jurors. 'Upon examining the body, I found no sign of external wounds that might have occasioned death.'

Philadelphia sat unmoving and silent as the surgeon paused to allow his audience to digest this information, while around her came the rustle of shifting bodies and the murmur of low whispers. The King's Head was bursting at the seams with her neighbours, some of the curious even relegated to the doorway. She had been allotted a seat on a bench at the front of the proceedings, a position from which all present could observe the widow's demeanour. Alongside sat her brother-in-law, and beside him her nephew, who kept shifting upon the bench at every second utterance.

The coroner presided at a table by the inn's fireplace, with the jurors seated around two long trestles to his left, while the surgeon stood to give his evidence at the coroner's right hand, the constable standing nearby. All other interested parties and potential witnesses crowded into the inn wherever they could find elbow room. The Tuppers were doing a roaring trade, providing the crowd with ale to wet the proceedings, and she noted Mr Tupper patting his waistcoat as he surveyed the hordes, from the doorway to the private salon, the very room where she had met Jasper for the first time. Meanwhile, her poor dead husband rested upon a trestle in the stables at the rear of the inn, only horses for company, his body required to be available for the jurors' inspection.

'I found evidence of vomit and faeces upon the deceased's clothing, and collected specimens of the vomit, which contained flecks of a green vegetable matter,' the surgeon continued once the murmuring had quieted somewhat. 'Upon opening the body, I found traces of the same undigested green matter in the stomach, which I later identified as the leaves of the plant *Digitalis*—'

'For the benefit of those present, could you give the common name for this plant, Mr Goodenough?' the coroner interrupted him to ask.

'More commonly known as the foxglove.'

There was a sound like a breeze sweeping under the doorway, a communal intake of surprised breath so noticeable that Philadelphia kept her eyes fixed upon the jurors to gauge their reaction. One in particular held her attention: Thomas Earle who, as the only gentleman to serve upon the jury, had been chosen as foreman. It was to him she looked now, hoping to find reassurance in his kind and sensible gaze, but he was considering the surgeon intently and did not catch her eye.

'And can you offer any reason why the deceased may have ingested foxglove?'

'Since Mr William Withering published his *Account of the Foxglove* last century it has become known as a treatment for the dropsy, but I found no signs that the deceased was suffering from the condition, no fluid collecting in his lower limbs and so forth, nor had he sought treatment from me for such.'

'And can foxglove cause death if taken in sufficient quantities?'

'If taken in the wrong dose, yes, it can induce violent vomiting, purging, convulsion and even death.'

The murmurs around her grew to a clamour at his words, the sound bouncing around the low-beamed parlour so that the coroner had to demand order. 'Thank you, Goodenough. Please take a seat while I transcribe your testimony. And I suggest the good people of this parish take their leave of this inquest if they cannot remain silent,' he said, with a stern look of admonishment for the unruliest of onlookers.

'I know how the tailor died!' a voice wailed from the rear, shouting in a high-pitched squeal to be heard above the hubbub of the inn.

All heads turned as a slight figure in a gown Philadelphia knew immediately – having taken its measure by her own hands when the wearer desired to add two lace flounces to the hem – insinuated her way through the press of bodies crowding the inn. Most stood aside as she passed, but one or two larger gentlemen required a tap on the shoulder to shift from her path.

'I know what happened,' the woman announced as she emerged into the only clear space in the room – the area directly before the coroner's bench and within a knee's length from Philadelphia – to claim the attention of the entire room.

'Sir,' she added, when the coroner frowned at the interruption, tugging at his wig in irritation. But all others in the room grew silent as it seemed the entire village hung upon the words of the diminutive woman standing before him.

'Is this person on your list of witnesses, Mr Puttick?' the coroner asked, turning to the constable who was looking equally put out.

Philadelphia was not surprised. The Lacy sisters, Dorcas and Lettice both, had a way of stealing attention that rightfully belonged to others.

'She is, sir, but later in the proceedings. Mrs Dorcas Glover, wife to the hatter and haberdasher, George Glover, and daughter of Edgar Lacy, owner of the brickworks.'

Wife to a man who believed himself a competitor to the Boadles, Philadelphia realised, as Dorcas took centre stage – a man with an itch to expand his business beyond mere hats and gloves.

'And what is so urgent that you speak out of turn, madam?' the coroner asked the woman.

Dorcas stood smoothing the skirts of her blue-and-white striped linen dress, and smiling prettily. 'I beg pardon, sir. I would not usually bring such attention to myself by interrupting such grave proceedings.'

'I should think not.'

'But my sister and I . . .'

'Mrs Lettice Tutt, sir, widow of the late Alfred Tutt, landowner, and daughter to the—'

'Brick maker, yes, I see. You and your sister have pertinent information to share about the deceased, Mrs Glover?'

'We do, sir. On the afternoon before the deceased . . . Mr Boadle's sad demise, my sister and I were taking a walk along the path by the Cuckmere, it being such a lovely afternoon. We were crossing the footbridge—'

'Which one?' came a voice from the crowd.

'The Old Bridge. I distinctly remember Lettice remarking upon a barge laden with wool passing beneath the bridge. When I looked back, what should I see but a hare sitting on the path in front of us. It looked straight at me before it bounded off into the long grass by the riverside. And just as it disappeared from view, black clouds covered the sun and the day darkened. It was then I knew something dreadful was going to happen.' She finished with a flourish of expectation, her eyes flicking in Philadelphia's direction.

'I fail to see your point, Mrs Glover,' said the coroner.

But Philadelphia knew exactly what she meant, as did most of those gathered, who now pressed even closer to the main actors in the drama, some with their eyes fixed upon Dorcas, others searching out the milliner. That Foord woman.

'A hare crossed our path, Mr Honeycett, sir. It was a warning,' Dorcas explained as the coroner, who had not been raised in Sussex, looked to the constable for explanation.

'Some folk hereabouts believe that a hare on the path brings warning of dire events to follow.'

There were murmurs of agreement in the crowd and a voice called from over by the doorway, 'I saw a will-o'-the-wisp flitting over the marshes at the back of the tailor's house.'

'A sure sign that death will follow,' said another among the assemblage.

Philadelphia noted nods of recognition passing between the mercer and the butcher at the jurors' trestle, while Thomas Earle looked on with an expression of incredulity. He caught her eye, nodded, and she relaxed her shoulders a little.

'I warned Mrs Boadle in May that it was ill luck to bring yellow broom into the house. But she said the flowers looked pretty, and such a saying was mere superstition.' Philadelphia recognised the voice of the shoemaker's wife, who still owed ten shillings for a basket hat of woven straw she had made for her last spring.

'I did tell my brother he should carry a hag stone on his person to protect against ill luck,' her brother-in-law boomed, giving her a look, while Isaac fidgeted with a button on the flap of his trousers, careful not to meet her eye.

Philadelphia felt more alone than ever.

'Enough of this,' ordered Honeycett. 'You may return to your seat, Mrs Glover, and the inquest will return to facts rather than superstition.'

Dorcas complied, but not before a lift of one eyebrow and a slow curtsey that a few in the audience seemed about to applaud. Her work done, she made her way back through the press of bodies. Philadelphia forced herself to gaze straight ahead, but she knew without turning that Lettice Lacy would be waiting for her sister at the small table by the window, reserved for ladies, where the light would show her complexion to advantage.

'Constable Puttick, please describe for this inquest the events of the morning of Mr Boadle's death,' the coroner resumed.

The constable took the floor, with a brief bow of acknowledgement, his eyes sweeping the assembled jurors, witnesses and onlookers, most of whom he knew. He proceeded to describe what had happened just two days earlier, so matter-of-factly that it might not have been her own husband lying dead on a bale of hay in the stables of this very inn. As if it might have been a stranger.

'And these leaves that the deceased's brother discovered on the kitchen floor of the tailor's house, did you recognise them, Constable Puttick?' the coroner asked, interrupting him when he reached the part of his story where Enoch fortuitously discovered the foxglove leaves on her kitchen floor. A kitchen floor she had asked her maid to sweep just a short while before.

'They were definitely foxglove. The purple ones grow wild all about the parish. My own dear wife has them planted in her garden. Tall they are, with spears of flowers like bells.'

'If I may, Honeycett?' The crowd hushed when they realised it was Thomas Earle who stood to speak, for none of the jurors were yet to say a word.

Philadelphia held her breath, hoping that he might have some words of support, or at least of good sense. Already, she could sense the mood of the room rumbling with suspicion, and with it the hot stares focused in her direction, for all knew she had learned the herbalist's art from her mother.

'Of course, Mr Earle. As I instructed before we began, jurors are free to question the witnesses if they feel the need.'

'Thank you, Mr Honeycett. Constable Puttick,' he began, 'given the common nature of the foxglove, would you say it is possible that *anyone* entering the Boadle house might have brought the leaves with them? Caught up in a pocket, say, or a cuff, or indeed a hat or bonnet?' He smiled at the constable, inviting him to agree.

'Why, yes, that is certainly possible, sir. The foxglove is most common hereabouts.'

There was a polite cough from the stool where the surgeon now rested after giving his testimony, loud enough to be heard above the muttering audience. He had remained at the inquest, out of curiosity, Philadelphia surmised, like the rest of the village. It's a wonder Mistress Tupper had not sold tickets to the event.

'Do you have information to add, Goodenough?'

'The flowers weren't purple,' the surgeon said, with a satisfied smile.

'Is there a colour other than purple?' asked Honeycett.

'I found a small remnant of flower spike amongst the leaves from the Boadle kitchen floor, a fragment of petal still attached.'

'And the colour, man?'

'It was yellow. *Digitalis grandiflora* rather than the native *Digitalis purpurea*. The flowers in question were golden in colour.'

'And the relevance of the colour?'

'*Digitalis grandiflora* is native to southern Europe, sir. It's unusual to find it growing wild in this parish, although it's quite popular as an ornamental. I believe Mrs Boadle has a delightful display of the yellow variety in her garden, for example.'

'Constable Puttick, did you see any signs that the deceased had ingested foxglove, whether of the purple or yellow variety?'

'Not that I saw, sir, but I did see signs of vomit upon the

The Heirloom

deceased's clothing. And it's well known that poison can be administered in the guise of medicines. Mary Bateman, the Yorkshire Witch, were hanged for such evil.'

At these words, the growing tension in the room became even more heated so that Philadelphia feared it might boil over. There was little attempt by those present to hush their voices as they prattled amongst themselves, of witchcraft and poison, no doubt – which, alongside the ever-present smuggling, was a popular subject of gossip in the parish.

'Yes, well, that may be so, but Mary Bateman has no bearing on this inquest, Constable,' the coroner said, raising his voice above the clamour. 'Did you question any witnesses to the tailor's death?'

'I spoke with the deceased's nephew, Isaac Boadle, who was with him at the time of his death, and to his wife, the milliner Philadelphia Boadle, formerly Foord, who discovered the body. It was Isaac's father, Enoch Boadle, who summoned me to the scene. All three are present at this inquest.' Puttick indicated the three with a nod of his head.

Philadelphia barely registered this nod, for she was still reeling from the mention of Mary Bateman, coming as it did after the surgeon's testimony. She had barely left her childhood when Mary Bateman was hanged for murder. The broadsides had been full of stories of her evil, and for a while the villagers had been even more suspicious of Philadelphia's mother, Susanna. Mary Bateman had convinced her victims that she possessed supernatural powers, before swindling them of their savings and murdering them with her 'magic cures'. Susanna had despaired of her giving the wise woman's profession a bad name.

Beside her on the bench Philadelphia sensed Isaac tremble, while Enoch glanced her way, a satisfied curl to his lip. Around her, she felt the tension in the crush of neighbours; aware of the rustling of clothing and shifting of feet upon the stone-flagged floor of the inn.

'Thank you, Constable Puttick. Unless you have anything further to add, we shall now hear from the other witnesses to the—'

'If it please your worship, I have pertinent information to offer the inquest.' A new voice chimed, high and clear above the din, and Philadelphia felt her heart sink.

Like her sister before her, Lettice Tutt sauntered through the gathered press of her neighbours, in expectation that they would part before her. She wore a smile on her face, her best silk gown, and a hat Philadelphia had never seen before perched upon a cascade of ringlets.

'There is little doubt the supernatural has been at work here, Mr Honeycett,' she continued as she swept her way towards the coroner's bench. 'For I have seen it at work. I have seen the tailor's wife communing with the supernatural before,' she announced, turning to Philadelphia with an accusatory stare.

'My sister saw the hare but we have both witnessed Philadelphia Foord practise magic. That is how she won the tailor in the first place. And if she used magic to win him, who is to say she did not use magic to be rid of him?'

At these words, the room erupted into a deluge of outrage that drowned out the coroner's calls for order. Philadelphia scanned the jurors' faces, searching for disbelief. What she discovered there brought no comfort, for their expressions ranged from mild interest to condemnation, while the mercer nodded along in energetic agreement. Only one juror regarded the speaker with a sceptical frown.

'It happened late one Midsummer's Eve, ten years ago,' Lettice continued, encouraged by her reception. 'My sister and I were returning late after taking food to a sick neighbour and took a shortcut through the churchyard . . .' She paused to let the audience absorb her words.

Philadelphia squirmed, for she knew what was about to follow. How could she forget that night, ten years before, when a young girl's eagerness triumphed over her good sense? She knew that Lettice had not forgotten either. Nor would she ever. Now, caught between the malice of this woman on the one hand and her brother-in-law's enmity on the other, she sought out the gaze of Thomas Earle. She hoped to find one ally among those present. He met her glance with a sympathetic smile and she took heart from this small encouragement, for there was little else to hold fast to in this room. Little else to hold fast to in the world, with her husband gone and her neighbours looking to lay blame for it.

Lettice fixed her gaze on Philadelphia. 'And who should we come upon in the churchyard, chanting her magic over a young man's grave?' she asked, and all present knew the unspoken answer.

The inquest had only just begun, yet already Philadelphia stood accused. It did not matter the accusation was unspoken. Her husband was dead, and someone would be made to take the blame – whether it be judged murder, misadventure or plain ill health. Well, it must not be her. She had her daughter's heritage and her own life to preserve, and she would do everything in her power to protect them. She could not let the likes of the Lacy sisters defeat her. She was her mother's daughter, after all.

Catching her one friend's eye for reassurance, she smiled back at this woman who had made herself her enemy, while deep within her breast her heart hardened.

She did not need magic to vanquish her enemies.

18

Sussex, England

1811

Despite the suspicions of half the village, Philadelphia was unaccustomed to loitering in graveyards – and certainly not at this hour. She stirred at every snap of twig or rustle of grass, ducking low when a whisper of sound swooped towards her from an ancient yew. A ghostly form shimmered in the moonlight and just for a moment, as the spectre skimmed her bonnet, she recalled her grandmother's tales of luminous nocturnal creatures that arrived in the night, heralding death, and she halted, rigid with dread. For several breaths she stood quaking, before good sense and a piercing shriek revealed that she had merely disturbed a barn owl.

'Oh, it is only an owl,' she scolded, drawing her cloak closer.

The evening was cold for midsummer, and the hour approached midnight. Beneath her cloak she wore a short gown of brown printed cotton, faded from years of wear, over a forest-green petticoat, with a hand-spun wool shawl crossed beneath her breasts. Her black linen bonnet, worn over a white cap, and thick wool stockings tied at the knees, shielded her from the chill air even if they couldn't guard her wayward thoughts or protect her from swooping owls. Picking her way through damp grass, she took

The Heirloom

care not to soak her stockings, for her mother would surely notice and ask where she had been so late. Susanna always knew when she was lying, so it was best not to give cause for unwelcome questions.

The gravestones loomed like grey shadows in the moonlight as she set out down the terraced slope. Some of the stones were ancient, etched with lichen, faded memorials remembering only nameless ghosts. Others belonged to people she had once known: women who had perished in childbirth; babies taken by the cholera; old men dead of apoplexy. And one, the earth only newly grown over, belonged to a lad not much older than her – dead after stepping on a rusty nail while shovelling manure in his master's stable. They had brought him to her mother when the surgeon could not be found, but by then he was wracked with convulsions and the poultice of dried puffball she applied was too late to save him. Philadelphia had stood at her mother's elbow, ready to fetch whatever was needed, but no one could fetch a miracle.

It was to poor John Cooper's grave she headed. It rested halfway down the slope, a cherry sapling sheltering it to one side, while his infant sister's grave lay to the other. Reaching it, she halted several yards distant and paused to remember the living boy and summon her courage. He'd had brown eyes with a crescent-shaped scar hooking the corner of one eye. Right or left, she could not recall. But she remembered the way his thick brown hair flopped over his forehead and how he would flick it away with the back of his hand. He had given her an apple once, too perfect for any horses, so he said. She hoped that he rested in peace and would understand her intent.

Above her, the church squatted upon the ridge, a hunched shape of sandstone rubble, its stone-tiled spire rising like a dark spear in the moonlight. While below her, the gabled silhouette of the manor house rose, arched windows glinting like watchful eyes. Still, she hesitated, wondering if it had been sensible to venture out so late on such a mission. For what if the priest or churchwarden decided to make a midnight reconnoitre and discovered her lurking amongst the dead? The churchwarden already looked askance at the Foord women, tut-tutting and clearing his throat whenever their names were mentioned amongst the congregation. And the priest made it a habit to single out her mother for his most searing glances during any sermon where he railed against Old Scratch. Her mother swore too that her grandmother had been made to enter the church through the north door, like a pagan of old, until they blocked it up some years before. But Philadelphia shook off her qualms, reminding herself that she did no harm, only asked the question all girls did at one time or another. Surely John Cooper would not mind?

His resting place bristled with long-bladed grass and clusters of tiny white flowers with feathery leaves, their scent sweetening the midsummer air. There was no sense in waiting longer. So, mustering her courage, she drew a deep breath and stooped to pluck a stalk of flowers, bringing the pretty white spray to her nose and inhaling its perfume. Then she closed her eyes, clutched the flower to her breast, and whispered this time-honoured plea.

Yarrow, sweet yarrow, the first that I have found,
In the name of the Lord, I pluck thee from the ground.
As Joseph loved sweet Mary, and took her for his dear,
So, in a dream this night, I hope, my true love will appear.

Even as she whispered the words, she only half believed them. For how could her mind conjure a beloved from thin air? She had lived in this village all of her seventeen years and knew no one to whom she could offer her heart. Though there were several who would take her for her beauty and youth alone, ignoring the more questionable aspects of her birth. But Philadelphia longed

The Heirloom

for an ally, a lover to shelter her from past misfortune or future mischief, and there was no sign of any such person in her vicinity. Perhaps belief was the thing if she wished to conjure her true future, rather than the phantom visions that sometimes visited her, unannounced and unwanted, at unpredictable hours.

Hearing the faint tread of feet behind her, she stiffened, her heart thudding, half expecting to see poor John Cooper's shade come to chastise her for disturbing his rest. She parted her lips, preparing to beg pardon for her trespass, her legs poised to run in the event that her words had little effect. But when she turned to confront whatever apparition had materialised, she only breathed out a sigh of relief. The newcomers were far too solid to be ghosts, although she could not know then that their appearance in the graveyard this night might come to haunt her in the years that followed.

'Good evening, Philadelphia,' said the first, a thin smile upon her face. 'What brings you out so late? Meeting old friends?'

The girl – for girl it was – posed this second question with a broad smile for her sister, who giggled behind her shawl in response.

'Good evening, Miss Lacy, Miss Dorcas, I might ask the same question,' Philadelphia said, with little pretence to the good manners and deference expected of her.

The sisters should be tucked up in bed in their fine muslin nightgowns, not roaming the churchyard in the moonlight. Unlike Philadelphia's father, who her mother had mislaid when she was an infant, and who had never thought since to claim his daughter, Edgar Lacy was a respectable brick maker with a kiln on the turnpike road and a house of three storeys in the village. His daughters were known to take tea with Lady Alcott. He would be most displeased to hear his daughters were roaming graveyards at midnight.

'Aren't you afraid your father will find you gone from your

beds and beat you when you return?' she added, with a slight curtsey for good measure.

'I told you that *she* would be here come Midsummer's Eve,' Lettice Lacy told her sister, smoothing down the skirts of her blue-and-white striped gown. It was new, Philadelphia noted with a pang of envy, its long sleeves capped jauntily, with several ruffles decorating the hem. And despite the crisp night air, Lettice wore her shawl draped loosely at the elbows to better show off her finery.

'I expect she finds the midnight hour the best time to cast her spells,' Dorcas replied, smirking. Her manner was defiantly nonchalant but she could not help glancing about, as if to check for wandering spirits, which caused Philadelphia to wish silently that the truculent barn owl might return.

'What can I do for you, ladies?' It was clear the sisters came with a purpose, and that purpose somehow involved her. Although what it could be she had no clue, for the sisters rarely took the trouble to greet her with more than a nod if they met her in the high street. And yet here they were, come to ambush her in a graveyard at midnight.

'We have a task for you,' Lettice replied. 'And coin to pay.'

'If you seek a cure for the pustules, you would do better to ask my mother,' Philadelphia answered, peering sympathetically at Lettice's face. She knew it wasn't wise to anger the Lacy sisters. Her mother was always warning her to respect her betters or, failing that, to stay out of their way, but Philadelphia's tongue had a habit of running away with her.

Lettice's hands flew to her face before she lowered them to glare at Philadelphia. 'It is merely a pimple or two that will disappear with the aid of some lemon water and salt. *You* would do better to look to those freckles marring your own complexion.'

The freckles arose from Philadelphia's work in the garden and the inn yard, which the other girl knew well.

The Heirloom

'We have already asked your mother,' Dorcas said, getting to the point. She was still jigging about, almost dancing from foot to foot now, in her eagerness to escape the graves.

'And she declined, though I cannot see why,' Lettice finished. 'It is a simple thing we require.' She shook her pretty blond curls so that the ribbons on her straw bonnet quivered.

'Well, I don't see how I can help you if my mother cannot. She is the one versed in cures and such. I am nought but a serving girl.'

'Yes, she is a very cunning woman, your mother,' Lettice said, her eyes narrowing. 'And you are her daughter.'

It was true Philadelphia was employed by the innkeeper as a general servant, but it was also true that she often served as her mother's right hand when need arose, caring for their garden of useful herbs and helping her mother to prepare tinctures, or treat those who came to their door. On occasion, she even accompanied her in aiding a baby to enter the world or an elder to leave it.

'My sister has need of a . . . a potion,' Dorcas said, her words lowering to a whisper. 'A special potion.'

'A love potion,' Lettice explained, unabashed by the request. 'Some gentle encouragement is all that is needed. The man likes me enough already.'

'I do not know any potions.'

'Of course, you do. Everyone knows what you and your mother are,' Lettice said, with an audible huff. 'Why deny it?'

'If you know what we are, then you should know to have a care.' Philadelphia took a step towards the two girls, her hips swaying, her chin raised.

'You c-c-cannot hurt us,' Dorcas exclaimed, fumbling beneath her shawl. 'For we carry protection.' She withdrew a small spherical object attached to a blue ribbon and thrust the amulet at Philadelphia.

Philadelphia laughed and took another step forwards. 'You

think a hag stone will protect you from a witch if she means you harm?' she asked, recognising the object for what it was – a smooth flint oval, with a natural hole through its centre, tied with the ribbon. Sailors wore them as charms against drowning. Farmers used them to protect their cattle. Cottagers hung them beside their doors to ward off evil. And many God-fearing country folk wore them to ward against fevers ... or witches. Her mother had been known to sell them, if she found one or two on her travels, and then laugh merrily at her good luck.

'Don't take another step!' Lettice hissed, producing a larger hag stone from her pocket and holding it to Philadelphia's face.

She laughed again. 'Do not fear, Miss Lacy. I am no witch, so you can put your hag stone away. And I don't know any potions, so you will have to lure the new tailor to your arms using other charms.'

She had heard the recent gossip about the way the Lacy sisters coveted a glance from the dashing young tailor who had set up shop in the village. He was said to be handsome, and they would probably make a fine pair. Only last week, Philadelphia had spotted him in the distance, striding down the lane to the Alcotts' manor with his apprentice hurrying along behind. It was said he already waited upon several other notables of the parish too, and he had only opened his workshop six months before. Lettice's father was known to have ordered two pair of breeches and an embroidered waistcoat just last month, necessitating several visits. No doubt the sisters made it their business to be at home when he called.

Well, Lettice Lacy could put her fancy gowns and winsome ways to work if she wished to win the tailor's love. Susanna Foord did not believe in potions for anything other than physic. She had no truck with spells, despite village rumour. Her mother did not believe in using her powers to manipulate others – those powers she always denied, in order to keep them both safe from the law and their neighbours – and neither did her daughter. Susanna saw to that. She claimed they must only use their powers in times of duress or great need. Yet, every day in small ways she used them unconsciously, despite her claims to the contrary. How else did she come to know all her daughter's secrets?

'We'll not forget this, Philadelphia Foord. We'll not forget how we offered you a kindness and you threw it in our faces.' Lettice's voice grew shrill at not getting her way.

'I'll bid you good evening then, Miss Lacy, Miss Dorcas,' Philadelphia said, bobbing her curtsey. 'I would not wish to keep you out on such a night when the skeletons of the dead be dancing about and the hobgoblins are abroad.'

She kept her back straight and her eyes fixed to the church spire, high upon the ridge, as she turned and strode away from the Lacy sisters, but inside she was shaking. Trembling with anger at being called a witch to her face – and worse, hollow with fear that it may be true. Not that she or her mother dealt in magical potions, only country remedies passed down from mother to daughter through the generations. Any other potions were mere rumour. No, it was the pricking in her thoughts of things seen but unseen, of events told but not yet lived, which unsettled her. These visions came without her asking, when all she craved was a printed cotton gown with ruffles and a straw bonnet blooming with flowers. These were the thoughts that chafed at her peace of mind.

She thought of poor John Cooper, whose death she had glimpsed in the tea leaves as her mother prepared that poultice; of old Grandma Barton, whose passing had appeared to her in a vision the week before her death. She wished she was as confident of what her future would bring as Lettice Lacy. She longed to dream of her future husband, not these harbingers of death. Staring down at the fist that had plucked the yarrow from a young man's grave, she considered the small white flowers, their delicate petals at the mercy of any stiff breeze. Then she tucked the spray of flowers into the hair beneath her bonnet where she could keep them close.

'I am no witch,' she declared to any soul, dead or alive, who cared to listen.

19

East Sussex, England
2024

There were several inns in her grandmother's village, so Mia had selected the one that looked least likely to fall down. Not that she blamed the proprietors, for their premises had seen five hundred years of custom, so they could be excused for walls that bowed into the street or stone-tiled roofs that looked about to implode. She just didn't want to be caught inside when it happened. No matter how quaint or historic. The King's Head appeared reasonably sound, despite its medieval origins. The ground-floor walls were pebbled with flint, the upper floor half-timbered yet comparatively straight, and the roof was finished with flat red tiles. She chose a room overlooking the cobbled yard to the rear, preferring it to the single-lane high street, where traffic jostled constantly to miss parked cars.

She hadn't taken much notice of the inn's interior when she checked in the night before, simply dumping her suitcase on the floor and falling into bed, exhausted. In the morning she had been in a flurry of tired excitement when she set out for Puckridge Cottage, and the afternoon had been spent exploring the village. It was only now, this evening, that she finally had a chance to investigate the inn, not to mention the sounds of good cheer emanating from the bar. Despite still being dead on her feet after the interminable flight, the exhausting journey from Heathrow and her day of exploring, she wouldn't say no to a pint.

Halfway down the creaking timber staircase she paused on the landing; her attention was caught by an arrangement of framed newsprints decorating the plastered wall. They were hard to make out in the dim light, but her bowerbird eye recognised them as examples of broadsides, the popular crime reporting of the eighteenth and nineteenth centuries. Unable to afford newspapers, most people of the time consumed their crime in these single-sheet pamphlets. She had always been fascinated by the graphic woodcuts and the florid headlines that were designed to shock, awe and entertain. Not so different to the TV news, really. The first framed broadside featured a ballad about a swashbuckling heroine known as 'The Female Smuggler', which chronicled the adventures of Jane, who:

> *In sailor's clothing young Jane did go,*
> *Dress'd like a sailor from top to toe . . .*

Alongside Jane, the female smuggler, a second broadside was illustrated by a handsome woodcut of a ship in full sail. Apparently, a mob armed with 'crowbars, pickaxes, hammers and saws' had attacked the unlucky custodians of Dover Gaol, back in 1820.

> *The full Account of the Riot and*
> *RESCUE*
> *of 11 Smugglers and others from*
> *DOVER GAOL*

There were several others revelling in the lurid details of a 'horrid murder' an 'awful suicide' and a 'true confession' that she mostly skimmed. Instead, she focused on the execution of the woodcuts that accompanied them, until her attention was caught and held by one particular image ornamented by a wide gilt frame. Her eyes narrowed as she scanned the first few lines, her hand straying to the gold chain she wore at her throat.

What she saw was a man with the bulging eyes of a corpse, sprawled upon a chair in what appeared to be a tailor's workshop. A youth stood to one side, head bowed, while to his other side was a woman who, for all the imprecision of the woodcut, was vaguely familiar. Mia felt an illogical stab of recognition that grew to a creeping sensation. It quickened her pulse and hastened her breathing so emphatically that she reached for the banister with her free hand. She had seen a picture of the woman – or someone very much like her – before, she felt certain. The woman wore a dress with a high waistline, a low neckline displaying ample cleavage, and long skirts that followed the contours of her body. A cloud of dark hair escaped a prim white mob cap in a riot of wild curls.

'Of course you've seen an image like it before,' she told herself. 'All the women wore ringlets and those empire-line dresses back then.'

Except no other portrait had ever had such a visceral effect upon her as this simple illustration; not at the Tate, nor the Rijksmuseum, the Louvre or even the Prado. She had been awed many times over by the power and artistry of the works she saw at these galleries. She had been moved by the beauty and emotion. But she had never experienced a reaction to those artworks like the punch in the gut this primitive woodcut had landed on her.

Despite her rational mind telling her that the woman's costume meant nothing, that the woodcut meant nothing, the wave of uncanny recognition continued to ripple through her body so that she clutched the gold talisman dangling from a chain at her throat even tighter. The pictured woman's crudely drawn eyes stared back at her, eyebrows arched like arrows, compelling her attention. As if she knew Mia, just as Mia recognised her. A woman who, at least superficially, resembled that apparition who had insinuated herself into the portrait of Mia's grandmother. She read from the broadside:

An Inquest into the
UNEXPLAINED DEATH
of Jasper Boadle, Tailor

Yesterday at 12 o'clock, a jury composed of 14 inhabitants of the Cuckmere Valley was empanelled before Mr W. Honeycett, coroner, at the King's Head Inn, in order to investigate the unexpected death of the above deceased. Once sworn, the jury accompanied the coroner to the inn's stables to examine the body. Upon returning to the inn, the coroner instructed the jurors to remove from their minds any rumours or reports they may have heard and to be guided by the evidence presented to them.

According to the parish constable, Mr N. Puttick, in the early hours of Monday morning the tailor's nephew and apprentice, Isaac Boadle, discovered him in a state of distress in his workshop. Upon the arrival downstairs of the tailor's wife, milliner and herbalist, Mrs Philadelphia Boadle, née Foord . . .

Mia stopped reading. *Foord*. She had to read the broadside again to convince herself she wasn't imagining things. That her gut reaction had been real. That it was true.

Yes, there it was – Philadelphia Boadle, née Foord. Milliner, herbalist and tailor's wife. Surely it couldn't be a coincidence?

'Can I help you with something?'

Mia jumped at the sound of a woman's voice from below the stairs. She was standing in the middle of the foyer with its tired

red carpet, and looked about the same age as Mia, if a little heavier, with her dark brown hair scraped into a topknot, wearing jeans and a neat cotton shirt.

'Sorry, didn't mean to startle you. It's just you've been standing there for almost ten minutes.'

It was Tessa, the receptionist who had signed her in. Although, in a small pub, she probably doubled as bar staff and accountant as well. She must have been at the reception desk in the foyer all this while.

'Oh no, I was just transfixed by these broadsides. You have quite a collection.'

'Yes, I see you're reading the one about the tailor's inquest,' Tessa said, joining Mia on the steps. 'Boadle's tailor's shop used to be just down the street from here, you know. The King's Head was the venue for quite a few inquests in its day.'

'You mean the inquest was held here, not a courthouse?'

'Uh-huh. They used to hold the inquest quickly – before the bodies decayed too much, I suppose. So they adopted whatever nearby premises could accommodate the coroner, jurors, witnesses and . . .' she paused for dramatic effect, 'the corpse.'

'They kept the corpse here, at the pub?'

'Apparently. Probably in the stables. It had to be available for the jurors to inspect . . . should they feel so inclined.'

'That's creepy.'

'The previous owners collected any broadsides they came across featuring the county. The one you're looking at is probably our most famous local case.'

'Really?'

'Infamous, actually. She was accused of witchcraft, you know, your Philadelphia. Kind of a local legend.'

Mia was momentarily taken aback by Tessa referring to the milliner as 'your Philadelphia', before she realised that it was only an expression.

'They didn't burn her, did they?' she gasped.

'Oh no, we didn't burn our witches in Sussex, lovely,' Tessa laughed, 'we needed them to fix our aches and pains. The local surgeon was too expensive. And occasionally we might ask for a charm or two, to help with our love lives.'

Mia was slightly taken aback at this but she only laughed, asking, 'Are there any more broadsides about the tailor's death? Or Philadelphia?'

'There would have been, no doubt. They loved their trials and executions, back in the day. But we don't have any here. You might find something online.'

'That's a shame.' Mia felt a stab of disappointment. She would have liked to know what happened to Philadelphia Boadle née Foord.

'Well, if you're set, Rob probably needs a hand in the bar right about now. It's roast night, if you're interested.'

'Can you save me a table? Or a place at the bar, if you're busy.'

'Will do.'

She set out to follow Tessa into the bar when her phone pinged politely (she had consigned the kookaburra ringtone to feathered oblivion) and she glanced down to see a message from her mother flash across the top of the screen.

Remember, darling, look to the future not the past.

What was she on about now? And when had she turned into such a worrier? Her warnings were dogging Mia across the world. What did she think Mia was about to do, join her grandmother's coven? Or was the past she referred to even further back in time? Generations of witches ago?

Mia was about to stow her phone in her jeans pocket, unanswered, when she had a thought.

Who was Philadelphia Foord?

She tapped out the message and pressed send. That should keep her mother busy.

20

Sussex, England
1811

Philadelphia did not know how many generations of her family had lived at Puckridge Cottage, but she could sense their lives in every pebble of flint in its walls and each soot-blackened rafter. Her grandmother's grandmother and all the grandmothers before her had left their marks, visible and invisible, beneath its roof. Sometimes as she lay beneath the thatch in her small attic chamber, she could hear their voices whispering in the walls, speaking of babies born and elders dead, of love gone wrong and love that endured a lifetime.

Once, she had thought she heard her sister, Mercy, calling in the night to warn of danger. Mercy's voice had sounded so insistent that Philadelphia tiptoed through the entire next day, waiting for something terrible to happen. Except the only event of note had been the goats getting into the herb garden and eating her mother's mugwort. Susanna was most displeased, as mugwort was an important ingredient in one of her tonics and useful to ward away moths, but Philadelphia doubted the dead took much interest in the doings of goats. Then again, her sister had spent long hours in that garden when she was still with them, so perhaps the warning rang true. She had always been their mother's pet, her companion in work – unlike Philadelphia, who was often nowhere to be found when the most arduous tasks arose. Already, Mercy had been gone five years, and still her little sister missed her every day.

That morning, she woke unsettled, an uneasiness hovering at the corners of her mind as if she had been dreaming for much of the night. She was late to wake too, after her covert excursion to the churchyard the previous night. Her mother would scold if she did not set the bread to rise before leaving for the King's Head. Perhaps this was the reason for her disquiet. However, she could not linger to puzzle over it, so she took the narrow stairs to the hall below two at a time, almost tripping in her haste not to be tardy. She lit two rushlights and placed them in holders, for only a thin dawn light filtered through the small windows. Her mother preferred rushlights to tallow candles; rushes could be had for the gathering, mutton fat was plentiful, and the addition of a little beeswax ensured a cleaner, longer burn.

Once she had light enough to work by, she laid a fire in the brick oven before turning her attention to the bowl of leaven left out upon the table. She lifted the cloth and sniffed expectantly, smiling to herself as the smell of old apples greeted her. Then, scooping rye and wheaten flour to make two loaves into a large earthenware bowl, she added a goodly amount of water and most of the leaven, while setting some aside for the following day. She had mixed the dough and was leaving it to rest on a stool by the oven when she heard the clank of the latch and the groan of the back door. A few moments later, her mother appeared in the hall wearing her old homespun cloak and much-worn bonnet, a haze of fresh lavender enveloping her.

'You've been in the garden early, Mother,' she said, looking up from her work.

'Midsummer morn is the best time to gather herbs. Had you forgotten?' Susanna said, setting her wooden trug on the table.

The Heirloom

She had crafted the trug herself from thin-shaved strips of white willow and a handle cut from a coppiced chestnut in the woodland beyond their cottage. The first vervain flowers of summer peeked from it in a tracery of lilac flowers alongside the bright yellow blooms of St John's wort and the purple spikes of lavender. Some called vervain the 'wizard's herb', for it was a well-known ingredient in love potions, but her mother brewed it as a tea to ease fever and crushed it in a poultice to treat wounds.

Susanna did not believe in magic potions, or at least so she said. Philadelphia was not so sure. Sometimes she also was not sure if her mother believed in romantic love at all. She certainly did not advocate for it. All her daughters ever knew of their mother's romantic past was not very romantic. She would say little of their fathers, other than that neither lived in the village. Mercy's father had been a Romani whose family camped outside the village one winter before packing up and moving on to spring farm work, without leaving a single word of farewell for his winter love. Philadelphia's father she had even less to say about. A foolish interlude with a visitor to the area was all she would say, leaving her daughter to fill in the gap with whatever romantic notion pleased her. A tinker? A tailor? A lord of the manor? She could be anyone's daughter she wished; claim any heritage she chose.

'And how did you sleep?' Susanna asked, peering at her daughter so intently that she had to turn away lest her mother perceive her thoughts.

The flickering light from the rushes caught the silver strands in her mother's dark hair and her eyes glittered so that she seemed to sparkle. Philadelphia had her mother's eyes, the midnight hue of dark blue violets, framed by winged black brows. Except that where her own eyes resembled a flower, her mother's shone with the hard gleam of a jewel. Susanna was obdurate enough to withstand the shame of her past, her daughter less so.

'Well enough,' she answered, although in truth her sleep had been troubled by visions. Twice she had wandered through the graveyard last night, once at midnight in the flesh and again in her dreams, trailed by the tolling of the church bells. In real life, she had defied her mother to do what many young girls did in defiance of their mothers, to recite a charm in the graveyard on Midsummer's Eve in order to see their future husbands. In the dream, she had skipped amongst the headstones, hand in hand with Mercy – alive again, and as keen to learn who her love might turn out to be as her younger sister. Later, she had woken with an ache, to find Mercy gone once more.

'You were not troubled by dreams?'

That earlier uneasiness, which Philadelphia had quieted with work, returned at these words and she saw before her eyes the image of a man, though she did not see his face, only his hands, fine-boned and nimble-fingered. Last night she had lain on her straw pallet beneath the tiled roof and dreamed of a tall man sitting cross-legged upon a low table, his back hunched over his work. She remembered hovering above him in her dream, like a bird, as he stitched a straw bonnet light as air. And later, she had watched as he plied his needle like a tiny silver rapier, piercing a river of red silk to make a lady's scarlet shift.

'Nothing of consequence,' she said to her mother, though she felt her breath quicken even now at the memory of the dream. She did not know if she could rely upon its truth. She had slept with the yarrow beneath her pillow and dreamed of a tailor, but her meeting with the Lacy sisters could have brought this to mind. All she knew for certain was she had been woken from the dream with a start, her arm stinging as if pricked by a needle. Then she had risen, tired and unsettled, to the weak dawn light creeping under the eaves.

'You slept so well that your eyes are lined with dark circles,' her mother insisted.

Philadelphia wondered what Susanna knew, or thought she

knew. She had been so careful to tread lightly down the stairs when she ventured out last night, avoiding the board that creaked, and choosing the door furthest from her mother's chamber to make her escape to the churchyard.

'I dreamt of Mercy,' she said, the words arriving out of nowhere.

Her mother's face told her that the feint had done its work, and she felt a pang of regret. Susanna rarely spoke of her eldest daughter, carrying her death like a leaden weight in her heart, so that Philadelphia was hesitant to speak her name lest she cause her mother more distress. Now, she had done just that. Her mother was a wise woman, yet none of her potions had saved Mercy from the lung fever. No amount of marshmallow or violet tea, no number of chamomile and poppy poultices could cure her. Susanna had nursed her daughter day and night for a week, only taking brief respite when Philadelphia sat by her sister's bed, covering her ears at the sound of the rasping cough she could do nothing to soothe.

In the days that followed her sister's death, it was as if Susanna had also died, so silent did she become. Only her patients could rouse her from her stupor. Only her work brought her back to the living and her remaining daughter, never to speak her dead daughter's name aloud, unless prompted. Philadelphia soon learned not to talk about her sister, unless she wished to send her mother back to that silent place inside her where Mercy still lived. Sometimes, though, she longed to relive memories of her sister, to speak of the things they used to do together, to recall the playful manner Mercy had about her. Memories were the only way to keep her close. Why couldn't her mother see this?

'Nothing else?' Susanna asked, recovering her composure.

Philadelphia shrugged and stared down at a house spider scuttling across the brick-flagged floor by her foot. She lifted her foot and brought it down with a stomp. She hated spiders, creeping unseen through the hidden corners of the cottage, plus it gave her a reason to avoid her mother's eyes. 'No, nothing I can recall.'

'You have not brushed your hair this morning,' Susanna said, ignoring the spider's fate, ignoring the mention of her other daughter. She closed the distance to Philadelphia in three swift strides, reaching out to pluck at her hair and present her with a wilted white twig.

'See, here are yarrow flowers tucked in your hair. I wonder how they got there on a Midsummer's Eve, with you safely abed.'

'I picked some on my way home yesterday from the King's Head and tucked a spray behind my ear for its sweet scent.'

'Aye, how sweet they are. The churchyard is heady with their scent, growing amongst the headstones on the lower terrace.'

'I had not noticed.'

'You did not notice when you plucked the yarrow from some poor dead lad's grave to speak your charm?'

Her mother fixed her with a glittering eye and Philadelphia wondered, as she often did, whether she divined thoughts with some secret spell. Although, if asked, her mother always denied the use of magic and pointed to common sense to explain her prescience, and a wide knowledge of herbs to explain her skill.

'You would do better to learn our craft, instead of wishing away your life, Philadelphia.'

Unlike Mercy, who had no chance to wish away her life.

'I was not wishing.'

She had been dreaming, not wishing. Dreaming of a different life to the one led by her mother and her grandmother and her mother before her. If she dreamed hard enough, perhaps she could make it come to pass. Will it into being.

'There's no good to be had dreaming of husbands. Though your name be written in the bastardy register, I have never felt the need of one. The Foord women can manage without husbands.'

Philadelphia did not want her children to be named bastards.

The Heirloom

She had lived with the shame of that. She had lived with the scorn of the Lettice Lacys of this world. She did not want that for her child.

'Perhaps I do not wish to manage without,' she said.

'Men come and go, but skill will keep a woman for a lifetime. 'Tis better not to hanker after what you cannot have.'

'I do not want to spend my life here in this cottage.'

Susanna still held the wilted yarrow. She took a step towards her daughter, tucked it back behind her ear, saying, 'Then you had better learn to guard yourself, sweeting, for the world has not always dealt kindly with the Foord women.'

Except that was the point, was it not? It had not dealt kindly with Mercy, and her foremothers' craft had not saved her. Philadelphia no longer wished to call herself a Foord, for the name carried too much history that could not be explained. Not to her satisfaction. It carried too much of the past and not a little of the future. Far too much of both for comfort.

21

East Sussex, England
2024

The keys jangled in Mia's hand as she hurried up the path to her grandmother's front door. Hers now, she reminded herself, conscious of an embarrassing glee. Reid followed a few steps behind, having given her a lift from the solicitor's office after their meeting. Puckridge Cottage and its secrets beckoned, and she could hardly wait to discover them. Without seeking guidance from the heir hunter on the right key, she selected a bronze key with an ornate bow and inserted it into the lock. She jiggled it for a few seconds, smiling when it turned with a satisfying click.

'You've got the knack,' Reid said.

'Must be intuition.' Actually, the key had felt alive in her hand, almost as if it knew it was coming home. Except that would be stupid, wouldn't it?

'How are you feeling?'

She stood on the coir welcome mat to collect her thoughts before answering. Her mother had rejected this house and the woman who lived here. Mia still didn't know why, not really. Should she be wary of what she might find beyond the door? But that was stupid, too. It was just a house, and for some reason she found herself believing the trite word of welcome on the doormat.

The Heirloom

Both her grandmother and her grandmother's house wanted her here, she felt sure.

'I don't know. Sort of excited and a bit nervous at the same time.' And yet, there was nothing to be nervous about – other than her mother's repeated warnings. Warnings she had grown so accustomed to ignoring that it had become a habit. If by chance they should turn out to be correct, she always put it down to coincidence. For by the law of averages, predictions had to come true some of the time, didn't they?

She stepped over the threshold with a flutter of anticipation. The house was hers to explore, down to each drawer and every cupboard – evil grandmothers notwithstanding. Pausing in the hallway, she closed her eyes, allowing her other senses free play. She became aware of an itchiness in her hands and a rush of warmth coursing through her body, as if she had waded into the tropical seas of Far North Queensland. It was the strangest feeling, not exactly unpleasant, but discomforting all the same.

'Right, let's reconnoitre,' she said, wiggling her fingers to shake off the feeling. 'I suppose you've already done a fair bit of exploring.'

She turned to Reid, with a look of enquiry. He had been all business at the solicitor's office, and she wondered if she had imagined his friendliness at their first meeting. But now he stood relaxed beside her, regarding her with that grin of his – a bit lopsided, head cocked to one side – its slight goofiness offsetting his physical appeal and somehow making him even more appealing. But she wasn't going to go there, she told herself in silent rebuke. She had vowed to be more circumspect. No more idle dalliances. No more men who were expert dalliers but couldn't commit to breakfast.

'Not too much exploring, I only rifled through your grandmother's desk and photos. Everything else, I left to its own devices.' He placed his folders on a worm-eaten Chinese-style console table in the hall and prepared to follow her.

'It looks like something ate chunks out of the table legs,' she said, nodding at the obvious repairs to the table's feet.

'I think the dealers traipse around old barns in the Chinese provinces, buying up broken furniture that no one wants, patching it up and shipping it off to the West.' He ran a hand across the cracked and scratched surface. 'Wabi-sabi or old junk, what do you think?'

'It depends on your perspective, I suppose.' She looked up at him speculatively. Most men didn't know their wabi-sabi from their wasabi. She kind of liked the Japanese philosophy – and her grandmother appeared to as well, judging by her furniture.

'Okay, lead away,' he said.

Where to first? She stood immobile for several heartbeats, as if waiting for unseen guidance. Then, with a shiver, she took a step towards the kitchen and the route to the back door. There was an entire house and garden to explore but an inexplicable force seemed to be drawing her towards the rear of the cottage, where she sensed her grandmother had spent much of her time.

'To the studio, I think. I mean . . . the conservatory.'

'I didn't venture in there.'

'Plants hold no secrets for the intrepid heir hunter?'

'I tend to follow the paper trail not the forest trail.'

'Let's head out back, then.'

The conservatory was relatively modern compared to the rest of the house, with a weathered timber frame fitted with glass roof panels and glass walls. Like a transparent lean-to, it cuddled up against the rear of the cottage, accessed only from the outside. Someone must have arranged for the plants to be watered because rampant greenery brushed the glass, through which Mia spied a tall wooden bureau, some shelving, a workbench, two wicker chairs and a small round table. She fumbled with the keys, selecting the newest-looking one in the bunch, and silently congratulated herself when the door opened first turn, as if it too had been waiting for her arrival.

Almost immediately, her head scraped against something and she looked up to see a length of thin rope dangling from the ceiling. The rope had been tied into knots at regular intervals and various bits of flotsam were slipped through the knots.

'Is it a dreamcatcher?' Reid wondered.

Maybe. Whatever it was, it was handmade. The cord, she saw on closer inspection, was actually three lengths of hemp twine plaited together and frayed for the last few centimetres, and the flotsam was a random selection of feathers, shells and twigs.

'That's weird,' she said.

'What?'

'I recognise some of these feathers. I used to pick them up in our garden when I was growing up.' She reached up to stroke a green and yellow feather with a flame of orange at its base. 'It looks like it's from a rainbow lorikeet.'

'Suitably colourful.'

'And this one,' she said, pointing to a fluffy white feather with a pink tip, 'looks like a galah feather. That long grey one could be from a galah's wing. And the grey-and-white striped feather might just be from a tawny frogmouth. Although, lots of owls have plumage like that, I suppose.'

She stood back to better see the top of the creation. 'And that's definitely the dried cone of a banksia flower.' Vivid yellow, red or orange when in flower, the grey-ish cone was bristling with seed pods like open clam shells.

So maybe not random flotsam after all.

'I'm guessing your grandmother didn't pick these up in *her* garden, then?' Reid said, raising his eyebrows so high that he looked almost comical.

'No, definitely not.'

It was strange, to say the least. Had her grandmother somehow discovered her mother's whereabouts and made a secret trip to Australia to lure her back? A meeting Celia had not bothered to mention?

'Maybe she ordered them online,' she said, non-committally. Or, if her mother was right in her character assessment, flew her broomstick all the way to Brisbane and back.

Reid was suddenly looking more thoughtful than comical as he stretched up to his considerable height and touched what looked very much like a twig of eucalyptus leaves.

'Except she told her solicitor, when she made the will, that she had no idea where your mother was,' he said.

Or had she? What exactly had Henrietta known? And how did she find it out?

'Maybe we should be looking for a crystal ball,' Mia whispered to herself and any unseen listening ears, 'Grandma.'

'What was that?'

'Oh, nothing.' She didn't want him to think she was a complete nutter.

'Actually, I think she kept her crystal ball in the living room,' he said, straight-faced, 'alongside her considerable collection of tarot cards. Your grandmother was quite a character.'

'Really, did you ever meet her?'

'Sadly, no. But I remember seeing her fortune-telling stall at a local fair. Apparently, she always obliged whenever one of the villages or schools in the area was raising money, either with the tarot or the tea leaves. She was quite a collector of teapots too, I noticed.'

So... her grandmother hadn't been quite the spooky witch that Celia made her out to be. She hadn't been shunned by everyone in the village. Rather, she was a much-loved eccentric and part of the local community. That was comforting to hear. Then why exactly had Celia run away? And how kooky could Henrietta have been?

Just then, a gust of wind sprang up outside, rustling the garden beds and wafting in through the open door of the conservatory to buffet the strange twine ladder of objects that appeared to have hailed all the way from the southern hemisphere. And in with the breeze drifted the faraway call of a flock of raucous lorikeets, a noise Mia had grown up with. She shook her head to be rid of a sound that could not possibly be there. Just as she had once shaken her head to be rid of the sound of rushing water. A sound she had also known could not be there.

What had Henrietta known?

And what did her mother know that she wasn't telling?

'Well . . . I'd better leave you to it, then,' Reid said, somewhat reluctantly, she thought. 'But if I can help with anything, give me a call. Any time,' he said, turning as if to leave.

Any time? That was a dangerous offer, especially to a woman with visions.

'There is one thing.'

'Yes?' He stopped mid-stride, considering her with that oddly infectious grin, and she was suddenly glad she had chosen to wear a long, floaty summer dress rather than jeans and a T-shirt, despite the goosebumps on her arms.

'Have you heard of a woman called Philadelphia Boadle?'

For a split second he seemed surprised, before saying, 'Philadelphia Boadle? The Witch of Sussex Downs? Actually, she's quite well known around here.'

'She is?'

'The shop where her husband was murdered is just down the street from the King's Head. Where did you hear about her?'

How could she tell him that Philadelphia had appeared to her out of nowhere on a canvas? Or that she was beginning to see her face in dreams?

'I'm not sure, but I think she may be my ancestor.' Her ancestor, the Witch of Sussex Downs.

'Hmm, that shouldn't prove too difficult to sort – for a genealogist.' There was that grin again.

If it had been two hundred years ago, she might have swooned.

'From things my mother said, probably through the female line.'

'Matrilineal, eh? That's interesting . . .' He paused, as if considering this idea, then said, 'Well then, I'll be in touch when I've looked into your connection to Philadelphia.'

'Oh, thanks, you're a sweetheart.' Without stopping to think it through, she flung her arms around him in a bear hug, only backing away when she realised that he might take it the wrong way. He had caught her in a moment of . . . happy anticipation, she supposed, but she didn't want him to think that she was interested romantically. Although, come to think of it, he might well be accustomed to women flinging themselves at him. She had no desire to add to their number.

'Sorry, too much excitement for one day,' she said, feeling flustered, wiping away a film of imaginary sweat from her brow and hoping her cheeks weren't flushed. He had felt good, she had to admit, kind of solid and athletic beneath his wool jumper.

'I'm not sorry,' he said.

'Anyway,' she added, 'you've been really helpful. Thank you. I hope I have a chance to reciprocate.'

'We could have dinner sometime.'

Okaaay, the hug had obviously been a mistake. She hoped he wasn't looking for some kind of hook-up. Because, if so, she was done with that. Funny, he didn't give off that vibe. He seemed . . . kind of genuine. Then again, her radar wasn't notable for its reliability, as her friend Kate was always telling her. It kept getting interference from wishful thinking.

'Well . . . I . . .'

'Or lunch,' he added quickly, before she could finish the

The Heirloom

sentence. 'I thought you might like to visit the café where Philadelphia once created her hats. It's at the other end of the village.'

'Oh ... um ... is that the same shop where Philadelphia's husband – the tailor Jasper Boadle – was murdered?'

'It is. But how did you know?'

'Tessa at the pub told me.'

'They do a great lasagne.'

It was only lunch, after all. What harm could lasagne do?

'Yes, thank you. That'd be nice,' she said.

The lasagne couldn't be haunted, so she had nothing to fear there – and surely Reid was harmless? It was only herself she needed to guard against, so she would just have to keep him at arm's length. She wasn't prepared to fall in lust or love any time soon. Either state might lead to complications she could do without. England was a long way from home, and she might need to put down roots in this lovely garden of her mysterious grandmother's – at least for a while, to get her affairs sorted. In which case, she would rather have a friend than a lover.

They arranged to meet at the café for lunch a few days later. Then Reid waved goodbye, bumping his head against the knotted rope of Aussie souvenirs on his way out and setting them dancing. It was only after he was gone that she recalled his comment about her grandmother's collection of teapots. Henrietta wasn't the only person Mia knew who collected teapots. Her mother had quite a collection too, currently taking up space in the pantry.

'Like mother, like daughter, hey, Mum,' Mia mused, eyeing the dangling arrangement of fragile knick-knacks. She stood on tiptoe, reaching up to straighten a spray of desiccated eucalyptus leaves in danger of falling loose after their brush with Reid's head, only to feel them crumbling to dust in her hand.

22

Darling Downs, Australia
2024

The route to Castle Rock began as an easy stroll (although this was not to last) as a sandy path led Celia and Mike through open woodland of eucalyptus, blackbutt and drooping she-oak. Patches of wattle blazed a brilliant yellow in the winter sun and pea flowers bloomed in a field of purple and yellow, while Celia also spotted some paper daisies beside the path. No wonder Girraween National Park was known as the 'place of flowers'; when spring arrived, it would be a veritable Eden. Her spirits lifted as they hiked, serenaded by the calls of yellow-faced honeyeaters and a chorus of melodious currawongs, and she realised just how miserable she had been lately.

On the Tablelands the morning had begun cold, but soon Celia was removing her jacket and tying it around her waist, glad they had brought plenty of water with them. They chatted companionably about their surroundings as they walked, watching a group of wallabies studying them through the trees, and Mike spied an eastern grey kangaroo bounding into the distance. But soon the way grew steeper and their conversation sparser as the path wound through fields of broken rock, tough mats of kangaroo grass and outcrops of granite.

The Heirloom

They mounted a rock and gravel staircase, pausing to marvel at a huge granite boulder balanced precariously on a smaller rock, while marshalling their resources for the climb towards a forbidding wall of rock ahead, which loomed before them like a fortress. Luckily, they didn't have to actually scale the fortress walls, as the path was revealed to squeeze through narrow crevices and between even more gigantic boulders until they reached the last segment of the walk – a clamber over a massive dome of solid granite – leading to the top. Despite her decades of yoga and gardening, Celia's breath was coming in gasps as they followed the painted white arrows across the sloping sheet of granite towards the summit.

'Oh my God, what am I doing here?' she panted, as she stopped to rest on a relatively flat perch, halfway up the dome of rock.

'You said you needed to get out of the house,' Mike said, annoyingly bright-eyed and bushy-tailed while she was about to expire. Why was her husband so relentlessly cheerful?

'Not this far out of the house,' she snarled, immediately feeling guilty. She had been so tetchy lately, and her poor husband was bearing the brunt of it.

'It'll do you good. You're fixated on Mia and the imagined machinations of your mother.'

'Imagined, my arse.'

'Come on, hon, you can do it. We're nearly there.'

'Well, I hope you're right, or you'll be the one carrying me down when my heart gives out.'

'Noted,' he said, with a grin and an encouraging punch to her upper arm.

Despite her complaints, or perhaps because of them, her husband was right. The climb was doing her good. Nature, the open air, the exertion and the excuse to complain, provided an excellent way to release some of her pent-up worries, legitimate or not. For she had to admit that, since Mia's letter from the heir hunter arrived, her anxiety had risen from its usual low-level white noise to an internal thunderclap. Not that most people would have noticed, for over the years she had become an expert at concealing her disquiet, even from herself. Most people, however, did not include Mike. Where she was concerned, his antennae were finely tuned.

She returned his gesture of encouragement with a reluctant smile. 'Okay, lead on.'

She was rewarded several minutes later – and after several steep climbs where she was forced to scramble on hands and feet – when they finally attained the summit of Castle Rock. She stood mesmerised, and literally breathless, at the magical vista extending beyond the park to the horizon. Then, as she pirouetted a full 360 degrees to take it all in, the rolling hills blanketed in eucalyptus forest panned before her eyes like a video, the dark green of trees broken by towering rock formations and granite outcrops.

'Worth it?' Mike asked.

'Yes. Thanks, darling.'

'For what?'

'For bringing me here. For putting up with my . . .' she sighed, '. . . my . . . um . . . obsessions.'

'You're a parent. It's part of the contract,' he said, with a shrug. 'And my motives weren't completely altruistic.'

'They weren't?'

'Well, only partly. I thought we could combine therapy with a little family history expedition. I was speaking to my cousin Barry last week and he was telling me our grandfather used to say the family once lived over that way,' he said, pointing to the east. 'Just over the border in New South Wales.'

'It's only bush.'

'Now, yes. But for a while Boonoo Boonoo was the site of a gold rush. So, some of my ancestors might have been born on the goldfields – in a tent, even. And over there,' he said, pointing south, 'could be where their parents came from. If I can trace their presence, I should be able to find out when and where they arrived in Australia. I guess I wanted to see the countryside where they might have come from.'

'Well, the hike worked a treat on me, anyway,' she said, with a smile, still out of breath from the walk. She loved how her husband had become so enthused about his family history. Ironic, given she had tried so hard to forget hers.

'I'm glad, although . . .' He hesitated, as if he didn't want to spoil the mood, but then decided to go ahead anyway. 'Don't you think it might be time to stop worrying about your mother and just focus on your daughter? Henrietta can't get to you now. Or to Mia.'

'Maybe.' Or maybe not. In her mind, the two were irrevocably entwined. Her mother's will had seen to that.

'Only if you let her,' he said. 'She's gone, hon.'

That was the trouble, letting go was easier said than done. She had been letting Henrietta get to her for a lifetime. She would go for weeks sometimes without thinking about her mother, and then – wham! The guilt, regret and anger would rage within, all over again. Even now that Henrietta was dead. Actually, now it was worse, because she would never have a chance to reconcile all those feelings. Her mother still haunted her. Infiltrating her peace of mind.

'Is she gone, though? Really?' she said.

'I thought you didn't believe in spirits and all things supernatural?'

It was her turn to shrug. There were more things on heaven and earth . . .

'You always maintained that the tea leaf thing was just a harmless hobby. And that Henrietta's witchery was more madness than magic.' He gazed at her with his head to one side, eyebrows lifting shrewdly.

She turned away from him to stare out at the vista before them, hoping its vastness might put her worries into some kind of perspective. For the landscape was real. She could see it, smell it, hear its bushland sounds, touch its trees and rocks. Her feelings about her mother were far more ephemeral. And not in a good way. For forty years, thoughts of Henrietta had only ever brought confusion. Such a maelstrom of guilt, fear and longing that she could hardly tell the difference between them. So that the only way she had managed her feelings was by supressing them. Now they were all raising their ugly heads again.

'I'm not sure any more,' she said.

He wrapped his arms around her from behind, not saying anything.

'I thought I saw her once, you know.'

'When?'

'Maybe twelve or thirteen years ago. Not long before Mia finished school.' She closed her eyes, rummaging for the memory. Although she didn't have to rummage far, as it wasn't buried deep.

'We were coming down the front steps, you, me, Mia, and getting into the car to go somewhere.'

She remembered exactly where they had been going; to a picnic down by the river with some family friends. Mia hadn't wanted to come, preferring to stay home with her laptop and her phone, but Celia had won the argument with some minor retail bribery. They had reached the car and were stowing the picnic gear in the boot when she glanced across the road at an unfamiliar car that had been parked there for some time. A nondescript, late-model car with a woman sitting behind the wheel.

'There was a woman parked across the road . . . staring at us. Her hair was tied back with a bandanna, but even so it was too wild to be contained, escaping in a riot of greying curls. And despite the road between us, I recognised her. It had been thirty years . . . but I would have known her anywhere.'

'You never said.'

'No. Because I didn't want to believe it. I wanted so badly to be mistaken. Then she drove off when she saw me looking at her.' She had wanted the woman to be a figment of her imagination. If she were mistaken, she didn't need to worry. But now, a decade or so later, she had to admit she had been right.

'She knew where I was. She may have known the entire time.'

'Are you sure?'

She nodded at the horizon. 'What if the will is her way of ensuring the legacy continues?'

'The legacy?' he said.

'Yes, the Foord women's legacy. Henrietta's bloodline. My bloodline.' Philadelphia's bloodline. Maybe all this was a way of drawing Mia into the fold. Already, her daughter had heard about Philadelphia's existence, judging by her messages. Already the glamour was drawing her in, casting its spell.

'If I rejected our heritage, maybe Henrietta decided to bequeath it to our daughter. And in so doing, punish me for taking away her own daughter. Me.'

Surrounded by beauty, ten thousand miles from her birthplace, she couldn't shake off the feeling that danger lay just ahead.

23

Sussex, England
1821

'Isaac Boadle!' Mr Honeycett read out his name.

Isaac held his knee in a tight grip, the only way he knew to stop it trembling. The coroner's announcement set his leg to jouncing of its own accord. Beside him on the bench, he was conscious of his aunt, her spine rigid, pretending not to hear the outcry of their neighbours, which had followed the surgeon's testimony and the Lacy sisters' revelations. Philadelphia stared straight ahead, so that he observed her in profile, with her short straight nose, curving cheek and delicate jaw. She pretended that she was oblivious to their neighbours' slights, strong enough to withstand their ill-wishing, but he knew better. He knew that beneath her calm exterior she was as fragile as a hummingbird's wing.

'Rise please, Boadle,' the constable ordered.

He wished he could reach out and touch Philadelphia's hand. Offer her the comfort she had given him whenever he was lost and afraid. Even now that he was grown, she always sensed when a kind word or deed would soothe the lash of his uncle's tongue or soften his blows. He longed to ease her suffering. But at his other side, his father observed his every move. Listened to his every intake of breath, just as he would parse each word when

The Heirloom

Isaac rose to give evidence. For they had practised together what he should say, his father making him repeat the words time after time, until he got them straight.

Tell the truth, but there is no need to tell what you ain't asked, his father had instructed him the night before as Isaac lay on his straw mattress next to his brother. *And make sure you tell how your aunt kept a physic garden at her mother's cottage as well as the herbs she grew behind your uncle's shop.*

Isaac kept his eyes upon the floor as he rose to tell his story for the coroner, hoping no one would notice the tremor in his legs. Behind him, he felt his father's eyes needling the back of his head and he knew a sudden urge to piss. He hoped proceedings would not take long.

'Isaac Boadle, you were the one to discover your uncle's body, is that not so?' Mr Honeycett asked, a scowl rendering his expression even more forbidding close to than it had seemed from Isaac's seat.

'Yes, sir.'

'And was your uncle still living when you discovered him?'

'Yes, sir.'

'Will you tell us in your own words what happened on the morning of your uncle's death?'

To his embarrassment, when Isaac opened his mouth, nothing emerged but a squeak, eliciting stifled laughter from his neighbours, and raucous laughter from his fellow apprentices who had gathered at the rear of the inn. Even with his back to them, Isaac knew their voices: Eli the butcher's apprentice, with his braying laugh; Thomas the blacksmith's son, whose voice was yet to break, with his high-pitched giggle; Samson the barber's apprentice, with his honk. Isaac would be laughing too, if it were one of them in his place.

'I came downstairs just before dawn, to find my Uncle Jasper in distress. I asked him what was wrong but he could not get his words out. There was vomit on his clothes and the smell of . . . well, I knew something was not right with him.'

'And had your uncle been unwell, lad?'

'He had complained of a wretched stomach the night before.' From the corner of his eye Isaac caught his father's glare, felt the heat of his wrath. 'My aunt . . . my aunt usually fixes a posset if someone in the household is unwell.'

And barely audible, the soft sigh from his aunt.

'And did she fix a posset for him that night?'

'I . . . I don't know.'

That wasn't what he was supposed to say. Not what his father had rehearsed with him. He was supposed to say . . .

'Perhaps,' he admitted now. 'She has receipts for many possets. Potions,' he added, the words tripping over themselves.

You don't want to be blamed, do you boy, for your uncle's death? For that is what will happen. You will be blamed and imprisoned. And then you will be sent to your death.

His legs would not stop their quivering.

If it came to it, your aunt could plead her belly. Beg for transportation rather than the noose.

'Why didn't you fetch help once you knew your uncle was unwell?'

And he felt a pressure in his abdomen where his bladder pressed.

'I thought he might need me. I fetched him some water and loosened his neckcloth. I-I didn't know what to do. I had n-never seen someone in his state before.' His body began to rock back and forwards without him thinking of it. 'I was greatly shaken. I was not thinking clearly.'

'Surely, you knew he needed help?'

'My uncle was already clawing at his throat and making gurgling noises. And then . . . and then he was gone.'

The smoke from the inn's enormous fireplace was making

The Heirloom

his eyes smart. He brushed an arm across his eyes to hide the evidence.

'And what did your aunt have to say when she came downstairs?'

Despite the crush of people crowding the inn, he could feel the tension twitching between his father and his aunt. He was the rope.

'She said that we must make my uncle presentable, for he would not wish to be seen like that.'

A stirring of the crowd told him he had said something disturbing. *Tell the truth. But there's no need to tell what you ain't asked.*

'Did she seem distressed by your uncle's death?' Honeycett asked, the scowl almost gouging his forehead now.

'My aunt is never distressed.' Philadelphia was his haven in rough seas. In her arms lay safe harbour.

'Is that so, lad? Why?'

Your uncle was as strong as an ox. He was poisoned as sure as day follows night. Do right by him, son, and have a care for your own neck.

He wished he could lie safe in her arms now. He wished she could save him – from the coroner, from the crowd, from his father. From himself.

'My aunt can see the future, sir.'

He was just a boy. And yet . . . Philadelphia had hoped she could count on him. Often, she would look up from a task to find that he trailed after her like a puppy. He seemed to be at her elbow every minute he could abscond from his tailoring. She should have known that his father would blow lies in his ear. Stir fear in his heart. How could she blame him for being a boy in a dangerous world? Harder hearts than his quavered in the face of it.

'The Foord women are known for their magic!' A shrill voice

rose above the sea of nodding heads, drowning out the coroner's calls for order.

'My wife swore by Mrs Boadle's potions. I always knew she was taken before her time,' shouted another onlooker.

She had no need to turn to recognise the farrier, whose wife had purchased more than the occasional bonnet from Philadelphia. Like most milliners, she supplemented her income by selling cosmetics, and the farrier's wife had been a regular user of her chamomile, elderflower and raspberry leaf lotion to keep her crow's feet at bay. Just as half the village women of a certain age swore by her recipe, with the other half swearing by her mother's elderflower infusion for their hay fever. No, it was the spotted fever that had killed poor Betty Bagot, not a simple receipt for a cosmetic.

'There are witches abroad here in the village. A witch rides my horses at night. I woke to find them tired and lathered in the morning, though they were tucked safely in their stalls when I went to bed,' Farmer Martin claimed loudly.

More like it was smugglers who had borrowed Farmer Martin's steeds to transport their barrels away from the prying eyes of the riding officers.

'She has read the future in my palm many times. It is not only hats that the milliner sells,' came a quavering cry from somewhere behind her.

The old woman's voice was barely audible in the clamour, yet Philadelphia swallowed back a gasp of dismay. The soft-spoken words did more to wound her than any shouted accusation, for they issued from the lips of one of her favourite clients, Goody Collins, who begged a look at her palm as often as a raising of her hem or a trimming of a bonnet.

As the accusations flew, poor Isaac grew paler and paler, and all Philadelphia could foresee was a dangling noose and a clamorous, expectant crowd. A crowd different in size only to the crush of neighbours who even now jostled the bench where she sat. It seemed the entirety of England had an appetite for a murderous tale. Jasper had taught her to read from the Bible and the broadsides – those rousing ballads and blow-by-blow accounts of horrid murders. Once, on the streets of Brighton, she had passed a patterer singing out his wares, tempting passers-by to purchase his broadsides full of murder and mayhem. She did not want to be the next villain of such a ballad. She did not wish to be another Mary Barton.

For hours, she had sat listening to the proceedings of the inquest in unmoving silence, but now she cast a glance about the inn, seeking a friend. There was Mr Tupper, with his roving eye and florid waistcoat, dishing out his best claret to select gentlemen. There was his wife, whispering tittle-tattle in the ears of several ladies. Over by the hearth stood the rector, upright in his disdain. For a second, she caught the eye of her maid, Jenny, who should have been at home keeping a watchful eye on Marjory. The maid looked away, but not before Philadelphia saw her fear. Whether fear of reprimand or fear of witches, she could not say.

Only one onlooker's face hinted at a speck of sympathy for her. Thomas Earle's eyes were wide with disbelief, concern, and something else . . . something she could not put her finger on. A series of expressions flitted across his features so that when their eyes met, she felt a wave of sensation shake her, as if whatever connected them to each other was too powerful to contain in a mere glance.

That glance, however, was enough to give her the strength to act. Without realising what she did, Philadelphia rose to her feet. She shook out the creases in her bombazine, freed a stray ringlet entangled in the jet brooch above her heart, and glided towards the inn's open door. She no longer saw the crowd, nor felt the brush of their coats against her sleeve as she threaded through the press of bodies. She heard only the rush of her own breath, felt only the rhythm of her heart, saw only the light streaming through the open door.

Ten years earlier, Jasper had wooed her with his handsome face and his prettier promises. Her mother had warned her against marrying him. She, of course, had not listened. Now he was dead, and she must find a way to escape the mob that was surely coming for her. If she did not take matters into her own hands first.

24

Sussex, England
1811

By their sixth meeting, Philadelphia had begun to see herself through the tailor's eyes, and she discovered that she liked what she saw. That evening, he had waited for her as she trudged beneath the arched gateway of the inn's yard after ten hours of drudgery at Mistress Tupper's beck and call. Her arms were sturdy from fetching and carrying, yet not so strong that her shoulders did not hunch nor her arms hang limp at her sides after a long day. So, when she saw him step into her path, she felt a small thrill at the thought that he had been waiting for the clatter of her pattens upon the cobbles. Then again, she thought with a disappointed sigh, perhaps he had merely been about to ride home and met her by chance. For as he swept his hat from his head and bowed low, she noted that the tails of his coat were folded and buttoned to the waist to accommodate his saddle.

'Good evening, Miss Foord.'

'Good evening, Mr Boadle, are you on your way home?' She nodded at his buttoned tails, then glanced beyond to his horse, tied to the hitching post outside the inn.

'I have been waiting for you. I hope you will not send me away.'

She inched back her shoulders and clasped her hands neatly at her waist at his compliment.

'That is kind of you, sir, but my mother is expecting me. She plans to prepare her remedies before we lose the light. We have picked and dried a great many flowers this summer.'

'I shall not keep you long then, for I do not wish to displease your good mother. She might lay a curse on me,' he added, with an indulgent smile.

It was meant lightly, she supposed, but she could not help taking it to heart.

'Do not fret, dear Philadelphia, I hold your mother in the highest esteem. How could I not, when she gave birth to you?'

At first his question did not register, for her attention was caught by his calling her Philadelphia for the first time.

'I will escort you home, if you will allow,' he said, without waiting for her answer. He unbuttoned the tails of his coat, brushed down a leaf that had caught on his sleeve, and gathered the reins of his mount to fall into step beside her.

They walked largely in silence for the first ten minutes of their journey; she through an uncharacteristic shyness, uncertain as to the true destination of this friendship, and he through concentrating on the muddy ruts left by the passage of carts and drays that were the usual traffic upon this lane. His riding breeches were a soft cream leather, and mud was most unwelcome. They headed towards the bridle path that ambled down the ridge from the village, bordered on both sides by a band of woodland, which served as a boundary for the fields thereabouts. It was somewhat sunken from centuries of traffic so that its verges sloped upwards like the banks of a stream. Occasionally, the distant lowing of a cow, the song of a nearby thrush, or the snorting of his horse interrupted the silence, but it was not until they were halfway to the cottage that she felt his hip brush her petticoat and his gloved hand slip about her bare one.

The Heirloom

'I would save these hands from rough toil,' he said, squeezing her hand with a gentle pressure.

'I am used to rough toil, sir.'

'But these hands are too precious to be scrubbing floors in another woman's kitchen. And *you* are too beautiful for such toil. Someone should be scrubbing your floors.' He brought her hand to his lips and kissed it with a feather-light touch that rippled along her arm.

She did not know what to say in reply. No man had kissed her hand, nor any part of her body – she was usually quick enough to evade them. The tailor had surprised her with his gallantry, an unaccustomed gallantry to a girl like her. Still, she could have snatched her hand away if she cared to. No one had called her beautiful either. But if she agreed with him, he might think her conceited. Then again, why shouldn't she be called a beauty, just because she was the daughter of a cunning woman and accustomed to hard work?

Her coal-black hair gleamed from the rosemary oil she applied to her scalp, and her deep blue eyes set her apart from the other pale-eyed girls. Her figure was trim, her curves shown to advantage by drawstrings at the neck and waist of her short gown. She might not go about dressed in silk, but why shouldn't she possess the charms to capture the interest of a prosperous tradesman? A man on the up, anyone could see that.

Before she could reply, he dropped the horse's rein and pulled her to him with his free hand. Perhaps she should have pushed him away, but all she could think of was the expression on Lettice Lacy's face if she could see them, followed by the strange sensation of his chest crushing her bosom and his silk cravat brushing her neck as he leaned in to press his lips to hers. They were soft and rather damp, but not unpleasant, and seemed intent on exploring. She parted her lips slightly to accommodate them, conscious now that one of his thighs was pushing against hers. She closed her eyes, breathing in the smell of his toilet water, the fragrant scent of lavender. It was a heady sensation: the smell of him, the gentle touch on her lips, the feeling of his body against hers.

A flash of gold floated like a firefly in the darkness behind her closed lids and she thought of that golden thimble, glittering on his palm as they had stood beneath the cherry tree in her mother's garden. What had the thimble meant? What had he meant by showing it to her? Or had he shown it as a ploy? Customers at the King's Head had offered her trinkets before, seeking more than conversation. She stiffened and made to draw away from him. Except before she could take a single step, a loud bellowing issued from the woods, followed by the sound of an animal rummaging in the undergrowth.

'What is that noise?' Jasper asked, reeling back from her a pace and looking to the trees just as a very large, very hairy pig came scrambling down the bank and halted directly in front of them. Its hackles were up and its mouth chomping as it squealed loudly in their direction.

'It is one of the village pigs, left to roam the woods for acorns.'

'You are sure it isn't a wild boar?' He took several more steps away from the pig, drawing Philadelphia along with him. 'Pharaoh does not like it,' he said, as his mount whinnied, tossing its head and pawing the ground with one hoof.

'I think not. See, he has no tusks.'

The pig lowered its head, trotting towards them.

Philadelphia pulled her hand from Jasper's to pick up a stray branch lying in the path. She brandished it at the pig, hissing, 'Get away!' as she lunged for the surprised animal. 'Be gone!' she bellowed, stomping her feet and flapping her petticoat with her free hand so that the animal backed away with a loud squeal before turning and scrambling up the bank once more in the direction from which it had come. They listened as it crashed through woods, grunting its dissatisfaction, until after a time they heard it no more.

When Philadelphia returned her attention to the tailor, he was staring at her in disbelief, his grey eyes huge and his mouth standing open. She felt warmth flush her cheeks, and lowered her eyes so he could not see her shame. He had named her a beauty. But what beauty stamped her feet and bellowed at pigs? What respectable lass hissed and shrieked in such a manner?

'I say, that was well done!' he said. 'You are a devil with that stick, m'dear. And have a way with pigs, I see.'

'There are always pigs loose in the forest this time of year. Perhaps we surprised it,' she said, unsure if he meant to compliment or chastise her. 'I did not mean to . . . to shock you.'

'Not at all. Sweet, earnest Philadelphia. You astound me.'

'I do?'

'You are like an uncut gem, m'dear, impermeable, formidable. The darkest sapphire, waiting for its true light to be revealed. I knew it from the first moment I set eyes on you, skipping nimbly out of the way of old Farmer Sutton's wagon, that first day we met. You were so concerned for your coarse wool stockings that I wanted you to have silk.'

'You did?' She had not known he was watching her, considering her even then.

'I would marry you, my dear, if you will have me.'

In the face of her stunned silence, he reached into the pocket of his waistcoat, withdrawing his mother's golden thimble between thumb and forefinger. Then, grasping her right wrist so that her stick clattered to the ground, he drew her close. Her heart quickened like that of a small bird captured by a human hand.

'What say you, m'dear? Will you have me? Shall you be my helpmeet?' He slipped the thimble upon her middle finger. 'Will you be mine?'

She searched her heart for an answer, uncertain if she loved him. She liked his easy manner. She enjoyed his flattery. She admired his industry. Could this be love? Then again, he had said nothing of love either. Perhaps this was the way of a betrothal. Perhaps it was customary. After all, her mother had never spoken of betrothals and the like. She had only warned of love's pitfalls. Susanna preferred shame to marriage, so what did she know? Perhaps if you found a man who suited your tastes and he asked, you accepted, expecting that love would follow in time. Jasper certainly suited her tastes. And she appeared to suit his.

'Together we shall become a formidable pair. One day, I shall be tailor to the gentry of three parishes and you . . . you, with your eye for a pretty costume, your nimble fingers and charming ways, you I shall teach to be my milliner.'

And Lettice would not have him.

'I shall need to ask my mother.' Philadelphia glanced from her golden finger to his expectant face. Susanna would have words on the matter, no doubt.

'Honour thy father and thy mother: that thy days may be long upon the land which the Lord thy God giveth thee,' he said, with a smile, chucking her under the chin.

The words seemed familiar, yet she could not place them with any certainty. They sounded like something the priest might say. Catching her betrothed's expression, she realised that she should know.

'The fifth commandment,' he explained, when she made no answer. 'Although, once we are married you must honour your husband first. You must give up this business with remedies and such.'

'What do you mean, Jasper?' she asked, testing the sound of his name on her tongue for the very first time.

He took her chin in his hand and held her eyes with his. 'There will be no cunning women in the Boadle family,' he said, low and quiet. 'That is all I mean.'

25

The sun was grazing the treetops when Philadelphia opened the gate and slipped through the herb beds to the rear door of the cottage. She hoped Susanna would be in a good mood. Better yet, she hoped that her mother might have abandoned her plan to blend potions that evening and opted for an early supper and bed. Philadelphia had lingered so long in the lane with Jasper that they would be crushing petals and steeping herbs by rushlight. Besides, she was tired to her bones and longed to retreat to her chamber and hug Jasper's proposal to herself, to contemplate the thought of leaving the Foord name behind and becoming Mrs Jasper Boadle, a respected tradesman's wife and, even more enticingly, a tradeswoman in her own right.

She entered the hall to no sign of her mother, but her hopes were soon dashed when that familiar voice beckoned her to the next room. She found her mother seated at the planked table in the bakehouse, bunches of dried flowers and herbs from the adjacent pantry heaped about her. She had her great mortar and pestle out and several flasks of oil and alcohol, while a congregation of bottles and jars stood ready to be filled with tinctures and oils, yet Susanna did not seem to be at work.

'Why, here you are at last,' she remarked, looking up from a dish of tea. She had finished drinking and for some reason had upended her tea bowl upon its saucer. 'See here what I found this morning, hiding in the grasses in Farmer Lowe's wood.'

Philadelphia released the breath she had been holding and crossed to the table, pulling out a three-legged stool, fashioned from three stout branches fossicked in the woods.

'I almost missed them. They are always few and mostly gone by the end of May. They cannot bear the heat. But these little fellows had found a cool, shady spot to flourish longer.'

Her mother indicated a bunch of fernlike plants that Philadelphia had never seen before, their leaves the shape of crescent moons.

'What are they?'

'Moonwart, most call them, for the shape of their leaves. They are said by some folk to open locks or unshoe any horse that might trample them,' she snorted. 'But their true power lies as a salve for fresh wounds. See, I have brought out some of the marigolds we harvested. A little moonwart and some ground marigold petals will make a fine ointment for old Mr Trickett's ulcers.'

'But why is your tea bowl upside down upon its saucer?' Philadelphia asked, noting the way her mother played with the bowl as she spoke.

'They are such delicate plants, and I was surprised to find them at this time of the year.'

'The moon-shaped leaves are pretty but . . .' Her mother had not answered her question.

'The moon brings change, Philadelphia. It governs the tides. It governs a woman's courses. It waxes and it wanes.'

Her mother often spoke in riddles; a practice her daughter suspected was intended to frustrate her, so she was not about to delve too far into this one. 'If we begin with Mr Trickett's ointment, we may finish it this evening,' she suggested.

The Heirloom

Susanna did not answer. Instead, she took her tea bowl in hand, rotated it once in a clockwise direction, before lifting it to leave a dribble of tea behind in the saucer. She peered at the leaves clinging to the inside of the bowl.

'The question is, change for the better or the worse?' she asked, as if her action was quite usual, as if she had not heard her daughter's suggestion about the ointment.

Philadelphia had never seen her mother read the tea leaves as the Romani were accustomed to do, although she had instructed her daughter in its rudiments. And she usually resisted calls from her clients to tell the future, saying the future was best left to itself. Why then this sudden clutching at leaves?

'Shall I pour you another cup?'

'Let us see what this one has to say first,' Susanna said, examining the bowl as if it might speak to her. 'When I spotted the moonwart sprouting from the grass, my stomach lurched for no good reason. It felt like something or someone was clutching at me from the inside. And such a pretty plant too, so small that I could have missed it easily.'

'Perhaps you are getting your courses early.'

'At first, I paid this unsettled feeling no attention,' her mother said, ignoring her, 'but it has followed me all day. I cannot shake it off.'

'I thought you paid no heed to foretellings. I thought you believed in the magic of plants and the power of nature.'

Her mother caught her eye and held her gaze, saying, 'I don't believe in manipulating people against their will, daughter, for that is *against* nature. And too much knowledge of the future can be dangerous. But when I feel the world telling me something is amiss, I am bound to pay attention.'

Both women stared down at the white tea bowl with its sprigs of pink and blue flowers. The largest leaves had clumped at the bottom, while smaller leaves and a few fragments of stalk had settled on the sides. The clump of leaves seemed to have arranged itself into a crescent, like the last sliver of a waning moon. And on the inner wall of the bowl Philadelphia discerned the shape of a cross and another that could be a crucifix. No, it was longer than Christ's cross – more like a dagger.

'The crescent moon is said to bring prosperity,' Susanna announced, glancing at her daughter's face.

Philadelphia felt for the thimble safely lodged in one of the pockets tied beneath her petticoats. Was now the moment to tell her mother of Jasper's proposal? Surely, marriage to a hardworking tailor would bring prosperity to the Foord women? Confirmation from the tea leaves might sway her mother's good opinion of the match.

'The moon is not the only thing that . . .' she began.

'Except here, casting its shadow upon the moon, lies a cross,' Susanna said, indicating an arrangement of leaves clinging to the porcelain, 'bringing a warning that all is not well.' She pointed to another pattern on the opposite side of the bowl. 'And see here, a dagger strikes, a sure sign that danger lurks. But where and when, I cannot tell.' She turned to her daughter, with a frown. 'Has something happened today? Something that will bring great change?'

It was Philadelphia's turn to feel her stomach lurch. And under her mother's gaze she felt her neck tingle and the tiny hairs lift, as if she armed herself like a caterpillar. She looked away, returning her attention to the small white bowl with its coating of wet leaves.

'It is only a dish of tea,' she said, conscious of the surly note in her voice. 'It is only leaves and sticks. It could mean anything or nothing. That is what you often tell those who knock at our door seeking knowledge of their futures.'

'Foreknowledge does not come to me at my choosing, you know that, and those who knock at our door seek solace more than anything.'

The Heirloom

In answer, she reached for her mother's chipped brown pot and splashed a stream of tea into the bowl so that any portents were washed away. The old leaves floated and swirled with the new.

'Once you choose a path, it cannot be washed away so easily,' Susanna warned, clasping the hand that held the pot and guiding it back to the table. Then she took it in hers. 'What has happened today to augur such change?' she asked, her voice tinged with fear.

Like any daughter, Philadelphia had toyed with concealing the truth more than once. But her mother always knew – although how, she was at pains to guess. Did her face betray her, or did her mother have a sixth sense? Whatever the case, it seemed she could no longer avoid the truth. She would have to reveal news of Jasper's offer sooner or later. What did crosses and daggers signify, anyway? Better to think on bolts of soft English wool and French silk, fine steel needles and golden thimbles. These would be her lot once she wed, not invisible daggers.

She cleared her throat and sought the right words. 'The tailor waited for me at the inn this evening, Mother. We walked the length of the lane together. He wanted to ask for my . . . my hand in marriage. This hand,' she said, drawing her hand from her mother's grasp and turning it palm upwards, the fingers splayed as if to encompass all that their future might hold.

'Did he now? A shame he did not think to seek my permission first.'

Philadelphia shrugged. 'What use to seek your permission if I would not have him.'

'Lettice Lacy would have had him, but her father said no to the tailor.'

'That isn't true! He has no eye for Lettice, for all her preening and primping.' Of course it wasn't true. Jasper had eyes only for her. He had said so. He could not help it that Lettice had set her cap at him.

'I do not say this to wound you. I say it to warn you. I heard it from Mrs Lowe and young Lizzie Wells, who had it from the Lacys' cook. Your tailor visited the brick maker several weeks ago, scurrying away red-faced and head hanging after a terse conversation in the brick maker's hall. Edgar Lacy would not have him for son-in-law. He did not think him a fit match for his daughter, nor his purse a fit match for the brick maker's coffers.'

Philadelphia let her hand sink to the table where it curled in on itself. No, it could not be true. She could still feel the imprint of his lips upon her hand and lips, the sensation of his chest pressed to hers. Jasper had wooed her for weeks. He met her at every opportunity. He praised her beauty and charm, declaring they would make a fine pair. He talked of the fine life they would fashion together. He could not be wooing another girl at the same time. She would not let it be so. She would not believe this rumour – for rumour it must be.

'The truth is, something is not right here. I feel it in my bones.' Susanna's voice was almost a whisper.

'The truth is, you do not want me to be happy. You want to keep me in this old cottage in the woods, planting your herbs, making your potions, ministering to the ills of our neighbours, while half of them whisper behind their hands about the Foord women being witches. Thrusting hag stones in our faces, nailing horseshoes to their doors, burying jars of pins beneath their hearths . . .'

Her mother flinched as if she had lashed out with her hand rather than her words.

'This is my chance to better myself. This is my chance to make my way in the world,' Philadelphia continued, pleading with her mother to understand.

She did not want to be whispered about or feared. She wanted to be admired. She wanted to be befriended for her talent and her charm. Learning the trade of a milliner would be just the thing. She would surround herself with straw bonnets and velvet turbans, with fine linen caps and silk ribbons. She would turn her hand to finery rather than drudgery. She did not want to be a cunning woman like her mother, and her mother before her. Like her sister. All the cunning in the world had not saved Mercy.

And who could blame her for that?

'I want to follow a different calling,' she finished, with a gulp indistinguishable from a sob.

Susanna cradled the tea bowl in both hands and brought it to her lips. She gazed at her daughter over the rim, a message in her eyes.

'Beware of betraying your true self for the lure of gold, poppet. For you cannot escape who you truly are, and you may give up more than you intend,' she said, before drinking deeply of the golden-brown liquid. 'Oh, my tea has gone quite cold.'

26

East Sussex, England
2024

Hearing a light knock, Mia slouched across to the door with a yawn. It had been a long day and she still had more to research before she hit the sack. So it was with some reluctance that she opened the door to find Tessa standing in the hallway with a tray in her hands.

'I've brought tea,' she said, and held out the tray.

'Oh, I didn't order any.'

'I thought you might like some.'

'Thanks.' Mia deposited the teapot and cup on a side table, before asking, 'Do you want to join me? There's another cup around here somewhere, although it might taste of toothpaste.'

'No thanks, there was a brief lull downstairs but it won't last. I hear you're moving to Puckridge Cottage.'

Mia smiled. Ah, here was the real reason for the cup of tea. 'Does everyone around here have psychic powers? You're the third person who's asked me today.'

'It's a small village.'

'Well, it looks that way. I saw the solicitor this morning, then Reid—'

'Reid Ellis, the heir hunter from Lewes?'

The Heirloom

'Uh-huh, he took me back to have another look around the cottage today. I plan to make the move tomorrow, after I check out and get a few groceries organised.'

'Henrietta's cousins had plans for it, you know.'

'Did they?'

'So I heard, Airbnb with a theme. You know, "charming medieval cottage", "once home to witches", that kind of thing.' She added air quotes to the descriptions.

'Witches?'

'You know, just old gossip. I'm sure your mother will have told you about it . . .' She paused, probably unsure now whether Mia's mother had in fact told her about the family history. 'Though no one believes that old rubbish.'

'The rubbish about me being descended from a long line of witches?'

'Something like that makes for a good story. Henrietta sort of played on it for her tea leaf and tarot readings. Anyway, I'll let you get on with it.'

She smiled, winked, and was about to close the door when Mia thought to ask, 'Does everyone in the village know that my mother ran away to Australia?'

'They do now. See you at breakfast.'

After she left, several thoughts jostled for space in Mia's head. Firstly, Tessa and her husband must work ridiculous hours. Secondly, how do you keep a secret in a village this size? Thirdly, maybe there was something in what Celia had said about Henrietta and witches.

Of course, this was the exact moment at which her mother chimed in on Mia's phone. She must have just woken up and be drinking her first cup of the day – sitting out on the terrace overlooking the river, with the dawn colouring the sky – and thinking, I must message Mia.

Hope your trip is going smoothly.
Send pics of cottage please. It isn't falling down, is it?
The messages pinged into her phone, one after another.
Please watch out for strangers in sheep's clothing.
Oh, and think of your grandmother as a stealth bomber disguised as Budgie the Helicopter.

Really, Mother? Mia shook her head in disbelief at the last message, although she shouldn't have been surprised. Clearly, her mother still thought she was twelve. And there was nothing about Philadelphia either. Whatever. She would reply in the morning.

There was something she needed to find out before she went to bed, something that had been niggling at her all day. The broadside on the stairs about the inquest into Jasper Boadle's death was nagging at the back of her mind, and she wanted to find out more if she could. Specifically, she wanted to find out what had happened to Philadelphia in the end. The missing pieces of the story were like an itch she couldn't scratch.

She settled herself on the bed with her laptop and typed in the words *Jasper Boadle broadside poison inquest 1821* and waited to see what surprises the internet would produce. She was hoping to discover further broadsides about the Boadles. She scrolled through header after header of 'Criminal Broadsides of 19th Century England', 'The Last Dying Speech of Mary Wright who committed barbarous murder by putting arsenic in her husband's plum cakes', 'The office and role of the coroner in England and Wales', 'Life, Trial, Confession and Execution of Catherine Wilson, The Female Poisoner'. Finally, 'Account of evidence taken before the inquest held at Mr Tupper's inn, the King's Head . . .'

Mia stopped scrolling, clicked and began reading. It began with the same preamble as the broadside hanging on the stairs but contained further details. It was illustrated with a woodcut of a corpse and a butcher standing over him holding a knife.

Actually, the butcher may have been the surgeon, she realised, one Mr Goodenough.

From the state of the body when the surgeon, Mr Goodenough, examined it, the deceased likely died by foxglove poisoning. The parish constable, Mr Puttick, gave evidence that leaves of the plant were found on the floor of the tailor's residence and that, furthermore, Mrs Boadle was known to grow the same variety of foxglove digitalis grandiflora *in her garden. The tailor's apprentice and nephew, Isaac Boadle, also gave witness that his uncle had complained of stomach pains the evening before and that his aunt, Philadelphia Boadle, would usually prepare a remedy for ailing members of the household. At several points during the proceedings the gathered crowd interrupted with accusations of witchcraft and suggestions that the deceased's wife was known for her supernatural gifts. The inquest was adjourned until nine o' clock the next day.*

Despite her weariness, Mia kept scrolling, compelled to learn more. At first, she scrolled past the heading 'The Milliner and the Tailor's Apprentice', then quickly turned back when she realised its significance.

The Milliner and the Tailor's Apprentice
1821
Printed by J. Catnach, Monmouth Court, Seven Dials
From Broadside Ballads Online at the Bodleian

'Well, let's see what you have to show me,' she murmured as she read. She clicked on the tiny image beside the catalogue entry and began to recite aloud:

There was a well-known tailor,
In Sussex he did sew.
His wife, she was a milliner,
Sundry skills she did know.
Of cures she knew many,
Of hats she knew some,
But for love and other charms
One and all to her did come.

The tailor had a nephew,
His apprentice, with the thread.
A tall and handsome lad,
Who took the milliner to bed.
'Not I,' he protested,
When the tailor did object,
But the uncle was no fool
And this lie, he did reject.

Before he could reap justice,
His stomach did complain.
So, he drank a likely potion,
To take away the pain.
Instead of giving aid.
His pain grew more severe.
And the nephew and the milliner
Did not even shed a tear.

'Whoa,' Mia breathed out in a soft whistle of surprise. 'Clearly they didn't sue for defamation in those days.'

According to the heir hunter, Philadelphia Boadle was notorious locally as the Witch of Sussex Downs. According to what she had just read, the husband had been poisoned and she was having an affair with his nephew. (Although, Mia had to admit, as well as bad poetry, broadside ballads were renowned for their salaciousness.) She was tempted to search further but after a long day, which had followed two even longer days, her eyes were coated in grit. Tomorrow would be soon enough. She put the laptop aside, about to prepare for bed, when it struck her. Philadelphia was a milliner. Her husband was a tailor. One of the tools both trades used was a thimble. Could her mother's gift – the thimble that had been passed down through the generations – once have belonged to Philadelphia? That would surely mean she was related to the woman.

She clutched at the thimble and brought it closer to her face. She'd had a jeweller attach a link through which she had threaded a gold chain so that the thimble rested against the skin of her collarbone. On the outside the gold was indented all over so that it resembled a basket decorated with flowers, while around the rim it was engraved with words. She peered closer, trying to make out the tiny, old-fashioned script, although by now she knew the words by heart.

Thine heart be mine.

If the thimble once belonged to Philadelphia, who had given it to her? Her husband, who was poisoned? Her nephew, who desired her? For the inscription declared it as a token of love. Or desire. Or perhaps – from her twenty-first century perspective – of ownership.

She closed her eyes, trying to visualise her long-ago ancestor Philadelphia Foord Boadle wearing the thimble upon her middle finger. But she was so weary now that she couldn't think clearly. She could only give in to the trance-like wave of lethargy that washed over her, blanking out her comfortable room at the inn and the events of the day, sensing the familiar weight of the laptop resting on her knees.

A boy crouches behind a door of thick, rough-hewn planks, his ear pressed tight against the wood. He is a good-looking lad, with chestnut hair and light brown eyes, tall for his age but yet to show signs of looming adulthood. He is dressed in clothing from bygone days; tan breeches and white stockings, what looks like a linen shirt and striped waistcoat, with a short jacket loose upon his shoulders. Despite his strange dress, there is something oddly familiar about him. And there is distress in those wide eyes and open mouth as he listens to the angry words being hurled about in the room beyond the door.

'You were seen, Philadelphia!'

'By whom? You know there are people in the village who have no love for me. Why would you take their word over that of your wife?' The woman's voice sounded defiant, with an edge of fear.

'Because I trust the source of this report.'

The boy drew in a sharp breath, before quickly covering his mouth, perhaps fearing to be heard by the man and woman beyond the door.

'Whatever was "seen" means little. People are prone to seeing what they wish to see.'

'You were seen reading Goody Collins' future in her palm!'

'She only asked me to deliver a balm for her callouses, that is what was seen,' the woman scoffed.

In reply came the sound of a loud slap and a thud as if the recipient of the slap had fallen to the floor. The boy moved to lift the latch upon the door but the man's angry voice stayed his hand.

'You made me a promise, Philadelphia, when I took you to wife. You promised to give up your mother's trade. You promised no more of your potions and charms and the devil knows what other cunning!'

'I have. I did,' the woman replied, with a whimper. 'I only practise the milliner's trade. I sell cosmetics, that is all, Jasper. I sell what is asked of a fashionable milliner. To help our business flourish.'

The Heirloom

Another thud and slap followed, before the man growled, 'See that you do. And let there be no more reports of this evil. I'll not have my name tainted by your mother's unchristian doings.'

'Yes, husband. There will be no more cunning business. I swear it.'

The boy flinched and was about to open the door when it was wrenched open for him.

'What are you doing here, boy?' the man barked, his face dark with anger in the dim light of the passage.

'I-I-I cannot find the dark green worsted for the butcher's new c-coat.' The boy shrank, his back scraping the rough plaster of the wall as he stammered out the words.

'It is on the workbench, numbskull, where it was left. And if I find you skulking around my chamber again, you will feel my wrath on your backside.'

'Yes, Uncle,' the boy said aloud, but as he took the narrow stairs to the workshop two at a time, he muttered so quietly that only a dreamer might hear the words. 'One day I will protect you. One day, when I am grown, you will have nothing more to fear, I vow.'

Mia jolted awake with a start, her head fuzzy, her neck complaining. For a moment she didn't know where she was. The low ceiling with its dark wooden beams and casement windows confused her. Where were the white, timber-lined walls of her bedroom and the shadowy trees that tapped against her window? Her head was full of a frightened boy listening at doors and longing to be a man. In her dream she had felt that longing deep within her, as if she were the boy. As if she felt the impotence of being a child in a man's world. She shook her head, blinked, took a deep breath and tried to reorient herself.

When her head stopped spinning, she remembered where she was, sitting slumped against the bedhead in her room at the King's Head in southern England. A notification must have woken her, for her phone was lit up on the bedside table. She picked it up to find that Kate had just messaged her. It was lunchtime in Brisbane and her friend was probably sitting in the park across the road from her office, eating her usual sushi or salad. Winter in Brisbane was often warmer than summer in London.

Hey gorgeous, what ya doin?

Look who I've got with me.

A picture of a grinning, waving man followed. Jase.

Yeah, we've been dating. I bumped into him a few weeks ago and it just kind of happened. Didn't mention it because you seemed kind of weird about him.

Why didn't you tell me he's such a sweetheart?

Mia had felt the buzz between them after drinks at the pub in the summer. She had been surprised when nothing appeared to happen between the two. Now she knew why; it turned out that Kate was more sensitive than she let on, that she had felt Mia's reluctance. Her . . . let's face it . . . fear of the past. And Jase *was* the past. Well, she was happy for them. They were both such easygoing souls – maybe even perfect for each other. That happened sometimes, didn't it? True love?

And why didn't you ever tell me about the river and what happened there?

You know, Jase said he still has nightmares about it.

Call me when you get a chance. Love you ♥

The last three messages threw her off kilter so that she dropped the phone. Her laptop slid from her knees to rest lopsidedly on the bed beside her. She had fallen asleep with it still open on her lap. Now its blackened screen stared back at her from a strange acute angle. She didn't want to think about the river or what had happened that day, thirteen years ago. She wasn't ready. Not yet. Maybe not ever. Maybe, despite his nightmares, Jase was stronger than her, more resilient. For clearly, he had told Kate about it. Or maybe he just had more self-belief. He was the one who had been

The Heirloom

there in the middle of it, after all, swimming for his life. She had been a minor character. Merely played a supporting role in the tragedy.

Yet, in a way, she could have been the protagonist of the story. If she had believed in herself. If she had acted. And because she hadn't, because she couldn't, she would have to carry the guilt, as penance, perhaps for the rest of her life.

She almost picked up the phone and called Kate. Almost. Instead, she retrieved the computer and returned to the last page she had opened. The distant past was safer than the more recent tragedy. History could distract her without touching her. Perhaps she would never be ready to deal with her own failings, the ones that kept her awake at night. Before she fell asleep, she remembered scrolling through pages of text about the dead tailor, Jasper Boadle. Then she seemed to remember a boy listening at a door, overhearing a tailor berating his wife. Her ancestor Philadelphia Boadle, she knew it. No, her *ancestors*, plural. If Philadelphia was her distant ancestor, then Jasper probably was too.

The question was, who was the boy at the door? And had she dreamed true? Had the dream been suggested by her online search, or was the past now reverberating through to the present and appearing in her dreams?

After all, it wouldn't be the first time she had dreamed true.

27

Sussex, England
1821

The kitchen was redolent with the scent of baking bread when Philadelphia returned home from the inquest. It seemed that the inquest would go to a second day, when most lasted but one. She feared there may be worse to come. She had been branded a witch by her neighbours and suspected of poisoning her husband. What 'worse' might be, she did not dare to contemplate. Yet contemplate she must, or be caught unawares. The hangman's noose dangled closer with each new witness, though she had done nought to deserve it. She had not poisoned her husband, though *he* had wished her dead more than once.

'You were quick returning from the inn, Jenny,' she remarked, removing her cloak and wrapping an apron of plaid linen about her waist.

'I only ducked out to ... to catch the tinker, mistress. The handle on the big ladle was loose. Martin kept a watchful eye on Marjory whilst I was gone.'

'Yes, I thought I spied you through the crowd at the inquest.'

'Only for a moment. I was curious, Mrs Boadle. I heard Isaac was to give witness today.' Jenny would not meet her eye as she replied. She was not usually so loath to offer an opinion. The girl had opinions on everything.

'And what did you think of Isaac's deposition? Of what he had to say?' She could not help wondering if Jenny believed her guilty of her husband's death. Perhaps she too believed the accusations of witchcraft. Perhaps she had always believed them.

'I thought . . . I thought . . .' Before the girl could get further words out, she dissolved into tears, rhythmic sniffs that escalated into wracking sobs, which shook her shoulders and set her nose to dripping.

'Have a care, or the snot will drip in the butter,' Philadelphia said, edging around the table to place her arm at Jenny's waist and set her upon a bench, which set the maid to giggling through her tears.

'There, my dear. It cannot be so bad, can it?'

'It can, mistress,' Jenny hiccupped. 'It can.'

'What can?'

'Isaac . . . he . . .'

Isaac had opened the door to Philadelphia being accused of her husband's murder, so what could be worse? That is what the boy had done, whether he intended it or no. Or more likely, whether his father, Enoch, intended it or no. And she was almost sure that Enoch intended it so. But could there be more to the story?

'What did Isaac do, Jenny?'

'He . . . I saw him preparing a posset for the master on the night before he . . . before he—' She broke off into another round of sobs. 'Before the master died.'

Philadelphia was silenced by her admission. Enoch had discovered the foxglove leaves upon the kitchen floor, but it was still possible to believe he had placed them there himself. It was also possible that someone else had dropped them there. And it did not necessarily prove that Jasper was poisoned – or by whom. Except she had not expected her maid to have witnessed

Isaac making that posset for his uncle. As to what the posset contained, it could have been innocent enough, she supposed. Yes, the boy often tarried by her side when he should be at his tailoring, watching her prepare remedies and lotions for her clients when her husband was absent from the house. At first, she had thought he sought to escape the tedium of the tailor's workshop, then several months ago she had come to realise that *she* was the attraction. She was the flower that lured him into her garden.

'And why didn't you tell the constable this?' she asked Jenny.

'Be-be-because I did not want to get Isaac into trouble.'

Philadelphia could not see the girl's eyes through the curtain of hair and tear-soaked lashes. 'You like Isaac, do you, Jenny?'

'I like him well enough, mistress.'

Well enough to bury such information, it seemed. 'He is a good boy,' she said.

'I was afeared, I would not wish to hurt him.'

Except we do not always get what we wish. Philadelphia could testify to that. And sometimes what we wish, we would rather not have, after all.

'None of us would *wish* to hurt, Isaac. But—'

A scraping of boots upon the stone flags outside the kitchen announced the arrival of a visitor at the door to the yard, and both woman and girl looked up in surprise. Visitors usually entered through the front door to the shop, not the kitchen door, their arrival accompanied by a good deal of bowing and scraping from the tailor and his apprentices.

'Forgive me for intruding, Mrs Boadle, I thought it best not to proclaim my visit to all and sundry,' the man said, with a polite bow, 'given the current circumstances.'

'Mr Earle,' she replied, curtseying with as much grace as her surprise allowed.

'I was concerned for your welfare.'

He stood just beyond the open door, inspecting her as if for

The Heirloom

signs of damage. His eyes roamed from the black velvet bandeau that kept her hair in order, to her dark eyes and the plaid apron tied about the formal black of her mourning dress. He let out an audible breath, before stepping across the threshold and into her house. She appeared to be in one piece, then – although shattered inside.

'Jenny, please set the water to boil for tea.'

'Yes, mistress.'

'I don't wish to trouble you,' he said.

'It is no trouble.'

He glanced around the kitchen, no doubt noting the bundles of herbs hanging from the ceiling, and the wood and stoneware jars ranged along its shelves, before pulling out a chair and seating himself at her table. She took a seat opposite, clasping her hands upon the table demurely to disguise the quaking in her breast.

'There are no witch's potions here, Mr Earle,' she said, with a rueful smile. Although some might say different of her mother's cottage, with its glass jars lined in neat rows, filled with their myriad remedies. But what did they know?

'I am sorry for what was said at the King's Head this morning. It was nothing but vile rumour. The work of the mob. Honeycett will not have it, I am sure.'

She nodded in silent acquiescence, all the while knowing that the coroner may very well have it, for that is the power of the mob, is it not? And who can stand against its conviction? Her foremothers had known it, forced to enter the church through the north door, the Devil's door. Philadelphia had striven to escape that fate her whole life, learning a respectable trade, marrying a respectable man, becoming a respectable woman. A woman of ordinary powers. Susanna had been respected for her skill, feared by some for her imagined powers. Yet she had never been respectable. Not that her mother had cared.

Philadelphia cared.

'They are frightened, I think, and look to soothe their fears,' he suggested.

'Perhaps. But there are also those who would do me and mine harm . . . given the chance.'

She knew Jenny listened as she hung the iron kettle upon the pot hanger and set it over the fire. She held her shoulders rigid, her chin raised. She would do well to realise the grim future they faced if Philadelphia were named murderess as well as witch. She would be taken from the tailor's premises and transported to the Lewes Gaol to be locked in a dank cell until the assizes. Who would care for her daughter then? Who would employ her maid then? Tainted, as she would be, by the witch's touch. They might both end up in the workhouse.

'And my husband's death has given them that chance,' she continued, glancing away from the maid to answer her visitor. Respectability had not protected her, after all.

Thomas Earle frowned. 'The lad has done you damage, I admit.'

'He suffers under his father's influence. Enoch looks to blame someone for his brother's death, and I am his nearest target. You do not believe it, do you, Mr Earle? That I had a hand in my husband's death?' Her hands flinched involuntarily on the wooden table.

He must have noticed, for he surprised her by reaching out to lay a hand upon them in comfort. Perhaps he surprised himself, because he stared at their hands for a moment, before saying, 'No, I do not believe it. I believe . . . I believe that you sought only to help, not harm. You helped my wife. You were always a good friend to her.'

'Mrs Earle was kind to me. And she had a great fondness for hats,' she said, smiling at the memory of Marianne Earle's cornucopia of headwear.

'I wish there was some way to repay that service.' His hand enveloped hers far longer than sympathy demanded or society sanctioned, so that she felt a quiver of recognition thread through her. He had always been there, this man, too far above her station to be more than an acquaintance, but that thread had always been there. In another life they might have been lovers. Except she could not think on that now.

She tore her eyes from his to glance at Jenny, busy with the good, white rose-covered teapot that she had inherited from Susanna.

'I shall prepare Mr Earle's tea, Jenny,' she said, rising from her chair to take the teapot from the girl.

She would prepare her finest blend for her distinguished visitor. He would see that she kept a respectable house, that she was no longer the cunning woman's daughter. She was a hard-working milliner with a busy trade. She was a mother and a widow.

As Thomas Earle talked on about that morning's events, she busied herself about the tea things, but her thoughts drifted elsewhere. Her maid had seen Isaac brew a posset on the night before Jasper died. A posset that may have caused his death. Yet no one would suspect her nephew of wishing to murder his uncle. He had no believable reason. So, what harm could there be in suggesting that Isaac was the one who had given Jasper the foxglove remedy, thinking to ease his discomfort? He may well have mistaken the leaves for comfrey, since they were quite similar and easily confused by a novice. He was only a lad, after all, a lad who could be mistaken.

A lad who feared being blamed for his uncle's death.

'Do take a sip of your tea, Mr Earle. It will warm you for your journey home,' she said, setting a cup before him and taking her seat once more. 'There may be a way to . . .' she began tentatively.

What if Isaac were blamed for his mistake?

'A way to?' Thomas looked at her expectantly.

Yet what if she were blamed? Carted off to Lewes, leaving Marjory alone, without protection. There was more than one person in the village who would be glad to see her gone. And none who wished Isaac ill. Surely, they would judge him mistaken rather than murderous.

'Perhaps if you were to suggest to the coroner that my maid, Jenny, has knowledge of events on the eve of my husband's death. That she should be called upon to give her deposition.'

From the corner of her eye, Philadelphia witnessed Jenny cower away from her, almost bumping the kettle at its place over the fire. She sympathised, she did. For she had felt the mob's wrath herself. Except the girl had done no wrong. She could not be blamed.

'Is that not so, Jenny?'

Philadelphia must save herself to protect her daughter, no matter the cost. She turned her head to nod encouragement at her young maid. 'You witnessed another person give my husband a posset.'

Still the girl hesitated.

'It is all right. You may speak the truth to Mr Earle. He doesn't believe you are tainted with witchcraft. None in this house be tainted.'

'Yes, Mistress Boadle,' the girl whispered. 'Yes, I saw another make a posset on the eve of the master's death.'

Thomas Earle looked up at the girl, with hope in his eyes. 'And you will testify to this, Jenny?'

'I will, sir,' she said, her eyes locked with her employer's. 'I will.'

28

Several yards of black gauze were Philadelphia's only armour against the world as she returned to the King's Head the day following her public denunciation as a witch. She had twisted the gauze into a turban towering upon her head, draping one end across her face as a veil. She owed the mob nothing and would not let them witness her shame. Or her fear. Her arm, sheathed in the dull black of mourning, was crooked through her maid's elbow to keep Jenny resolute. The girl was twitchy as a bird, although Philadelphia could not say she blamed her.

As they crossed the village square, she stopped in her tracks when she caught a glimpse of a man emerging from the lane beside the mercer's store. The hair on her arms bristled and a familiar dread crept up her spine as an image of his face flashed before her eyes like an apparition. She felt sure she had seen him before. With his long angular face, hooked nose and eyes of a very light blue, he was quite distinctive, but she could not quite place him. He cast a swift glance behind him, before hurrying off at a brisk trot.

She was about to walk on when another man emerged from the lane after him – a lane that led only to the rear of a rough tavern – and this man she knew well. It was her brother-in-law, Enoch. Although what business he might have at the tavern early on a Tuesday morning, she did not know. But it looked very much like he had been meeting the first man. Enoch hurried off in the direction of the King's Head, no doubt to find his place before the onlookers arrived. She decided to think no more about it, at least for the moment, following after him with Jenny in tow. Perhaps the memory would come to her later.

The two women had almost reached the inn when their path was blocked by another woman wearing the lavender silk of half-mourning, a woman Philadelphia did not wish to meet, this day or any day.

'Good day, Mrs Tutt,' she said, dipping her knees in an effort to forestall any further public assault upon her reputation. For Lettice Tutt and her sister had done their worst at the inquest yesterday. Philadelphia wasn't sure she could remain silent if the woman were to accuse her to her face. She might be tempted to retaliate in kind.

Unfortunately, her courtesy was not reciprocated, for Lettice darted forward as if about to peck out her eyes. 'He never wanted you. It was me he wanted,' she clucked.

Philadelphia took a step back, astounded at so public a lack of decorum. For a heartbeat she imagined the sight of Lettice Tutt, tearing at her hair in a fever of passion. 'I am sorry, I do not take your meaning,' she said, as calmly as she could, while every sense was telling her to fight or flee.

'I speak of your husband. It was me he courted. Me he wanted. And now he is dead,' Lettice said, her voice clearly teetering on the precipice of unreason. She had lost her husband more than a year before, so loss wasn't a new thing to her. It wasn't raw like Philadelphia's widowhood. It offered no excuse for her behaviour or the hatred she had shown at the inquest. How could so much venom reside in so small a body?

The Heirloom

The Bible said to love others, yet the milliner could find no love for this woman in her heart. She could not dredge up one iota of sympathy for her obsession with an imaginary ancient slight. Ten years ago, they had been girls, blinded by the tailor's glamour and fancying themselves in love. Lettice Tutt was a grown woman now, a widow still chasing a youthful fancy. Chasing someone else's husband. That is the person Philadelphia saw standing before her in the village square. The same girl who had accosted her one midnight amongst the graves.

She lowered her voice to a whisper, saying, 'And now you will never have him. Unless you have had him already.'

On any other day she might have felt ashamed of her retort, her lack of kindness. Certainly, Susanna would have chided her for her words, she who had always counselled quiet restraint, for their own sakes as well as others. Except for the response that followed.

'*I* am no whore,' Lettice sneered.

'Is that so?' Philadelphia wasn't so sure. Her husband *had* been late returning home more often in recent months. She had not thought to question him at the time. Jasper did not like to be questioned. But now . . . now that she felt the widow's hatred, she set to wondering.

'And I did not stoop to witchcraft to win him,' the other woman added, her white-gloved hand straying to the tiny amber cut-glass bottle that she wore about her neck. Her hand lingered there for a moment, before dropping to her side.

'No? Yet I recall one Midsummer's Eve when you asked a certain favour of me . . .'

'He took you because he could not have me,' Lettice said, stepping towards Philadelphia with a curl of her lip so that Jenny tried to pull her mistress away. 'My father would not give his consent. He did not love you then. And he does not love you . . . he does not love you.'

'Perhaps it is your father you should rail against, not me.'

'When my husband died, Jasper would have taken me for wife then, if it were not for you. He told me so.'

She stood so close that Philadelphia could smell her anger beneath the scent of her perfume, the scent of orange blossom.

'That is a pretty scent you wear, Mrs Tutt.' It brought to mind the whiff of cologne that had hung about her husband after his late-night forays in recent weeks. The sweet and sickly scent she had determined not to remark upon whenever she caught a whiff. She had determined to remain blind to his roaming. Deaf to his dissatisfaction when he spoke to her. Resolved not to sniff out betrayal. For what would be gained from drawing attention to his betrayal, when he would simply deny her accusations and indulge his temper all the more as punishment?

Yet she could not help taking note of a particular conversation she and Isaac had overheard not long before Jasper's death. At the time, she had determined to shrug off the conversation as yet more grumbling from her disgruntled brother-in-law, though it had shocked her nephew enough that she had to stay his hand.

Perhaps fate will lend a hand and free you to marry again, her brother-in-law had said, sitting in the tailor's shop, quaffing her ale.

Oh well, what was done, was done. And nothing could change it now. Still ... that did not mean Lettice Tutt should escape unscathed.

'Did *you* order that perfume from J. Floris in London?' She asked the question that she had not asked Jasper when she found the receipt in the shop accounts for two 8oz bottles of eau de cologne from J. Floris, Comb Maker and Perfumer, of 89 Jermyn Street, St James, London. 'Or was it a gift from my husband?'

'Once I was free to marry, he wished to be free of *you*,' Lettice spat.

Beside her she felt Jenny stiffen, heard her gasp in surprise.

The Heirloom

Philadelphia stared at Lettice, seeing her clearly for the first time. Seeing in those wild eyes, which belied her soft lavender disguise, the danger she posed. She had known the woman her entire life but had never perceived her as a threat. A hindrance and some-time rival, yes. An irritating gossip, certainly. The inquest had made her dislike plain, but Philadelphia had never believed the woman would do her real harm. Until now. Do every harm she could.

'And he did not care how that came about,' the woman spat.

The words were like a blow to the heart, and she found herself leaning back from their force. So, Enoch wasn't the only one whispering in Jasper's ear then, sowing his seeds of malice. Plotting to be rid of her. Lettice had been prompting her husband, too. Philadelphia had discounted her brother-in-law's words as all talk, on the night that she and Isaac had overheard them. But perhaps Jasper had done more than agree with his brother. Perhaps her husband truly had done more than simply wish her dead. Perhaps he had acted upon those words.

The world is full of mishap, Brother.

All she could do then, and all she could do now, was take measures to protect herself and her daughter. Whatever measures were needed. Susanna would have done the same, wouldn't she, to guard against those who wished her dead?

She patted Jenny's arm in a show of confidence she did not feel, and said to the woman who laid claim to her husband's love, 'That must have proved difficult, since I am very much alive.'

'Fortunately,' Lettice said, stroking the amber glass at her neck, 'there is more than one way to kill a witch.'

She turned with a swish of her lavender skirts and swept in the direction of the King's Head, leaving Philadelphia to follow, towing a reluctant Jenny behind her. It was only when they arrived at the door to the inn a few minutes later – the rumble of the crowd already evident – that she thought of the lurking stranger once more and remembered where she had seen him before. One afternoon, not long before he died, she had witnessed Jasper through the window of the tailor's shop, talking earnestly with a hawkish-looking man on the street. She had thought at first that her husband enquired after Flemish lace or French silk from one of the local smugglers, since he had spoken of such arrangements. But when no new silk or lace appeared in the shop, she had put it from her mind.

Now she suspected that he was a man with a more perfidious service to sell.

29

East Sussex, England
2024

Mia's clothes were still sitting unpacked in the low-ceilinged bedroom upstairs but the art supplies she had brought all the way from home were neatly stowed in ceramic jars from the kitchen, and arranged on a small cane table in the room she had christened 'the studio'. She had purchased a modem, scanner and printer and set them up on her grandmother's workbench. Now, it was just a matter of getting the WiFi installed, for it was apparent that Henrietta had not approved of twenty-first-century technology.

She paused in her labours to admire the room she had chosen for her workspace. The potted plants her grandmother's neighbour had tended so thoughtfully seemed to invite the outside garden in, creating a haven of greenery. Even in midsummer, the light streaming into the studio felt soft and golden, so different to the hard, bright light she was accustomed to in Australia. She loved the uncompromising light of home, loved its heat and clarity, but this gentler sun had her dreaming of the past, hazy as it was. It wasn't surprising, given her grandmother's eclectic taste in furniture, and the photographs and prints decorating her walls. While the esoteric collection of other, weirder objects scattered about the cottage pointed to another world altogether.

The handmade knotted rope entwined with found objects, which she and Reid had found suspended from the ceiling, was a case in point. Mia had done some internet trawling to discover it was probably a 'witch's ladder'. Although the jury was out on whether these artefacts were actually historical practice, they had become incorporated into the craft of some contemporary witches. The objects braided into the ladder were said to symbolise the intent of the witch's spell. And from what she understood, the braiding was usually accompanied by a spoken charm. Her discovery of the knotted rope; the presence of numerous books with mysterious titles like *The Discoverie of Witchcraft*, *The Magus*, *The Sixth and Seventh Book of Moses* (she had actually found one called *The Petit Albert* lying on the bedside table, as if left there especially for her to find); plus kitchen shelves laden with apothecary jars of dried herbs; all this lent credence to her mother's claim that Henrietta might indeed be a practising witch.

Mia could only wonder what spell her grandmother had been casting with her witch's ladder of miscellany from down under. It was too fragile to be taken down, and she had become fascinated by it, snapping numerous photographs of it suspended from the ceiling and experimenting with manipulating the images in Photoshop. Although she wasn't exactly thrilled with the results; the artefacts had lost their vibrancy with age, and she couldn't get the light to her liking.

She had also scanned hi-res images of an antique print she had found on the sitting-room wall – a landscape depicting Pevensey Castle – and taken numerous photographs of the exterior and interior of Puckridge Cottage. She didn't know exactly what she was doing with them yet, but something was forming in her brain, some fledgling idea that she knew she had to nurture. For the moment, she had printed out low-res images – hoping to crystallise the forming ideas – and was about to begin cutting them up and playing around with them when she realised that she hadn't brought anything other than nail scissors with her.

'Now where would you have put the scissors, Granny?' she said, having taken to talking aloud to Henrietta as a way of filling the silence.

Her flat in Brisbane was rarely silent, always alive with the distant rumble of traffic, but her grandmother's house was quiet except for the odd bird call.

'That old bureau, maybe?' She had noticed the desk the first time she visited the cottage with Reid, placed against the rear masonry wall of the conservatory, rather than by the glass walls where temperature fluctuations would be more acute. She was no expert on furniture but she guessed it was much older than her grandmother; possibly Georgian, and scuffed about by the centuries. It was taller than Mia, with two decorative arches forming the top. She opened the panelled doors to reveal an array of pigeonholes and small drawers, finding none of them contained scissors. The desk was actually quite exquisite, though, and it looked out of place in Henrietta's humbler abode. Apart from the scratches, it could have belonged in a grander, more stately home. A bevelled drop-down cover appeared designed to form a desk when opened. The problem was, it was locked. That didn't deter Mia. If her grandmother used it regularly, she probably kept the key nearby. Or on her person.

'The bunch of keys.' Of course, it would be on the bunch of keys the solicitor had given her when she moved into the cottage. So far, she had only needed the front and back door keys but there were several other antique keys in the bunch that she now kept in her satchel.

The second key she tried, with a simple oval bow and sawtoothed bit, produced results and she opened the drop-front desk with a flourish. Behind it she discovered further drawers, pigeonholes and decorative columns.

Rummaging through these hidey holes in search of scissors, she discovered a bowerbird's nest of pebbles, papers, pencils, shells, metal and wood trinkets, ceramic figurines and scraps of fabric. In one drawer she found several lengths of rolled ribbon, the wonderful colours of the faded silk inviting her to take them out and lay them flat on the desk. One particular ribbon of finely woven yellow silk jacquard roses on a cream background tempted her into tying it around her hair, corralling her curls into a low ponytail. She wondered where the ribbon had originated, since it didn't match her grandmother's personal style. No, the ribbon was refined and elegant – and by the look of it, very old. She risked damaging the antique silk by wearing it, she supposed, but it felt like the ribbon was meant to be tied about the wild melee of her hair.

Which was all very well, except she still hadn't found the scissors. And she hadn't noticed any in her grandmother's kitchen either. By the time she had investigated all but the last drawer, she was almost ready to simply tear the printouts with a ruler, and purchase some scissors tomorrow. The final bureau drawer was proving singularly stubborn – either the wood had swelled or something was caught between drawer and cabinet – so that she needed to apply brute force to her mission. Bracing herself with one hand against a decorative column, she heaved on the drawer. But instead of freeing it, she felt a click, and the wooden column popped free from its housing beneath her hand.

At first, she thought she had broken it, then she realised she must have triggered a mechanism of some kind, for as it turned out, when she grasped the edges of the column and pulled, a wooden compartment slid free of the cabinet. The mechanism appeared to conceal a secret hiding place.

'Of course it does,' she told herself. 'You're staying in a medieval cottage, complete with supernatural texts, on the edge of a forest, in a magical garden, ostensibly home to generations of witches. Of course the desk has a secret compartment. All you need now are Hansel and Gretel, and you'll be living your own fairy tale.'

The secret compartment was about the size of a large book, an atlas for example, or a cookbook. Even before she peered inside, she could tell from its weight that it wasn't empty. Holding the piece in her left hand, she turned it over carefully so that whatever it contained might drop into her right hand. And so it did – a small book the size of a paperback. She recognised immediately that it was very old, bound in scuffed black leather, with that old book smell of dust, dry grass and a faint hint of vanilla. The book felt just the right size for her hand, as if it called out to be opened and its pages written upon. But first . . . it wanted to be read.

She set the book down on the desk and considered it. Placing her palm flat on its cover, she inhaled the smell of it, as if it might deliver up its secrets through all her senses. For surely any book of this antiquity, concealed inside a secret compartment in a fairy-tale cottage, must hold secrets? Except nothing came to her other than the same vague sense of belonging that she had felt when it dropped into her palm. Clearly, she would have to look further to discover its mysteries. She opened the book to find an inside cover and end leaf decorated in a swirling pattern of colours, dulled a little by time. Flipping over the page, she found written in old-fashioned script the words *Philadelphia Foord Boadle's Book of Receipts*, with a ruled and numbered table of contents opposite.

Stunned for a few seconds, she read the title a second time to convince herself that she wasn't imagining things. No, there it was in faded brown ink. The script was large, the penmanship heavy and uneven, with rounded letters, as if the author had laboured over the words, unpractised in the act of writing: *Philadelphia Foord Boadle's Book of Receipts*.

There was that name again, her mother's family name, handed

down through the generations, according to Celia, its longevity overshadowing any other surname, any mere husband's name. Or lack of husband for that matter. She had wanted to know if Philadelphia, the Witch of Sussex Downs, could have been her ancestor, and here she had found the woman's book, written in her own hand, hidden in her grandmother's cottage. Had her grandmother known it was there? Planted it there even, as a puzzle for her granddaughter to unlock? Well, whether she had or not, Mia's question about her relationship to Philadelphia had been answered in a way she could never have expected in a thousand years.

Almost of its own volition her finger traced over the title, as if she might connect with this long-dead woman through her fingertip. Perhaps she imagined it, but for a millisecond she did feel something akin to the buzz of static electricity in the pad of her index finger – a jolt of recognition – and with it an image of a woman in a high-waisted dress of printed cotton with a white scarf tucked into its neckline flashed before her eyes. Her hair was covered by a lace-edged white cap, curling tendrils of black hair escaping from beneath it. Yet she couldn't see the woman's face as she sat at this same desk writing in a book. This book.

Mia took a deep breath as she scanned the first page of contents. Several entries caught her eye with their list of common and not-so-common complaints.

A Medicine to quicken a woman
An Emulsion for a cough
Receipt for the dropsy
An Ointment for rheumatic pains
A Remedy for the biting of a mad dog
A Receipt to make hair grow
A Simple Receipt for a painful menses . . .

Philadelphia could have made a fortune if her cure for baldness actually worked. Not so much call for the mad dog bite remedy in England these days. She flipped to the receipt for a painful menses and began to read.

A simple Receipt for the painful menses

Take a handful of fresh peppermint leaves and a handful of fresh yarrow leaves and steep in three cups of boiling water for ten minutes. Drink one cup three times a day.

Susanna's Receipt for the painful menses

Take a handful of fresh nettle leaves, a handful of rose petals and a knob of grated ginger and steep in three cups of boiling water for ten minutes. Strain and sip through the day.

Now she was even more intrigued, for who was this Susanna that Philadelphia referred to? Another relative? She continued to leaf through the recipes, until her eye was caught by a heading that seemed out of kilter with the other more medicinal remedies.

A Charm to see a future husband

At midnight on Midsummer's Eve pluck a sprig of yarrow from the grave of a man who died young and speak the charm. Place the yarrow under the pillow and you will dream of your future lover.

Yarrow, sweet yarrow, the first that I have found,
In the name of the Lord, I pluck thee from the ground.
As Joseph loved sweet Mary, and took her for his dear,
So, in a dream this night, I hope, my true love will appear.

Wow, if only she had known this spell as a teenager, she could have saved herself a lot of trouble. She could have skipped a retinue of failed boyfriends she believed herself to be in love with, if she had known about the yarrow charm and gone straight to her forever partner. But she wasn't going to think about that possibility, was she? She had promised herself there would be no more of that, at least for now – she was here to concentrate on her work, on her future.

Strange that both seemed to have become caught up with the past.

She smiled to herself, thinking, wouldn't Reid be surprised when she showed him her discovery? She had asked him to use his powers of genealogy to research her connection to Philadelphia Boadle, and now she had material evidence to suggest that the connection was in fact very real. That Philadelphia may have lived in this very cottage. And she was possibly as witchy as her local reputation suggested, judging by this 'receipt' for a love divination. She wondered what other charms the manuscript might hold.

'Whoa!' she said aloud, in a thunderclap of clarity, her ideas suddenly coalescing as a fledgling plan began to form. She knew what she wanted to do with her art now – what stories she wanted to tell – and maybe, just maybe, how she might accomplish it. She was going to explore the present through the medium of the past. Hers, and this mysterious family she had inherited, no thanks to Celia. And she would do it using what she found – and perhaps what she made – around her.

Excited now, she was about to grab her camera and head out into the garden to throw herself into the work, when she remembered. Reid. Oh, shit! She was supposed to meet him at the Tailor's Café in . . . what, twenty minutes. It was a thirty-minute walk into the village, and she was still wearing old jeans and a T-shirt stained with that morning's endeavours. Oh well, she thought

The Heirloom

with a disappointed sigh, she would just have to postpone her work until later that day – if the light held. She closed the book, written in her ancestor's own hand, and returned it to its hiding place. Its secrets would have to await her return.

30

Sussex, England
1821

As the constable introduced her and began the questioning, Jenny kept her chin down and her eyes on the floor, except for flicking a glance in Isaac's direction through lowered lashes. He did not know why she looked to him for reassurance, as he could do nothing to help her. He did feel a moment of sympathy when her cap slipped, giving her a lopsided look, and she clasped her hands white-knuckled before her. He knew that beneath her linen skirts her legs would be quaking, because his legs had trembled like saplings in the wind when the constable questioned him. Puttick spared no one from his inquisition. But if Isaac could not save his aunt from lies and accusations, how could he protect her maid?

He stole a sideways glance at his father, expecting to find his eyes fixed on Philadelphia, as they had been throughout the inquest. Except his father's eyes were on the maid, his brow wrinkled, as if waiting for something.

'What is that girl up to?' he muttered, turning to his son. 'What does she know?'

Isaac shrugged. 'Nothing. I do not know, Father.'

'She knows something. Let us hope it is to our advantage.'

His whispering was cut short by the constable. 'You have told

The Heirloom

us of the fateful morning of your master's demise, Jenny,' he growled, glaring at her, as if she had played some part in her master's death. 'Now, tell us what happened on the evening prior to Mr Boadle's untimely death. And mind you tell the truth, or there will be consequences.'

'Mr B-B-Boadle was feeling poorly, sir.'

'We have heard this from his nephew. What happened *before* Mr Boadle took to his bedchamber feeling poorly?'

'Well, the mistress served a soup at dinner with the bones from Sunday's joint, a head of celery, turnips and a quart of split peas.' She counted the ingredients off on her fingers. 'Some shallots, a handful of herbs from the garden . . .'

'Yes, yes, but what else happened?'

Isaac sensed the constable growing impatient, and his father leaned forward, frowning at poor Jenny.

'We ate it with a new loaf, warm from the oven, sir,' she said, looking to him again for reassurance while the crowd tittered and Isaac looked down at his shoes to avoid both his father's and the girl's gaze.

'Get on it with it, Puttick,' the coroner ordered testily. 'What is the point of this questioning? We have been here too long already.'

'Now, Jenny,' the constable said, taking another step closer, 'tell the gentlemen what you saw when you returned to the kitchen after your repast?'

'What re-repast, sir?'

'The dinner, girl, what did you see in the kitchen after dinner?'

The silence that followed stretched so long that Isaac prised his attention from his shoes and looked up to discover Jenny flicking panicked glances from Philadelphia to him, for all the world like a trapped rabbit. It was then that a hint of what was to come glimmered, just out of Isaac's reach. Something . . . something . . . she knew something. But what?

'I-I returned to the kitchen to look for my mistress's receipt book that she had mislaid.'

'And . . .?'

'And I saw Isaac, the master's nephew,' she nodded in his direction, 'crushing leaves to make a tea. Fresh leaves that looked to have come from the mistress's garden.'

'And do you know *which* herbs that came from your mistress's garden?'

'I saw only leaves, sir.'

'What did these leaves look like?'

'They were green, sir.'

Another eddy of laughter rippled through the room and Isaac shivered despite the fug of warm bodies pressed close. Beside him, he sensed his father's anger seeping from his body like a red haze. He had not thought. He had not noticed the maid enter the kitchen that night, too busy at his task. Too busy about his aunt's business. And even if he had, he would have thought Jenny was not clever enough to notice. That she had eyes only for him, not herbs from her mistress's garden.

'Describe these leaves, young woman,' the coroner ordered. 'I am sure you must have seen more than their colour.'

Jenny's head jerked towards the coroner. 'They were quite large leaves, sir. Shaped like a-a spearhead, I-I recall.'

'Like this?' The constable rounded on the maid, producing a wad of leaves from the pocket of his frock coat and waving them beneath her nose in his gloved hand. 'Were the leaves like this?'

'I cannot say for certain . . .'

'But . . .' He glared at her.

'They do look s-s-similar, sir.'

This time, instead of laughter, the room resounded with a collective gasp, and Isaac sank further into himself. He felt his innards spasm as if someone twisted them from without.

'Your honour, these are the very same leaves that the deceased's brother, Mr Enoch Boadle, found on the floor of the tailor's kitchen on the morning of his death. The same leaves identified by the surgeon as being from the plant *Digitalis grandiflora*, or the yellow foxglove, a plant known to cause death if administered in even minor doses. A plant which Mrs Boadle grew in her garden.'

The coroner cleared his throat. 'Are you suggesting, Mr Puttick, that the deceased's nephew may have . . . poisoned him?'

'I am but questioning the witness, sir. I leave any question of culpability to the jurors.'

Isaac wondered that his heart did not beat out of his chest, so hard did it hammer to be free. Free of this room, of this throng of people, of his father pressed up against him, even of his aunt draped in her widow's garb, seated at his other side. His aunt, his lovely aunt, with her cascade of silken black hair, her skin the velvet of rose petals, her voice with the sweet crispness of an apple, her scent heady with jasmine, his aunt who he . . . who he . . .

'She has damned you, boy,' his father hissed into his ear.

He flinched, twisting in his seat to stare at the soot-blackened beams above the jurors' heads, his father's hot breath on his cheek. Was he right to call him a boy? He was eighteen and had thought himself a man. With a man's desires. A man's strength. Ready to take on the world. To become a journeyman tailor and set out on his own, a woman at his side if the stars aligned. But was he, in fact, still a boy? Too naive to make his way in this world alone?

'She has you lusting after her like a dog. And you will hang for it, if you do not fight back.'

He had believed . . . nay, he had trusted in his aunt, in her love. In *their* love. At first, her kindness had taken him back to his childhood when his mother was alive. A feeling, more than a memory, a hazy recollection of his mother shielding him from his father's offhand slaps and beatings. Just as Philadelphia had diverted his uncle's temper with flattery and smiles. Once or twice, she had even stepped between Isaac and his father, taking a glancing blow for her pains. Soon he had longed to feel her arms wrapped about him in comfort, to hear her lovely voice tending to his hurts. It was only later, much later, when he had outgrown his boyish frame, that despite all his vows, all his shame, he felt his cock stiffen at her touch. It was only then that he came to burn for it. Would have done anything to feel her hand upon him.

Now he saw that perhaps his father was right, it was not love he felt. Perhaps it was lust that raged through his body, keeping him awake at night, teasing him, taunting him – testing him. A burning ache that she had conjured. For such an ache could not be natural, could it? Such an ache must surely emanate from the Devil.

He stole a glance at his aunt, to find her regarding him sadly. Shifting an inch or so upon the bench, he squirmed away from this woman he had longed to hold close. What woman possessed eyes of so deep a blue? Surely, they were not natural. And surely, it was not natural to lust after your uncle's wife? No, a love like that could not be a thing of God. She had bewitched him with her spells, with her book of strange lore, and her mysterious charms. Yes, that was it. She had bewitched him into ridding her of her husband. His uncle, who she claimed to fear. Who she believed would do her great harm.

'She has counted on your naivety to do her evil bidding,' his father whispered, a breath away from his ear.

He raised his eyes to his father for as long as he dared.

Was it not also true that his father and uncle had talked of some harm that might befall her? How could he forget the evening he and his aunt had happened upon the men when they believed themselves alone in the tailor's shop. They had stood there on the threshold of the brothers' secrets. He had not imagined that.

The Heirloom

Perhaps fate will lend a hand and free you to marry again, his father had said.

Your wife may not live forever. She may take sick.

Or fall victim to an accident.

The world is full of mishap, Brother.

He could still hear his father's words ringing in his ears. Yes, perhaps Philadelphia had been right to fear her husband. To fear what he might do to her.

And yet, whether true or not . . . whether she had bewitched him or not, he knew he was not ready to hang. Not even for her. He was only eighteen, his life just begun. He was not ready to dangle from the hangman's noose, his legs jerking, his tongue turning blue. No, he was not ready at all.

On quivering legs, he took to his feet, resisting the touch of his aunt's hand upon his arm as she reached for him, those nimble fingers that plied a needle with such skill, that soothed a boy's hurts with tenderness. They grasped at air where just a moment ago he had sat at her side. Ignoring the pit of fear and desire warring in his body, he stepped forward into the circle of judgement, his action silencing the heckling crowd and drawing all eyes to him.

'My aunt bewitched me. She bewitched me,' he said, and he felt her flinch in his very gut.

The constable took the few yards between them in three strides, crossing the rush-strewn stone floor to glower at him, leaning in, nose to nose. 'Do you declare that your aunt bewitched you, boy? How did Mrs Boadle come to bewitch you?'

'She made a special tincture. For a winter cough, she said.' He steeled himself to hold the constable's gaze, for he could not look behind him.

'And what was in this tincture?'

For the next few breaths, the crowd stayed quiet, awaiting his answer, not even a clearing of throats or shifting of feet disturbed the room.

'It was a potion, sir, of dried herbs pounded and mixed with wine. I watched her make it, with the leaves of vervain, the berries of mistletoe and the dried root of the elf-dock flower, she said.'

'And did it cure your cough?'

'My cough righted itself, sure enough, but a powerful feeling for my aunt also overcame me so that I would look for her at all hours of the day and night. I could not sleep for thoughts of her. I was shamed by my . . . my lust for her.'

Even now, he was conscious of her every movement on the bench behind him, the shifting of her legs, the soft gasp. And despite the new mutterings his words provoked amongst his neighbours, he heard the rustle of silk bombazine as his aunt rose from her seat for the very first time at this inquest.

He heard the pain in her voice as she said, 'It was only a cure, Mr Honeycett. Strong herbs to cure a stubborn cough and troubled throat. Nothing more sinister than any good housewife would know.'

Still, he could not face her.

'No, it were a spell. She spoke a chant as she mixed the tincture, in a language I did not understand,' he said, grasping to make them believe. 'She cast her spell over me and I could not resist. Then she showed me the deadliest plants in her garden so that I would make the posset for her. To rid her of her husband. To rid her of my uncle who had been good to me.'

He dropped his head, standing in full view of his neighbours and judges, and denounced his aunt's wickedness. Denounced their love. Yet in truth, all he wanted was to lay his head upon her breast and rest in her arms.

'It is true!' a woman's voice shouted from the other side of the room.

Isaac glanced up to find heads turning as Mrs Tupper, plump arms working to gather speed, pushed her way to the front of the

The Heirloom

crowd. Her voice was stern but he saw that one side of her mouth crooked up in a pleased smile.

'If it please Your Lordship,' she said to the coroner, 'I do not like to interrupt, but I have important corrob— corrobor—'

'Corroborating?' suggested Mr Honeycett.

'Yes, I have important corroborating evidence.'

The coroner sighed but waved a hand in her direction. 'Do go on, then.'

'Thank you, sir. As I was saying,' she began, 'I saw the boy with his aunt in the garden behind the tailor's shop one day about a month ago, when I called to enquire of Mrs Boadle whether the straw for my new capote bonnet had arrived. Mr Tupper and I were hosting a picnic for some notables of the parish and—'

'Do stick to subject of the Boadles' garden, if you please, Mrs Tupper,' the coroner interrupted.

'Yes, I well remember being surprised that they stood very close to one another, their heads almost touching,' she said, turning to ensure her audience was listening, 'as if they were lovers.'

'I do not know that standing close to one another is a crime,' Honeycett drawled.

'*She* was pointing to the yellow spears of the fairy thimbles in her garden and explaining their uses.'

Isaac remembered the day in question. How could he not? It was a day he wished he could wipe from his life forever. For it was then that the plan first came to him, the plan to be rid of the man who endangered his aunt, to make her a free woman. In his madness for her, he forgot the man was his own uncle.

'*All* parts of the plant are poisonous, she told the boy, and the leaves brewed in a tea will kill a grown man if given in sufficient quantity. I particularly remember her saying this last. Yes, there is no doubt about that,' Mrs Tupper said, rounding on Philadelphia.

Isaac could not help but think that she had been saving her

words especially for this moment. He watched, his feet glued to the spot, as his aunt cried out.

'No! It is not true. I was warning my nephew of their dangers. That a small dose given in a tea cures the dropsy, but a large dose can kill. I never imagined the boy might harm my husband. I never imagined he would think himself in love with me. He must have mistaken the foxgloves for another plant. You must believe me. I knew nothing of this.'

He did not want to look at her but he could not help turning. Strands of hair had come loose from the yards of black gauze twisted about her head, and she was breathing so hard that he could see her chest rise and fall beneath the silk of her mourning dress. She was so beautiful in that moment, her despair so powerful, that he almost recanted. Perhaps he could agree with her, say that he had mistaken the correct dosage. Perhaps the jurors would understand. Forgive.

Out of the corner of his eye he caught the look on his father's face, a twisted effigy of anger and fear. His father shook his head. 'Do not be deceived by her, boy,' he mouthed.

His father was right. If he took back his words, he would condemn himself to the noose. The jurors would never believe him, he saw that now. Perhaps she had bewitched them, too.

'I had no power to resist,' he croaked, barely able to speak the words. 'No power to stop her evil.'

His love. His Philadelphia, the woman he had sworn to protect, to save from his uncle's wicked plot. In his mind he could still hear Jasper's voice as clearly as he had on that night as he listened from the other side of a door.

Then who had he betrayed? His uncle or his aunt?

31

Isaac had been in the garden with his aunt that evening, some weeks before his uncle's death. When his uncle was gone from the house, he was in the garden with his aunt as often as he could manage. On occasion, he would even sneak away while Jasper was taking a mug of ale in the shop before supper. He liked to watch her tending the plants, bending to snip a sprig of marjoram or rosemary for the cooking pot, or reaching up to pick a spray of mugwort for her remedies. Sometimes her sleeve would fall back to reveal her slender arms. If it were a hot day, like this one, she might remove the kerchief at her neck to wipe away the sweat between her breasts. If it were cold, she might shiver and he would fetch her cloak from the hall and wrap it about her shoulders, accidentally brushing his arm against her body as he did so. He liked to listen to her voice and imagine her whispering words of love to him. He never told anyone of these thoughts. Not even Philadelphia, to whom he told everything.

The light was almost gone by the time they entered the house and his aunt set her trug upon the kitchen table. They must have supposed the household all safely abed – all except his uncle who had gone to the inn to drum up business, so he said. Philadelphia searched for a length of twine to tie the herbs into bundles and hang them from the rafters to dry, while he went through to the workshop to ensure that all was in order for the morrow. His uncle would be twitching with rage if he found his tools scattered about or bolts of fabric left out. He crossed the hall and was about to open the door that led through to the shop, when he was surprised to hear his father's voice.

'The widow Tutt will soon be free to marry again, Brother,' his father said, his voice smacking of ale and good cheer.

At first, Isaac thought he was simply reporting local gossip, for all knew that Tutt had died of the scarlet fever the year before. A year was barely respectable to remarry, but Lettice Tutt and her sister had little care for what others thought. Even so, he halted where he stood until the men finished speaking. He had not known his father was visiting that night, and Jasper did not like to be surprised, especially by his apprentices.

'The widow Tutt is a fine-looking woman with a handsome inheritance,' his father observed. 'And when her father dies, she will inherit more.'

'That she is,' Jasper replied, and Isaac thought he caught a wistful note in his uncle's voice. 'No doubt she will not stay a widow long.'

'Any suitor will have to be swift. If only *you* had waited – or forced the brick maker's hand. If only you had not wed the first pretty face that came along,' his father said, in a tone he often used with Isaac's uncle, an older brother chiding the younger. No one else dared speak to his uncle in such a manner. It wasn't so different to the way Isaac's brother spoke to him.

'I offered for Lettice but the brick maker would not have me for son-in-law, you know this. Though I pleaded my case more than once,' his uncle said, the disappointment evident. 'Lacy made it clear he would disinherit his daughter if she disobeyed him.'

The Heirloom

'The girl wanted you. If you had waited, she would have worn her father down.'

'I was in need of a wife. Philadelphia had a pretty face, a fine figure, and the makings of milliner.'

'She always lusted after you,' his father said, and Isaac felt a rush of blood to his head. Why did he say such things about Philadelphia, who was a chaste and loving woman?

Jasper laughed. 'You are jealous, Brother, that your new wife is too God-fearing to take pleasure in your bed.'

'At least my wife brought a dowry to our marriage.'

If Isaac was shocked by the men's revelations about his stepmother and his aunt, he was even more surprised by his father's next words.

'Perhaps fate will lend a hand and free you to marry again.'

'And how might that come about, Brother?'

'Your wife may not live forever. She may take sick.'

'Philadelphia is as healthy as an ox.'

'Or fall victim to an accident,' Enoch said slowly, sounding out each word as if he spoke to the hard of hearing.

Isaac jerked his head. Perhaps *he* had not heard right. Surely, his father could not mean what his words implied. He could not be suggesting what Isaac thought he was. So disturbed was he by his father's declaration that, for once, he ignored his instinct for self-preservation and reached for the latch. He was about to lift it and push the door open when he felt a light touch upon his forearm.

His aunt held a finger to her lips and begged his silence with her eyes. He wanted to ignore her plea. He wanted to demonstrate his courage, his . . . manhood. To stand up in front of his father and his uncle and defend her in the face of their disrespect. To be a man for her.

'What purpose will it serve?' she whispered, turning him to face her, a tiny frown wrinkling her forehead.

She stood so close that he caught the scent of lavender from a sprig she had placed between her breasts, and the freshness of mint upon her breath. He felt the warmth of her hands as they traced the length of his arms through the linen of his shirt, and hoped she did not notice the tremor in his limbs or the swelling of his cock in his trousers. Perhaps she was right. Perhaps they would do better not to reveal themselves.

'The world is full of mishap, Brother,' he heard his father say, his voice like gravel.

The tailor's workshop was silent for several moments, as if allowing time for this world of mishap to be imagined, before his uncle replied, 'You are right, Brother, as always.'

Isaac looked to his aunt. His uncle would not heed his father's hints, would he? Surely, *he* did not wish her dead. She was his wife. She shared his bed. She was the mother of his child.

'There are smugglers and brigands at large in the parish. Any one of them might set upon a poor milliner going about her business on a lonely lane,' Jasper mused.

Isaac imagined his uncle nodding in agreement with himself, as he often did.

'Yes, there are flooded rivers that might claim the careless, horses that might kick the unwary, rocks that might trip the unlucky.'

'The world is a dangerous place indeed, Brother,' his father agreed, before the two fell to discussing the new innkeeper in the next village and the quality of his ale, as if murder was only a passing fancy, as if the death of a wife was nothing of note.

And just for a moment, Isaac thought he may have imagined the entire conversation. His father getting in his brother's ear. Planting his wicked ideas. Then he looked to his aunt's face, where tears trailed her cheeks like twin rivers, and he knew that he had heard true. He supposed that she must have loved his uncle once. Perhaps her smiles had once been true, even if the man had soured that love with his hard words and vicious slaps. He supposed that she might love him still, in her way, though the thought pained him.

'He cannot mean it,' she whispered, 'can he?'

Isaac did not know how to answer her. Her husband had betrayed her with his words. With worse to follow, if he spoke true. She who had been so chaste and loyal, when Isaac knew in every sinew of his being that she wanted to love *him*. To take him to her body. To love him as a woman loved a man. He felt it in every soft touch, every smile, every chaste kiss of kinship. A fire burned in her as it did in him. And he knew then that he would do all that was asked of him to save her. Whatever it might take to protect her. To make her his own.

His uncle could go to the Devil.

32

'Look at this, Mama!' Marjory was kneeling in the garden of her grandmother's house, where several small plants with tiny leaves were in flower.

'Do mind your new dress. It took hours with my needle – and several shillings for the best crêpe muslin we could afford,' Philadelphia reminded her daughter, although she could not help smiling at the child's delight in her grandmother's garden.

It had been months since she had brought her here. Jasper did not like her 'filling our daughter's head with your mother's nonsense'. That afternoon had seemed like the perfect opportunity to escape the cloud of suspicion that hung over her in the village. Perhaps in her mother's garden she might find clarity and a way forward.

'Black does not show the dirt, Mama, so there is no reason to worry. And you promised never to leave me. Soon I will put away the dress and never take it out again.'

When had her daughter become so clever in her arguments? She did not remember getting the better of Susanna so easily at her age, despite her many efforts. Her mother had been full of lectures on the practice of the wise woman's craft and how

The Heirloom

to use it wisely. Lectures Philadelphia did not always heed, for what was the point in having a skill if you could not use it to full advantage?

'What are these called?' Marjory said, leaning over to sniff at the tiny white flowers.

'They are called lemon balm, or bee balm, because the bees like them so.' Philadelphia smiled as her daughter drew back at the mention of bees. She had been stung once before in her grandmother's garden when she disturbed the bees at their foraging, for Susanna kept two straw bee skeps in her orchard. She used the honey in many of her cures, the bee glue to heal warts and wounds, and the wax to seal her jars. Which reminded Philadelphia that it would be time to harvest the honey again soon – a chore she had avoided, if she could, as a girl.

'It is the leaves you smell more than the flowers,' she said, pointing out the mint-like leaves.

'And what are they used for, Mama?'

Despite Jasper's warnings, it was clear her daughter was a Foord through and through. She was drawn to her mother's and grandmother's secrets without any tutelage whatsoever. Philadelphia sometimes wondered what other arts she might possess.

'A tea made from fresh leaves is good for calming the stomach and the nerves,' she said.

'Then I will make you a tea,' Marjory said, and set about plucking a handful of leaves from the lemon balm plant. 'You have been greatly upset since Papa died.'

It was true, she had been greatly disturbed since Jasper's death, as any wife would be, and the inquest had only piled fear and suspicion upon her grief. But she thought she had hidden her fears from her daughter. Marjory had her own grief to contend with. She did not need her mother's worries to add to her sadness. She thought she had protected her child.

'You do not need to be afraid, Mama,' her daughter said,

smiling up at her confidently. 'We will be fine. They will not take you away.'

'How do you know we will be fine?'

'I saw it.'

She was about to question her daughter further when she was hailed loudly from the front of the cottage. 'Mrs Boadle! Philadelphia! It is I, Thomas Earle. Are you about?'

She did not need to hold her fingers to her wrist to know that her heart quickened at the sound of Thomas Earle's voice. She could feel it as a flutter in her chest and a flush of warmth to her cheeks.

'Wait here while I greet our visitor,' she said to her daughter, 'and stay away from the bee skeps.'

'You have gone red, Mama,' her daughter observed, with a frown.

'It is only the sun kissing my cheeks,' she called behind her, as she hurried around the corner of the cottage, twitching the black gauze of her turban more becomingly and loosening the white lawn fichu tied at her neck. She had almost reached the front garden when she spotted their visitor. He had let himself in through the gate of hazelwood twigs and was making his way around the side of the cottage. His horse was tied to a fence post, shifting its weight from one foreleg to the other as it cropped the foliage growing through the fence.

'Ahh, Mrs Boadle,' he said, sweeping her a bow, 'do forgive me for intruding. I asked at your house but your maid informed me you had gone for a walk in this direction. I wondered if I might find you here at your mother's cottage. It is such a peaceful spot.'

And she in need of peace, after that day's events at the inquest.

'If somewhat overgrown, I am afraid. I have not devoted the time to it I might like. My mother always kept it so neat. Thank you for your concern, Mr Earle.' She kept her eyes glued to the

The Heirloom

hat he gripped in his right hand, afraid of what she might find in his eyes.

What if he should believe her nephew's accusations? He had named her a whore and witch. Coldness from Thomas Earle she could tolerate, though barely; disgust she could not bear.

'I-I . . . your nephew . . . his accusations were alarming. I hope you do not think I would believe them.'

He frowned, she did not know whether at her or Isaac. In any case, she could not summon the words to reply, merely shaking her head. She needed his support on the jury. She needed the support of an educated man who would do his best to quash the superstitions of his neighbours, especially after Isaac's accusations. Yet, more than this, she realised that she wanted his trust. She needed him to believe in her as Jasper never had, she realised now. Once, she had thought she and her husband were a team, in work and life. She had nurtured infatuation and admiration until they grew into a kind of love, telling herself that his harsh treatment was only what most wives bore. Yet, seeing the love that this man, Thomas Earle, bore for his poor wife Marianne had made a lie of that, hadn't it?

'I admit I was dismayed by the response of my fellows,' Thomas said now. 'I thought to find less superstition amongst our neighbours.' He waved his hand in frustration. 'Such credulity. And from persons from whom I expected good sense. I thought this persistent belief in witchcraft had had its day.'

'Old beliefs die hard, sir,' she remarked, Susanna could have told him that.

'Still, we must remember that the lad is young. He has confused a boyish infatuation with something more sinister. I cannot say the same for others in the room.'

She found the courage to meet his gaze again, saying, 'Unfortunately, nothing but pain can come from this now. For one or other of us.' For both her and Isaac, she feared. But she could not dwell on what this pain might entail. Dwelling on it would only sap the courage that she needed to save her little family.

'I thought when I encouraged Constable Puttick to question young Jenny, that the boy would claim he mistook the herbs for some other harmless plant. Or that he was mistaken in the dosage. Then the jury could have delivered a verdict of misadventure. I did not think the lad would . . . would go so far as to . . .' He shook his head at the course events had taken.

'To denounce me as a witch? Accuse me of betraying my vows and soliciting my husband's death? Believe me, Mr Earle, this is not the first time I have been accused of witchcraft.' No, she wasn't surprised at the accusations, only at the person who had made them, a boy she had raised as if he were her own son.

In her despair, she forgot she spoke to the gentry. She forgot she spoke to one of the most important landowners in the parish. She abandoned all her neat and tidy words and spoke from her heart. 'My mother helped people when they had no coin to pay the apothecary or the surgeon, and for that service she was called a witch. I forsook my mother's trade and learned to fashion hats rather than cures. I thought this would bring respectability, that I could escape the slurs my family has endured for generations. But I see now that I can never escape that heritage. I will always be a witch to the people of this parish.'

Her mother had been right. She would always be one of the Foord women, no matter that she had changed her name and sought to escape her destiny.

'So, I may as well embrace it. I may as well cast my spells, weave my magic, brew my potions,' she said scornfully. 'I may as well become the witch they believe me to be.'

Finally, she ran out of words and shuddered into silence, waiting for some sign from the man to whom she had opened her heart. Apart from the faint sound of bees gathering nectar, and

The Heirloom

the warbling, tuneful whistle of a nearby blackbird, the garden and the man remained quiet.

'There he is,' he said, after an interminable minute, pointing in the direction of Susanna's small orchard where the summer fruits were an open invitation to birds and insects alike.

Despite her despondency, she turned to look where he indicated.

'See, high up in the cherry tree,' he said, and she felt his gloved hand enclose hers in a reassuring grip. 'Perhaps he is singing for his love. Charming her with his song.' He smiled as he brought her hand to his lips. 'Even the birds are not above a little enchantment when the occasion calls for it.'

Philadelphia allowed herself to look directly into his eyes. Was this his answer to her unspoken question?

'Do you remember that day, ten years ago, when I called at your cottage seeking help for my Marianne?'

She nodded. It had been the same day Jasper first showed her the golden thimble and set her upon the path that would change the course of her life.

'You gave me a handful of cherries to take with me. They were the sweetest cherries I ever tasted . . . I often wondered if your lips would taste as sweet.'

Still holding her hand, he stepped forward, seemingly intent on taking her in his arms. With only inches between them, he hesitated, while she remained perfectly still, not wanting to disturb the blackbird's song or the man's intent, yet confused about the nature of its meaning. Thomas Earle's arms promised safety, but she had been deceived by the promise of a man's arms before. Better to wait and let love's spell complete its work – if that was what was at play here. If that indeed was what she wanted.

There he stood with his head bowed, so close that she could feel the whisper of his breath upon her face. Yet he moved no closer. Perhaps he too waited. Perhaps he waited on her response.

Then before the bird trilled its last note, they heard Marjory call excitedly from the rear garden.

'Mama! Come and see! I have found some pretty yellow flowers. I have found some fairy thimbles growing in grandmother's garden.'

At the sound of the child's voice, Thomas Earle made to draw back, to retreat into respectability once more. He squeezed her hand with a reassuring pressure and looked to the path where his horse was demolishing the leaves of her mother's comfrey plants.

'Perhaps one day I will find out,' he said with a sigh. 'Now does not seem to be the time.'

No, now was not the time, with her husband lying cold and stiff in the stables of the inn. Despite what she now knew, or suspected, about his plotting, she would mourn him as a devoted wife should. She would also marshal every resource at her disposal to save herself from imprisonment and possible death. The great problem was that saving herself might mean condemning Isaac.

She dipped her knees in a curtsey and watched as Thomas Earle returned to his horse. The dark green wool of his frock coat and cream leather of his breeches strained against his body as he mounted his horse, the animal's head still deep in the comfrey.

'We must ensure that science and enlightenment defeat ignorance and superstition, Mrs Boadle.'

'Yes, superstition must be defeated at all costs. Good day, Mr Earle, and thank you.'

Thank you for what you have done and what you will yet do, she thought, as he dragged the reluctant mare's head from the foliage and steered her towards the lane and home. The horse knew what she needed. Knitbone, as comfrey was often called, was just the thing for her sore shins. The mare did not need a witch to tell her that.

33

East Sussex, England
2024

Mia breathed a sigh of relief when she spotted Reid through the casement windows of the Tailor's Café. He didn't look at all annoyed with her for being forty-five minutes late. There was no tapping on the table or glancing towards the door impatiently. No, he appeared totally at ease. A blue teapot with pink roses and cute little birds was set in front of him, as he sipped from its matching teacup and studied his iPad, a smile playing at the corner of his lips. They were nice lips, wide-mouthed with a hint of a Cupid's bow, and a shading of stubble around them. The stubble suited his white T-shirt, tweed flat cap and the olive-green suede jacket thrown over the back of the chair. She much preferred this look, she decided, to the tennis vibe he had been sporting when they first met.

Like the King's Head, the café had obvious medieval bones – pebble flint walls, plastered and half-timbered, with a clay tile roof – but she suspected the casement windows were more recent, maybe only a couple of centuries old. A bell tinkled as she pushed open the glass door and entered the busy café. There were nods to its tailor's shop origins with a large pattern-making table surrounded by stools, shelves spilling spools of ribbon and bolts of fabric, a collection of gigantic scissors in a glass case, and a tailor's dummy wearing a vintage velvet jacket and bow tie. Vintage prints of tailor's and milliner's shops from the eighteenth and nineteenth centuries decorated the walls.

On the surface it appeared a warm and inviting environment, except the moment she crossed the threshold she felt something she could only describe as a pall of dread shudder through her. She knew the description was straight out of gothic fiction – but it was as true to the sensation as she could get.

'Mia, you made it,' Reid said, rising to greet her. 'Is something wrong?' he added when he noticed her expression.

'No . . . I . . . sorry I'm so late.' She blinked, shaking her head to throw off the sensation of dread. 'I just got a kind of déjà-vu thing happening. Which is weird.'

'Happens to me all the time,' he said. 'I can't decide if I've lived before or spent far too much time scrolling the internet. Not that I'm making light of your feeling,' he added quickly. He must have noticed the distress she was trying, not very successfully, to hide.

'I think I actually shivered when I walked in here. There's something about it that . . . I don't know, you'll think I'm imagining it.'

'Not at all.'

'It's a cliché but I felt like someone was blowing cold air down the back of my neck. It was such a strong feeling of . . . presence.' Spooky presence. As if someone wished her ill.

'Maybe it's because Philadelphia's husband was found dead right here. In this room, I think. You could be sensitive to it,' he said, with a shrug that implied he was open to contemplating the viability of all kinds of phenomena. 'I sometimes get a sense of presence when I visit ancient churches, or even old houses.'

Or maybe she had talked herself into it, with all the thinking about Philadelphia and the Witch of Sussex Downs. After all, the eponymous tailor of this café was Philadelphia's dead husband. Murdered husband, if the broadsides were to be believed.

'Anyway, I'll be fine when I get a coffee into me.' She sat down opposite him and summoned her best smile just as the waitress arrived to take their orders; a latte and Cornish pasty for her, lamb moussaka and another pot of tea for him.

'So . . .' she began, when the woman had gone.

'So . . . you look . . . different.'

'Do I? Good different or bad different?'

'Obviously good, or I wouldn't have mentioned it,' he said, with a laugh that animated his whole face, right up to his eyebrows. 'Although, am I allowed to mention a woman's appearance these days? I've heard that complimenting shoes is acceptable.'

'Compliments on outfit, hairstyle, et cetera are fine by me, thank you.' She smiled, especially since she had thrown together her outfit and given her face a quick lick of make-up in ten minutes flat.

The outfit consisted of a white cotton shirt with the cuffs turned back and a long, pinafore-style dress with a high waist that she had found in her grandmother's wardrobe. Her hair was tied back in a low ponytail by the antique ribbon she had found in the bureau. She realised that he was still looking at her. Why the intense scrutiny? It was unnerving in one way, yet also strangely satisfying to be the sole object of another person's attention. She wasn't used to it. She wasn't used to such a concerted gaze trained on her face like this.

'So . . .,' she began again, trying to break the spell, 'I'm pretty sure now that Philadelphia and I are – were – related.'

'You were,' he said, frowning slightly. 'Descended directly through the female line. But how did you know? I spent a bit of time tracing your ancestry and was going to show you the line of descent I drew up.' He pointed to the iPad sitting beside his cup.

'Strangely enough, I found an old book in a hidden compartment of my grandmother's bureau. Now I'm sounding like a movie, aren't I? Except . . . you don't seem surprised,' she added, studying his face.

'Hidden drawers and pigeonholes were common in Georgian furniture, so I'm not surprised about the secret compartment, no. But the book, what was in it?' He leaned forward ever so slightly.

'*Philadelphia Foord's Book of Receipts*. A handwritten manuscript. By her own hand, I guess.'

'Wow, that's a real family heirloom. I mean, there are a number of extant manuscripts for recipes and remedies, but to have come across one from your own family is a really nice find. Especially since your family didn't have the benefit of a great house and family name to preserve it. I'd love to see it one day.' He actually sounded excited about the prospect of reading a bunch of recipes written by a woman who had lived two centuries before. Mia was excited, but it was her family, her ancestry. An ancestry that was revealing more secrets than she could have imagined.

'How did you come to be a probate genealogist?' she asked, as the waitress arrived with their food.

Genealogy seemed like an unusual profession but kind of fascinating in its own way. At the intersection of history and family, trying to connect the past with the present, the personal with the public, fact with story – and all to, well, solve a puzzle, she supposed. She wondered what had brought him to it, rather than to law or finance, or some other more usual profession.

'A series of serendipitous events, I suppose,' he said, taking a bite of his moussaka. 'I took history at university . . .'

'Oxbridge?' she guessed, without stopping to think. There were probably hundreds of universities in the UK, yet his accent immediately suggested Oxford or Cambridge to her. After talking to him on the phone, all those months ago, she had imagined a crusty old professor type. Even now, she realised with an inward grimace, she wasn't seeing him for who he really was. With his light brown hair, blue eyes, polite manner and Ryan Reynolds' wardrobe, she was seeing an expectation. She should do better. It was unbecoming.

'University College London,' he answered, confounding that expectation. 'I grew up around here, and I suppose I was more attracted to the bright lights of the city than a university town – no matter how charming and historical. Charm does wear off, you know. What about you, did you study in Australia?'

'I started at art school in Brisbane for a while, and then . . .' She shrugged, not sure now exactly what had happened to derail her studies. At the time, it had seemed obvious – get out and see the world if you want to make art – but now she wasn't so sure. How do you explain the kind of uncertainty that invades your very being so that you lose yourself for a while? For years, actually. How do you explain the ghosts that haunt you so that you spend almost a decade hiding from them? From yourself? However, lunch at the Tailor's Café with a new acquaintance wasn't the moment for this kind of revelation, that was for sure. No matter how charming the acquaintance revealed himself to be.

'Anyway, I got sidetracked, took off travelling, doing casual jobs, never quite got around to finishing my studies.' Lately, she had been telling herself that she needed to return to school. But in reality, she didn't need a degree to make art. That was merely an excuse. She just needed to get on with it.

'Sometimes I wish I'd free-ranged more,' he said. 'I took the straight route, BA Hons, MA, thought of doing a PhD then got tired of being poor and started looking around for a way of putting my history degrees to work. I kind of fell into genealogy after helping a solicitor mate trace the beneficiaries of a will. Found that I liked it, liked the research, the puzzle, the human element and . . . the rest's history.'

They chatted over lunch about his work, her tentative foray

back into making art, and (weirdly) the origins of Australia's State of Origin rugby competition, until she realised that her plate was clean, her cup empty, and she was leaning over the table, resting a chin on one hand while gazing into his eyes as he told a story about finding the clue that solved one of his cases amongst a bundle of letters stuffed into an old biscuit tin. He was funny and thoughtful, and pretty hot in his preppy Oxbridge way.

No, no, no. This wasn't allowed. She had promised herself she wouldn't let this happen again. She was going to stay away from men, all men, until she had re-calibrated her life. She was going to get her finances in order, sort her career, and come to terms with her demons (if that were possible) before allowing love back into her life. Now, one nice pair of eyes and a minor show of interest later and she was forgetting all her rules. Well, she wasn't going to let it happen. She owed it to herself.

'Oh, I just remembered,' she said, feigning surprise. 'I'm expecting the . . . the internet guy at three. Sorry, I really have to go,' she said, almost knocking over the chair in her haste to escape.

'I can walk you home, if you like. I need to get some exercise, and it's a beautiful day.'

'That's okay. It's a long walk back for you.'

'Right, well. Before you leave, I was going to show you this.' He took up his iPad, flicking to a page as he turned it towards her. 'I thought you might be interested. Here, I'll enlarge it.'

She was about to ask him to send whatever it was to her, if he didn't mind, that she really needed to go, when she caught a glimpse of a name that leaped out at her from the looping script of an old manuscript.

Jasper Boadle.

'I remembered I own a book about coroner's inquests published by the Sussex Records Society. Since the Boadle murder was such a notorious case, I thought the record might have survived, that it might be included in the book.' He was so earnest, so helpful, and he was gazing at her with that hint of sexual interest that could waylay even the best of intentions.

Oh no. No, no, *no*.

'It's the coroner's report into Jasper Boadle's death.'

Oh *yes*. For how could she resist an account of the events that had denounced her ancestor as a witch? Had she also been branded a murderess? Reid hadn't said when exactly Philadelphia died – admittedly, she hadn't given him a chance, she was so excited about the receipt book. So, despite her best intentions to escape while the going was good, while they were still barely acquaintances, she resumed her seat and began reading, trying to put all thoughts of the man sitting opposite her to bed once and for all. No, *not* to bed. That wasn't what she meant at all.

An Inquisition taken for our Sovereign Lord the King at the King's Head Inn on the seventh day of July in the twenty-first year of the reign of our Sovereign Lord George the fourth King of Great Britain and so forth before Honeycett, Gentleman Coroner for the County of Sussex, on view of the body of Jasper Boadle now lying dead by the oaths of . . .

34

Sussex, England

1821

Puttick motioned to Philadelphia with a nod of his head. She took a deep breath and walked forward to face the coroner, hands clasped at her waist to prevent them shaking. Although she did not look in the direction of the jurors' bench, she knew that Thomas Earle would be there and took some comfort from that fact. There was little comfort to be taken from the presence of anyone else.

'Gentlemen, this inquest has dragged on too long.' The coroner directed his remark to the jurors' bench, ignoring Philadelphia for the moment. 'I am determined that this shall be the last day we sit. The public purse is not bottomless, and already the costs of constable, surgeon and witnesses are mounting. Most of my inquests are concluded in hours, not days.'

He rounded on the crowd of onlookers, adding sternly, 'Let all here understand that I will tolerate no further gossip dressed up as fact, and interjectors will be removed. Mr Puttick has one more witness for us and then the jury shall consider their findings.'

He nodded in the constable's direction and Puttick began, 'Mrs Boadle, in your own words—'

'And as briefly as possible,' the coroner interrupted, taking up his pen to transcribe her testimony.

The Heirloom

'Tell us what happened on the evening before and the morning of your husband's death.'

There were mutterings amongst the crowd but the coroner quelled them with a sharp look as Philadelphia cleared her throat and began.

'My husband, Jasper Boadle, complained of feeling ill in the evening with a queasy stomach. He took to his bed soon after dinner, which was most unlike him. Later that evening, his nephew offered to prepare him a light supper and a dish of tea. To save me the trouble, he said, as he knew I had a bonnet to complete for the dame. My husband was asleep when I came up to our chamber and gone from our bed when I woke in the morning. The next thing I knew was finding him in the workshop dead in his chair, with his nephew standing over him. There were signs of vomit upon his face and clothing. I asked my nephew why he hadn't raised the alarm and he said that he did not like to wake me.'

She sensed a hundred eyes scorching the black crêpe of her mourning dress but she determined to ignore them and concentrate on the men of reason assembled for the jury. Or at least, so she hoped. There were a couple among them who were Jasper's particular friends, and several like the brick maker and the apothecary who did not approve of her. But there were others whose families she or her mother had helped and whose wives sought out her hats and occasional other services. She scanned their faces with a confident glance she did not feel, lingering for a moment upon one face in particular, one man of reason who she hoped might convince those inclined to more credulous, superstitious views. Hoped that they would listen to a reasoned argument, and perhaps be swayed by his standing in the community.

'And what do you say to your nephew's accusations that you bewitched him into poisoning his uncle?'

'I am no witch. And I am surprised that my neighbours would

believe such popular superstition. They have known me my entire life. I am a simple milliner. A tailor's wife. I have a little knowledge of herbs, that is all.'

'And yet, the question of witchcraft aside,' the coroner said, looking up from his notes, 'Mrs Tupper, the proprietress of this very inn, assures us that she observed you teaching your nephew the use of poisonous herbs. Of the very herb that killed your husband.'

'It is a fact,' she began, looking directly into the coroner's eyes, 'that when young Isaac showed interest, I taught him the properties of various plants in my garden. And that may be what Mrs Tupper witnessed, but I also warned of their dangers. That I bewitched him . . .' she paused, frowning, to let her words find their mark, 'I can only suggest that he is young and perhaps mistook a motherly care for something that it was not. Just as he may have mistaken the leaves that he brewed for my husband's tea for something they were not. The leaves of the foxglove are not dissimilar to those of borage, for example. He may well have intended a tisane of borage for my husband's fever. All who know him, know that Isaac is a kind boy. I cannot believe he wished his uncle dead.'

Philadelphia let out a shaky breath. She felt as tired as if she had spent an entire day hunched over her needle. Yet she had denied any guilt, and defended Isaac in the same breath. She had done her best to protect them both. Perhaps there was a chance the jury might yet find that Jasper died by misadventure. Then she and Isaac could both go free of any taint. Perhaps.

'I am no witch, gentlemen. I am a milliner and now a widow. That is my only crime.'

The coroner had no tolerance for time-wasting that morning and bade her take her seat as soon as he had taken her deposition. He declared the questioning complete and bade the jurors retire to consider their verdict. She kept her eyes focused on those fourteen men of good character as they filed out of the inn's hall to deliberate in the adjacent private chamber.

Despite her suggestion that Isaac had mistaken foxglove leaves for borage, she could not forget the evening when she and the lad overheard Jasper and his brother in a disturbing conversation. That conversation had been difficult to put from her mind, though she had tried for the sake of her daughter. Isaac had taken it to heart. The brothers had planned her death – a passing fantasy, she had declared at the time. Then, not long after, she had observed Jasper meeting with a local ruffian. To purchase fabric, he had said. The same ruffian she had seen emerge from the lane that morning, ahead of Enoch. Now, she knew for a certainty that they had meant to put their plan into action. What they could not have known was that Isaac would take matters into his own hands.

Her husband had died for his wicked plan. She did not intend to be next.

'Gentlemen, what say you?' the coroner asked, as the jurors returned from Mr Tupper's private chamber.

Judging by the raised voices issuing from the inn's parlour, their discussion had been heated. The scowls upon their faces suggested only an uneasy agreement.

For the first time in two days, the villagers crowded into the King's Head were quiet. Not a shuffle of feet or a clearing of throats to be heard. So quiet were they that Philadelphia could almost hear the beating of her own heart, and she felt a tremor ripple through her body. Despite her resolve not to waver, she flicked a glance to her nephew, sitting shoulder to shoulder with his father. One old, one young. One she had thought her friend, one she now knew to be her enemy. She realised that Isaac wore his father's clothes this day, though the coat was too large for his young man's flat belly, and the style was from a decade earlier. As the father bent his head to the son's ear, the boy's face appeared thin and sallow in the meagre light of the inn. He appeared to have lost his youthful glow in a matter of only days.

He was so young. Once, she too had nurtured dreams of finding love, though her mother warned against it. She had been wooed by a handsome man with a golden trinket and believed herself to be in love. Perhaps Isaac too had thought her gentle hand and motherly attention were something they were not, and believed himself in love. Perhaps he had been bewitched by her beauty, as he said, though she had never sought such admiration. Nor had she planned to beguile the boy. And now that he faced the noose, he accused her of witchcraft, no doubt at the urging of his father. No one could blame him for being mistaken in that love. Yet who would not blame him for an act of murder?

These thoughts weighed heavily on her, squeezing her skull like a giant hand so that she shut her eyes against the pain of it. When she opened them again, a powerful sense of foreboding pulled her gaze back to the jurors tasked with determining the truth of her husband's death. They sat in two rows upon rough wooden benches, fourteen men of good character. She knew each and every one of these men. As a girl, she had watched as they sought out her mother's services for their ills. As a woman, she had plied her needle for their wives and read those same women's futures in the leaves. Occasionally, when begged, she had brewed a potion to help them attain their desires. Each of the men had heard the same testimony, listened to the same accusations made against her. But she saw now that each would reach his own truth, according to his beliefs and superstitions. Whatever this truth might be, she knew that no good could come of it. The hardening of their faces told her that.

In the smoke-filled air above their heads, she watched as a hangman's noose slowly materialised, its rough hemp fibres like glowing filaments in the dim light of the inn. The noose seemed

The Heirloom

so real as it hovered there that she knew someone was about to be blamed for Jasper's death. Someone was about to become acquainted with the hangman's knot. There would be no verdict of misadventure here. And although she felt a tenderness for her nephew – a tiny flame that, even now, despite his betrayal, flickered in the cold light of day – although she felt sorry that he had misread that tenderness, she prayed that the blame did not fall upon her.

'Mr Earle, what say you and your fellows in the matter of Mr Jasper Boadle's death?'

Thomas Earle kept his gaze locked on the coroner as he stood to read from the sheet of paper he held in both hands. Even so, she knew that he was drawn to her, that a shimmering thread of light bound him to her, a thread that wound all the way back to a single morning beneath the cherry tree in her mother's garden, a thread that now stitched them together. How could it not, when she also felt its fastening? She could only hope that he would be true to his word, that he had persuaded his fellows to listen to reason rather than superstition.

'Mr Honeycett, gentlemen,' he began to read in a firm clear voice, 'we the jurors find it so happened that Jasper Boadle did on the evening of the third day of July drink of a tea containing the leaves of the foxglove plant in a toxic dose, which on the morning following caused his heart to fail in his tailor's shop in the presence of his nephew Isaac Boadle. We further find that said Isaac Boadle did cause his uncle's death by preparing and giving the deceased the poisonous tea, believing himself in love with his uncle's wife, the milliner Philadelphia Foord Boadle. And so, upon our oath, we do say that Jasper Boadle was in the manner and by the means aforesaid murdered by his nephew Isaac Boadle.'

'Nooo! You shall not take my son as you took my brother!' Enoch roared, his voice thundering through the inn.

If it had not been for the quick thinking of Thomas Earle, her brother-in-law might have murdered her then and there as he leaped from the bench and pounced, his hands clutching for her throat. But Thomas had crossed the floor between them in three swift strides and prised Enoch's hands from her neck before he could do more than bruise her with his grip.

'Come now, Boadle, this is no way to treat your good sister-in-law!' Honeycett shouted. 'I shall have Puttick put you in irons if you do not take your seat forthwith.'

'She has bewitched my son as she bewitched my brother!' Enoch cried out to the crowd. 'Is there no end to her evil? Is there no justice to be had?'

Philadelphia put a hand to her throat and stared at him. 'I am not the evil one here, Brother.' She spoke so softly that none but Thomas and Enoch would hear. 'I am not the one who wished his brother's wife dead. I am not the one who planted the leaves on a kitchen floor, the very leaves which condemned my son.' And softer still, her lips barely moving, so that only she knew what she spoke, 'It is only just that you be punished.'

Around them, the crowd erupted in a volcano of sound and fury. Even so, she would have recognised Lettice Tutt's shriek anywhere as she screamed at the assembled jurors, 'Can you not see? She has cast a spell on all of you! She has killed her husband as surely as if she brewed the tea by her own hands.'

'You will all come to order!'

Throughout the ensuing hubbub, the barrage of accusations and exclamations of outrage that flew across the room, Isaac, the poor boy, sat crumpled in his seat, oblivious to his father's rage. Both his neighbours' indignation and her danger went unnoticed. He was heedless to all but his own peril. She could not say she blamed him. In some ways, she blamed herself, for she had not succeeded in saving him from his own folly. No, it was his father who deserved to be punished.

'Constable Puttick, you will take charge of the accused man, Isaac Boadle, until he can be transported to Lewes Gaol, there to await a trial for murder at the next assizes,' the coroner shouted, struggling to be heard above the din.

She could hardly bear to watch as the constable dragged the boy to his feet by his wrists and marched him from the inn, waving his truncheon in warning to any who might interfere with the King's business.

'Out of my way! Keep clear!' he growled.

She felt the hot eyes of her neighbours burning the back of her neck. Throughout it all, Thomas Earle remained standing beside the boy's father but even his presence could not stem her brother-in-law's hatred.

'Have a care, Earle. For who knows who her next victim will be,' he spat, aiming his spittle at her feet. 'Are you sure it was only hats she fashioned for your wife?'

Philadelphia gasped. She was near enough to see a muscle twitch in Thomas Earle's face but she could not peer into his thoughts. She could not know if he believed the poisonous words. And despite her gift, she could not see what was in his heart. She could barely understand what was in her own.

35

East Sussex, England
2024

Mia and Reid slipped down a narrow lane beside the café to emerge on to the village green. He had promised to show her a shortcut to the cottage, and despite her misgivings and staunch resolve to remain aloof, she found herself agreeing. His attention was difficult to resist, almost courtly, like a character out of a Jane Austen novel. Not an overly proud Darcy or a wounded Captain Wentworth, but a sensible George Knightley or loyal Edward Ferrars. In fact, she did not want to resist. She found herself enjoying his company more each time they met. Nevertheless, she reminded herself sternly, she remained committed to Rule Number One – no falling in love. And definitely no sex.

The shortcut turned out to involve traversing the grounds of the parish church adjacent to the green and following a path that meandered alongside the Cuckmere River. The church itself stood on a rise, built in the shape of a cross, its pebble flint exterior rising to a square tower and tiled steeple. The graveyard descended the slope below in a congregation of ancient, off-kilter memorials, wild flowers peeking from the long grass between the stones.

'Are you going to give me the history tour on the way home?'

she asked, smiling up at Reid. 'I've been too self-involved to do anything touristy yet.'

'Sure. Built in the fourteenth century, possibly the site of an older pre-Christian place of worship. Ahh . . . are you interested in legend?'

'Why not?' she said, as they picked their way through the graves.

'Legend says that, each night, the building stones miraculously appeared on the green. The villagers didn't know if this was the work of God or the Devil, until one morning when four white oxen were discovered lying on the green in the shape of a cross. That settled the matter.'

'Of course, it did!' She laughed, then spotted a patch of tall flowers like white lace growing around one of the graves. 'Is that yarrow?'

'Uh-huh, it grows everywhere around here. I think I noticed some in your grandmother's garden.'

'You did. Handy for wounds if you're caught without a Band-Aid, so I've read.' And love divination, if Philadelphia's book was right, although she wasn't about to suggest this.

He, though, was on a roll of popular superstition. 'And, apparently, a favourite herb of witches and druids,' he said. 'And an aid to second sight.'

'Really? Have you tried it?'

'Me? No,' he laughed. 'I have trouble seeing beyond my next appointment.' He was staring at her again.

'What?' she asked, thinking she must have sprouted a pimple on her nose or lady hair on her chin.

'Nothing. You have very unusual eyes, you know. I thought they were dark brown at first. In this light they look almost purple.'

She snorted in reply. 'I used to think I was a changeling. Or adopted. No one else in the family has them. Except . . . apparently, the grandmother I never knew existed.' There was a hint of bitterness in her voice that she couldn't quite disguise. Since she had arrived in Sussex, she had begun wondering what else she may have inherited from Henrietta beyond a cottage and eye colour.

Not long after, they joined a well-kept dirt path bordered by wild shrubbery and trees, which led to a rough plank bridge across a stream. By silent agreement they paused to lean on the bridge's railing and look out across the stream to the marshy fields and rolling Downs beyond.

'The Cuckmere Valley,' he announced, waving an arm to encompass everything.

'I thought it was supposed to be a river. It doesn't look big enough.'

'Not at the moment. But it does have a habit of surprising us. Two years ago, it was about a hundred metres wide, right here. This bridge was completely drowned. And down at the mouth—' he broke off. 'Are you okay? You suddenly went very white.'

She couldn't catch her breath to answer, her skin had broken out in a cold sweat as she began to tremble violently. It was as if her body no longer belonged to her, limbs shaking and shivering, lungs gasping for air, mouth filling with water – as if she had been plunged beneath the cold, swirling waters of a river. A flooded river.

She felt a rising panic, unable to stop the shaking. She felt as if her heart might explode. What was wrong with her?

'I . . . I . . .'

'Here,' he said, taking her by the shoulders and holding her still. 'Breathe. Just breathe. You'll be all right. In . . . and . . . out. In . . . and . . . out.'

She fixed her eyes on his face, turning her gaze away from the river as she tried to catch her breath. Breathing in slowly, and then out even more slowly. In and out. In and out, for several minutes, as he stood perfectly still, waiting for her. When the tremors began to ebb a little, he gathered her closer so that her face pressed against his white T-shirt, her senses filling with the scratchiness of the cotton and the commonplace scents of laundry detergent and deodorant.

'Should I call for help?' he asked, quietly.

'N-no-o,' she managed to stammer.

'We can stay here as long as you like, then,' he said, relaxing his body a fraction.

She meant to pull away, she really did, but just couldn't manage it.

They stayed like that for minutes which could have been hours. His calm acceptance, his unhurried stillness and lack of questions were soothing. She stayed where she was, letting the seconds do their work until she felt the tremors ease and her breathing return to something approaching normal. He must have sensed her recovery, for he leaned back a fraction further, allowing more space between them, space she immediately regretted.

'Whew,' she breathed out, fishing for a smile as she put a hand to her chest. 'I don't know what came over me. You must think I'm nuts.'

After all, this wasn't the first time she had behaved strangely in his presence. There was the moment in the café when she had felt a disturbing presence. And in the cottage garden – it was starting to become a habit.

He didn't question her but his eyebrows almost hit his hairline and his cheeks puffed out sceptically, like a cartoon animal. His exaggerated expression suggested a lack of vanity that was more appealing even than his looks or his affable manner. It also had the effect of disarming her, chipping away at her reticence so that she found herself inexplicably wanting to reveal the *thing* to him. Or was she really wanting to acknowledge the thing to herself? She wasn't sure which was true.

'I think you might have had a panic attack.'

The thing she never, ever talked about. The thing she tried not to think about. The thing she tried to relegate to the past. To bury so deep that she didn't need to look at it. The river thing.

'It happens sometimes,' he said. 'Was it the river?'

She nodded.

'The flood?'

She nodded again. And then, against all previous reluctance, all sensible precaution, she began to speak. And once she began, she couldn't stop. Until it all came out – strange and disturbing, or not. She no longer knew.

36

Brisbane, Australia
2011

Of course, she was stupid to go along with it in the first place. It had been raining for days, with more to come, and Brisbane knew what rain was about. The plan was to stay the night in Toowoomba for her boyfriend Nick's cousin's eighteenth, then head to the Granite Belt to camp for a few days in the national park. It was a dumb plan, but they were at a dumb age. School was out forever, and they had weeks before they needed to get serious about work or study. Even so, she had tossed and turned that night, before waking to a sensation of suffocation, only to find that in the night she had tangled the sheet around her head and buried her face in the pillow.

Her mother buzzed about in her dressing gown all through breakfast, quizzing Mia about where they were going and insisting that she check in on her phone every few hours.

'I'm not a child, Mother!' she snapped.

'Look at the rain, Mia! It's bucketing down. Who goes camping in a downpour?'

'We're not camping!' At least not that night, but her mother didn't need to know that. 'We're staying at Nick's cousin's house in Toowoomba,' she answered.

All the while a little voice inside was telling her exactly the same thing as her mother. Of course, she ignored it.

'I have a bad feeling about it,' Celia insisted, staring into her teacup with a frown.

'You have a bad feeling about a lot of things, usually things to do with me.'

The argument had ensued for some minutes, but by the time Nick's station wagon pulled into the driveway, Mia had won. She was eighteen now, she informed her mother righteously for the hundredth time, and there was nothing Celia could do about it. They picked up Jase and Amy before heading west, rain slashing the windscreen, wipers battling the onslaught valiantly and in vain. Traffic was sparse yet slow-going when they stopped for coffee about half an hour out of Toowoomba.

Years later, she would remember the exact moment vividly, like a video rolling in slow motion. She was simply sipping her latte, watching the rain pelting down outside the café, when a cold sweat of dread drenched her. Her ears filled with the sound of rushing water and an icy chill shivered through her limbs. She knew in that moment of fear that she wasn't going to get back into Nick's car and drive on to Toowoomba. She was going to stay right where she was, at least until she found somewhere better to be. Somewhere safer.

'Let's hit the road,' Nick said, when she didn't look like she was getting up from her chair.

'I don't think we should go. It's too wet. I think we should turn back.'

'Come on, Mia,' Amy groaned. 'It's not that bad. And it's not far to Nick's cousin's place now.'

'Nup,' she shook her head. 'I don't feel like it. I'll catch the bus back.'

She could tell that Nick and Amy were exasperated with her.

Jase stared at her, frowning, and said, 'What is it, mate? What aren't you telling us?'

'I just have a bad feeling about it.'

'Come on, babe, don't be a drag,' Nick said, through gritted teeth.

And she just crossed her arms and shook her head. She had known in her bones, through every pore of her skin, that doom lay ahead, but she hadn't fought hard enough to dissuade them. Too worried about looking stupid. Too cowardly. For what eighteen-year-old wants to tell their friends that they've had a premonition? If that's what it had been. That the hair on her arms standing on end, the film of cold sweat breaking out all over her body, and the sick feeling in her stomach, was telling her that something really bad was going to happen. They wouldn't have believed her anyway.

'Come on, Mia. It won't be the same without you,' Amy said.

'It's so wet,' she said, lamely.

'I don't believe this!' Nick said, scraping back his chair and nearly knocking it over as he stood up to leave.

'Are you sure?' Jase asked. He was still frowning. Not an angry frown but puzzled, as if he sensed there was a lot more going on than she was admitting.

For one brief moment she contemplated telling them that she just 'knew' it was a bad idea. That she felt it in her fingers and toes, in the beating of her heart, in the prickling of her skin. But Nick was already heading for the door and Amy was shaking her head and giving her a 'look'. Clearly, she was just being stupid.

'Okay, then. Give us a call when you get home, hey, mate?' Jase said to her.

Nick walked out the door without saying goodbye.

She hadn't believed in her gift, and people had died.

Her boyfriend and her best friend, both dead. Her mate Jase, barely surviving.

12 January 2011: Two teenagers died and one barely escaped with his life when their car stalled on a flooded road near Toowoomba, yesterday. They had driven into a section of water across the road, before realising it was deeper than first thought, and attempted to reverse. The vehicle was washed from the road, the floodwaters carrying it into the nearby creek. The three teenagers managed to climb on to the roof of the vehicle but a collision with a floating log knocked them into the fast-flowing creek. One of the teenagers managed to swim to safety but the bodies of the other two were later recovered several hundred metres downstream. The victims' names have not yet been released.

Mia knew their names. For how could she ever forget?

37

Sussex, England

1823

The carriage danced up the lane at a steady pace, drawn by two matched pairs of greys. Thomas had bred and trained both pairs himself – a hobby of sorts, he said. Where other gentlemen employed a horse dealer to find and match their teams, he liked to breed his own. It had taken him several years to train the horses to the harness and drill them to work together; changing gaits in unison, cornering smoothly, their tails flicking elegantly. He was proud of his team and – she suspected – secretly envious of his coachman, Sheppard, who drove them every day. Sometimes, he would hitch one pair to the curricle so that he might drive himself about the countryside just for the fun of it. Philadelphia found his enjoyment endearing and could not help but smile at the pleasure he took in his turnout, especially on this day of her daughter's first ride in a coach-and-four. The very first time Marjory was to visit his home.

She had fashioned new hats for them both in honour of the occasion: a silk capote bonnet in lavender silk for her, now that she was in secondary mourning. She had designed the bonnet herself, saving a length of fabric when the contents of the tailor's shop were sold up. She folded and pleated the silk until she achieved a pleasing result, then arranged a bow in the same fabric around the brim. More often than not, Marjory's bonnet hung down her back, ribbons clinging precariously to her neck, so Philadelphia had perched a simple bonnet of woven straw upon her daughter's head and hoped it would remain there for the duration of the visit.

'Are we nearly there, sir?' the child asked now, bobbing up and down excitedly on the upholstered banquette beside her mother.

'Strictly speaking, we are already there,' Thomas said, smiling at the excited little girl sitting opposite him.

'I do not see a house anywhere about.' The day being fine, Thomas had ordered the hoods folded back upon the carriage and she swivelled about, searching for the house beyond the avenue of trees that lined the lane.

'When we passed the farmhouse a while back, we were already on the estate. We shall see Kell Place very soon, I promise,' he said. 'In fact . . .' he announced, indicating the lane ahead with a flourish, as a forest of red-brick chimneys came into view above the treetops.

'Oh . . . there are so many chimneys!' Marjory squeaked. 'Our cottage has but one chimney. I count one, two, three, four, five, six, seven, eight . . . nine!' She counted them off on her fingers. 'Who cleans all your fireplaces, sir? Mama makes me sweep our hearth,' she said, to Philadelphia's chagrin.

The owner of Kell Place did not need to be reminded that they cleaned their own fireplace now, since her brother-in-law had seen to it the shop was lost and her trade now dying. Jenny and Martin forced to find other employment, the young maid's sleeve damp from wiping away so many tears. She and Marjory banished to dwell in Susanna's cottage on the outskirts of the village. No, she did not need to be reminded of their precarious state or their losses. There was gossip enough about the friendship between the tailor's widow and the master of Kell Place.

'Marjory! Do not be so rude.'

Thomas laughed. 'No need to be concerned, Marjory, no one will make you sweep the hearths at Kell Place.'

Of course, Philadelphia knew the house well, since she had visited Marianne Earle many times before her death, but until its master had taken her under his wing, she had not ventured beyond the morning room, and only then under sufferance from Robertson, the butler. It was a handsome house, not a great house, Thomas had once corrected her gently, but far greater than anything she had ever known. Built of warm sandstone, with a tiled roof, it spread over two storeys with a gabled attic. The windows were mullioned with diamond panes, and an arched porch welcomed visitors – most visitors, anyway. A stream meandered through the estate, substantial enough to support a working mill, and there were two farms. One of Thomas's ancestors had commissioned the building of the house two centuries before, although the family name had changed through marriage several times.

'Are we to live in the house with the chimneys, Mama?' Marjory asked as the coachman drew the carriage to a halt on the drive.

A groom hurried from the stables to hold the lead horse's head as the butler and a footman emerged from the house to stand to attention on the gravel.

'Marjory!' she chided.

Her daughter was too precocious for her own good – the image of her grandmother – and since her father's death, did not bother to restrain her comments or behaviour in the least. What did she know or think she knew?

'I'm not sure your mother will have me, Marjory. She has been quite coy, thus far.' Thomas caught Philadelphia's eye across the carriage, his gaze roaming her face as if he might find an answer in the curve of a cheek or the contour of a lip.

A court of law had seen the beginning of his courtship, for she supposed that was what this was. Not a propitious beginning for any marriage – and certainly not from the manner in which the inquest had ended. Yet she could not deny that, with Jasper's death and Isaac's imprisonment, she felt a sense of relief, a feeling of freedom that she had never known before. Her husband was dead, and despite the change in her circumstances and the censure of her neighbours, she was oddly happy. Her mother's cottage a haven. She no longer feared the loud voices and angry words, the sudden cuffs about the head, or the promised beatings for some misdemeanour or other.

Yet could death ever be fertile soil for marriage? Or indeed for love? Thomas had been drawn to her long before the inquest, she knew. And she to him. And the longer he waited, the greater the yearning she saw in his eyes, the stronger their bond became – too powerful to be broken by anything less than death. It was almost time to finish what had begun all those years ago under a cherry tree.

She was saved from answering her daughter's question by the footman opening the carriage door and unfolding a step for them to descend, although Marjory ignored the step and leaped to the ground in her excitement. Thomas descended next, taking Philadelphia by the hand and leading her past the waiting butler and through the front door as if silently announcing his intentions for all to see. A mill, two farms, three hundred acres of hedged fields, several cottages, a house of twenty rooms, and the love of a good and kind man. What more could a poor widow ask?

They crossed the black-and-white tiled entrance hall before the master of Kell Place ushered her into the morning room, a lady's room – Marianne Earle's room, in fact – with its day bed of green damask and its dainty occasional tables. Philadelphia would choose something more cheerful, if this were her room: the golden yellow of a daffodil, perhaps, or the sunset-hued silk

The Heirloom

of a patch of marigolds. Something that did not remind her of Marianne as she had seen her last – wan and white and dying.

'Oh! I see Robertson has ordered tea.' She glanced up at the butler, with a polite smile.

The scalloped silver tea service was placed on the side table, with Marianne's cups blooming upon their saucers like a garden of lilies, tulips, lilac and irises. Those she would not change. Those she remembered vividly from her many visits, accompanied by her hatboxes, cosmetics and her other skills. No, she would keep the tea set, for it reminded her of her mother's garden and the talents she would pass to her own daughter and all the daughters who came after her. For she saw now that Susanna had been right, she could never truly escape who she was. Milliner, cunning woman or gentry, no matter who she became, she would always be a Foord. She would always have her gift. A gift to bequeath to her daughter, and her daughters, and all the daughters to follow.

'I instructed Robertson to ready it for our arrival, though it is not yet the dinner hour. I know how much you enjoy a cup. Will you do the honours, m'dear?'

She nodded obligingly, spooning tea from the caddy into the silver pot and filling it with hot water from the urn.

'May I have a cup, Mama?'

'Not chocolate?' asked Thomas. 'I have requested a cup of chocolate for you.'

Marjory considered the question for a moment, before sighing. 'Hmmm, perhaps I should like a cup of chocolate. We may not have it for very long.'

Philadelphia turned to stare at her daughter. What did she mean? Sometimes the child said the strangest things. 'Mr Earle,' she reminded her.

'Mr Earle, sir.'

By the time the chocolate arrived from the kitchen in its tall silver pot, the tea had brewed and Philadelphia poured for them all. Thomas gave Marjory an account of his favourite hound's litter of newborn puppies while she sipped her tea, her thoughts drifting to her last meeting with Marianne, where she had seen that poor woman's future in the leaves. Was it a kindness, that death had taken her swiftly, before she could waste away to nothing? Who but the Lord could know with any certainty? It had been a kindness to Thomas, of this she was certain.

Without conscious thought, she saw that her hand had begun turning the teacup of its own volition, twirling it around and around, the painted flowers a kaleidoscope of colour upon the saucer. As the cup twirled, she listened while Thomas Earle entertained her daughter, the child's laughter tinkling about the room. She glanced up, to find him smiling happily, so handsome and at ease, his hazel eyes alight with mischief. This man was hers now, and she was his, although she had never intended it to be so. And for the first time in her life, she too was happy and at ease.

Trembling inwardly at this realisation, she inadvertently knocked her cup with the back of her hand so that it fell on to its side, a dribble of tea draining into the saucer. Then, her hand moving by rote, she upended the cup, leaving it so for several breaths before setting it upright again – just as she had learned as a child from Susanna. A ritual she had performed so many times for her clients, but never for herself, for she had vowed that only she would determine her future. Only she, not her husband for all his edicts, not his brother, not even her sweet-natured nephew, and definitely not Fate in a teacup. Her mother always claimed that too much knowledge of the future was dangerous and that warning her clients of their futures could be a self-fulfilling prophecy, not a kindness. The future was a thing to be treated with caution. Yet sometimes knowledge came to Philadelphia unbidden, thrusting its way into her conscious mind and demanding to be heard. Unlike Susanna, she believed the future was a thing to be grappled with.

The Heirloom

Out of the corner of her eye, she noticed Thomas glancing at her curiously, a question in his eyes. She smiled, letting her eyes answer him, before peering down into the dregs of her cup. Now that it mattered, now that love truly mattered, she was even more afraid to look. Yet she could not help herself. She needed to see the happiness she had toiled so long to find.

Taking up the cup, she cradled it in both hands, so that the leaves would be disturbed no further. The leaves patterned the interior of the cup in a series of dots and dashes, patches and swirls, large leaves, tiny sticks and a smattering of dust – a meaningless collection of leaves to most people but a guide to the future if you knew how to read them, how to let your senses run free to find the future. She turned the cup slowly this way and that, in order to inspect it from every angle, adopting an expression of carefree daydreaming should Thomas – or, God forbid, Robertson – interrogate her actions.

What did the future hold for her and for Thomas Earle? What could the leaves tell her about love? She needed to let her mind roam free to find pictures in the scattering of leaves, like a child finding shapes in the clouds.

Near to the cup's golden rim, the future indeed appeared rosy. A posy of dots upon slender stems materialised from the chaotic leaves, surely a sign of success, a sign of a happy marriage. She smiled to herself at this thought, so that Thomas looked up, asking, 'What are you smiling about so mysteriously, my dear?'

'I am thinking about us. I am thinking about the future.' There . . . she had dared to speak it. *Us.*

'Well, then . . . if that is the case, I am *most* happy to see you smiling.'

She turned the cup again, compelled to look further, peering down the sides and even to the very bottom. She saw what at first appeared to be a bird with wings outstretched, but then she noticed the hooked beak and the grasping talons and knew she was seeing a hawk readying to pounce. An enemy approaching? That was old news, except . . . except . . . there, at the very bottom of the cup, lay a series of writhing lines, a nest of what she saw now were vipers.

'Oh!' she gasped, letting the cup clatter to the floor.

'What is it?' Thomas rushed to her side. 'What has upset you?'

'It is nothing, my hand slipped, that is all, dear Mr Earle.' My dearest Thomas.

'Marjory, shall we take a walk to the kennels to visit the puppies?'

'Yes please, sir!'

'And shall we allow your mother to accompany us?'

'I suppose so,' her daughter said, glancing thoughtfully from one adult to the other.

As she and Thomas strolled across the wide cobbled yard towards the kennels, Marjory skipped ahead, only turning her head once or twice to ensure they followed. He walked so close beside her that their shoulders nudged each other, their fingertips touching. She wondered that so small a part of her as her fingertip could contain so much feeling. Like a lightning rod of sensation.

'Dear Philadelphia,' he said, bringing her hand to his lips, ignoring any watchful servants' eyes. 'We have waited long enough. I believe you know how I feel.'

She answered him with silence, needing him to put his love into words. She needed to be sure of its truth if they were to be happy. She needed his heart to be hers.

'I have always admired you. And after watching you deal so bravely with your husband's death, and the slights and suspicion inflicted upon you by your neighbours, I admire your strength even more. Desire you even more.' His voice trembled a little on this last.

She did not need words to read the desire in his eyes.

'You are so far above my station,' she said.

As if to prove his words, he pulled her to him, crushing her against his chest and encircling her with his arms so that she felt the hardness of his body through the thin silk of her gown. Then, bending his head, he kissed her briefly on the lips before releasing her, saying, 'How can I be above you if we are one? How can I be above you when you hold my heart in your hand?'

Now she was the one to tremble, wishing he had not released her. Wanting to feel his body pressed to hers once more. Wanting him to take her to his bed. To make love to her. To feel his flesh on hers. To feel the magic of their desire.

'There will be those who seek to break us,' she whispered, suddenly afraid. She had thought to gain *his* love. She had not counted on him gaining hers. What if they should be torn apart? How could she keep them safe?

'My dearest Philadelphia, do not worry, for I am by your side. And by your side I shall remain – for as long as you will have me.'

Yes, he was his own man, she had learned that over these last two years. A man who held to his convictions. A man of his word. And she had striven so long to find happiness, had made mistakes and paid for them along the way. She must take that happiness now, she realised. She must ignore the vipers and leave the future to take care of itself. If she did not, it might prove too late for them.

38

The carriage slowed to a halt; the lane ahead was blocked by a wagon stacked high with summer hay. Philadelphia did not know why the wagon had stopped – there was little daylight left – but its four draught horses and tower of hay blocked the lane so there was no option of going around. Perhaps an axle had come amiss or the driver had taken sick. She did not like to think of any more ominous threat.

'Look, Mama, may I see the draught horses?' Marjory was already opening the door and leaping to the ground before her mother could say yay or nay.

Her heart in her mouth, Philadelphia scrambled after her skipping child, descending from the carriage in a whirl of skirts and hurrying past Thomas's handsome greys, to circle around the wagon with its sweet, dusty scent of fresh scythed hay and find her daughter standing beside the wagon's driving seat holding aloft an apple.

'Uncle Enoch! May I give your horses an apple?'

Instinctively, Philadelphia clutched her daughter to her body before she could venture any closer to the horses, or her uncle. A kick from one of the huge draught horses could knock a child to the ground or worse. And at the sight of Enoch Boadle, she wished momentarily that Thomas had accompanied them on the drive back to Puckridge Cottage, to provide a bulwark against her erstwhile brother-in-law's hostility. Then again, what could the man do in broad daylight with the Earle's sturdy coachman in attendance?

'What are you doing here, Brother Enoch?' she said, more shrilly than she had intended.

'It is a public byway, Sister,' he answered, his lip curling on the word 'sister'. 'Mr Earle can have no objection to an honest man going about his business.'

'You are taking up the road, sir,' Sheppard, the Earle's burly coachman, said.

He joined Philadelphia by the wagon, his eyes narrowing slightly at the carrier, his legs in a wide stance. Luckily, the groom rode at the rear of the carriage and could hold the Earle team steady.

The coachman took up a position by the wheelers – the pair of draught horses closest to the wagon – and took them in hand, speaking to them softly. The wheelers were a safer proposition than standing at the leaders' heads, who might rear if they took fright, or their driver agitated them in some fashion. Clearly, Sheppard had no more faith in Enoch Boadle's motives than she did.

'Marjory, please wait for me in the carriage.'

'But, Mama, I want to give the horses my apple.' Somehow the apple had appeared mysteriously in her hand, as if she knew there would be a need for it on the journey home. Or perhaps Philadelphia was imagining things, and her daughter had intended it for Thomas's team.

'You may give Sheppard your apple and he will give it to the horses.' Although how he would prevent the first lucky creature from gobbling the whole, she did not know. 'No argument now.'

'Better heed your mother, sweetheart,' Enoch said as he turned to Philadelphia, with a smirk. 'You think I would harm an innocent child? I am not the one who murders children.'

'I have never harmed a child in my life, you know that well.'

'You have caused the murder of my son – my child! You have caused him to be hanged by his neck until he is dead, when it should be you swinging from the rope.'

'It was not I who planted the foxglove leaves on the floor of my newly swept kitchen. It was not I who led the surgeon to suspect poisoning. And I know for a fact that your wife grows yellow foxglove in her garden, Brother, for it was I who gave her the seeds. She wanted to cheer you with their vivid colour. If any is to blame for your son's sentence, it is his father.'

'You blame me? You, a woman who solicited the murder of her own husband!' His face was the picture of hatred, brow contorted, mouth twisted and eyes like twin fires, so that Philadelphia recoiled from him.

'That is enough, sir!' Sheppard growled. 'You will remove your team now, or I shall have our groom run for the constable.'

'And you care not a jot for the boy who you profess to love. You bewitched him and left him for dead once he had done your evil work.'

She could not hate young Isaac for betraying her in the end. He was only a boy, a boy under duress from his father. And she did love him still, although not quite as a mother does, which she had discovered when it came to it. Not enough to hold his life above hers, as she would have done for Marjory. For all her care for his hurts, her regard for his needs, she did not love him so well as her daughter. She wished that she could have saved him from himself, from his foolish admission, but not enough to sacrifice her life for his. No, not enough for that.

She felt a drop of spittle land on her cheek, and the heat rose in her belly. 'Have a care, Enoch Boadle.' She spoke in a low growl, her fury barely under control. 'If I am a witch, as you say, are you not afraid? Are you not afraid this "witch" will curse you?'

'You are the one who should be afraid, Philadelphia Foord. You are the one who should quiver in your dainty boots. Your husband had too many debts, and what little was left came to me. I have poisoned the well of your business by destroying your reputation. Ask yourself, what might I take next . . . or who?'

She shrank back as he spat again, a smattering of drops flying through the air to land upon her face and body.

'You have a care!' he snarled.

Before she could reply, he flicked his whip at the lead horse's ear and shouted, 'Walk on!' as Sheppard released the wheelers and stepped away, taking her by the elbow and urging her to step back with him.

Momentarily, she resisted, resentment and fury stiffening her entire body, before relenting and allowing the coachman to lead her away.

'Best to leave him be, Mrs Boadle. Best not to pile tinder on his anger.'

What about me? she wanted to ask. Enoch should fear to pile tinder on *her* anger. She knew that he had been the one to convince Jasper to bequeath the tailor's shop to him alone. He had denounced her as a witch before the entire village so that few now called on Philadelphia Boadle to fashion them a new hat or trim the old. Even fewer required her help in refurbishing their gowns. But there would always be those who sought out her other services, the skills she had learned from her mother. Those they could not do without.

Now the man had threatened her. Worse, he had threatened those she held dear. Well, he should look to his own and have a care. He should look to his own house. For a Foord, once threatened, does not forget. A Foord, once injured, will have her vengeance.

39

Brisbane, Australia
2024

The moon emerged from behind a blue gum, a silver disk hovering in the midnight sky, just as a group of flying foxes flapped past. Celia smiled to herself at the bats silhouetted against the full moon, like an illustration from a tale of things that go bump in the night. There were thousands of flying foxes in Brisbane and a dozen giant roosts, which they frequented like bat airports, flying from one to another, pollinating trees and distributing seeds over vast distances. The bats and owls were her neighbours and far more interesting than any fairy-tale witches and goblins.

Yet here she was, sitting glumly on her terrace, sleepless in the wee hours as if, despite her scepticism, the full moon was messing with her emotions, while the overhanging branches of a silver wattle overwhelmed her senses with its cloying honeyed scent, its thousands of blossoms like tiny yellow puffballs of pollen. She had thrown an old jumper around her shoulders, for the night air was cool, but her bare legs had broken out in goosebumps. She felt frozen to the spot, unable to get up and fetch a dressing gown or blanket. She was immobilised by anxiety, as if threatened by an unseen entity or force.

'Where's your teapot?' Mike said, wandering out on to the

back terrace in his pyjamas and dressing gown. He carried an alpaca throw from the sofa, which he draped over her legs, before plonking himself down in the chair next to her. 'I thought I might find you consulting the leaves.'

'I think they might just make me more anxious,' she said, with a rueful smile. 'I don't think I've slept at all.'

'You were asleep for a while, darl, bundled in the sheet like a mummy. I had to unwrap you in case you smothered.'

'Sorry. I don't know what's got into me.'

'I do. You're worried about our daughter.'

Celia shrugged. That went without saying. Don't all parents worry about their offspring? 'I can't help feeling that she's in danger. I know it sounds silly, but I don't think she ever got over Nick and Amy's deaths. She pushed it somewhere deep inside and locked the box. Something tells me that Henrietta's influence, even from beyond the grave, might unlock it in unexpected ways.'

'Would that be such a bad thing?' Mike asked. 'She never wanted to talk to us about it – or to anyone, as far as I know. She refused the counselling we suggested. Unlocking the box might set her free.' He gave his wife a knowing look, as if he wasn't only referring to their daughter.

'I don't know. Maybe you're right. You know what woke me tonight?'

'What?'

Celia stared out at the bulbous hanging moon where a lone bat was flapping across its face. 'I had a dream. I dreamt that Henrietta and I were standing in the garden of Puckridge Cottage – except she was Henrietta, yet not Henrietta. She was dressed in a long black gown, but rather than one of my mother's flowing robes this garment had a high-waisted, fitted bodice, with military-style frogging down its front, and she wore a straw bonnet swathed in metres of black gauze on her head. A style from two hundred years ago.'

'What did she do to you?'

'Nothing. She offered me her hand, gloved in black, holding the golden thimble she gave me on my twenty-first birthday.'

'So, she was your mother?'

'Maybe. But she might have been my ancestor Philadelphia Foord too, the one whose husband died of foxglove poisoning. The one accused of being a witch. It was the right era.' And perhaps the thimble had indeed come from her. A milliner married to a tailor. In Celia's dream, if not in fact. A symbol of her heritage.

'Did she say anything?'

'She said, "It's a gift. Take it."' Celia looked into her husband's eyes. 'The funny thing was, I didn't know whether I was me, or Mia.'

The thing Celia had always appreciated most about her husband wasn't his sexiness, or his sense of humour (although he was sexy and funny), it was that he took her seriously. He didn't say 'it was only a dream' or 'you'll feel better in the morning'.

He said now, 'Let's go, then.'

'Go where?'

'To Sussex. To your childhood home. Let's go and see how our daughter is faring in the house of the evil witch.' He grinned at her. 'You have school holidays coming up in September. I can take a couple of weeks off work.'

'She won't like it.'

'We'll tell her I wanted to do some family history research and you wanted to visit the place where you grew up, now that Henrietta is gone. Nothing to do with her,' he said.

'She still won't like it.'

'She'll survive.'

Besides, Mia might not be the only one who didn't like it. Then again, how much harm could the dead really do?

40

East Sussex, England
2024

The Sinking Woman: The woman descends beneath the water, her hair like a cloud of black netting, her inky dress trailing into the depths. A log floats upon the surface of the water, its branches reaching to the sky, its roots a web entangling the woman's hair. The sinking woman's arms are weighted with spherical rocks, ropes tied through holes at their centres. It is night and a full moon casts a silvery light upon the water, bats and magpies swarming the sky. If you look closer you see that three tiny people crawl like water striders upon the surface of the river. And in its depths, cars swim amongst the reeds like fish, bubbles rising from their open windows.

The Beauty in the Woods: The woman stands at the door of a cottage, holding a broomstick, on guard. She wears a gown from two centuries before, white muslin through which her legs are faintly visible. A castle rises in ruins on a hill in the distance, a procession of tiny people dressed in bygone fashion waiting outside its crumbling arches. Around the cottage a tangle of giant yellow foxgloves climbs the walls and twines through the twigs of the hazelwood fence. The only entrance to the woman's cottage is through a hole in a round stone the height of a man.

Mia arched her back, stretching her arms above her head. She had been hunched over her laptop for what seemed like hours, and she knew it was time to take a break or she might find herself permanently bent into the shape of a pretzel. Yet she was reluctant to break her concentration. There was something missing from the second piece she was working on, but so far it eluded her. She had been working on the two pieces for several weeks, collecting old photographs she found on the internet, antique prints from her grandmother's walls, selecting from hundreds of photographs she had taken herself over the years – some she had taken recently, including self-portraits in costumes she put together from her grandmother's wardrobe – combined with a few old family photos she had found amongst Henrietta's belongings. She took various elements from these sources, sometimes an entire background, sometimes a single leaf or item of clothing. Each of the digital collages she created consisted of at least thirty or forty images, layered one upon another to create the work. But already she could see a day when she might include hundreds of images. The most frustrating part was finding or taking pictures where the size, lighting and camera angles blended seamlessly. That and wondering if it was all pointless when AI could magic up images in a blink of the eye. But then, where was the artistry in that?

Clasping her hands above her head, she stretched to one side and then the other, her neck bones cracking. Maybe it was time for a cup of tea. She had taken to using an ancient china teapot she had found in one of Henrietta's kitchen cupboards, and actual tea leaves, sometimes adding a sprinkle of chamomile or chrysanthemum petals from the garden. Turning towards the door,

The Heirloom

she jumped back in surprise to find a face peering through the glass wall to the garden. The face was pressed so close, nose to the glass, that she didn't recognise it at first.

'Hiya! It's just me!' The figure waved a hand and stood back from the glass, revealing its identity as Tessa from the King's Head.

'Tessa! You gave me a fright,' she laughed.

Tessa was only her second visitor after Reid, who had taken to popping in on a regular basis, usually with a bottle of wine and some document or other he thought she might find useful.

'I knocked but no one answered. Henrietta never answered if she was in the conservatory, so I came around back.'

'I didn't realise you knew her.'

'Oh, everyone knew Henrietta. You know, if you had a stubborn cough, she'd brew up a tonic. Or if you had an important decision to make, she'd read the leaves for you.'

'I see. She was like the local . . . um . . . wise woman.'

'Well, once upon a time we might have called her the local witch, I suppose. But we just thought of her as . . .' Tessa shrugged, 'I don't know, our resident psychic maybe? And she didn't charge as much as a counsellor, so that was a bargain. My grandmother told me she used to consult Henrietta's mother.'

'So, it was the family business?'

'I suppose so. Hey, what's that you're working on? I saw your laptop screen through the window.'

Mia hadn't shown anyone her work yet, although Reid might have an inkling. The old photographs he just happened to find at home – and think she might like – told her that. She wasn't sure how she felt about showing the results to anyone yet.

'Just some digital collages I'm working on.'

'Can I see?' Tessa had sidled closer to the workbench before Mia realised and now stood peering at 'The Beauty in the Woods' on her screen.

'I really need a bigger monitor.'

'It's . . . ah . . .' Tessa began, searching for the right words to let her down gently, and Mia's stomach clenched. 'It's astounding. Stunningly beautiful. And also, quite . . . I don't know, otherworldly. Kind of spooky.' She rounded on Mia. 'You didn't say you were an artist. I came here to ask if you wanted to work at the pub. We're really, *really* short staffed. But—'

'No! I'd love to work at the pub. I'm running out of money *very* fast and about to trawl the wanted ads.'

What a godsend. Tessa and her husband were so nice, and she could walk to the King's Head from the cottage. Luckily, she had sorted a UK passport before she left home, so she was able to work legally. Thank you, Celia. 'The art is . . .' She searched for the right way to describe it. Therapy? Vocation? Family history? Clairvoyance? All of the above?

'A gift.' Tessa said. 'You really have a gift. Do you have any more pieces you're working on?'

'Only one more, so far,' she said, bringing up 'The Sinking Woman'.

Tessa studied it for a while, before saying, 'You should talk to Lucy. She runs a gallery in Rye. She'd love your work. She also happens to be my sister.'

Mia smiled. Tessa appeared to have connections everywhere. And the idea of showing her work, while terrifying, was also exciting. 'Maybe I will,' she said. One day. When she had worked out what she was trying to say. Or was her art an ongoing process of discovering what she thought?

'By the way, how's Reid? You've been seeing him a bit, I hear,' Tessa said.

'Where did you hear that?' Mia squeaked, alarmed at the idea that people might be talking about her. People she didn't know. 'Anyway, we're just friends.'

'It's a small village, remember. Suresh at the Tailor's Café mentioned it. Reverend Paul at the church. Graeme at the mini-mart . . .' She reeled off a list of names. 'Plus, Reid and I were at school together. I was friends with his ex . . . I mean, his best mate.'

His ex? Now that was something Mia would like to know more about, purely out of neighbourly curiosity, of course. 'He has an ex?'

'Mmm. I thought they'd probably marry but . . .' She shrugged. 'It wasn't to be.'

'Oh, why, what happened?' she asked. Then, feigning a casual disinterest that wouldn't fool anybody, added, 'Would you like tea?'

'Thanks. Strong, with milk. Where was I? Oh, yeah, Sarah fell for her boss and moved to New Zealand.'

Well, that wasn't what Mia had been expecting. 'New Zealand?'

'I'm not sure if it was the boss or the career move that was the selling point.'

'Was Reid . . . disappointed?'

'Crushed. But that was three years ago.' Tessa met her eyes with a questioning look.

'Anyway, when would you like me to start at the pub?' Avoidance was a safe course of action, Mia always found.

'How does Monday sound?'

'Great! Let's get that cuppa.'

After Tessa left, Mia returned to the studio but she couldn't settle to work. Images of Reid and his love-rat ex kept battering at her concentration. What was wrong with her? Of course the man had an ex. Any man in his thirties had an ex – or, more likely, several exes. So, instead of adding to her frustration, she decided to abandon the project for the day and relocate to the garden where the scent of flowering herbs and the warm afternoon sun beckoned. She would take Philadelphia's manuscript, a sketchbook and one of her grandmother's herb almanacs with her, and see if inspiration might strike.

After spreading a rug on a patch of lawn beside her grandmother's garden beds, she placed the manuscript on the rug, wrapped in a length of faded silk she had found in a trunk beneath her bed. Then, with the almanac open beside her, she unfolded the silk wrapping and turned to the rather haphazard index in Philadelphia's *Book of Receipts*. She scanned the first page, frowning as she deciphered the old-fashioned script. She wasn't exactly sure what she was looking for, just something that might catch her eye and her imagination. There were numerous remedies for common medical complaints, even several for treating livestock, and then on the second page of the index she spotted one that piqued her curiosity: *Great-grandmother's receipt to Charm a Man*, a title which sounded suspiciously like a love potion to Mia. And the idea of a love potion was inherently interesting – as much for what it suggested about the person who would commission such an aid as the person who created it – whether it worked or not.

Taking great care with the fragile pages, she turned to the requisite page and began to read.

Take a handful of fresh peppermint leaves and a handful of vervain leaves, add three dried hawthorn berries, a sprinkle of rose and heartsease petals, and steep in three cups of boiling water for ten minutes, taking care to think of the man as you prepare the infusion. Stir a spoon of honey into a cup of the tea and offer to the man you wish to charm. Several cups may be necessary.

Mia read the recipe three times over, wondering if its author actually believed in the efficacy of the recipe. It hardly seemed likely that a few handfuls of leaves and petals could induce either love or lust. Then again, if the person preparing the potion believed in its power, perhaps her confidence might do the trick. Mia's friend Kate was a case in point. She believed she could attract any man she wanted (or at least any unattached man) and she did. Not that the romance necessarily lasted, but that wasn't the point – it was the gleam of love, even if transitory, in his eyes that validated her confidence. Perhaps it was some long-gone woman's desire and confidence that charmed her man, rather than the magic tea. Mia had never had that kind of confidence. She always seemed to be the one who was charmed. Bedazzled by each bright, new, shiny boy-man who came along. Why did her friend believe in her charm and she didn't? Mia would probably need litres of great-grandma's recipe. Yet she wasn't unattractive. In fact, she had been told more than once that she was beautiful. She had an engaging personality when she chose, and heaps of friends. It didn't make sense.

Or perhaps she was asking herself the wrong question. Perhaps a better question would be: why did she fall for the charmers in the first place? Why pick dazzle over substance, when she knew deep down it was unlikely to last? Why start relationships that were doomed? Relationships that would never progress to anything resembling intimacy? One-night affairs that would not leave a gaping wound where a heart should be when they ended?

Mia gasped as realisation hit her. Was this all she believed she deserved? Fake love. Unworthy of anything more real. Is that what 'The Sinking Woman' was telling her? That her boyfriend and her best friend had drowned, and she was still drowning all these years later, weighed down by their loss and her own culpability. She gripped the edges of Philadelphia's book with the intensity of thirteen years of remorse. Maybe, just maybe, it was time to let go.

She drew in a lungful of air and flexed her fingers, wriggling them and shaking out her hands, when she noticed a sliver of paper caught in the gutter of the book. At some point in the past, a page had been ripped out. Right between *Great-grandmother's receipt to Charm a Man* and *Susanna's pomatum for Wrinkles* – a kind of ancient face cream, apparently. The missing page tore her from her introspection and set her to wondering what it may have contained. But since it could have been removed at any time in the past two hundred years, there was little point in searching for it. Better to focus on the immediate enigma of the love potion. Better to set insights about her own life aside and distract herself with action. She had been holding on to these beliefs her entire adult life. Maybe it *was* time to let go of past losses but for the moment she didn't know how she might go about it. Except . . . perhaps . . . through her art.

Peppermint she had noticed growing in a bed by the back door. Roses rambled all over the front garden. Hawthorn grew in hedges, she thought. Vervain . . . not so sure. And what was heartsease? Henrietta's herb almanac might hold the answers. She flipped to the page indicated for vervain and set forth, almanac in hand, to hunt for the ingredients in the tangle of her grandmother's garden. Her lovely neighbour had kept it watered and an occasional paid gardener had forestalled complete chaos, but since Henrietta's death the garden had still taken on a life of its own.

She found the vervain, 'a sacred plant of the Druids' (thank you, Gran), in a rear garden bed, its clusters of tiny mauve flowers spiking above a patch of marigolds. The heartsease turned out to be wild pansies with pretty purple, yellow and white flowers, which she discovered growing amongst the rose beds at the front of the cottage. While her next-door neighbour's field turned out to be bordered by a hedge of hawthorn, she realised, after consulting the almanac.

An hour later, she was standing at the studio bench congratulating herself on finding all the required ingredients for her ancestor's tea, when it struck her that she didn't know why. Why

The Heirloom

was she assembling the ingredients for a love potion? She didn't believe a tea could make someone fall in love. Even if she did, she had vowed to avoid the whole messy business for at least a year. She had no candidate to inflict the tea on anyway, she thought, as an image of Reid with his china cup and pot of Darjeeling popped into her head uninvited.

'Yet here I am, like a witch of old – sorry, Gran – mixing up a magic spell.' What on earth had got into her? It was as if intuition were driving her; not a compulsion exactly, but an impulse akin to the creative instinct that drove her art. She wasn't sure where it had come from, or where it would lead; she only knew that if she heeded it, inspiration must surely follow. And that was the mystery of creativity, wasn't it? It needed to be nurtured. It needed freedom to wander. And then it needed to be trusted. She had ignored her intuition for so long, hiding from past storms so that she'd lost sight of the sunshine, too. Without that light, her art had shrivelled to a poor, insubstantial thing. Without nurture, her gift had not thrived. And neither had love.

Now she felt like she was rediscovering her gift, and in the process, maybe rediscovering her true self, the self she had hidden away for too long. The self she had never forgiven. So today she would listen to her intuition, rather than her preconceived notions about potions and charms and all manner of witchery. She would set out to photograph the herbs in the places where they flourished, photograph them in all their wild growth. And then she would see what this long-dead great-grandmother's love potion might set in motion.

41

Sussex, England
1824

The donkey paused at a particularly luscious patch of grass, and nothing could persuade her to move – not the girl sitting on her back or the groom standing alongside, or the woman lazing on the lawn nearby. She was a pretty brown jenny, with white belly and muzzle, and circles about her eyes that gave her a look of intelligence (whether deserved or not, Philadelphia was yet to decide). Thomas had purchased her especially for Marjory when they first moved to Kell Place after the wedding, saying that she looked like a young lady who was going places and a donkey would do quite nicely.

To begin her lessons, she rode astride – her pinafore hitched up a little on her legs, not that Philadelphia cared a jot – but Thomas had promised a side saddle and habit when she became proficient. He took it upon himself to begin teaching her to ride too, but since he had left on some business early that morning, Henry, the youngest groom, had taken up the mantle.

With Millie still stubbornly munching, Marjory abandoned the reins. Holding them loosely in her left hand, she leaned over the jenny's neck. It appeared to Philadelphia that her daughter was whispering in the creature's ear. For although she continued to crop grass, one tall ear turned towards the girl on her back, while the other pointed forwards, as if she were listening intently but not about to give up her treat. Henry, meanwhile, frowned as he walked around to the donkey's head and was about to take her by the halter when Marjory sat up once more, saying, 'It's all right, Henry, she says she will be ready to go in a moment.'

The groom looked as stunned as Philadelphia, who was watching from a rug on the lawn with the luncheon picnic basket and a bottle of elderberry wine. She was so surprised, in fact, that she snorted the wine from her nose and had to pat it dry before saying, 'My daughter has a vivid imagination, Henry, pay her no mind. She does love little Millie.' It would only inflame gossip if the lad were to tell all and sundry that Philadelphia Foord's daughter talked to animals. Those fanciful old tales – of bats and cats, owls and hares, and witches who roamed the night – were still taken seriously in the parish, especially since the inquest, and she would not have her daughter subjected to the smears she had suffered all her life.

'No, Mama, she told me—' Her daughter broke off as the donkey suddenly lifted her head and ventured forward a few steps, turning her head to the groom as if enquiring where he meant for her to go. 'Do you see?'

'Millie is thirsty now, that is all. Henry, you may lead her down to the stream while Miss Marjory and I picnic.'

'Mr Earle said at breakfast that he would join us for our picnic,' her daughter reminded her.

'He has asked you to call him "Papa", remember?'

Marjory wrinkled her nose, saying, 'I had a papa. I don't want to lose another one.'

'What do you mean, child?' Philadelphia asked, her concern aroused. Her daughter was coming out with such odd things that day, even for a daughter of the Foords.

Marjory sighed, such a burdensome sound from a child of eleven. 'It does not matter, Mama, for there is nothing to be done.'

'Come,' Philadelphia said, standing of a sudden, 'I have changed my mind. We shall take our luncheon at the house. Perhaps your papa will have returned by now. Run and ask Henry to return with the donkey. He has not gone far yet.'

'Yes, Mama,' Marjory said, with another sigh and an expression that her mother could only describe as resigned.

She watched her daughter skip across the lawn, her figure growing smaller as she neared the stream where she caught up with the groom and the donkey. Philadelphia's trepidation grew as she watched. She placed a hand upon her heart, conscious that it beat faster than usual and her breath came unevenly. Had her daughter's fatalistic words provoked this fear? Or something else? Whatever the cause, she knew that she must return to the house. She bent forward, meaning to tidy the picnic basket and fold the spread rug, and then thought better of it. The servants would no doubt whisper behind her back if they spotted her. Their new mistress had no idea how to be going on as a gentlewoman ought, they would tell anyone they chanced to meet. Little wonder, they would whisper, for the woman was merely a milliner – even worse, a cunning woman and reputedly a witch.

She stood watching the trio: the donkey continuing along her path to the stream, reluctant to return now that she smelled water, the humans determined to thwart her. A shadow in her peripheral vision caught Philadelphia's attention and she turned her head towards the avenue of trees shading the lane, where a man emerged from behind a large oak. For a moment she thought it might be Thomas, because that is who she wanted to see, who she needed to see, but this man did not have her husband's purposeful stride. He slunk from the trees, a tall and wiry figure, then halted when he noticed her looking, and returned her stare. She could not see his face from where she stood, could not make out his smirk, but she had no doubt that he would be smirking. And she knew in her bones that he came to execute his threat.

'Marjory!' she screamed, with all the power of a mother's lungs. 'Marjory!'

At the sound of her mother's voice, Marjory set off at a sprint, her pinafore billowing about her legs, her bonnet flying. The groom abandoned the donkey's reins and caught up with her within a few strides. Even the donkey, sensing danger, had flattened her ears at the commotion and started after them. Philadelphia picked up her skirts and reeled towards the man who would rip her heart from her chest if he could, she knew, but he was nowhere to be seen now. He had disappeared beyond the trees, gone back to his lair. Except she knew without a scrap of doubt that he would return soon to reap his vengeance.

If he had not reaped it already.

'Has Mr Earle returned home yet, Robertson?' she gasped, when the butler appeared in the hall upon their arrival.

He barely contained his expression of disapproval at her bedraggled, breathless state. 'Not as yet, Mrs Earle.'

'Do you know if he took the curricle? Or was he riding?' She hugged her daughter close as she spoke.

'I believe he rode, madam.'

'Then we must find him. We must find him now. We must send Sheppard and Henry to look for him.'

'I am not sure ... I don't know that Mr Earle would think that necessary, madam. He is accustomed to returning when his business is finished. We always hold luncheon for him,' he said, making no effort to conceal his disapproval at her request. What wife sent the servants to hunt down her husband on a whim?

'Then I shall look for him myself. Order the carriage or I shall walk. But find him I must!'

She knew she screamed like a banshee but she did not care.

Enoch Boadle had the look of a man deranged. And if Marjory was safe here in her arms, then it was her husband who must be in danger.

'Perhaps there will be no need, after all,' the butler said, without moving a muscle to do her bidding, 'for I believe I hear the sound of a horse approaching now.'

Woman and child turned towards the door at his words and, indeed, it was true. Philadelphia heard the clip clop of hooves upon the drive, slowing to a halt now that horse and man had arrived home.

'Thomas,' she breathed and, taking Marjory by the hand, ran for the door, too fast for the ageing butler to get there before her. She hauled at the heavy oak with one hand, while gripping Marjory with the other, before stepping out on to the entry porch.

'Thomas!' She shouted his name in relief as she felt her daughter's hand slip free of hers.

To her dismay, she realised that the horse's back was bare of any rider. She recognised the chestnut mare, and the saddlebags embossed with her husband's initials, but the mare's reins dangled freely about her neck as she stood panting in the drive. And her beloved husband was nowhere to be seen. The pain in her breast was as sudden as it was acute. She felt as if Enoch had taken a dagger to her heart, plunging it deep into her chest where her love lay bleeding. She could only pray that Thomas might have escaped his trap, even as her senses warned otherwise.

42

Portsmouth, England
1824

Guards in red coats herded Isaac and his fellows along the riverbank, past gangs of convicts labouring under the weight of stones and timbers, like a thousand reluctant Hercules. Hundreds of men were engaged in the back-breaking business of building new docks and embankments around Portsmouth's harbour, a veritable army compared to the band of men imprisoned at the Lewes House of Correction. Isaac's erstwhile prison had been a small affair, where he knew the names of all his fellows. Knew and feared them, if he were honest. But honesty was not much valued amongst convicts. Better to find the right lie, the one that would keep you out of trouble. Or bring only as much trouble as could be managed.

The harbour stretched for miles before him, dozens of ships and boats dotting the swill of muddy brown water. A flotilla of broken-down vessels was moored upon a mudbank in the shallows, and it was to these piteous hulks that he and his fellows were directed. All knew of the hulks, but to see them close up was to strike fear into the shrivelled hearts of the most hardened of men. Isaac huddled miserably on his bench as they were rowed out in a fleet of ageing longboats. The condition of their new home became even more apparent as they drew closer: the gunwales barred with iron, ramshackle accommodations erected upon the deck, a line of washing flapping between the masts, and the creaking and groaning of ancient, barnacle-encrusted timbers.

Oars docked, he scaled a rickety staircase that clung precariously to the hull, climbing after his fellows, to the shouted orders of a sentry and loud cursing from one of his neighbours who copped a kick to the head from above. It was the smell Isaac noticed most, a rancid mixture of salt air, rotting wood, stale sweat and mould. A different rankness to the dank confines of the gaol, but surviving here would no doubt prove much the same. He had learned the hard way to guard his meagre belongings, avoid the gaolers' blows, fend off the vermin that would share his daily bread – and the vermin who would steal more than bread if he did not keep his wits about him.

He had learned that, for all his height, he was a boy amongst men. To survive he must become as vicious as they were. Become as shifty-eyed and vigilant as his fellows. Thinner, scrawnier and meaner. And sometimes, in his darkest moments, when the night seemed endless and all he yearned for was a sharp knife, he had learned to keep any thoughts of Philadelphia at bay or risk going mad. With desire. And hatred.

She who had been his love and his nemesis.

A wicked breeze blew in from the sea but that did not prevent their gaolers from ordering them to strip to their drawers and wash in buckets of cold, grimy water. They dressed in slops of coarse grey wool, none-too-new, that scratched the skin and affronted his tailor's dignity, and he could not help remembering the fine jacket Philadelphia had helped him sew for his seventeenth birthday.

They were each handed a canvas hammock and a scrap of blanket by their gaolers, before being shackled with leg irons and led below, where the stench was worse, if that were possible.

The Heirloom

As the sentry unlocked the great iron padlock that secured the hatch, Isaac drew a deep breath before descending into the hell below. They passed through two decks before landing at a deck where the groan of the hulk's timbers, the slap of water against the hull and the rattle of chains were to be his bedfellows until the day he was taken out to be hanged. Or a pardon was granted, by some miracle. Except his life had been short on miracles thus far. The inquest and the trial at the assize court had proved that.

'Now listen up, you mangy devils,' his new gaoler shouted, waving his bayonet for emphasis, 'a belting will be the least of your worries if you cross me or my colleagues.'

They assembled in a corridor that ran the length of the ship, lined by cells walled with iron railings. This was to be his home.

'You will rise every morning at half five, muster at six, followed by breakfast. The deck is to be swabbed every second day, and at a quarter of seven you will stow your hammock and muster above deck. Then it's off to work ashore.'

Some of his fellows cursed loudly at this announcement. They had all seen the scraggy inmates bent under the weight of their labours and had no desire to join them.

'And there'll be no shirking,' the man threatened, 'or you will feel the weight of the cat on your backs. But if you work hard, you will dine on fine biscuit and oatmeal, good bread and cheese, with a bit of ox cheek and a tot of beer.'

The gaoler grinned at the largesse of the Crown as Isaac muttered, 'Aye, a bag of crumbs, putrid meat and a bite of mouldy cheese, more like.'

'Better than some poor devils who ain't committed no crime! Count yourself lucky, you scaly cove. I've got my eye on you. There's them that will thieve just to get their three meals a day.'

He prodded Isaac with the tip of his bayonet to make his point, but so accustomed to violence was he by now that he took little notice. The fleas were a more immediate hazard, for by the time the gaoler finished growling his orders Isaac was scratching fiercely at his new slops. But he was not dead. At least, not yet. The crowd had not gathered to watch him swing. The hangman was not selling scraps of rope from around his neck as talismans just yet. He must suffer for his sins, while hoping that, given pen and paper, he might beg mercy of the King. Or his father might petition the powers that be on his behalf. Until then, he must survive.

Perhaps his King would be more merciful than his God, who had punished him for a deed that was not of his doing. For who can withstand the power of the Devil when he tempts you in the guise of a beautiful woman? A woman with the creamy arms of a goddess, the warm laugh of a siren, a net of hair to snare the unsuspecting and an ink-black heart to condemn them. Not young Isaac Boadle, tailor's apprentice and murderer. Not he. He had not been strong enough then. And now it was too late. His uncle was dead by his hand, and the hangman's noose dangled closer with each passing day.

To His Most Gracious Majesty, the King

This humble Petition of a desperate father residing in the county of Sussex, on behalf of his son, Isaac Boadle, convicted of murder.

I humbly beg pardon for taking the liberty of writing to you but my desperation at the plight, and prospective execution, of my son emboldens me to beg clemency. I truly believe that through various circumstances, which I will outline below, my son has been the victim of an evil plot to lure him into committing the sin of murder. That at the time of the offence he was under the malign influence of another and not responsible for his actions.

The Heirloom

Isaac Boadle was only eighteen at the time of his trial at the Lewes Assizes in January, the year of our Lord eighteen hundred and twenty-four, having caused the death of Jasper Boadle through poisoning in July of the previous year, and was sentenced to execution. He now languishes in the hulks at Portsmouth Harbour, awaiting execution.

The said Isaac Boadle is an honest, industrious boy of good habits, as was well known in the parish. He was apprenticed to his uncle, Jasper Boadle, a tailor, and living in his home at the time of the offence. That his uncle's wife practised witchcraft was well known throughout the parish and several folk testified to this fact at the inquest, that she and her mother Susanna Foord, having been in the business of selling magic cures for many years. Isaac swore on the Bible that his aunt had cast a spell on him and lured him into committing this terrible sin on her behalf, instructing him on how to brew the foxglove leaves in her garden to make a poison.

This humble petitioner deplores the crime of murder which this spell provoked his son into committing but he was an innocent boy who, though he tried, could not resist the Wickedness of his aunt, for all know that witches do consort with the Devil.

Your Gracious Majesty, I have stated my son's miserable situation to you in the hope that you will take his case into your merciful consideration and bestow upon him a reduction of his sentence, if you do not think him deserving of a Royal pardon. I pray and trust in your Judgment and humbly submit myself to your authority.

Your most loyal and obedient servant,
Enoch Boadle

43

East Sussex, England
2024

The lunch service had been hectic but that didn't prevent Mia from spying a certain person seated at the bar, lingering far longer than needed over his pint. She gave him a friendly wave on one of her many trips across the dining room to the kitchen, silently chastising herself for wishing she had washed her hair that morning and lamenting the drabness of her black skirt. 'Remember the rules,' she told herself sternly, while simultaneously feeling relieved that at least she was wearing a new white T-shirt, rather than the one with the tomato sauce stain down the front.

'First time I've seen Reid in here for months,' Tessa observed as Mia did her last fly-by to the kitchen, carrying a stack of dirty dishes, at the end of her shift.

'Oh?'

'He does live in Lewes. Bit far for lunch alone at the bar with a jacket potato, though. Unless he happened to be meeting someone, of course.'

'Well, he's probably meeting someone, then,' Mia shrugged.

Tessa made an ostentatious sweep of the room with her eyes. 'Not that I've noticed.'

The Heirloom

'These dishes are heavy, if you haven't noticed, boss.'

'Go on then, run away.' Tessa shook her blond bob in disgust.

Mia was about to do just that when she heard her name being called.

'Mia! Good to see you. Could we have a word when you've finished your shift?' Reid asked, abandoning his stool and walking towards her, smiling broadly.

If there was a twitch of uncertainty about his eyes, most people wouldn't have noticed. But for some reason, Mia had become attuned to the slightest quirks of his expression. How had that happened? She had only met the man a handful of times. Six, if you counted today – but who was counting?

'Sure, I'm . . . ah . . . about to finish.'

'Here, let me take those,' he said, relieving her of the plates and backing his way through the swing doors to the kitchen, with Tessa calling after him, 'Feel free to wash them, too!'

'I know my way about this kitchen,' he said, when he saw her puzzled frown. 'Dish pig for one very long summer between school and university.' He scraped and loaded the dishes into the basket of the dishwasher, before saying, 'So? What's next?'

'I thought you wanted a word.'

'Ah, well, I might want more than a word.' Somehow, he had ended up leaning on the stainless-steel counter, his elbow adjacent to hers, with the din of the kitchen clattering around them.

'That's a bit presumptuous, isn't it?' she said, although she didn't move her arm, and her eyes were locked on his mouth. It was a nice mouth.

'I meant . . . I might need more than one word.'

'Oh.'

'It depends how many you have time for.' He made as if to move towards her.

She thought he might be going in for a kiss. 'I'll get my bag,' she said, almost leaping sideways. 'We can talk on the way out.'

A few minutes later, she found herself on the high street, bag on shoulder, Reid Ellis by her side. 'So, what did you want to talk about?' she said. She began walking, heading in the direction of the lane that led to the village green and beyond that to the church.

'I wondered how you were getting on at Puckridge Cottage. You were waiting on the internet being connected.'

'All done, thanks. A bit slow but I'm getting by. How's the heir hunting business?'

'A bit slow. Not enough dead people,' he said, deadpan.

She smiled. 'Too many zombies?'

He laughed. 'Are we taking the shortcut?' he asked, as she started across the green, a questioning look in his eyes.

'Don't worry. I've made my peace with the river,' she said. At least with the Cuckmere. That other river from her past she was still working on.

'The past can be hard work sometimes,' he said, 'and I don't mean genealogy.' She wasn't sure if he was referring to her confession that day on the bridge, or to his own past. This time she was the one to give him a questioning look.

'I mean, we all have regrets, *mia* Mia. Things we wish we'd done differently. Losses of one kind or another. I'm sorry about your friends, by the way. Too young.'

'Yeah, me too,' she sighed. 'I think I've been sorry for a very long time.'

'Regret can be debilitating if you let it.'

Even now, she could feel the regret like a hard lump in her throat. She swallowed it back. For so long she had avoided talking about Nick and Amy, because talking about them forced her to confront those feelings. It was easier to function in silence. Except life was about more than functioning, wasn't it?

'What do you regret?' she asked, peering up at him intently.

'Mostly I regret the things I didn't do. The risks I didn't take

The Heirloom

because of . . . uh . . . I don't know . . . fear of rejection, fear of failure . . . all the usual bogeymen.'

'Hmmm. Fear of loss,' she said, wiping away a tear, surprisingly unselfconscious. 'Anyway, today I'm digging up a different kind of past. Doing a little family research in the church graveyard.'

'Then you've come to the right person. Graves are my speciality.'

'What are—?' She halted, turning so swiftly that her bag swung into his hip.

'What *have* you got in that bag?' he said, rubbing his hip.

'Camera. And lenses. Sorry. But . . . what are you doing here?'

Tagging along beside her, getting up close and personal. It was too much, when all she wanted was to smooth out the rough edges of her life. And maybe do a little bit of digging into her subconscious. Oh, why on earth had she done something so stupid as revealing herself to him that day on the footbridge? And why did men seem to think that opening your heart a crack meant you were up for opening anything else? She was done with that. It was exhausting.

'Strange as it seems, given your less than welcoming manner, Ms Curtis, I thought we might be on the verge of becoming, I don't know . . .' he paused, searching for inspiration in the clouds, 'more than acquaintances? Not-quite friends?'

She couldn't decide if he was being sarcastic or funny, or both.

'Dare I add – almost pals?'

'Oh God,' she sighed, pressing a hand to her forehead.

What had possessed her to take him into her confidence? Did he really think they were friends now? Were they actually friends? Did she want to be friends with him? No. What she really wanted was . . . no, she didn't want to think about that. Not at all.

'Okay, you can tag along,' she sighed again, even more dramatically this time. 'We can be "almost pals", if we really must.' She could have simply told him to leave her alone but somehow, she couldn't quite find the words. They refused to be spoken.

'Excellent!'

'But you have to promise – no kissing or anything of that nature.' This last was presumptuous, but she felt a certain relief that it was out there now and could not be unsaid.

'I wouldn't dream of it,' he said, holding up his hands in surrender.

'No arms around the shoulders.'

'Not even at the football?'

'I don't do football – of any code.'

'Good to know.' It was his turn to sigh. 'No arms around the shoulders, then. Any other preconditions?'

She thought for a few seconds, hand on chin. 'Not at the moment.'

'And may I say, you are a very difficult woman to—'

'Chat up? That's the general idea.'

'Get to know.'

Was she? She had never thought of herself that way. She had always been on the move, meeting new people, making lots of new friends. Was she really all that difficult to get to know?

'Right then, how can I help out with the grave-digging?'

'I want to find Philadelphia.'

The thing about an old churchyard was that death always teemed with life. The headstones might be faded and leaning with time, the dead might have decayed to bones, their shrouds crumbled to dust, but beneath the earth, worms and beetles thrived; while above ground the grass grew green and lush, and the wild flowers bloomed. Mia thought about the life and death around her as they wandered amongst the graves, tramping through ankle-high grass scattered with pink and white summer flowers, searching for the final resting place of the Witch of Sussex Downs. Thought about it and found it comforting.

The Heirloom

'It's so hard to read the gravestones,' she said, bent almost double, peering at a lopsided, lichen-encrusted cross.

'If we can find one Boadle, there'll probably be others nearby,' Reid suggested.

'I doubt the Foords and Boadles were on good terms – not if the village thought she bewitched them. Philadelphia might be buried with the Foords.'

'That's true.'

After ten minutes of searching, Mia found herself at the far edge of the churchyard, beside a yew tree.

She called out, 'Oy! Over here!' hailing her new pal with a wave. She could just about make out the name F-O-O-R on a small headstone peeping above the long grass. Presumably, a D had been eviscerated from the stone with the years. 'It's Susanna,' she said when Reid joined her at the grave site. '1771 to 1818.'

'Philadelphia's mother.'

'Yes, but how did you know?' she asked, looking up at him in surprise. She had read several of Susanna's recipes in the receipt book, and put two and two together.

'I only drew your matrilineal chart going back as far as Philadelphia, but I did note her mother's name.'

'If Susanna is here, Philadelphia might be not far away,' she said, turning her attention to the nearest grave, where a narrow column crowned by a ringed cross rose obliquely from a scattering of white daisies.

'A Celtic cross,' Reid said.

Mia knelt, pushing away daisies and grass to read the faded words inscribed on the pedestal.

Philadelphia Foord Boadle Earle
1794 – 1867

'She married again, then.'

'Looks like it. I wonder if this Mr Earle survived her? I might look it up,' he said.

'That's an awful thing to contemplate.' Philadelphia like a black widow spider, consuming her mates. Mia didn't want to believe it.

Carved below the dates, the letters wildly uneven, and chiselled into the stone by no stonemason's hand, she deciphered a single word.

W-I-T-C-H

'So, she was vilified even in death,' she said, resisting the urge to cry out as a black mist suddenly blotted her vision and she felt herself wavering on her feet.

'Except she had the last laugh,' Reid said. 'She lived into her seventies, whereas the nephew was sentenced to be hanged.'

'So, he really did poison his uncle?'

'Well, the courts said so.'

'And did they end up hanging him?' For some reason she felt an inexplicable sadness, that *her* ancestors were at fault for the young man's death, even tangentially. Despite his murderous act. He was so young. 'Can we find out?'

'I can search the records on my phone. We have subscriptions to most of the archives.'

By silent agreement they wandered over to a stone wall that terraced the sloping graveyard nearest the church and sat, a little too close together for Mia's complete comfort. Reid set to searching records, skimming the search results until he held up one index finger with a smile, saying, 'Here it is: his name appears under the England and Wales Criminal Registers. Blah, blah, blah ... "register of all persons charged with indictable offences, showing the results of the trials, the sentences in case of conviction, and dates of execution of persons sentenced to death; some of the registers contain personal information respecting the prisoners."' He kept skimming. 'Ah, yeah, I can see his name come up under both a Petition for Pardon and . . . in the Hulks Register. So, he must have spent time on the hulks.'

'Would he have been hanged after that?'

'Possibly not. About half those condemned to death escaped the noose in the end. Even murderers. Let's see . . .'

She breathed deeply of the perfumed summer air, thinking that the church and its graves probably looked little different to two centuries before, when a boy of eighteen poisoned his uncle and then claimed that his aunt had bewitched him. What psychological demons could have driven him to do such a thing? And what part, if any, had Philadelphia played in his downfall? It was almost Oedipal. Like a Greek tragedy.

Reid was immersed in his phone, his face a study in concentration, eyebrows scrunched together, eyes focused. 'Yes. Here it is, in the Hulks Register for the *Leviathan* at Portsmouth in 1826 . . . I tried a few dates in order to find it. "Prisoner details: Isaac Boadle, aged twenty-two, received 1824, convicted at Lewes, Sussex on 20 July 1822 for murdering his uncle by poisoning. Sentenced to be hanged. Annotated "has been very useful gangsman for two years". Commuted to fourteen years' transportation.'

'Transportation? So, he ended up in Australia.'

Then there would be no gravestone for Isaac Boadle in the graveyard of the church where he had been christened. Surely there must be something more tangible than a few lines of text stored on a cloud, or a ribbon of microfiche filed away in a metal drawer, to testify to his existence? She closed her eyes for a moment, picturing him just out of reach behind her closed lids. A lanky boy, on the edge of manhood, his flesh still catching up to his bones. The image she conjured was the same boy she had seen in her dream that night at the King's Head inn, she knew it. A boy listening at a door as a man chastised his wife. Isaac Boadle, Jasper's nephew. Philadelphia's lover. Or so it was claimed. Still, she found it difficult to accept that a young man would murder his uncle because he believed himself in love. Believed his uncle to be his rival. Could Jasper Boadle have done something so terrible that Isaac felt compelled to protect the woman he loved?

Mia didn't know why exactly, but she felt a need to commemorate that boy's existence, to metaphorically bring him back from the dead. As if somewhere, sometime, her family had played a part in his eventual fate. She wanted to make it up to his memory.

'It depends,' Reid was saying. 'Plenty of convicts sentenced to transportation never made it to Australia. Too sick to be put on a ship, or they died before they could embark.'

'But we could find . . .' In the middle of the sentence, she lost her train of thought, glancing down at her phone to see a message from her mother floating across the top of the screen.

She didn't need a vibrating phone to alert her that something was up; the sudden twitching in her fingertips told her that. She should have realised that Celia had been too quiet of late, which probably meant that either she was hiding something or she was busy plotting. She knew her mother well.

'Sorry, family drama,' she said, opening the message.

Your father and I have decided to visit. Arriving next week. I've emailed the details. Love and kisses.

'Oh no,' she groaned.

'What?'

'She's coming. Here.'

'Who?'

'Celia. My mother. Dragging my father with her for reinforcements, no doubt.'

Well, either Celia was coming to make her peace with Henrietta, just a tad too late. Or – and this was far more likely – to make trouble for her daughter. Neither prospect appealed to Mia. She wasn't ready for visitors, and she certainly wasn't prepared to fend off an inquest into her affairs. She was too busy finding her way, to be able to explain herself to someone else.

The Heirloom

'Not to worry,' Reid said. 'I can give them an exhausting list of local places of interest to visit. That should keep them out of your hair for at least a week.'

He was so obliging, the way he regarded her with his lopsided, conspiratorial grin, that she couldn't help wondering who was going to keep him out of *her* hair and – more disturbingly – out of her head?

44

Sussex, England
1824

Philadelphia rode with her skirts bundled about her thighs, hair escaping from its pins, the silk bonnet long gone. She rode with her backside bouncing on the saddle, her feet clinging precariously to the stirrups. She was a terrible rider but she rode the chestnut mare like the wind, letting her have her head, hoping desperately that she would lead her to her husband. Lying close to her neck as she cantered down the lane, Philadelphia urged the mare on, whispering, 'Find Thomas. Find your master.'

Thomas had mentioned recently that he had business with the newly established coastguard at the cottages they were building near the river's mouth. Perhaps that was where the mare would take her. Perhaps that was where she would find him.

In the distance, she heard the grooms calling after her, trying to catch her up. Let them shout; they could follow, for she might need assistance when she found her husband, but short of wrestling her to the ground they would not stop her. Even when her foot came out of the stirrup when the mare careened around a corner at the boundary of the estate, she did not stop. She flailed about, searching for the stirrup with her leg. She could not fall. Falling would keep her from Thomas.

The Heirloom

They turned on to the road that led downstream of the Cuckmere River, heading towards Cuckmere Haven and the sea. There were smugglers abroad on the estuary but she paid them no heed; her thoughts were for Thomas and how they had reached this point, how she had aroused the enmity of the Boadles and put him in danger. As her body jounced in the saddle, Isaac's face came to her mind. She saw it in such detail that she could count the freckles upon his nose. There were twelve, she recalled, twelve freckles sprinkled over a snub nose, with a lick of hair that was always falling across his forehead. He had been a good boy, a loving boy – and, once upon a time, an innocent boy. But that face was no longer the face of an innocent; it shifted and transformed as she watched into an expression of anger and violence – the look of his father. Her enemy, she saw now. Isaac had tried to protect her from Jasper; the law had punished him, and now his father meant to punish her in revenge. Enoch's soul was tormented by the havoc he had wrought when he planted the foxglove leaves on her kitchen floor. Perhaps the only way he could live with himself was by blaming her. Punishing her.

The mare cantered along rutted cart tracks, keeping as close to the river as possible. She seemed to know what was needed of her. The Cuckmere was fast flowing but it wound in switchbacks and loops from the southern slopes of the Weald to the English Channel; across the lonely coastal meadows and salt marsh, home to the smugglers who traded goods from across the Channel, and owlers who ferried fine English wool abroad. She would not let mere smugglers stop her from finding her husband.

Henry had fallen in behind the mare while Alfred, the other groom, had seemingly gone for help. Philadelphia clung to her mount's back, scanning the roadside and the river for any sign of Thomas as they cantered towards the sea. They must have travelled about two miles from Kell Place when they slowed, coming to a halt beneath a group of alders shading a bend in the river. Both horse and woman were breathing heavily, the mount snorting disapprovingly when Philadelphia nudged her with a knee to encourage her onwards. It seemed she was not about to move.

'What is it?' she said to the mare as Henry drew up beside her. 'What should I do now?'

The mare snorted again, turning her head towards her rider, nostrils flaring as she panted from her hard ride.

'Help me dismount, please, Henry,' Philadelphia said, her legs weak from the unaccustomed ride. She would follow her instincts and that of her husband's horse. There was some clue to his whereabouts here, she felt sure.

'Yes, ma'am,' the young man said, dismounting and coming around to hold the mare's reins.

Philadelphia kicked her feet out of the stirrups and Henry looked away as she swung her left leg over the saddle, her skirts hiked to her knee. 'I'm unsure of my legs. You may hold me as I dismount, Henry,' she said, so that he dared to take her by the waist and ease her to the ground.

He steadied her by the elbow for a few seconds, so she could find her legs, before she drew her arm away and looked to the river. The mare had led her here for a reason. Trailed by Henry, she stepped through the long grass to the reed-lined bank of the river. Here, where the river slowed its run to the sea, the white, yellow-hearted flowers of threadleaf crowfoot floated, while the leaves of water soldiers speared the surface.

Her breathing had not slowed, though her ride was ended, and the trembling in her legs had spread to her hands. She strode across the damp ground by the riverbank, heedless of her fine boots, sweeping a low-hanging alder branch from her path. There was something floating in the water amongst the water soldiers, a long brown shape, half submerged in the shallows. She did not stop when her boots met the water but waded into the river, the water soaking her ankles, then her knees, seeping up the fine cotton of her gown as the mud sucked at her boots. She reached the floating man – for in her heart she knew it was a man – and pushing aside the plants, pulled him to her with all the strength in her arms.

'Madam,' said Henry, a few steps behind her. 'Let me.'

She could not release this man garbed in her husband's brown wool frock coat and favourite buckskins, for her hand gripped his coat sleeve in a vice. If she did not let him go, she could keep him with her.

'Madam, please.'

It was funny; women were the ones commanded to float, to learn if they were witches. Yet here she was – a witch by most definitions – and her husband was the one floating upon the river.

'He may still be alive, Mrs Earle,' Henry said, risking a light touch to her arm.

'Yes, yes, he might,' she agreed, uncurling her fingers with a determined effort. She allowed the groom to turn him over so that her husband stared up at the sky, his hazel eyes brimming with river tears, his eyelashes soaked. He did not blink.

'I'm sorry, madam. He is gone, but only just, I think. His lungs still hold air, or he would have sunk.'

'When will he return?' she asked, confused for a moment.

The groom stared at her. 'I shall take him ashore, shall I?'

'Yes. Take him home for me.'

'Alfred has gone for the parish constable. Perhaps we should wait here with Mr Earle until he comes. See, there is a gash upon the master's forehead . . .'

'A gash? I see no blood.'

'The river has washed away the blood. And the bleeding has stopped now Mr Earle is . . .' He did not finish his sentence, bending to take a good hold upon her husband.

'Is dead?'

The lad nodded. He could not bring himself to say the word to her.

She watched as he dragged Thomas through the water to the bank of the river. He was not much older than her nephew had been when she last saw him, although Isaac would be three years older now, she remembered. A grown man, if a boy can grow, festering in the bowels of a hulk moored at Portsmouth Harbour. That was where they had taken him now, she had heard. As far as she knew, he had not faced the scaffold yet.

'Perhaps he fell from his horse,' she said.

'There be smugglers about. Not averse to a bit of robbery if opportunity knocks,' Henry said, gazing at her husband's chest where she saw now that the silver buttons of his waistcoat had been cut free. No doubt his snuff box would be missing, too.

'But murder?'

'They may not have meant to kill him, ma'am,' Henry said, lifting Thomas on to the bank as gently as possible.

None of it rang true. Her husband dead in the river? How had he come to be there?

'Search his pockets,' she said, crouching over his prone body.

There must be some clue. Some reason for such unreason.

The groom complied, finding no sign of her husband's enamelled silver snuff box that he had from his father. He loved that little blue bird singing upon its branch, and carried the snuff box with him always. His gold watch and chain were missing from his fob pocket, his card case and wallet gone. The only item Henry found in his pockets was a piece of folded brown paper, which he handed to her. She unfolded it carefully, trying not to tear the waterlogged paper. The ink was blurred, making it difficult to read, but there was no mistaking the word R-I-V-E-R, which was written twice, and what looked like L-I-T-L—

'Litlington,' she whispered.

Someone had lured him here to the riverbank, near the village

The Heirloom

of Litlington. This was not the thin white paper, woven and hot-pressed, used by ladies, but more akin to the thick brown paper a tailor used in his pattern making. The kind she knew well. The note could not tell her who had sent it, for most of the words had been washed away, leaving only the suggestion of a message. But she knew. She was meant to know.

'I hear horses, Mrs Earle,' Henry said, standing and walking back the way they had come, a hand shading his eyes from the afternoon sun. 'And a wagon.'

Had she been here so long? It felt like mere moments. She did not stand. Instead, she sat down in her sodden, striped-silk gown on the muddy bank of the river and held her husband's hand in hers while she stroked his cheek with the other. His skin was cold from the river, if not death.

'What have I done?' she keened softly. 'Forgive me.'

They did not leave her alone with Thomas for long. A short while later, a small party of men marched across the damp grass to the riverbank: two young grooms, Constable Puttick with his truncheon, and then a tall, thin man, whip in hand.

'We happened upon Boadle as we were leaving the village,' Puttick said, staring down at Thomas. 'He offered to bring his wagon.'

'No trouble,' said the man who had intruded on the park at Kell Place earlier that morning, the man who had haunted her since the death of his brother. 'I thought the wagon might be of use carting a body.'

'You found your husband, Mrs B— Earle?' Puttick asked.

'Henry and I found my husband. His horse led us here.'

'Is that so? His mare led you, did she?'

'Mr Earle has a gash upon his head, Mr Puttick, and his watch and such is gone,' the groom said.

'He did not drown of an accident, then?'

'I do not think so, sir. The water is shallow here.'

'Well, let us get him in the wagon and send for the coroner,'

Puttick said, with a sigh. 'It appears that another of your husbands has been murdered, Mrs Earle,' he scolded, as if she had been careless in some manner. As if she had courted death. 'The coroner will not be best pleased.'

'I'll see my sister-in-law to her horse,' Enoch said, gripping her arm and hauling her to her feet as the other men picked her husband from the mud. The man's fingers held her arm in a pincer grip and his breath was hot on the back of her neck as she let him lead her away, too distraught to resist.

'I told you I would have my vengeance,' he hissed. 'Death can always be had for a price. There is many a rogue happy to commit murder for the price of a silver snuff box and a gold watch. Just as a curse can be bought for the price of a leg of mutton. You would know that.'

She felt her heart crack into pieces at his words. He had plunged in the knife and now it broke. She did not have the strength in her for speech and watched silently as the men lifted her husband and carried him to the cart. One of his arms slipped from his chest where they had placed it and dangled to the ground. She wanted to rush to his side and hold his poor hand so that it did not scrape across rocks or thorny plants. But it took every vestige of will to stand upright unaided. He was dead and nothing could save him.

Enoch had taken his vengeance for her sins, though it was her husband who had paid the largest share. Who had paid dearly for his love of her. Susanna had warned her against using the craft to master others, and she had ignored her mother's warnings. She had betrayed her husband and her mother's memory. Yet Philadelphia knew she would do it all again, if needed. She knew she had that rod of iron in her. She had not climbed so far to fall back again. Not she.

A curse be on the man and his sons for all eternity.

A curse be on him and all his issue.

The Foord women would endure. She would endure.

The Heirloom

'And now you will have nothing,' Enoch Boadle told her, as the men placed her husband in his cart.

And she would have her vengeance on Enoch Boadle in the end, too.

45

East Sussex, England
2024

'Well, that was silly!' Mia scolded herself in frustration, her only audience a solitary sparrow sitting on a branch outside the studio window. Who knew that string could be so tricky to braid? On her first attempt she had cut the hemp into three one-metre lengths, discovering that it quickly dwindled in length before her eyes. Of course, she should have thought, but she was accustomed to braiding her own curly hair. Once her curls were stretched out, the braids ended up about the same length as in the beginning. String just didn't abide by the same rules.

So, she did a quick internet search, and began the painstaking process again with 1.5 metre lengths, having knotted one end of the prospective cord around a hook on the wall to hold it in place as she worked. Her plan was to knot a series of objects into the braided cord. She had laid them out on a wooden tray balanced on a trolley beside her. Some of the objects she had found in the cottage, others in the garden or by the roadside. They were chosen randomly, intuition her only guide. Since the walk in the cemetery with Reid, Isaac's fate had been bothering her. Actually, she felt as if he was haunting her, waking her at night and intruding on her thoughts in the daytime as she worked. So much so that she had become obsessed by a single idea, another in the series of digital collages she was working on.

The Hanging Boy: The boy stands upon a large stone in a cottage garden. Inside the cottage, the shadowy form of a woman can be seen through the window. Outside, two ravens and a screech owl sit upon the ridgeline of the cottage roof, looking down at the boy's hands. The boy is clothed in a billowing white muslin shirt and knee breeches, with bare feet. In one hand he holds a spear of yellow foxgloves. In the other he holds a posy of peppermint and vervain, violet and rose, with a sprig of hawthorn berries. He smiles as he offers the posy to a person beyond the artwork; perhaps it is the observer. A noose dangles from the branch of an oak tree above his head. The noose is of braided string, knotted with a strange assortment of objects – a stone with a hole at its centre, a faded yellow ribbon, a large needle, a golden thimble, a spray of yarrow flowers, a twist of brown paper, a black feather, a spray of golden wattle and a tiny ceramic jar.

It was this string she braided now, intending to photograph the strange noose when she finished. As she worked, her thoughts meandered with the repetitive twisting and twining of the string. She pictured the boy from her dream standing in the cottage garden, but for some reason he would not stay where she put him. She saw him, thin and huddled in a dark cell, then rolling with the movement of a ship, and lastly turning his head to look back at her as he hiked across rugged country. She did not know what these visions meant; she only knew that in some fashion she was weaving them into the knotted cord. And as she braided, she began to hum, the melody creating itself as she sang.

'What are you doing!'

Mia jumped as her mother's voice broke the spell. She turned to the door, moving sluggishly, disconcerted by the interruption. It took her a moment to focus on the two people standing in the open doorway to the glass studio. Her mother's expression could only be described as one of horror, an expression she had never seen on Celia's face before. And it was there because of her.

'I'm making art,' she said, frowning.

'No, you're not. You're crafting a spell. I know a spell when I see one.'

Standing just behind her mother, Mia's father raised his arms. She wasn't sure if it was an elaborate shrug or a gesture of surrender.

'I'm making a sort of . . . um . . . dreamcatcher to photograph for a piece I'm working on. Why are you getting all worked up over a bit of string, Mum? You haven't even said hello yet.'

'Hello.' It was ungracious, even for Celia.

'Hi, darling,' her father said.

'I thought you were coming tomorrow,' she said, turning to her father.

'Your mother got the dates mixed up. It *is* tomorrow back home.'

'Where are your bags?'

'When you didn't answer the door, we came around back. I left them in the garden,' he said, watching his wife who had gone a shade paler than her usual winter gardener's tan.

She was shaking her head, and appeared to be quite distressed. 'I told you, didn't I?' she said to her husband. 'I told you Henrietta would get her claws into Mia from beyond the grave.'

'What?!'

'The witch's ladder. You're making a witch's ladder. Who showed you how?'

'The internet, Mother. Do you think Henrietta is haunting the internet?'

'Quite possibly.'

The Heirloom

'And don't you also think you're *quite possibly* overreacting?' Mia said, with an exasperated sigh.

'Not from my point of view. It's not the first time I've watched someone knot a spell in this room.'

'You mean your mother.'

'Yes – and that other time, the spell was directed at me.'

'What do you mean?' Mia asked, quite concerned now.

'I mean that I've been through this before. That I watched someone craft a binding before.'

'When?'

'A long, long time ago. In another lifetime,' her mother said.

'I think it's about time you came clean, Mum. If you want me to listen to your warnings, you really need to tell me the solid truth, not some tracing paper version of it.' She looked her mother in the eye, frowning in puzzlement as much as frustration.

Celia stared back at her for several moments, then with a resigned glance at her husband said, 'All right. But not before we have a cup of tea. It's been a very long day. I swear the seats in Economy get tighter every year.'

'And I'm pooped, darling,' her father admitted.

'Sorry,' Mia said, 'the kitchen is through here . . . but of course you know that, Mum.' Puckridge Cottage was beginning to feel like her home; she had forgotten that it had been her mother's home for two decades.

Once they were all settled around the kitchen table and Mia had set a pot and cups before them, Celia began to tell her story. Hesitantly, reluctantly at first, and then with a gathering urgency as the story progressed.

By the time Celia opened the gate of hazelwood twigs and skirted around the cottage, through the garden, she was almost drained of energy. It was a Thursday, and she usually only went home one weekend a month, but that afternoon she had left her flat share in

London on a whim, feeling teary after a fight with her boyfriend the night before and a very rough attempt at her final exam that morning. 'Cosmology and the Supernatural in the late Middle Ages' (a subject she ought to have had a head start on, given her family history). So, after a train journey, a bus ride and a long walk through the churchyard and along the river to the cottage, tears of exhaustion threatened, ready to brim over if she didn't choke on them first.

There was no doubt that her feelings about home were conflicted – her friends told her that, all the time. Living in London was ridiculously expensive and tiring, so home should have been a refuge. Yet every time she walked up the lane to Puckridge Cottage her heart fluttered in anticipation – and not the good kind. She never knew what she might find when she arrived, what surprises Henrietta might spring on her, what involvement she might demand. Whether it was being sent out to forage for wild herbs or dead animal parts, or being dragged to a midnight full-moon meeting with other local witches because winter colds had left them short of numbers, her mother simply expected her to comply.

'You're a Foord, darling. You can't escape your heritage,' she would say if Celia complained.

Several times, Celia had been embarrassed when a client of her mother's turned up for a reading, insisting Henrietta had said her daughter would read the leaves because she was indisposed. Reeling Celia into her world without her consent. London, with all its complications, freed her from the constraints of home.

By late afternoon, her mother was usually reading in the living room or discussing her esoteric work on the phone with a member of her coven. Celia hoped to avoid her by sneaking in the back way and holing up in her bedroom for an hour or two to marshal her resources, before facing her mother's interminable questions about what was going on in her life. But as she tiptoed towards the back door, she spotted Henrietta seemingly talking to herself in the conservatory. She was standing at her workbench, hands busily engaged in braiding a witch's ladder, while chanting rhythmically to herself.

Of course, Celia stopped in her tracks. Her mother wasn't shy about her work and often treated her daughter like an apprentice of sorts; reading the leaves, brewing herbal cures (and Celia used the word 'cures' loosely, for some of the recipes belonged more to the realm of fantasy) and explaining other esoteric interests, but she had never initiated her into the darker aspects of what she called her 'spell craft'. The secrets she had learned from her own mother, and her mother before her. Rather than the protective charms Celia knew about, Henrietta had kept the love spells, the hexes and the bindings to herself. She always said that Celia wasn't ready. And as a teen her daughter had no desire to argue, being more interested in the magic of parties and boys than spells. But now she was older, and if she was going to be treated as a flunkey, she wanted to know what her mother was up to.

'Ready, my foot,' Celia muttered under her breath as she crept to the door, crouching low so that her mother wouldn't see her behind an array of indoor plants that blocked the view through the glass walls of the conservatory. She didn't actually believe that a person could alter the course of the world with a magic spell, not even in a minor way – and nor did she wish to – but it would be interesting to know why Henrietta thought that she could do so, and why on earth she might wish to.

From her crouching position, she could just make out the coloured rope her mother was working on, a rope that appeared to be braided with a mixture of ribbon and cord. Actually, one of the ribbons looked a lot like the shoelaces with coloured hearts from Celia's childhood roller skates, another was reminiscent of the pink organza hair ribbon she had worn to her Sixth Form dance, while the third was almost certainly her old school tie.

She would have recognised those hideous red stripes anywhere. Her mother had also knotted various odds and ends – flowers, feathers and bits of fabric – into the braided rope.

Now her daughter was definitely interested.

Henrietta was still chanting to herself as Celia began to pay attention to the actual words.

'I call on you, Goddess, Lady of Life. I call on you, Mother, I call on you, Maiden, I call on you, Crone, to bind Celia Foord Sutton, daughter of Henrietta, granddaughter of Elisabeth, and inheritor of the powers of her forebears, Philadelphia and Susanna Foord. I call on you to bind her to your service. Let her believe in her powers. Let her follow our calling. Let her be one with our purpose. As this lace binds a shoe, as this ribbon binds hair, as this tie binds a shirt, I call on you to bind my daughter to her inheritance, to her place, to her history.'

Henrietta's hands moved in time to the rhythm of the chanted words, braiding the strands of her daughter's childhood into her spell. Or did they? What Celia would not bring herself to tell her own daughter, all those years later, was that from where she crouched, it appeared her mother's hands did not touch the strands she was braiding. Bathed in a nimbus of silver light, the ribbon, the shoelace and the old school tie seemed to move of their own accord, one strand winding about the others, over and over. Henrietta's hands merely suggested the movement with a light gesture. The braid materialised as if by magic, binding Celia's future to her mother's dubious purposes. The worst thing was, she seemed happy about it, smiling pleasantly all the while. For several long minutes, Celia could only crouch behind the pot plants, numbed by the act of betrayal she was witnessing. She could only listen in silence as her mother repeated her spell, over and over, plaiting and knotting her twisted intentions. She could only recoil in horror as her mother betrayed her.

She must have made a sound of some kind, loud enough for

The Heirloom

Henrietta to hear her, for she broke off her chanting, and lifted her head, for all the world like a fox, ears pricked and nose sniffing the air. Then she slowly turned her head to stare in her daughter's direction. Celia instinctively shrank back, not wanting to witness whatever madness lurked in her mother's eyes. Not wanting to see whatever craziness had led her to betray her daughter in this way. But it was too late. Her mother had seen her, and she had seen Henrietta. She had witnessed the shame mixed with confusion and sorrow on her mother's face. And yes, a strange sort of triumph.

'Celia,' her mother called, her hands tightening around the multi-coloured rope. Her eyes were as dark as the midnight sky, despite the sun filtering through the glass walls of the conservatory.

Except her daughter had already gone. Never to return while her mother lived.

What Celia could not say even now, more than forty years later, was that she still wasn't sure if what she had seen was magic or madness. Had her mother's hands braided that spell without touching the physical strands – or, in her shock, had Celia imagined it?

'Oh, Mum, what did you do?' Mia said, when Celia had finished her story. The tears were already spilling down her cheeks at the pain she heard in her mother's voice.

How could a mother do that to her daughter? It didn't matter whether you believed in magic spells, or thought it was all hokum, Henrietta believed. Yet she still attempted to use binding magic on her daughter.

'I left. I didn't confront her. I didn't enter the house. I just turned around, walked back down the lane, got on the next bus and took the train back to London,' Celia said, her voice croaky, as Mia's father took her hand in his.

'You never went back? You never talked to her about it?'

'No. Uni was finished. I moved out of my flat and went to stay with a friend where she wouldn't find me. Then, when I'd saved enough for the airfare, I took off on a working holiday to Australia and never returned.'

'Until now,' her father said, as Mia crossed the few steps between them to give her mother a hug.

'Why would she do such a thing?'

'I don't know. I've thought about it a lot. In the end, I let it go. What did it matter why? She did it.' Celia's voice was uncompromising.

Unless Henrietta had experienced a premonition of some kind. Had seen her daughter running away from her and created her own self-fulfilling prophecy. It was a tragedy, of course. The story of her mother and her grandmother. Mia didn't understand why Henrietta had tried to control her daughter's life to such an extent. Nor did she understand why Celia hadn't confronted her mother. Hadn't told her, in no uncertain terms, to butt out of her life. Not that telling your mother to butt out of your life was foolproof; but it was a start.

'You know, I wasn't trying to work magic or bind anyone, Mum.'

'I know.'

'I was only making art.'

'I know. It was just the shock of it. Of seeing my daughter, who looks so much like my mother—'

'Weaving her grandmother's spells?' Mia finished the sentence for her.

Mike looked to his wife; his eyebrows were raised in a silent question. When she nodded, he said, 'Your mother has, rightly or wrongly, been worried that Henrietta's bequest was a way of influencing you, of dragging you into her world. The world your mother travelled so far to escape.'

The Heirloom

Had her mother thought Henrietta was reaching out from beyond the grave? In a way, she supposed she had been.

'Don't worry, Mum. I'm not about to join a coven,' she said, tightening her arms around Celia's waist. 'And I don't believe in magic.'

At least, not in Henrietta or Philadelphia's brand of magic, the kind that sought to bind others with their potions and their spells. The world was magic enough all on its own.

She released her mother from the bear hug to find that Celia was still staring at the witch's ladder.

'I'll take it apart once I've finished photographing it,' she promised. She had never seen her mother so upset about an inanimate object. Just as well she hadn't seen the crumbling witch's ladder Mia had found hanging from the studio ceiling when she moved in. Surely, she didn't actually believe in the power of a piece of string?

Except Celia wasn't staring at the witch's ladder.

'Where did you find that bottle?' she asked, reaching out to touch a salt-glazed, brown stoneware jar sitting on Mia's work trolley. She was using it to hold her largest paintbrushes. About twenty centimetres tall, with a rounded belly, the jar was moulded into the face of a strange-looking bearded man, his belly wrapped in motifs of leaves and flowers.

'It's a Bellarmine jar,' Mia said. 'Reid and I found it buried beneath one of the flagstones outside the back door. The stone was wonky and he helped me dig it up and level it out.' Only after she said this did she realise she had mentioned Reid's name. Now there would be questions. 'They were made in Germany from about the sixteenth century onwards, and later, here in England. For drinking wine.' She tried to distract her parents from her slip-up – to no avail.

'Oh, did *Reid* tell you that?' her mother said, with raised eyebrows.

'Uh-huh, the heir hunter, remember? History is his thing.'

'Did he also tell you they were used as witch bottles? Scatter in a handful of nails and pins, urinate in the bottle, seal it up, then burn or bury it. If you found that one buried beneath the threshold of Puckridge Cottage, it means someone put it there as a ward against one of our ancestors. Someone believed a Foord woman wished them harm. Quite possibly believed she had cursed them. The Foord women have always been witches, after all.' Her mother said this in a half-joking manner, but all the same, Mia shivered as if someone was walking over her grave. It was one thing to read about these superstitions, but to discover they had been used against your own family was another.

'Well, no need to worry. The fabric and hair were rotted, and I threw out all the pins and needles,' she said, determined not to let Celia's revelation disturb her. 'They were all rusted, anyway.'

'I guess that means there's no need to worry, then,' Mike announced, beaming at both women.

Celia and Mia turned to each other and shook their heads in silent agreement. He was such an optimist.

46

Sussex, England

1824

No woman expects to be made a widow twice in a matter of three years. Philadelphia barely needed to refurbish her mourning gown, although she did re-trim a bonnet, for a moth had got into the silk. Marjory had grown out of her mourning clothes, so she dyed two of the child's pinafores and covered her braided straw bonnet with black crêpe. The housekeeper had suggested asking a milliner from Lewes to call. The irony was not lost on Philadelphia. But plying her needle was one way of keeping the grief that threatened to overwhelm her at bay. She could stitch her sorrows into her mourning clothes, leaving her heart empty.

Susanna once told her that she could not escape who she really was, and Philadelphia had not believed her. She had determined to become a wife, a milliner, and later a fine lady, while dallying with her mother's profession. But if Thomas Earle's grand house and carriage were taken from her, who would she be? No longer a milliner or a fine lady. She would be her mother's daughter. Her husband's nephew was even now ensconced in the library with the Earles' solicitor and man of business, Mr Campbell. She had met the nephew, Phillip Sparrow, once before too; on that last day she had seen Marianne Earle. He had not attended Philadelphia and Thomas's wedding. Struck down by a fever, and too sick to travel, they were informed.

'Ah, Mrs Earle, may I ask you to step into the library?' The solicitor she had also met previously, a jovial fellow by nature, with wildly overgrown side chops and a penchant for plaid waistcoats. 'I have taken the liberty of ordering tea,' he said.

He ushered her to one of the mahogany chairs with scrolled armrests, leather seat and cane back. The chair rested on brass castors, and Marjory had taken to rolling down the hall on it when the butler was away on an errand. An occasional table had been set with Marianne's tea service, and her husband's nephew was seated in the companion chair across from her, while the solicitor took up a position by the fireplace, leaning an arm on the mantle.

'I hope you do not mind that Mr Sparrow and I had several matters to discuss before we met with you regarding your husband's estate and your future.'

Philadelphia glanced from one man to the other. At least the solicitor made a pretence of sorrow, with his downturned mouth and frown, whereas her new nephew could barely restrain his grin. She suspected her future would not look rosy if he had his way. And why did they meet to discuss her future without her?

'I should like to read my husband's will,' she said.

'Oh, forgive me, I was under the impression that you did not read, Mrs Earle,' the nephew said. 'That your trade as a . . . er . . . milliner – was it, Campbell? – did not require it.'

At first, she was shocked at his rudeness and was about to explain herself, to take rightful pride in her accomplishment in learning to read and write (she had to thank Jasper for teaching her the fundamentals, even if it was for the benefit of his business), before realising that she would only be playing this man's game. She was not sure what other tricks he might have up the

The Heirloom

sleeves of his worsted frock coat but she sensed their presence in his eyes.

'I will have a copy prepared for you, madam,' the solicitor said, agreeably.

'Thank you, sir.'

'In essence, however, the will is quite straightforward. As per the marriage settlement, your dower property herewith known as "Puckridge Cottage" reverts to you in the event of Mr Earle's death.' He cupped his hands at his waist and smiled at her. 'And the remainder of the Kell Place estate becomes the property of Mr Sparrow.'

'I thought... I understood that as a widow I would have other rights.'

'Ah, you speak of your dower rights under the law. A one-third life interest in your husband's property and the income thereof?'

'Yes, I suppose I do,' she said, although she wasn't sure. Not really.

Her years as a milliner had made her privy to many a confidence and no lack of gossip from her clients, but the legal fine points were not known to her. She knew that widows should get something; a 'widow's bench', the women of the parish called it. Although, as executor and heir, Enoch Boadle had seen to it that she had nothing from her marriage to Jasper but her hat blocks, straw splitter, petal dies and scissors – the tools of her trade – the clothes off her back and her precious book of receipts. No widow's bench for her, as there was nothing to be had. The shop had been sold out from under her to pay her husband's debts.

'Unfortunately, Kell Place and its surrounding farmlands were not owned by your husband, as such. Under the terms of his father's will, he inherited a life interest only in the property. The estate would pass to his eldest son upon his death, or in the event that he had no sons, to his eldest daughter, and in the event that he had no offspring, to his nearest male relative. Mr Philip Sparrow, his sister's eldest son.' He inclined his head to the nephew, who was tapping the fingers of one hand upon the scrolled arm of his chair and smirking in her direction.

'Never fear, m'dear,' the nephew said, 'you shall not be evicted from Kell Place precipitously. You shall have at least a week to pack up your belongings and remove yourself to your cottage. Surely it took less than a week to snare my uncle, so a week to remove yourself from his life should be more than adequate?'

'Sir, I do not think it the appropriate occasion for such talk,' the solicitor said, in rebuke. 'Mrs Earle is in deep mourning.'

'Thankfully, this particular nephew is beyond Mrs Earle's snares.' Sparrow could not refuse one last jibe.

'Mr Sparrow!'

Even as Philadelphia swallowed her tears, she thought of the hex Susanna might have called down upon the man if she were alive. The power of the spell was in the subject's fear, her mother always said, fear being a most terrible weapon. Her mother did not use such spells lightly, and only when mortally threatened. Philadelphia was surely threatened now. Her very survival could be at stake. Enoch had taken away her husband and her livelihood. No one had sought out her services as a milliner since the inquest. She would have to bring up her daughter in poverty, and all knew that one poor harvest and a cold winter could kill as surely as any knife or poison. In any case, it appeared to be too late for Philadelphia. The deed was done when the estate was entailed. The law was immune to hexes. Why hadn't Thomas explained these facts to her? Why hadn't he prepared her?

'There is also a sum of five hundred pounds, a proportion of your husband's personal property, that will come to you,' the solicitor was saying. 'A nice sum that if invested wisely should yield twenty-five pounds per annum, say. Since you will have no rent to pay on your cottage, the sum of twenty-five pounds . . .'

The Heirloom

'Twenty-five pounds?' She didn't know whether to be relieved or indignant.

'Why, yes, a very respectable sum.'

Only last month, Philadelphia had ordered five yards of moiré silk at six shillings the yard to have a new walking dress made up. If she were to be a lady, she required a special dress for walking, her husband had said. Yet once upon a time, she and Susanna had lived on their garden and their wits. Once upon a time, they had survived alone.

'I see,' she said.

Yes, she saw that her mother had been right, all those years ago, when she plucked the sprig of wilted yarrow from behind her daughter's ear, saying, 'Men come and go, but skill will keep a woman for a lifetime.' The world had not always dealt kindly with the Foord women. It seemed that no matter how Philadelphia strove to provide safety for herself and her daughter, no matter what measures she took, the world kept demanding its dues.

'May Marjory take her jenny with her when we leave?' she said. The child had formed a great attraction to the creature and would be devastated to leave her behind.

'Her jenny?' said the nephew.

'I believe your uncle purchased a riding donkey for his step-daughter,' Campbell said.

'Well, I am sure that could be arranged for a small sum, Mrs Earle. After all, you will have five hundred pounds.'

Philadelphia did not understand the disgust in the nephew's eyes, the quiet loathing in his voice. She did not know what she and Marjory had done to earn such enmity. All she had done was marry his uncle. Now her husband was dead and she had lost her home. All she had left to bequeath her daughter was her mother's cottage, her knowledge and her gift. Would they be enough?

She stared down at the tea service with its garden of painted blooms. Well, she would take Marianne's teacups with her when she left and dare these men to stop her. She would have something belonging to that poor woman, even if she had lost her husband.

Leaning forward, she took up the silver teapot and tipped the spout towards her husband's heir. 'You have Kell Place, nephew,' she said, smiling, though her eyes were as cold as a moonless winter night. 'Are you not afraid that this witch will have her vengeance in the end?'

But it was a hollow threat from a hollowed-out woman. She saw in his eyes that this man did not believe in her powers. He was a nineteenth-century man who believed in the power of steam and the magic of electricity. He cared not a jot for witchcraft.

47

East Sussex, England
2024

Mia hadn't invited Reid to dinner through any particular inclination for his company, of course. It was just that her father wondered if the heir hunter might consent to help him trace his missing ancestors. She had obliged by inviting him to dinner, and the two men huddled over a laptop in the living room while Mia and her mother put the finishing touches to the meal, chatting about Celia's years growing up at Puckridge Cottage. Despite Henrietta's evil spell, those years hadn't been all bad, Mia was relieved to learn. How could they have been, in this fairy-tale cottage? In fact, now that the truth was out there, Celia seemed inclined to reminisce: describing early morning rambles to gather dew-laden herbs, when Henrietta insisted on wearing an old mac over her pyjamas; summer holidays in Scotland visiting every witchy site known to history; getting a sex education by eavesdropping on Henrietta's readings with the lovelorn.

In a way, Celia's storytelling helped heal the rift that had appeared between mother and daughter since the arrival of the parcel. It was the most her mother had ever said about her childhood, and Mia was disappointed when the food preparations were complete and her mother called, 'Mike, Reid! Come and eat.'

Once they were all seated around the kitchen table – surrounded by her grandmother's cupboards bursting with apothecary jars of dried herbs, and shelves laden with ceramic jugs of fresh herbs Mia had cut from the garden – she placed a hot pastry on the table alongside some salads, saying, 'We have a walnut and date paste with haloumi and green apple; pumpkin and feta tart; and a crisp green salad courtesy of grandmother's garden.' Lately, she had been experimenting with greens from Henrietta's garden. Unfortunately, her salads sometimes turned out quite bitter – but thankfully, this one seemed okay.

'No dessert?' her father asked, glancing forlornly at her mother. He had always had a sweet tooth.

'Maple-glazed roast figs and ice cream,' Celia said, blowing him a kiss across the table.

'Excellent,' he said, and rubbed his hands together.

'I must invite myself more often.' Reid eyed the spread appreciatively.

'Do you cook, Reid?' her mother asked.

'By necessity, since I live alone. Stir-fries and steak and chips, the frozen kind, are my specialities. But not up to your daughter's standards, obviously.'

'Years in hospitality, something had to rub off on me,' Mia said, shrugging off the compliment.

'So, what did you find out, love?' Celia asked her husband, as she piled her plate with salad.

The two men glanced at each other, their expressions verging on mysterious. 'Reid here has access to just about every online genealogy database and archive there is,' Mike said happily.

'Tools of the trade.'

'So, we've actually discovered the birthplace of my great-great-grandmother, Matilda. I've been searching for weeks and getting nowhere. Haven't had much luck with her husband either.'

'That's wonderful, Dad.'

'The spelling was the culprit,' Reid said. 'Or misspelling. A common trap in genealogy. Names were often transcribed incorrectly on official lists and documents – shipping lists, registers of births, deaths and marriages, census records, et cetera. You could find two or three spellings for the same person. Sometimes because the informant was illiterate, and sometimes because the recorder made assumptions.'

Mike explained, 'It was the family name. I was searching for Curtis, of course, and it turns out her married name – my ancestors' original family name – was recorded incorrectly. My great-great-grandparents were originally Curteys. My ancestors were the Curteyses! That's why I couldn't get any further back.'

'So, I'm a Curteys too, then?' Mia asked, turning to Reid.

'You could have been,' he said.

Her father was on a roll. 'Once Reid alerted me to the possibility, we found the details of her marriage. It wasn't very difficult to trace her birth name, place and parentage from there.' He applauded their diligence with a nod to his partner in crime.

'So, what did you find out about her?' her mother asked.

'Matilda was the very first of my family on either side to be born on Australian soil. In Tenterfield, New South Wales, 1843, mother Fanny Witcombe.'

'And Matilda's father's name?' Mia said, wondering if this could be the reason for the men's mysterious air. Did she have an infamous ancestor on her father's side of the family, too? Maybe she was related to the bushrangers who once roamed the Granite Belt. Or a convict?

Apparently, she had witches on her mother's side. And her father always insisted there were convicts somewhere along his line. According to Mike's grandfather, one of *his* great-grandfathers had been transported to New South Wales. Unjustly, so the story went. Australians do love having a convict or a bushranger in the family, as avidly as the British seem to love having a titled ancestor.

'Well, that's not the biggest surprise,' Mike said, in the midst of tackling a slice of tart with gusto. 'Do you want to do the honours, Reid?' he added, a forkful of pumpkin and cheese halfway to his mouth.

'Sure,' the heir hunter said, catching Mia's eye. 'Matilda's father's name is listed in the New South Wales Registry of Births, Deaths and Marriages as . . . Isaac Boadle.'

For a moment she wasn't sure that she had heard right. She had been dwelling on the young man convicted of poisoning his uncle since the day she found Philadelphia's grave in the churchyard. Wondering what had happened to him. Wondering how an eighteen-year-old had come to commit such a terrible crime, a Greek tragedy of a crime. He had entered her dreams and she could not escape thinking about him, channelling his story into her work. So much so that she had begun to wonder if Philadelphia had indeed put him up to the crime as he claimed.

'You're not joking?' she said at last.

'It's an unusual name,' Reid said. 'We can do a little more research after dinner, if your father is up for it. I can search some of the digitised convict registers. And Matilda's birth, death and marriage certificates should tell us more once we order them from the New South Wales Registry. But yes, I'm fairly sure.'

'Absolutely, I'm up for it.' Her father's voice emerged, muffled by pumpkin.

'I can't quite believe it,' Mia said, looking to Reid in puzzlement. 'That would mean I'm related to both Philadelphia and Isaac.' Philadelphia, who had been denounced as a witch. Isaac, who had been her accuser. It was ancient history and yet she was so shaken by the revelation that she had to put down her knife and fork.

'Are you all right?' Celia asked.

She didn't answer at first. Perhaps it was her imagination but she could almost sense these long-dead ancestors' presence in the room. Philadelphia had always been here in the cottage, her life bound up in the very fabric of its walls. Now, Isaac was haunting the cottage, too. Or haunting her. The tragedy of the past seemed to have found its own circuitous path to a resolution. It was almost spooky.

'I'm fine. Just surprised.' Was she really, though? No wonder she had begun working on the hanged man piece. Isaac Boadle was as much a part of her DNA as Philadelphia. A tiny fragment of their lives flowing in her veins.

The conversation flowed around her as she tried to take it all in. Then, once they'd finished eating, Reid insisted on helping clean up – despite Mia's protests that he was a guest – before he and her father retired to the living room and more research, while Celia joined Mia out in the studio.

She opened her laptop and was showing her mother a new piece that she was working on when Celia remarked, 'You've put Mum's old bureau in the piece.' She glanced from the image on the computer screen to the other side of the room where the oak bureau with its secret drawers huddled against the wall.

During the last few days, Mia had been fiddling around with a couple of nineteenth-century photographs of women, which she had found in a local antique store. She was experimenting with placing the women in a room where they stood alongside the oak bureau. The bureau and the room were from shots she had taken in the cottage, as she tried to find images that might work together. She was toying with an idea that revolved around secrets, but it hadn't come together yet. The idea in her head wasn't gelling with the photographs at hand. The era of the clothing was wrong, for a start. She might have to find a willing and cheap (preferably free) model. The more proficient she became with the techniques and software, the more complex the layers in her artworks were becoming.

'Have you found the secret drawers yet?' her mother asked, stirring her from her reverie.

'You know about that?'

'Well, I guessed. Mum always kept the desk locked up tight, with the key hidden so that I couldn't investigate.'

'Didn't that make you more determined to find it?' Mia said.

'Henrietta had her ways of knowing things, so I didn't quite dare.'

'Do you want to look? I have the key. And you'll never guess what I found there.' Mia hadn't mentioned Philadelphia's book of receipts to her mother yet. Her response to the witch's ladder had been so ... extreme ... that she had decided to save it for later, after Celia had settled in.

'What?' Her mother drifted over to the bureau and was running her hand over the aged patina of the wood. 'A book of spells?' she said, rolling her eyes.

'Almost.' Mia produced the key to the bureau from under the potted pink Cymbidium orchid where she kept it, and inserted it into the lock. She opened the drop front, then pressed on the scrolled column, saying, 'Ta-da!' when it popped free.

After removing the hidden compartment, she handed over Philadelphia's precious book, wrapped in silk, to her mother.

'Voila! *Philadelphia Foord's Book of Receipts*. Apparently, she cancelled her married name, Boadle. There was talk that she had her husband murdered, but you probably already knew that.'

Celia stared at the silk-wrapped bundle in her hands as if momentarily in shock. She looked at Mia, saying, 'I always wondered what to make of Mum's claim that we came from a long line of wise women. Sometimes I thought she made it up to give herself more authenticity.'

'I've been using it as inspiration for my art. I think I'll photograph the actual book for this latest piece I'm playing around with. It features the bureau and the secretive woman ... oh, I just thought . . . she should be wearing a black veil, and mourning clothes.' Mia drifted off into another daydream suffusing her brain with ideas.

Celia unwrapped the book and set it on the bureau, caressing the faded black leather. 'Have you read it?'

'Uh-huh. Most of the entries are for herbal remedies, but there are some slightly suspect, purportedly magic potions,' she said, coming back to earth once more. 'And I discovered that her mother's name was Susanna. She's buried next to Philadelphia in the churchyard. There are several of Susanna's receipts in the book, too.'

'Can I read it?'

'What? Of course.'

'She left it to you.'

You didn't want it, Mia was about to say, but her mother's expression was so regretful that she bit her tongue. Maybe she would have rejected her heritage too if Celia had put a hex on her. Her mother's stream of texted warnings was mild by comparison.

'Thanks,' her mother said, hugging the book to her chest. 'I'll take great care with it.'

'Mum . . .' Mia began, 'why have you ignored your gift? I mean, it's obvious to me now that all those so-called daily horoscopes you sent me over the years came from you. Not the *New Idea* or the *Courier Mail*. I understand why you might have cut ties with Henrietta . . . but why ignore a part of yourself?'

Celia considered her daughter for long seconds, before saying, 'I suppose I didn't want you to feel the weight of it that I did, growing up. I wanted you to be free of the burden. Free to be yourself.'

'Except it isn't something that you can ignore, is it? It comes to you, whether you want it to or not, doesn't it?' Mia had finally admitted this to herself. She had finally begun to forgive herself for not trusting her instincts, all those years ago. No one had told her she could. No one had helped her understand that part of herself. She'd had to learn to trust her gift all by herself. It was part of her – and part of her mother, too.

'I suppose so. I only wish that it hadn't driven me away from my own mother. I wish I'd been strong enough to stand up to her and tell *her* to get lost. I wish I'd put my foot down, rather than pushing her away and almost losing myself.'

'Oh, Mum,' Mia said, kissing her mother on the cheek. 'You've still got me.'

'I know.' She gave her daughter a lopsided smile. 'And maybe . . . a future son-in-law?'

'What are you talking about?'

'The heir hunter,' Celia said, nodding towards the inside of the cottage. 'He likes you.'

'*Phhttt*,' she said. 'Anyway, I've sworn off men.'

'Then he must *really* like you if he's still hanging around.'

'We're just friends,' Mia answered airily. 'We have a pact.'

Celia raised her eyebrows. 'Have you now?' she snorted. 'So, you're passing up an intelligent, helpful, funny, good-looking man who doesn't take himself too seriously and obviously likes you? Smart move, darling.'

'Mum! I know he's – well, quite cute, I suppose. And he does make me laugh,' she added, thoughtfully. 'He's gone out of his way to help, without much encouragement but . . .'

'You must have put a spell on him, then.'

'That's ridiculous,' she huffed, rolling her eyes at her mother's suggestion. What a lot of nonsense. The sort of thing you'd only read about in a dusty old manuscript.

She was about to flounce off into the kitchen to make a pot of tea and escape Celia's prying when she noticed the tall figure standing in the entrance to the studio, casually leaning against the door jamb. Oh no, why was her family always so embarrassing?

'I just came to say goodnight,' Reid said, a grin plastered on his face.

'How long have you been standing there?'

'Long enough. I was . . .' he shrugged, 'spellbound.'

'Very funny.'

He glanced at Celia. 'I'm growing on her.'

'Like a weed?' Mia said, only half-jokingly. He was proving annoyingly difficult to remove.

He laughed, thankfully changing the subject and relieving her of her embarrassment. 'We've discovered more about Isaac Boadle, if you want to come see,' he said. 'It turns out he was a ticket-of-leave man.'

Well, that changed things. Isaac was a ticket-of-leave man. Free, or almost free, to roam the New World and find his own path. He had escaped the hulks and been transported across oceans to the other side of the world. He wasn't hanged. He was shipped off to the Antipodes. Eventually, he had gained his freedom with a ticket of leave – and, in a weird turn of fate, become one of *her* ancestors. She was descended from a murderer *and* a witch. Or, if Isaac was telling the truth about Philadelphia, she was descended from a murderer and the man who she bewitched.

'It's all very strange,' she said, shaking her head at the uncanny turn of events.

'Nothing is strange when you have a self-proclaimed witch for a mother,' Celia muttered under her breath. She hadn't forgiven Henrietta yet, it seemed.

'Life is strange,' Reid agreed, still smiling at her from the doorway so that her stomach suddenly did a flip.

Oh no – maybe he *was* growing on her. This wasn't what she wanted at all – stomach flips, goosebumps and the hot ache of desire. This had always led her astray. She had thought she was protecting herself with her Rules of Engagement. She had thought that 'no sex' meant no romance. Yet here was this man, standing in her grandmother's cottage, laughing and smiling at her, and all she wanted was to bask in his laugh, snuggle into the warmth of his smile.

Her rules were suddenly in clear and present danger of being broken.

48

New England, Australia
1839

TICKET OF LEAVE
No. 31/1024   15 June 1837

Name............. Isaac Boadle
Ship.............. *Mangles*
Master............ Cogill
Year.............. 1824
Native............ Sussex
Trade or Calling.... Tailor
Offence........... Murder
Place of Trial...... Sussex Quarter Sessions, Lewes
Date of Trial....... 25 March 1822
Sentence.......... Death (commuted by the King to life)
Year of Birth...... 1803

General Remarks:
Granted for serving 12 years with two masters.
Allowed to remain in the District of Upper Hunter River
On recommendation of _____ Maitland _____ Bench

Dated: *15 September 1837*

Isaac finished the last of his damper and boiled beef, tipped the dregs of his pint pot of tea on the ground and stowed his tin plate and pot in his saddlebag. He was not taking chances with the most vital of his meagre belongings. His ticket of leave was wrapped in oilcloth and stowed in the midst of his bundle, with a spare pair of grey slops and red cotton shirt wrapped around it. If it was 'His Excellency the Governor's Pleasure to Dispense with his Attendance at Government Work' he was not about to be caught by a trooper without his pass. Although, thankfully, this far from civilisation, troopers were bound to be thin on the ground.

He doused the fire and saddled up his pony, preparing to resume the trek north, following the leader of their small party. It was barely light but already he could feel the steaming air, and the ground still held some of yesterday's heat. He donned his cabbage-tree hat, glad of its shade, relieved he was no longer required to wear the dreaded leather cap that branded him a convict and offered no shelter for his sunburned skin. He wet his handkerchief in the creek and tied it around his neck, then mounted his pony and set off behind the boss as he led their party northwards once more.

They were in search of a suitable run, on behalf of a prospective squatter with pockets deep enough to acquire the cattle and sheep necessary to stock it. They followed a route described in his journal by Mr Cunningham, when he travelled south after his discovery of the Darling Downs to the north. There were no roads, not even a track, merely rivers and mountains to mark their way. Once they returned with news of a likely location, the squatter would set out with his crew of men, his wife and children, their bullocks and drays piled high with provisions to last half a year, their horses and dogs herding the sheep and cattle purchased to occupy the run.

Isaac did not know what the Aborigines he had spotted several times on the journey up from the Hunter might have to say about it. Presumably, they had occupied this territory long before Cunningham travelled through and may not wish to be evicted. He had heard tell recently of a battle the Faithfull brothers fought with a band of Aborigines in Central Victoria, where fifty of the Aborigines had been killed. There was trouble in the Murrumbidgee territory, too. He knew enough about killing to be disturbed by the stories, but it wasn't his problem. Other, richer men would make those decisions. He had been exiled to this blasted land, slaved for the government and later for his assigned masters, and now he was free. So long as he did not run or try to return home to England, he could make what he could of his life here until he had served out his full fourteen years.

The country they travelled through was beautiful in its own way, though nothing like the rolling green Sussex Downs. At times, their ponies picked a path over mountainsides and through forests of towering eucalyptus, the ground below dense with ferns and brush. At other times, they skirted swampy ground or wound their way through massive formations of granite, shaped by the hands of giants, where stringy bark trees and native cypress thrust up through the stony ground. They crossed clear-watered creeks and picked their way past cascading waterfalls, searching for a likely prospect for a run north of the Mole River.

The countryside was grandly beautiful, he admitted, but it was not home. Sometimes, when he thought of the tailor's house, with its work table and shelves, its plastered walls and stone-flagged floor, he could not help thinking of her. Philadelphia. Milliner, tailor's wife, witch. Even after all these years, her face came to him; heart-shaped yet heartless, her hair dark and wild, her mind cold and calculating. And if he closed his eyes he could smell her breath, fresh with peppermint leaves, warm upon his neck, as she unlaced his shirt, her sweet white hands nimbly unbuttoning the flap of his trousers so that they dropped to his ankles.

At first, he had been shy. Despite the evidence of his longing, he did not know how to proceed. But she had shown him. She had shown him everything; her milky breasts that fitted his cupped hands as if made for them, her rounded hips and plump thighs, her twining arms. All for him. She had called him her darling boy, her sweet saviour, and whispered her need in his ear. Then she had lain back on the grass of her mother's garden and invited him to take her. And in the doing she had made him hers.

Even now, half a world away, his manhood stirred at the thought of her. His breath quickened. His hatred flared. Would he never be free of her? Would he never rid himself of his guilt?

'Whoa!' the command came from up ahead, shattering Isaac's reverie.

They had watered the horses at a stream a good half-hour earlier, before the route began to climb once more. They were not due to rest a while yet. His pony crested the rise and he came abreast of his fellow travellers. They had halted their mounts on a ridge high above the surrounding country, the ground beneath the animals' hooves a vast sheet of granite, pebbled by giant boulders. From their position on the ridge, the men could look northwards over a series of low hills and valleys covered in open forest, towards distant purple-shadowed mountains that blended with the sky.

'I have a good feeling about this next valley,' the boss said. He took off his hat and wiped his forehead with his sleeve before shading his eyes with his hand as he looked out over the land spread before them. It appeared to go on forever.

Isaac swung from the saddle to shake the stiffness from his lanky frame in a brief reprieve. He was as slight of build now as he had been in his youth. Then he had been yet to grow into his manhood; now it was all stringy, hard muscle that clothed his frame, and his skin was as a tough as cow hide. He had come so far. He had come so far and endured much. His body was even leaner after weeks in the saddle; his soul was lean from his years as a convict. It needed sustenance.

Standing high on this granite table, his eyes found the glint of a stream winding through the bushland below. He thought of the cold, clear waterholes they had camped by on their trek north. He thought of the wide-open spaces of this never-ending land. Perhaps he could claim a bit of it for his own, build a slab hut to shelter here under the stringybarks. He sighed and scratched at a bite on his calf that had been bothering him since an ant took objection to him sitting on a log the day before. Perhaps he could build a future out here for what was left of his life. There was a woman back in Maitland, an ex-convict like himself, who might wed him if he wooed her right. She had hinted with her eyes, those dark brown eyes that danced with laughter.

Yes, finally, perhaps he had paid enough. He could find a new home, a new love, and relinquish Philadelphia Foord and the deeds of the past once and for all. Or at least he could try.

49

East Sussex, England
2024

The warm September sunshine tempted Mia outside, making the most of the tail end of a British summer. The mornings were cooler and she was trying not to miss home and sunny Queensland. (At times like this, she was prone to forgetting about the cyclones and summer storms.) Her parents had returned to Australia, both happier for the revelations the visit had brought them, and she had the cottage to herself again. A state of affairs she surprised herself by having mixed feelings about. She was enjoying working with Tessa at the pub; she was immersed in her art making, and her discoveries about her ancestry were intriguing – if a little alarming – yet she couldn't help feeling she was missing something.

Earlier that morning she had combed through a stack of books her grandmother kept on a shelf in her bedroom. Whether they were often-used references or current reads, Mia didn't know, but the thought that her grandmother may have read them in the days before she died might help her get to know the woman beyond Celia's stories. There must have been more to her than cruelty and eccentricity, she felt sure.

She ran a hand over the dusty spines, passing over relatively recent titles like *The British Book of Spells and Charms*, *West Country Ritual and Magic*, *The Book of English Magic*, *The British Witch*, much older works such as *The History and Practice of Magic*, *The Sixth and Seventh Book of Moses*, *The Book of Abramelin* and other esoteric titles. She was more interested in her grandmother's collection of herbals – where a reproduction of Nicholas Culpeper's seventeenth-century *Complete Herbal*, Elizabeth Blackwell's eighteenth-century *Curious Herbal* and Hildegard von Bingen's twelfth-century *Physica* rested alongside several well-thumbed recent works on gardening.

Closing her eyes, she reached out a hand and chose a book at random, a sensation like static electricity racing up her arm as she picked it up.

'Elizabeth – looks like you're up,' she said aloud, shaking the pins and needles from her hand before taking book, picnic rug, a bottle of Chardonnay and wine glasses outside, where she spread herself on the lawn in Henrietta's sweet-smelling garden and began leafing through Volume One of the *Curious Herbal*. It wasn't a very fine edition. Mia had come across Blackwell's botanical prints previously and they were intricately detailed paintings. This was a black and white reproduction of text and illustrations, a digital scan of the original. But how incredible that almost three hundred years after Elizabeth had completed her handbook of the botanical wonders at the Chelsea Physic Garden, Mia could hold a copy in her hand.

She opened the book to a beautiful rendering of a dandelion, with botanical details of the flower, root and seed, followed by the red poppy with flower, fruit and seed. The book was set out with a page of handwritten text explaining each of the four following plates. Already, Mia was imagining how she might incorporate a representation of the book and her grandmother's garden in a series of digital collages. She flipped to a few pages further along, where it appeared that Henrietta had placed a bookmark, what appeared to be an ancient sheet of paper folded in two. It marked an illustration of a tall spear of foxglove flowers, accompanied by smaller illustrations of the flower, fruit and seed. She flipped back to the earlier page of text that pertained to the plate, squinting as she tried to decipher the poor-quality print.

Plate 16. Fox-Glove. Digitalis.
It grows to be three Foot high; the Leaves have a little Down upon them; the flowers are red, spotted with white, and grow all on one side of the Stalks.
Fox-Glove grows in Hedges and Lanes; and flowers in June and July.
This Plant is but rarely used inwardly, being a strong Emetic, working with Violence upwards and downwards . . .

A violent emetic? No wonder it had killed Jasper Boadle – violently. But why had her grandmother marked the place? Had she been researching their ancestors, too? Mia couldn't believe that Henrietta had been plotting to poison anyone, despite the ancient rumours about their notorious ancestor.

'You look comfortable.'

She looked up to see Reid coming around the corner of the cottage, carrying a picnic basket of woven willow.

'And you look very pleased with yourself,' she answered.

'Why not? It's a beautiful day, I have the company of a gorgeous woman, I've borrowed my mother's antique picnic basket to impress her. Along with a couple of slices of her famous apple cake.'

'And I have a bottle of the pub's finest Chardonnay to impress you,' she laughed.

'It almost feels like a date.' He lowered himself to the rug beside her, placing the basket by his other side so there was nothing between them but space. Quite a small space, actually.

'Don't get too excited.'

He eyed her questioningly, and she wondered why she had agreed to a picnic when she knew it would involve a perfect storm of romantic possibility.

'I don't mean to sound full of myself, but do you think you might be resisting your own feelings, rather than me?' It was lightly said, but he was clearly in earnest, a tiny frown settling between his eyebrows as he considered her.

'I'm not looking for romance, Reid. I've been really bad at it so far,' she said. 'I'd rather be friends.'

'Maybe that was because you weren't ready. You hadn't sorted your shit out yet.'

That was one rather elegant way of putting it.

'You know, I may deal mostly with dead people,' he continued, 'but dead people – even the ones who appear to have no one in their lives – were moulded by their pasts and, to a lesser extent, by their family history.'

'I suppose you have sorted your shit, then?'

He laughed. 'Not really. But I'm working on it. I had a pretty good plan once, but my plan took someone else's cooperation for granted. When she decided that her own plan lay with someone else, I was shocked. I couldn't believe it. I blamed her for a long time, and I don't mind admitting it made me cynical.'

'About love?'

'Yeah. I was probably pretty arrogant, too,' he said, with a rueful smile. 'Broke one or two hearts. Of which I'm not proud.'

'No shit?'

'No shit.'

'And you think I'm arrogant, then?' Did he think she was so full of herself that she wanted to keep him dangling, was that it?

'No. I think you're hurting. I think you're blaming yourself for something that was outside of your control. Something that you don't want to risk happening again. You don't want to feel responsible for anyone else's life. Or death.'

'Thank you, Dr Freud.'

'And now I've spoiled a perfectly good day by being too honest.'

'Not quite,' she admitted, despite herself.

He had leaned closer to her as he spoke, as if the intimacy of his words were mirrored by his body. She wasn't sure if it was deliberate, but it didn't matter. She felt his nearness in every pore of her body, pulling her inexorably towards him. She reached across the last few centimetres, cupping his face with her hand and bringing his mouth to hers. His lips were harder than she had imagined (and she had imagined them a lot), taking her invitation and running with it, pressing his mouth to hers until she drew back, breathless, her limbs shaking.

'I don't understand what's going on here,' she said. 'I don't know why you've been pursuing me. I haven't given you much encouragement. And I really hope you don't think I'm a vulnerable maiden in need of rescuing, or any of that shit.'

'That would be the day,' he said, breaking into what could only be described as a guffaw.

'You actually brayed! Like a donkey.'

'We're all vulnerable, in our own way, Mia. You just have to find the sensitive spots.'

A gust of wind chose that moment to ripple across the garden, setting the echinacea flowers to nodding, and flipping the pages of *A Curious Herbal*, so that her grandmother's bookmark escaped up into the air. She lunged for it but Reid's long arm caught it before it could blow away.

'Here,' he said, handing it to her. 'What are you reading, anyway?'

'Elizabeth Blackwell's herbal. My grandmother was using that piece of paper as a bookmark. I didn't want to lose it. Maybe she wrote on it.'

'It's quite old,' he said, unfolding the yellowing paper, 'and someone has written on it.'

'She bookmarked the page about foxgloves.'

They both peered at the writing on the makeshift bookmark, Mia realising that she had seen the uneven, painstaking script before. 'I think it's a page from the book of receipts I found. Philadelphia's book of recipes. Apparently, she wrote down all her remedies, as well as some from her mother.'

'A Proven Receipt to Kill a Man,' Reid read, his voice tapering into silence on the word 'man', before clearing his throat and continuing. 'The foxglove leaves being bitter, sweeten the tea with honey for best results. Take—'

He stopped reading and they stared at each other.

Mia sighed, 'Wow, are you thinking what I'm thinking?'

'That maybe Isaac was telling the truth when he accused Philadelphia of wanting her husband dead? That maybe she did cast a spell on him to do it? Or at least gave him the tools to complete her mission.'

'There's not much magic to inciting the lust of an eighteen-year-old boy,' Mia said. Every girl knew that.

'Inciting him to actually kill his uncle should have taken more than a little encouragement.'

'True. Except if she promised him a life together, free of his uncle's shackles, that might have done the trick,' she said, remembering her dream of a boy listening at a door and vowing to protect the woman he loved.

For a boy on the precipice of manhood, aching to prove himself to his lover, it may have proved a powerful motive.

50

Sussex, England
1829

The cherry tree was heavy with fruit; its slender branches bowed with ripe necklaces of ruby fruit. Marjory reached up to pluck a handful, slipping one into her mouth, her smile confirming its sweetness. She was such an agreeable child, enjoying all that life brought her even as she saw far more than any other child her age. Saw far beyond most adults. She seemed to take life in her stride, unlike her mother who had to fight it at every turn. More like her grandmother, Philadelphia realised. She watched her daughter finish eating her cherries, wiping the juice from her lips with the back of her hand. Her cheeks were flushed from the sun, and she had removed her chemisette so that her collarbones showed.

Philadelphia sighed at life's inevitability. Her daughter was becoming a woman. She was sixteen; almost the age Philadelphia had been when she met Jasper Boadle and left her mother's cottage to pursue her desire for a different life. To better herself, so she had thought.

'You cannot escape who you truly are,' Susanna had said to her on the day she told her mother of her betrothal.

Philadelphia had believed that in marrying Jasper she would become who she was meant to be. Except he had wanted her to abandon so much of herself that she became only half the woman she was meant to be. He expected her to bury her gift, stifle her vision, hide her inner light. Could she be blamed for wanting to reclaim that other half? No matter the cost?

For the cost had been greater than she could ever have foreseen. To Jasper, to Isaac, to Thomas and to herself.

'Have some cherries, Mama,' Marjory said, plucking another bunch and tossing them to her mother.

Philadelphia caught them, with an exclamation of surprise. Her daughter looked so much like her, with her mass of black curls, heart-shaped face and deep blue eyes, but she was far kinder, more accepting ... more innocent. Far more like her grandmother – who had served this village her entire life, despite the suspicions and prejudice of so many.

It did not seem so very long, after all, since Philadelphia had stood beneath this same cherry tree and plucked its fruit. She too had been an innocent. Offering the cherries to a man out of kindness. A man she came to love for his kindness, in the end. A man who was stolen from her. Just as the life she had hankered after was stolen from her. All that remained to her was her gift, the knowledge bequeathed by her mother, and her precious daughter. Sometimes when she thought about the past, she could taste its bitterness like yarrow upon her tongue. She did not want her child to suffer as she had.

'Come, Marjory,' she said. 'You are old enough to learn some of my secrets.' She smiled as she beckoned her daughter close.

The girl paused, a cherry halfway to her mouth. Her lips were stained purple and there were red smears upon the gigot sleeves of the dress Philadelphia had fashioned for her birthday. 'You don't have any secrets from me,' she said, with a laugh.

'Everyone has secrets, my sweet.'

'Your secrets are all locked away in drawers, Mama, and I

know where you keep the key.' Her daughter's eyes gleamed with mischief.

Of course she did. But Philadelphia also knew her daughter well enough to know that she would not pry open her mother's hidden cabinet without asking.

'Come, let me teach you about some of our garden's secret uses.' She took the girl by the hand and led her to a patch of plants with green-grey leaves and masses of tiny mauve flowers. 'Vervain, sacred to the ancients.'

'An infusion of the flowers, leaves and stalk are used in your nerve tonic, Mama,' Marjory said, regarding her mother with a puzzled frown. This was old news. 'Or as a daily gargle for sore throats and gums, or a wash for painful eyes.'

'And yet, there are other uses . . .' Philadelphia hesitated. Did her daughter need to know? Their use was not without consequence.

'Yes?'

'A tea brewed with the leaves of vervain, peppermint, hawthorn, rose and heartsease is a powerful love tonic,' she said. Knowledge, after all, was only dangerous if wielded unwisely.

Marjory listened raptly as her mother explained the use and preparation of *Great-grandmother's receipt to Charm a Man*. Then, before she could ask too many questions, such as whether her mother had ever put the receipt to use, Philadelphia beckoned her to the rear of the garden where the last spears of yellow foxgloves were fading with the summer.

'Fairy's thimbles,' Marjory said.

'Yellow foxglove. *Digitalis grandiflora*. Less common than the wild *Digitalis purpurea* that grows in the hedges and lanes, yet both having similar properties. Also known as fairy bells, goblin's thimbles . . . dead men's bells.' She held her daughter's gaze as she spoke this last name.

'A preparation of either can be used in the treatment of dropsy,

Mama,' Marjory recited the lessons of her ancestors. 'Yet it is a most dangerous herb and must be used sparingly and with great caution.'

'That is true. And yet, my sweet child,' Philadelphia said gently, placing her arm around her daughter's slender waist and drawing her close, 'there may come a time when a woman needs to harness the full strength of the dead men's bells. She may need their deadly power.' She had craved respectability, yet in the end it was power that she needed most.

To save herself from one who would do her harm.

To avenge herself on one who had wronged her.

To rid herself of one who would be rid of her.

'Yes, Mama,' her daughter said, 'I know. But I shall never need them.'

51

East Sussex, England
Midsummer's Eve, 2025

The dew was heavy on the long grass as Mia picked her way across the sloping churchyard from the footbridge. The church steeple, silhouetted against the night sky, loomed over her like an accusing judge cloaked in dark stone. But she paid it no heed for her excursion was no adventure in the black arts, merely a *divertissement*. An experiment in popular folk beliefs. Nothing that a twenty-first-century woman could take seriously. Nothing too witchy. She wore an old Nike hoodie, unzipped, with a white singlet and black leggings for the outing – very twenty-first century. All the same, she flinched as a ghostly white shape dive-bombed her head, screeching, before realising that it was probably only an owl. She was intruding on its territory, after all.

'Sorry, mate,' she said, with an apologetic wave.

She had scouted the churchyard days earlier to ensure her midnight ramble proceeded without any major hiccup. Spraining her ankle in a rabbit burrow or tripping over a fallen headstone would lead to questions she would rather not answer, and any surprised squeal might bring unwanted rescuers. Finding what she was searching for in the dark could have proved a major operation without prior reconnoitering. Instead, she found her way sure-footed through the graves, skirting around all obstacles until she arrived at her destination: the grave of a young man.

Here lies the body of John Cooper
Died 10th September 1809
In the 19th year of his age

John Cooper wasn't the only young man buried in the churchyard, but the winged skull on his headstone had drawn her to him with its grinning death's head and fine feathered wings. She had been surprised by the image at first, but after a little metaphorical digging she discovered that it was meant to represent an angel or a winged soul – the spirit of the deceased finding its way to heaven. She liked that idea. Poor John Cooper, who died so young, on his way to heaven.

His grave lay in a bed of long grass scattered with clusters of small white flowers that glowed in the moonlight. She wasn't exactly sure why she was standing here in a graveyard on Midsummer's Eve, only that she felt the need for some kind of ritual to complete the journey she had begun a year earlier. Although she had travelled ten thousand miles, it was nothing compared to that other journey – of finding her way to self-acceptance and a willingness to open her heart.

'Ah, what the hell,' she muttered, 'here goes nothing.' Leaning forward, she plucked several blossoms, tucking the stems into her bra so that they clothed her skin like white lace, as she silently thanked the young man who had been taken from this earth too young.

The stairs in her grandmother's house creaked no matter how soft the footsteps that trod them. Mia climbed the narrow staircase, finding her way to the bedroom in the dark. It was her bedroom now; she had made it her own with several of her latest pieces hung on the walls, forest-green linen encasing the bed, and her clothes overflowing from the aged wardrobe and chest of drawers. She stripped off her hoodie, runners, leggings and singlet, letting each garment lie where it fell. She crept towards the bed, clad only in her bra and underwear, to sit on the edge of the bed and remove the flowers from her bra. Then, lifting the pillow, she placed the yarrow beneath it before taking off her bra and slipping in between the sheets. She lay her head upon the pillow, whispering, 'Good night, fair yarrow, thrice goodnight to thee, I hope before tomorrow, my true love to see.'

She smiled as she recited the words that she had found in an old text on Sussex folklore. She didn't really need to place the yarrow beneath her pillow to dream of her true love. His face came to her clearer than a 300 PPI digital photo. She was conscious of his body heat imprinted upon the bedclothes. She heard the soft hush of his breath deep in sleep; smelled the mandarin soap on his skin, felt the hard muscles of his thigh as she snuggled a little closer.

Somehow, in her adherence to the rules, she had forgotten about the magic of love. That it could cast its spell despite rules. Love was a gift. And Mia had other gifts, too. In fact, she found herself replete with them. She had the gift to create art. And she had inherited the gift of sight from her mother, her grandmother, and their mothers before them – though she had spent years denying it, she and Celia both.

She hailed from a long line of wise women. A legacy of witches. Their presence was all around her, seeded in the herbs that perfumed her grandmother's garden, pebbled in the walls of an ancient cottage. Those seeds were part of her life now, just as her ancestors' secrets had become her secrets. Sometimes she

The Heirloom

wondered how far back this heritage extended, into what misty realms of the past. But even more so, she wondered how far it might abide into the future – this mysterious legacy she had been bequeathed.

Acknowledgements

Every book is a team effort, and *The Heirloom* is no exception. As always, I would like to thank my very persuasive agent, Judith Murdoch, for representing me faithfully. Thanks also to the team at Headline UK who have been so enthusiastic about this title: my wonderful editor Nicola Caws, Sophie Keefe, Shân Morley Jones. And a big thank you to the team at Hachette Australia who ensure my books sit nicely on the retailers' shelves.

Thank you to my husband, Vincent Kwok, who so patiently drove me around the towns and villages of East Sussex for a week to research its landscape, architecture and history. And to my family, Ru, Kit and Joice, for being so enthusiastic when I tested out my ideas for the story that became *The Heirloom*.

Author Q&A

1. *The Heirloom* is a dual time period book – how do you set about keeping the two stories flowing together and yet retaining their distinctive elements?

Some authors write each timeline separately then weave the stories together later but I prefer to write the two stories concurrently. Although I conceive of each timeline as a separate narrative, with its own protagonist and story arc, the protagonists' journeys and the events of each time period are intimately connected. So, the only way I've found to convey that connection is to write them together. Each chapter needs to link with the chapters around it. And many of the events in one protagonist's life will resonate with events in the other, often mirroring them.

2. The Australian and English settings both provide vivid backgrounds to the novel. Did you feel the way you wrote each section was influenced at all by each particular location, in the sense that it helped you shape the scenes?

Most definitely. I spent a week driving around East Sussex, researching the locations, the architecture, the feel of the countryside. Then once I was back in Australia, I pored over maps and photographs I had taken. A visit to the Weald and Downland Living Museum near Chichester was particularly influential in how I pictured the cottage where Philadelphia grew up, and the garden she and her mother Susanna tended. Although I don't name the village in the novel (so that I have some fictional elbow room), I did have the village of Alfriston in mind for the setting.

For the Queensland settings, I lived in Brisbane as a child and have spent many holidays there since. The Brisbane River is a powerful presence throughout the city, winding through many suburbs, it's impossible to ignore really. And the architecture of Brisbane is quite different to the other Australian capitals. Much more tropical, so that influenced the story as well.

3. Mia, the Australian character, and her ancestor in 1811, Philadelphia, are both strong women, yet also show a vulnerability. How important is it for you to create female characters that have independence and spirit?

I take pride in saying that I write so-called 'Women's Fiction'. And I do see myself writing for women readers, more than men. So, I think I owe those readers independent, spirited protagonists whose journeys they can connect with in some fashion.

4. There's a strong element of mystery in *The Heirloom* – do you think all families have secrets?

I have to laugh a little at this question because dig just a fraction into the past (or sometimes the present) and I think you will find a secret or two in most families. In researching my own family history, I discovered that my great-great-grandmother's second husband was actually her first husband's nephew, who according to the census lived with them as a teen (although I never did find evidence of a legal marriage with the nephew). The pair emigrated to Queensland with the two youngest children, leaving the adult children from her first marriage in England. Both husbands had the same surname and first initial. From what I can deduce they lowered her age and upped his on the passenger lists then settled in Queensland with no one the wiser. If you're reading *The Heirloom* this fact will ring bells.

5. Is the idea of inheritance – whether traits or artefacts – important to you?
I don't know about important, but I will say I believe inheritance is unavoidable. I'm in my sixties now but I'm still discovering aspects of my life that I can attribute to my parents. Apart from the more obvious ones like eye colour or athleticism, little health niggles for example. I also see certain traits in my children that are similar to me or my partner. Our parents' and grandparents' life experiences affect the way they interact with us as children, and so on, and so on. We all inherit traits and beliefs from our forebears, it's what we do with them that's important.

6. As you delve further into the novel, how do you control how much of the mystery you can reveal at certain stages?
Although as a writer I'm not a detailed planner, I do a great deal of research and brain storming before I begin writing and I usually have a framework of revelations on which to build the story. These revelations, or plot points, help me structure the mystery. And of course, many more events and details arise as the story progresses so in a sense the mystery unfolds organically. I do sometimes go back and tweak a little in revision, adding or deleting information.

7. Philadelphia is a milliner and seamstress, and her use of fabrics and colours is vividly described. What inspired you to give her these skills?
I suppose I was inspired by both the present and the past in giving Philadelphia these skills. Firstly, we need to remember that two hundred years ago clothing was handmade rather than mass produced so there were many women working in this field. I have a number of ancestors (in particular, several generations of tailors and milliners in Wales) who made clothing for a living, so the past inspired me. But also, my daughter is a fashion designer and I'm constantly astounded by her creativity and the way her mind works as an artist, and the training she has undergone to hone those skills.

8. In this book, as well as other works that describe historical reactions to women using herbs and 'witchcraft', the men are often adamant that the women with such skills should be suppressed. Was this an element you wanted to expose and explore in *The Heirloom*?
I did want to explore this element, but I also wanted to show how women with these skills formed an integral part of village life in centuries past. They ministered to the health and well-being of their neighbours. They helped to bring children into the world and ease the passing of the elderly. They were respected (and sometimes feared) for their skill. Unfortunately, they could also be scapegoats when things went wrong.

9. You write so well about specific plants and their uses. Is this a subject you have always been interested in, or did it develop with your writing of the novel?
I have to admit I'm not much of a gardener, although recently we have acquired a country garden and I've been doing some digging and planting. All Australian natives, however, and mostly indigenous to the location of the garden. I made a giant leap into herb lore to write this book, including obtaining copies of books that were extant two centuries ago.

10. Do you feel that including elements of love, and redemption as you close a novel are important for both you and the reader?
I think that all my books are about love of one kind or another – and its opposite, hatred. Usually, the hatred in my books is a bitter reversal of a love, or the hope of love. The reversal of this love brings about the most harrowing kinds of conflict, I think. The most bitter. A dark kind of conflict where love turns to hate demands an ending that promises redemption and a newer, happier love, so that the reader – and the writer – can still have faith in love's power.

**Don't miss Julie Brooks' thrilling dual-time novel
with a complex family mystery to be solved
in the present day.**

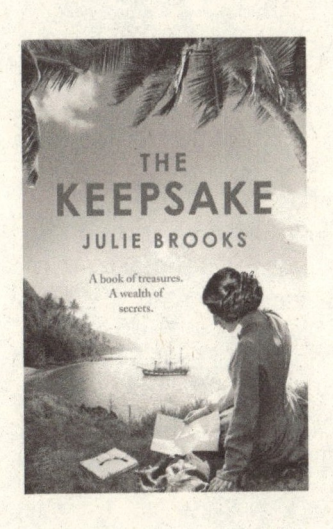

A book of treasures.
A wealth of secrets.

Order now!